REBECCA LEVENE

The Hunter's Kind

THE HOLLOW GODS
BOOK 2

HODDER

First published in Great Britain in 2015 by
Hodder & Stoughton
An Hachette UK company

First published in paperback in 2016
1

Copyright © Rebecca Levene 2015

Maps by Clifford Webb

The right of Rebecca Levene to be identified as the Author of the Work has been asserted by her in accordance with the Copyright, Designs and Patents Act 1988.

All rights reserved. No part of this publication may be reproduced, stored in a retrieval system, or transmitted, in any form or by any means without the prior written permission of the publisher, nor be otherwise circulated in any form of binding or cover other than that in which it is published and without a similar condition being imposed on the subsequent purchaser.

All characters in this publication are fictitious and any resemblance to real persons, living or dead is purely coincidental.

A CIP catalogue record for this title is available from the British Library

Hardback ISBN 978 1 444 75374 5

Typset in Plantin by Palimpsest Book Production Limited,
Falkirk, Stirlingshire

Printed and bound by Clays Ltd, St Ives plc

Hodder & Stoughton policy is to use papers that are natural, renewable and recyclable products and made from wood grown in sustainable forests. The logging and manufacturing processes are expected to conform to the environmental regulations of the country of origin.

Hodder & Stoughton Ltd
Carmelite House
50 Victoria Embankment
London EC4Y 0DZ

www.hodder.co.uk

For Fiona Singh,
who remembers our childhood for both of us

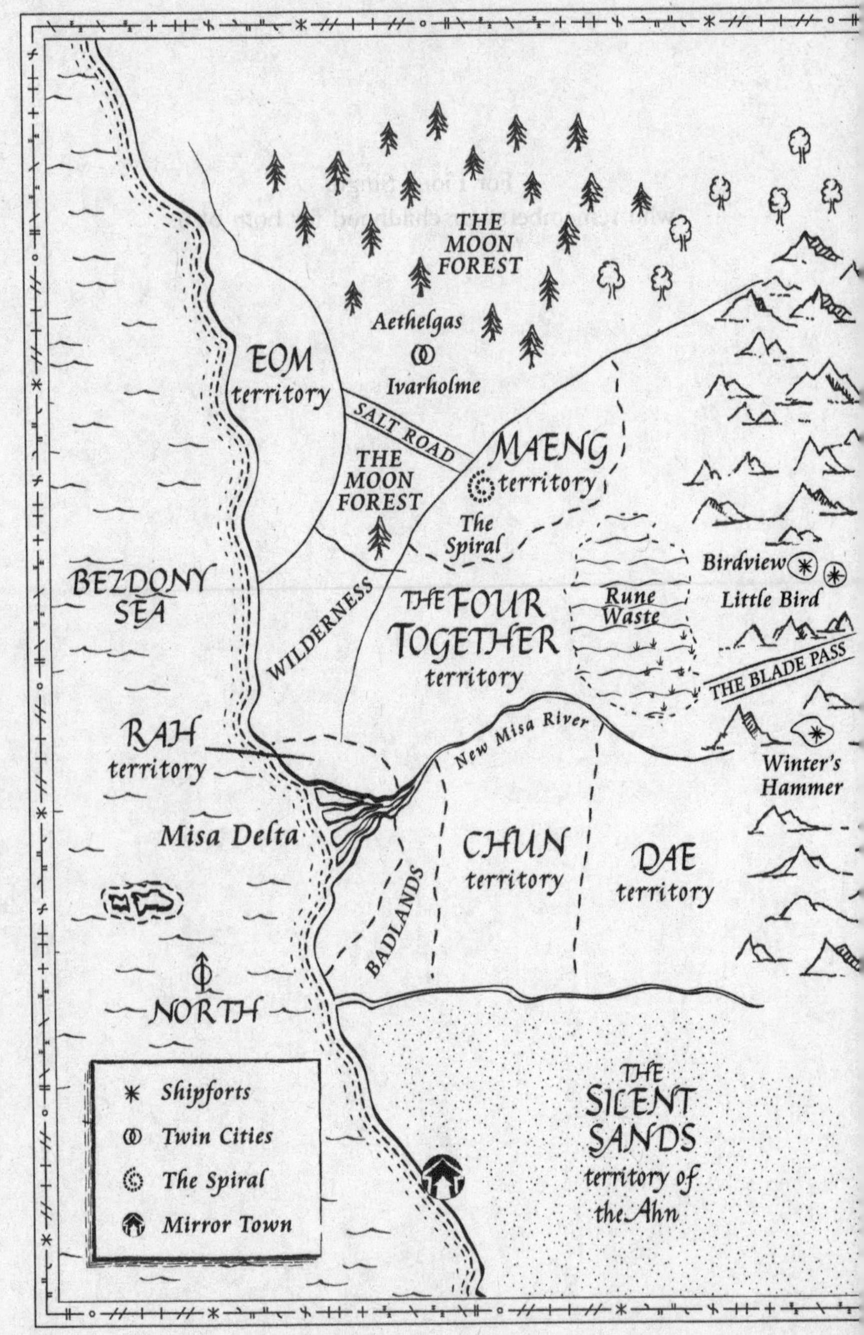
THE MOON FOREST
Aethelgas
Ivarholme
EOM territory
SALT ROAD
THE MOON FOREST
MAENG territory
The Spiral
BEZDONY SEA
WILDERNESS
THE FOUR TOGETHER territory
Rune Waste
Birdview
Little Bird
THE BLADE PASS
RAH territory
New Misa River
Winter's Hammer
Misa Delta
CHUN territory
DAE territory
BADLANDS
NORTH
THE SILENT SANDS territory of the Ahn
Shipforts
Twin Cities
The Spiral
Mirror Town

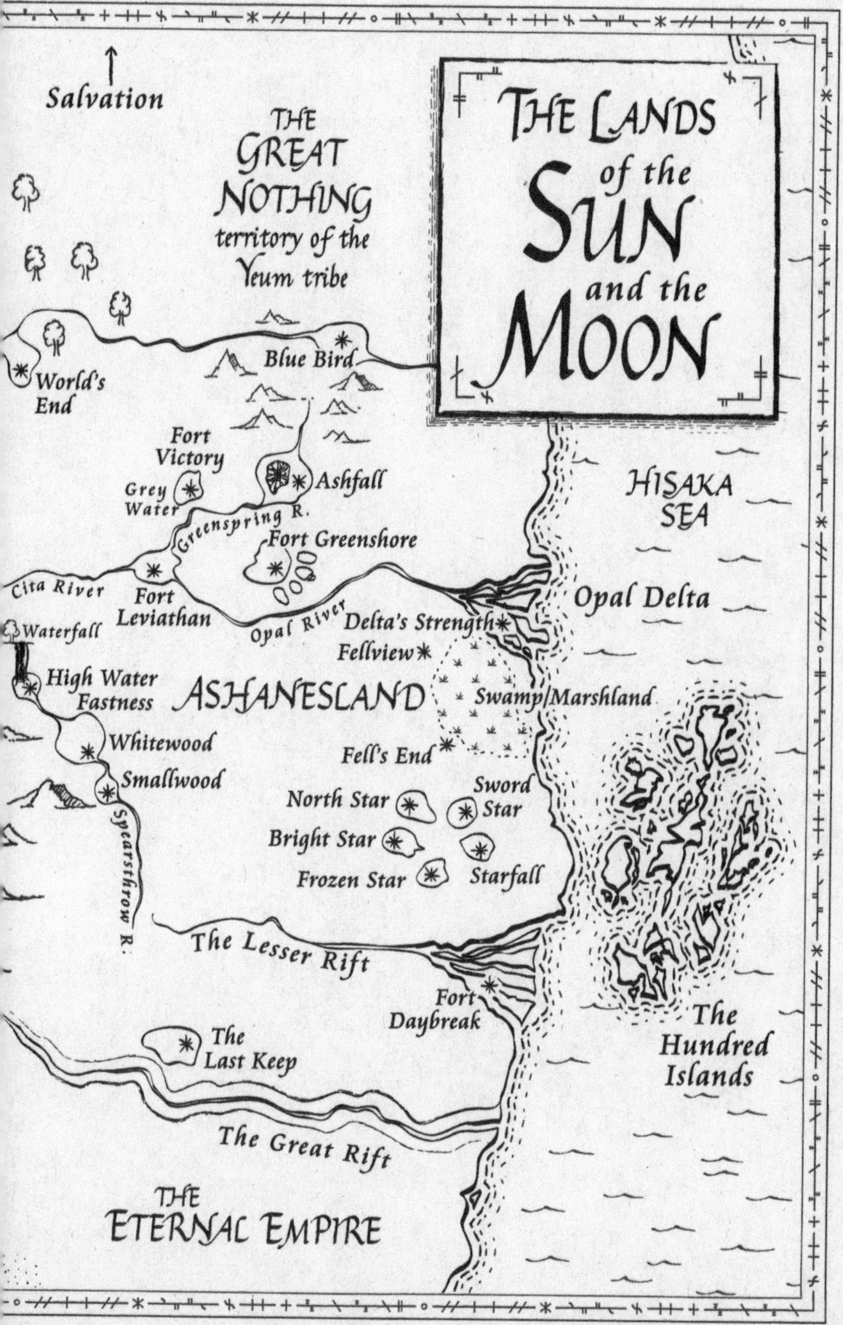

The Lands of the Sun and the Moon
Salvation
The Great Nothing territory of the Yeum tribe
Blue Bird
World's End
Fort Victory
Grey Water
Ashfall
Greenspring R.
Fort Greenshore
Cita River
Fort Leviathan
Opal River
Delta's Strength
Opal Delta
Hisaka Sea
Waterfall
Fellview
High Water Fastness
Ashanesland
Swamp/Marshland
Whitewood
Fell's End
Smallwood
North Star
Sword Star
Bright Star
Frozen Star
Starfall
Spearsthrow R.
The Lesser Rift
Fort Daybreak
The Last Keep
The Hundred Islands
The Great Rift
The Eternal Empire

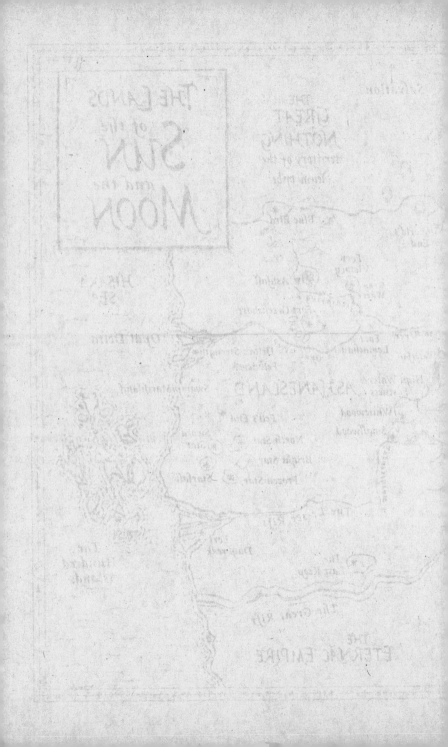

The Hunter's Kind

Prologue

For as long as she'd understood what a birthfeast was, Cwen had dreaded her twelfth. She woke up on the morning it finally came, turned her face to the wall and kept her eyes tightly shut, as if she might be permitted to sleep it away and never suffer its consequences.

She heard Griotgard approaching her bed, but he wouldn't be able to shake her awake. Everything she touched must be washed before a warrior could handle it, and any food she left was thrown into the forest, too defiled even for the pigs. She rolled over and looked up at him.

'Hawk day for you, girl,' he said. His face was very red and very square, without any softness in it.

'They told me I'd have a feast before I go.' She dropped from her bed to the wooden floor of the longhall. 'And you're not invited.'

Last night she'd laid out the clothes she was to wear today. Her father had provided them, looking to the left of her head as he set them out one by one on the bed: woollen trousers and shirt, hide boots and belt, a linen jacket and a hooded cloak in forest green. The jacket had been embroidered with a portrait of the Hunter, smiling and golden. Cwen hated it. It was the Hunter who'd put the hawk mark on her cheek while she was still inside her mother's belly, and singled her out for this fate.

The other Jorlith were rising too. She'd crossed practice swords with some of the youngest in her training and they smiled at her now, but it was with pity. Her pride wouldn't allow that and so she straightened her back and nodded gravely back, like a thegn acknowledging the village churls. She *was* a thegn, whatever else the mark on her cheek made her.

Her mother was waiting outside the longhall. She stared for a long moment at the birthfeast finery she'd embroidered with her own hand, and then her face tipped upward to cast a beady eye over Cwen's wildly curling orange hair, which she'd forgotten to comb. Cwen was startled to realise she was the taller by a head. Her mother was, as always, perfectly neat: hair plaited, an embroidered scarf draped round her neck and a silver acorn brooch clasping her gown tight across the plump breasts at which Cwen had never been permitted to suckle.

'My darling,' her mother said finally. 'So beautiful.'

'Who cares about beautiful? I'm the strongest my age. I beat Osbeorn at staves yesterday, and he's near to being a warrior full.'

'Yes. That's good. I wouldn't . . . Cwen, if there was any way – if I could have stopped this, kept you for myself . . .' Her mother looked away, seeming to war with some strong emotion, and when she looked back her face was calm. 'Come then. The food grows cold and the sun's already risen.'

The guard owls swivelled their golden eyes to watch as they walked across the swaying platform that led between the Jorlith longhall and the village square. The great moon pines' trunks stretched into the sky above and far down to the forest floor below, where the thegns would never walk and the churls grubbed in the dirt of their farms. The wind was light today and scented by wild rose.

Westleigh housed 122 bodies, nearly the most the Hunter permitted, and it seemed as if every one of them had come from their homes to stare at Cwen as she passed. Only the thegns had been invited to the feast, but the churls would be given the meal's scraps and besides, she'd always been a curiosity. Other villages had three hawks or half a dozen; sometimes every child in one family bore the mark. She'd waited and waited for another hawk to be born into Westleigh, but she was the only one.

Her training had suffered for it; she had been unable to touch any of those she sparred with. Unable to touch anyone. She'd sometimes stroked her own arms, wondering what it would be to feel another's skin against them, but that was childishness. Today she needed to put all such weakness aside.

Her parents' manor sat in the crook of the largest branch of the largest ice oak for miles in any direction. No one had ever been allowed to doubt their wealth. The thatch was fresh and the plaster bright white between the supporting beams. Inside, the tables were already laden with meats. The smell was as thick as gravy and she kneed aside two hounds who had been drawn by it to loiter in the doorway.

The babble died away as the guests noted her presence. Some looked like they felt they should speak, but what could they say to her on this of all days? Nothing. She felt as if she'd lived her whole life in that silence.

She whistled as she walked to the head of the table, tuneless and loud. Her mother drew away from her, embarrassed, but her father watched stern-faced until she sat at his right side. She leaned away from him and tried not to let his disdain spoil her appetite. A bullock and two lambs had died for this meal, and she didn't know when she'd have such plenty again. Everyone gobbled their food, the sound of the chewing and slurping like a kennel. If she'd let the dogs inside their manners could barely have been worse.

The sun was climbing and she must be gone before it reached the top of its daily hill. When the feast ended, the thegns formed a corridor down the length of the great hall for her to walk. She watched her boots take each stride and tried not to shake. Why should she be afraid? She'd been trained for this since the moment she could walk.

Outside, the rest of the village had gathered. Someone had laid a knife and a spear on the wooden platform and she picked them up. Her mask would be last of all; she turned to see her mother holding it. The wooden face was placid, a sharp-beaked bird with round eyes and scarlet cheeks. Her mother's face was equally calm, but Cwen could see the turmoil in her eyes and longed to reach out to her.

She didn't. She wanted her mother to be left with a good,

strong memory of her and so she put on the mask, her fingers fumbling to tie the leather cords at the back. Suddenly she was crying, her eyes hot with tears. But it didn't matter: the mask hid them.

It was an awkward climb, with a spear in one hand and the knife clenched into her armpit because she'd forgotten to hang it at her waist. At the bottom, she couldn't stop herself taking one last glance at her home in the treetops high above. Only one figure remained in sight, leaning forward to watch her descent. It might have been her mother but she was too far away to be sure.

The trees clutched darkness around them. Cwen knew better than most what it held. Leaf mulch squelched beneath her boots, its decayed stench banishing the memory of her feast. The whole thing already felt very distant. Fifty paces on and the village did too, lost to sight in the treetops.

The path was broad enough that the sun would strike it at noon and keep it safe from the worm men and the moon beasts, but now everything was in shadow and nowhere felt safe. She'd never seen one of the monsters but she'd seen pictures. Griotgard had shown her the bestiary when she was four and she'd wept at what was painted there. He'd told her these were to be her prey when she joined the Hunt. It seemed more likely she'd be theirs.

The forest was filled with noise. In the village there had been other sounds to drown out the bird calls and insect skritches and rustle of unseen things, but here they seemed far too loud. She jumped at the snap of a twig to her left, scolded herself for behaving like a child – and then jumped again at a howl to her right.

She'd soon drained her leather flask dry and her throat was parched. She could hear the maddening gurgle of a stream to her left. It must be the Briarburn, which wound through the farmland to the west of the village and then headed down towards the distant plains, where the savage tribespeople lived. To be so loud it must be close.

She peered between the oaks, but the undergrowth was tangled and wild and hid what lay beyond. She took one step from the path and paused, shaking, but no attack came. Of course it didn't. The moon monsters slept during the day; that was what everyone said. And what kind of warrior was she, afraid of a few trees?

The ground was thick with brambles; they caught at her trousers and scratched her hand. She took out her knife and sawed vainly at the knotty stems until the sap set her cuts stinging and she abandoned the attempt. She wasn't sure at first if the flecks of light were tricks of her eyes or true sunlight, but as she moved they kept their shape and gained in brightness until she was sure that what she saw was daylight dappled through leaves.

A tension she hadn't been aware of loosened in all her limbs and her spine. She flung her head back and yelled in triumphant relief.

Something, very close, called back. It was a high-pitched scream, almost human. But there was a strange quality to it, a tone both high and low that could never have emerged from any person's throat. A moment passed and a second cry came from her other side, and then another from behind. They had surrounded her, and the undergrowth was too thick to wield her spear.

'You've got a head full of shit and air, Cwen,' she hissed to herself and drew her knife. It looked too small in her hand, its blade not even as long as her forearm.

The screams came again, closer, and she caught her first glimpse of what pursued her as it shook the branches far above her head. Its own was lost in shadow but an eye flashed green and huge and then was gone.

She backed up until the trunk of a moon pine braced her upright. She needed its support. Her knees had weakened with fear and she gritted her teeth and locked the joints. The beasts would hardly care how she died, but she imagined Griotgard laughing at her cowardice and it stiffened her resolve.

Then the first of the beasts pushed through the undergrowth into plain view and she couldn't stop a whimper of fear. The teeth were the length of her hand; the eyes shone with their own internal flame, brighter than the scarce daylight; and when it lifted one clawed foot she saw the glint of scales. It looked like no natural animal, but like a stitched-together thing made of the worst parts of all the rest.

The monster sank to its front knees until its head was only a few feet above hers. There was intelligence in its eyes, as much cunning as she'd ever seen in Griotgard's. Its lips peeled back, as if to show her the full length of its fangs. It was mocking her, she was sure of it.

She raised her spear and snarled back at it. 'I've a fang too!'

It howled, reared back to strike – and then screamed again. She braced for the blow, frozen, and only slowly realised that its scream had changed into a desperate sound. A dark stain spread from its open jaws down to its chest. Blood: all that the creature had or at least more than it could spare. It fell back to its knees and then on to its side, crushing bushes and plants beneath it, and the smell of its gore mixed with a sudden puff of wild garlic.

There were more screams and other cries: human sounds, and these ones were triumphant. There was a great creaking and cracking and snapping of branches all around her as the smell of blood grew thicker. The beasts were dying. They were being slaughtered.

Before the screams stopped she knew who'd come to her aid and her face burned beneath its mask. It would have been easier to die an idiot than live to see her idiocy witnessed by the Hunt.

The beasts had crushed so many trees and bushes in their death throes that the sun was blazing down on her unchecked when the first of the hawks emerged. Their expressions were hidden behind masks, wide-eyed blanks. The nearest tilted its head sideways, so exactly like the bird its mask resembled that Cwen giggled helplessly and couldn't stop. And then the final figure emerged from the trees and the laughter dried out in her throat as all sound died in the forest, birdsong quieting and insects stilling, as if the whole world held its breath where this figure walked.

She'd seen a hundred paintings of the Hunter, a score of tapestries. She'd hated that face from the moment she knew who owned it. Now the hatred melted under the strength of that calm regard and left something formless behind.

'Cwen,' the Hunter said. 'Youngest of my hawks.'

Cwen knew she should bow. She didn't.

Some of the gathered hawks hissed behind their masks and the two wolves that flanked the goddess raised their hackles and growled. The Hunter neither frowned nor smiled. Beneath the golden curls of her hair, her face was terribly scarred. None of the paintings showed that and Cwen felt a stab of terror as she imagined a beast so powerful it could wound a god. 'We looked to find you miles from here, child,' the Hunter said. 'You wandered from the path.'

'I was thirsty. No one said how far I had to go. No one told me anything.'

'They warned you, I am sure, of the dangers in the dark.'

Cwen looked down, abashed. 'Yes.'

The Hunter said nothing further, but when she turned and strode away, Cwen felt compelled to follow, trotting on the heels of the Hunter's wolves.

When the sun began to set, they turned aside from the path into a clearing three hundred paces across. Cwen was shocked to see a building in its centre, rooted to the ground like a tree. Her steps faltered but the other hawks walked towards it and she couldn't bring herself to seem a coward in their eyes as well as a fool.

Closer to, she could see that the building was open on one side, its peaked, wood-tiled roof overhanging a large open space full of shadows as dark as those beneath the trees.

'The monsters will not come here,' the Hunter said. 'The ground is safe from them.'

For the first time, one of the other hawks turned to speak to Cwen. He pulled off his mask to show the face of a boy little older than herself with the fair hair of the Jorlith. 'Our bodies keep it safe,' he said. He gestured at the sharp-featured statue of a man that stood in the hall's entrance. 'That was Wulfsin, one of us. He died nearby and we buried him here. His body has the Hunter's magic in it – it keeps the beasts away.'

He grinned but she wasn't sure what message he wanted her to take from his words: that she was safe, or that she too would one day die to make a haven for the rest. The statue's face was young. That day of death wouldn't be far off, if she only lasted as long as him.

There were fewer hawks than she'd first realised, only two dozen or so. This couldn't be the whole Hunt, but she had no idea where the rest were and too much pride to ask. She watched as they led their mounts into the enclosure and gaped as the nearest turned its beaked head towards her, blinking beneath its shaggy golden mane. It was every bit as monstrous as the beasts the Hunt had saved her from.

'You'll have your own too,' the Jorlith boy said. 'We all catch one to ride – it's the first thing you'll do.' He smiled again, entirely friendly this time. Maybe he'd meant to be friendly before.

'The moon's monsters can be made to serve us,' the Hunter said. 'I bent the greatest of them to my will a millennium ago, and these dumb beasts are more easily swayed.'

Cwen studied the creature, which looked far less fearsome saddled and under harness than its brothers had wild in the woods. She reached out a hand and its forked tongue flicked out to lick it, just like her father's hounds when in her loneliness she'd sometimes crawled to their kennels to sleep among the warm, stinking press of their bodies.

'What's his name?' she asked the Jorlith boy.

'He doesn't have one.'

'We do not name the things we mean to kill,' the Hunter said.

'But . . .' Cwen stared at the beast, which stared back, its red eye more soft than fierce in the twilight.

'When all their brethren are gone, they too must die. How else will the world be rid of the moon's curse?'

Cwen watched in silence as the hawks made camp, laying out blankets beneath the wooden roof and building a fire whose smoke rose to fill its rafters. The sun set out of sight behind the trees and the sky darkened through purple to a pinpricked black. There was a lot of laughter as the hawks worked, but she couldn't see what any of them had to be happy about.

Blankets were provided for her, and a place close to the fire. She supposed it was a kind gesture. All the hawks had unmasked now and several tried to speak to her, but she shrugged off their questions and pulled her blankets to the furthest corner of the room. Their eyes followed her beneath frowns but no one moved to stop her and no one spoke to her again.

It was easier to sleep than she'd expected. The surge of fear she'd felt earlier had washed away to leave behind exhaustion and she'd barely closed her eyes before blackness came.

She woke with the same abruptness to find the Hunter leaning over her. It wasn't a sound that had woken her, she was sure; the goddess's presence alone had been enough. The fire had burned down to embers and in the near darkness Cwen could see that her new mistress glowed with a faint golden light of her own. It outlined her curls like the promise of sunrise.

'Come,' the Hunter said.

Cwen thought of refusing. She hesitated for a long moment while those bright eyes gazed down at her and the generous mouth remained silent. It was the silence that defeated her in the end, as it had beaten her down her whole life. She rose to her feet with a sigh and followed as the Hunter strode to the boundary of the camp.

The scars on the goddess's face were softened by night into four long shadows. They shifted like serpents as the Hunter spoke. 'I dreamed of the new moon last night,' she said.

Moon dreams were ill-luck, everyone said so. Cwen had never imagined that a goddess might be haunted by them.

'Something I thought long banished has been born again,' the Hunter said. 'And on the same day you came to me, the youngest of my hawks. There must be purpose in this, but . . .' She frowned, studying Cwen's face in a darkness her eyes could perhaps penetrate. 'You are angry, and your anger is not with the moon.'

Cwen couldn't find a safe reply, but the Hunter nodded as if she'd given one anyway.

'Your skin is very dark,' the goddess said. 'As dark as an Ashane's. Do you know why?'

'Yes,' Cwen said, her voice vibrating with anger. 'Griotgard told me. My mother fucked one of your Wanderers, and I was what came of it. She could have lain with anyone, he said. Women do it all the time. But she had to go and choose a half-foreign mongrel so everyone would know I wasn't my father's.'

'Yes. Yes, that is the truth.' The Hunter reached out and rested her fingers against Cwen's cheek.

Cwen froze, more shocked than when the moon beasts had ambushed her in the forest. No one had ever touched her that way. No one had ever touched her at all. The goddess's skin was smooth against hers, far different from the coarse hair of her father's hounds, and burning hot. Or perhaps fiercely cold – the sensation was so strong and strange she couldn't tell. She wanted to flinch away from it and to hold the Hunter's hand against her so she could never let go.

'Do you know what this is?' the Hunter asked, tracing the outline on Cwen's cheek with her fingertip.

'It's the hawk mark,' Cwen whispered.

'No, only the ignorant call it that because of its shape and because it singles out my hawks from the common flock. It is a rune, *my* rune. Do you know why it was put on you?'

Cwen shook her head. It made those fingertips brush across her cheek and she shivered.

'I only mark those whose parents pray for it,' the goddess told her. 'Your mother did not want you. Your father did not want you. They prayed for me to take you as my own.'

Cwen jerked back from the words and the Hunter's touch. 'That isn't true! Of course she wanted me – it was you that took me away from her!'

'No. I would never steal a child from a parent who loved her. Your mother could not love you, because of what you were –

because the day your growth showed in her belly was the day your father knew that she had betrayed him.'

Cwen felt a sensation so strong, she couldn't tell if it was rage or grief. Perhaps it was both. 'You're lying! You're lying to me!'

'I will never lie to you. It was your mother who deceived you, because she could not bear her own guilt.'

'She didn't want me?'

'Never. But *I* want you. And do you know who I am?'

'You're the Hunter.'

'So your people call me. The Hunter, the Lion of the Forest, the Sun's Right Hand and the Moon's Bane. All these words and none of them my name, as if they fear that merely speaking it might pollute their tongues.'

She paused a while and Cwen knew what she was supposed to ask. Eventually she did. 'What *is* your name?'

'Bachur, which is eldest in the eldest tongue.' She cupped Cwen's cheek, and this time Cwen leaned into the hot-cold caress, into the comfort of it. 'This rune's true meaning is "beloved of the eldest". Bachur is a name only my hawks know, my beloved, just as only I see your bare faces. When you die in my service, your mask will be sent back to your family to hang above their hearth. But in the clearing in which we plant your body, we will carve a statue of your true face, because only we truly see it. Do you understand?'

'My mother asked you to take me away before I was even born?'

'*I* wanted you, Cwen. You belong with me.'

It was the first time the Hunter had spoken her name. It sounded more musical on her tongue than it ever had on any villager's. Cwen nodded and was shocked to feel the splash of tears. She clenched her fists, angry with herself for the weakness, but Bachur took her hands and gently loosened her fingers.

Cwen gasped, half a sob, and the goddess put her arms round her and pulled her against the gold-chased armour on her chest. Cwen's cheek pressed awkwardly against the junction of the armour with her neck so that it was half against leather and half against bare skin.

'The moon is rising,' Bachur said. 'Will you fight him for me, Cwen? He cannot be allowed to live.'

'I'll do it,' Cwen promised, her voice muffled against flesh. 'I'll kill him for you.'

PART I

Betrayal

I

Here and there, embers still glowed in the ruin of Smiler's Fair. The corpses were everywhere, pitiful black twiglike bones grasping through the wreckage for a rescue that never came. And worse, far worse, the meaty red mess of those the fire hadn't entirely consumed.

The heat and his exertion bathed Sang Ki in sweat and soot coated him, turning his fair hair as black as the dye his fellow Seonu used. He would have done much to avoid this task. He'd seldom had to heave his great bulk so far, or over such difficult footing. He wished he could have left his men to the search, but he didn't trust them to do it properly.

King Nayan's son had been here, of that he was quite sure. Did the boy's corpse now lie as fire-flayed as the poor unfortunate to his left, trapped beneath an ash-black sculpture of the Smiler himself? That remained to be seen. Close questioning of the fair's survivors had revealed that a boy who was almost certainly Sang Ki's quarry had been wearing manacles on his wrists, a legacy of his brief imprisonment by Gurjot. His body, if it lay here, should be easy to identify.

One more day, Sang Ki had promised himself, and if neither his scattered scouts nor his own search uncovered the prince, he would return to Ashanesland and declare the job done, confident that Krishanjit would never return to contradict him.

Alas, he wasn't entirely alone for the hunt. The carrion bird strutted beside him, its head bobbing above his. Its feathers were only a shade greyer with ash and its stink was sadly in keeping with its surroundings. Gurjot had never returned from Smiler's Fair, but his mount had flown to safety and landed at

Sang Ki's feet while her old master was no doubt still aflame. The lack of loyalty in the creature was disappointing, her new attachment to Sang Ki even more so. The bird refused to be parted from him.

'Well, Laali,' he said, 'what do you think that might be?'

Something glittered in the rubble, beautifully ornate where the fire hadn't softened and deformed it. He used Laali's knobbly leg to steady himself as he knelt beside it. He'd always enjoyed pretty things, and had already pried several jewelled treasures from corpses with no further need of them.

This, he realised, had once been a strongbox, but its melted lock sprang open at his touch. The coins inside looked worthless until he wiped one clean with a finger and saw the sparkle of gold beneath the soot. His cloak served to polish the rest and he was soon back on his feet, cradling a sizable collection in his shirt. The coins weren't wheels – they were no currency he recognised. The face on their reverse was a woman's. Queen Kaur's perhaps, but no: the Iron Queen had never smiled so freely.

He was pondering how he might determine their provenance when he heard the voice, pitifully weak and calling for help in Ashane. The cry came again and he saw a small heap of rubble shift. A hand emerged, fingers wiggling feebly.

Sang Ki hesitated. He'd grown used to the mutilated corpses but he'd yet to reconcile himself to ending the torment of those still clinging to life. And this was a woman's voice; he could be sure that the lost prince didn't lie trapped here. There was no need to dig this time and she'd die without his assistance soon enough.

The cry came again, a little stronger this time, as if the woman sensed his presence. Perhaps she'd heard his footfalls. Another whimper, and he could stand it no longer. His knees creaked as he lowered himself to the ground once again and pulled the half-burnt planks and shattered tiles away.

The body he revealed was far smaller than he'd expected. It seemed incredible that she'd survived, buried, for three days. She was hideously burnt, of course. The skin of her face and arms had crackled like mammoth fat. Her hair was mostly scorched away and her breasts were an obscenity. But she was breathing and her eyes were open, though clouded with pain.

If she'd survived this long, it seemed feasible that the attention of a physician could save her. Sang Ki slipped one arm beneath her body, resting her weight against the folds of his belly and bracing himself before he attempted to rise. Her clothing was almost entirely burned away and she whimpered as he touched her ravaged skin. Only her thick leather belt had survived the fire, and the knife suspended from it.

No, not a knife. It hooked and held his eyes as he froze with her body cradled in his arms. It was a sword in miniature, tarnished by the fire yet clearly finely made. When he wiped it clean, he felt the sharp facets of jewels beneath his fingers and then saw their glitter. And along the golden hilt itself there was script, worked in platinum. Some of it had melted in the intense heat but it didn't matter. He knew what was written there. He'd seen it a dozen times hanging at the waist of the woman who'd murdered his father and then fled Winter's Hammer. This knife belonged to Nethmi, who'd once been known as Little Blade.

By a fluke of wind and the will of the gods, one small segment of the fair had survived the inferno unscathed. Its residents hadn't wanted to remain latched on to the ruin of their home like maggots on a rotting body, so had taken what few beasts of burden remained, disassembled their houses and moved them to a hillock some thousand paces away, where they'd reconstructed a sad echo of the once mighty fair.

Sooty children and drooping whores turned to watch as he led Laali through their streets with Nethmi resting on the bird's back. He'd heard there was an Eom healer here. It seemed quixotic, he knew, to bring a woman to be healed whom he soon meant to see hanged, but he wanted her conscious and in her right mind when she paid for her crime.

The healer's rooms weren't difficult to find; Sang Ki followed the sounds of screams through the mud-choked passages to a small, ill-made house. After staring for a second at the walls, one brightly painted with pictures of grape and grain and the other with a huge portrait of Lord Lust, his member swollen angrily red, Sang Ki concluded that it had been cobbled together from the wreckage of two or more different dwellings.

The physician looked as patchwork as his home. The man's hair was long and purple, caught in no topknot but instead allowed to fall to his hips. He'd painted his face the precise shade of orange best designed to clash with his hair and his hands were red, though whether from blood or dye, Sang Ki couldn't tell.

The Eom seldom left their lands. They were somewhat like the Seonu in that, although unlike the Seonu they had never spent centuries wandering lost and separate from the other tribes at the start of the great exile. They'd simply found a place that suited them and stayed within its borders, doing whatever it was they did when no one else was watching. They'd last emerged in any numbers more than seventy years ago when they'd decided to broker the peace that ended the Five Tribes War. No one knew why they'd come then nor why they'd returned to their home after.

'She may live,' the Eom said with a quick glance at Nethmi, held awkwardly in Sang Ki's arms. 'Leave her on that bed and go.'

'I'd rather stay,' Sang Ki replied.

'Does it seem likely I care for your wants?'

There were six beds in the cramped room, five home to victims of the fire. Sang Ki placed Nethmi on the sixth and turned back to the physician. With some reluctance, he drew out a handful of the gold hoard he'd found earlier. 'Perhaps this will increase your interest in my desires.'

'Am I to eat gold? Someone burned down the only market in a hundred miles. You'd have done better to bring me food. Are you an Asheneman or a tribesman? The worst of both, it seems to me: sure that gold will solve every problem and too ignorant to know that those are Kardosi sovereigns. You'd have to cross the wide ocean and a thousand years to find a country where you could spend them.'

'I . . .' Sang Ki said, and found no further words. He watched in silence as the Eom knelt by Nethmi's bedside. His touch was far gentler than his words as he held her chin between his fingers to turn her head and inspect the damage. Nethmi groaned in agony all the same.

'If you must stay, bring me water,' the physician said as he continued his inspection. 'That's the worst loss fire brings, worse than the pain, though I'm sure she doesn't think it now.'

There was a barrel in one corner of the room. Sang Ki was sorely tempted to drink himself, but at the Eom's glare he ladled some into a goblet and brought it to Nethmi.

She choked on the first mouthful and then screamed in pain as trickles leaked from her mouth over her raw skin.

'Carefully!' the Eom snapped.

Sang Ki slowed the flow of water to drips and watched as Nethmi's swollen tongue darted out to lick them from her lips. The Eom used her distraction to begin spreading a pungent lotion over the worst of her burns, frowning at her whimpers. Within seconds some of the raw redness had leached out of them, and Sang Ki opened his mouth to ask the composition of the unguent and then snapped it shut again.

'Your lover?' the Eom asked as he set aside her belt and pulled off her few remaining rags of clothing.

'The woman who murdered my father.'

'You're a generous man. When you bring me coin I can spend, my work on her will cost you dear. Did you dislike your father?'

'He was the best man there could be. She'll hang for her crime when she's well enough to look me in the eye as I kick away the stall.'

The Eom stopped his ministrations and turned to stare at Sang Ki. His eyes looked almost black against the orange of his skin. 'You're Ashane, aren't you? Mixed blood, but you have the accent. And this woman is Ashane too.'

'I am Seonu Sang Ki, son and heir to Lord Thilak of Winter's Hammer. This woman is Nethmi, formerly of Whitewood and wife to my father.'

'Definitely Ashane then, and so you certainly can't hang her.'

Sang Ki felt the first stirrings of anger. 'I think you'll find that I can.'

'Not according to your own laws. This woman is pregnant.'

*

Sang Ki brought both Nethmi and the reluctant Eom physician to his own encampment. It was meticulously neat, as anything in his mother's charge must be, but worryingly small. Only a bare two hundred of his men had survived the immolation of Smiler's Fair and, though their numbers had been swollen by the remains of Gurjot's troops, it was still a much diminished force. They'd dug a ditch around their tents and seeded it with bitter-thorn caltrops, but there was insufficient wood for a palisade. The sooner they departed this place, the safer he'd feel.

His mother was slow to answer his summons and frowned as she entered the tent. The frown deepened when she saw the mutilated woman he'd laid out on his own cot.

'Look at her knife,' Sang Ki said. He'd placed it beside her on the bed.

His mother stared at the weapon, her expression hardening into something grim. 'Nethmi.'

'Indeed. And this fellow here—'

'Eom Min Soo. And you are Seonu Hana – an honour, elder mother.' The physician bowed with far more courtesy than he'd ever shown Sang Ki. But then, his mother had a way of commanding it.

'Min Soo assures me that she will live, if given the proper treatment,' Sang Ki told her.

His mother knew him too well. She folded her arms and silently waited for the rest.

'She's pregnant,' Sang Ki said, 'which apparently means we can't hang her. Although who's to tell if we do? I doubt any of my men would much care.'

'*I* care.' Min Soo flicked his long purple hair over his shoulder. 'And I *will* tell.'

'Of course we won't hang her,' his mother said. She turned to Min Soo and added, 'Please wait outside.'

Min Soo folded his arms in turn and stood stubbornly still. It occurred to Sang Ki that the Eom and his mother were remarkably similar. 'You gave her to my care. I won't let you kill her.'

'I don't plan to,' his mother said flatly. 'You can treat her in a few moments. Now wait outside.'

Sang Ki had yet to see his mother lose a battle of wills. The Eom grunted and strode through the open tent flap, pulling it closed behind him. In the sudden gloom the smells of unguent and scorched flesh seemed far stronger.

'Why don't you plan to kill her?' Sang Ki asked.

'The baby, of course.'

'Are you really so sentimental? There are two of Gihan of Fort Greenshore's anatomy texts in our library. If you recall, the man dissected pregnant mothers before one of their fathers put a trident through his eye. Nethmi can't be more than a few weeks gone. I've seen the pictures, and what lives inside her now is little different from a tadpole.'

'A tadpole that in a few months' time could inherit Winter's Hammer. A tadpole that will need you as its regent. Without this child we could lose the fort entirely – King Nayan would have the right to pass it to another lord.'

'But this child isn't my father's. How can it be? There's no roundness in her stomach, no milk in her breasts. Thilak's child would be showing itself by now, more than three months later.'

His mother shrugged. 'Some babies grow slowly.'

'Even if that's true, even if it is Thilak's, its mother is *the woman who killed him.*'

'Do you think I've forgotten?' Her face twisted for a moment in pain and he looked away. He found her grief hard to bear, too much a reflection of his own.

'Then must we really care for her?'

'Yes. You won't be disinherited when I can prevent it. Thilak wouldn't have wanted it and he wouldn't want his own child dead. It's . . . it might be the last thing we have left of him. We need to remain here while she gets well, but we'll take her back to Winter's Hammer for the birth.' His mother looked down at Nethmi, writhing in pain on already bloody sheets. 'Then we can hang her.'

2

The smoke of Smiler's Fair lingered in the east. The blue of the sky was smudged with grey across the horizon and in places flocks of crows thickened it to black, while the smell of burning wood and flesh lingered in the endless grass of the plains. Three days' walk from the ruins of her former home, and Olufemi felt as if she would never escape the shadow of its destruction.

Ah well, better to look ahead, where Krishanjit and Dae Hyo were outlined at the top of a small rise. The boy was regaining his strength more slowly than she would have liked. Her salves had stopped the wounds on his legs from festering, but the blood he'd lost wasn't easily replaced. Dae Hyo had his arm slung round the younger man's waist and was half supporting him as they followed the river seaward. Earlier the warrior had been scouting their route ahead, but he'd reappeared as soon as the boy needed him. Olufemi suspected he'd been watching them from a distance, like a mother with a newly walking child.

Adofo shifted on her shoulder, tightening his scaly tail round her neck. The lizard monkey's moon-coloured eyes were fixed on Krish, as they had been since she'd found the boy. 'I know,' she said. 'The sun's still hours from setting but we'll have to stop. Can't have him dying of exhaustion.' Not now, after everything she'd been through to find him.

Adofo chittered in what she took to be agreement and she pushed herself to catch the others up, her arthritic joints protesting the use.

'We can stop here,' she told them. 'There's water and that copse of willows will shield us from hunting eyes.'

Krish sighed in relief and sank to his rump on the rocky ground of the riverbank. His eyelids drooped and there was an unhealthy pallor to his brown cheeks. Adofo screeched and unwound his tail from her neck, galloping across the ground to deposit himself in the boy's lap. Krish absently stroked the lizard monkey's head as their mirrored eyes met.

Adofo had been deserting her more and more in the last few days. The jealousy she felt was absurd, of course. His affinity for Krish was the evidence she'd sought that the boy was indeed everything she'd hoped: Yron's new avatar in the world. But the creature had been hers for so long. And with Vordanna and Jinn gone – with Vordanna and Jinn *dead*, she had to face it – Adofo was all she had left of her past. The future Krish opened to her seemed very uncertain.

As she watched Krish and Krish watched her pet, Dae Hyo set about making camp. He'd done the same every night since their first night together, though back then he'd been spattered in the blood of the men who might have been their allies. He'd bathed in the river since, but she still saw their senseless slaughter whenever she looked at him. And Krish had permitted it. He'd encouraged it.

But he'd also wakened the runes, after long centuries of silence. She remembered the astounded joy she'd felt as the flames had died at the moon rune's command and went to kneel beside Krish, pulling unguents from her pack.

'My legs are feeling better,' he said. 'I don't need the ointment.'

'You'll stop using it when I tell you and not before.'

He sighed and coloured but undid his trousers so that she could pull them down to expose the deep cuts scoring his thighs. There'd been a time when a young man would have blushed with joy, not shame, at the thought of undressing before her, but that time was many years past. His penis remained unflatteringly limp as she smoothed the honey-scented paste into his skin.

'If I'm a god,' he said, watching her fingers and not her face, 'how can I be hurt?'

'You *are* Yron.' She felt sure of it now, and not just because of his strange silver and black eyes.

'I'm Krish. Krishanjit. I was born, I grew, I raised goats.'

'Yes – you were the son of a goatherd, but also the son of a king. A person can be more than one thing at once.'

He pushed her hands away to tie his trousers himself. 'But I *wasn't* my da's son. That was a lie. King Nayan was always my father, I just never knew it.'

'Well . . . maybe not that, then.'

'And where was Yron when I wasn't here? Was he someone else?'

'You were made flesh a thousand years ago, and again long before that.'

'And when he wasn't me or, or whoever that was before, where was he? What is he? What does it *mean* to say I'm a god when I'm still just me?'

As she studied his face she saw a bright curiosity and maybe enough intelligence to understand. 'Yron is an idea,' she told him. 'A very deep idea, one of the two most profound that exist in the world, and both the source and the solution of the runes. A concept is eternal, its physical manifestation in the world transient, but they are two aspects of the same thing.'

'Like . . . like talking about a meal and the actual food itself.'

'Yes! Very good, Krishanjit. It's the same with your mother – your real mother. She died when you were born, but that didn't change the relationship between you or end the concept of motherhood itself. If all the mothers in the world were killed, the idea of motherhood would still exist until someone else gave birth and became a mother of flesh again.'

He stroked his trousers over the cuts on his leg. 'Yron is immortal, but I can die.'

'Yes.'

'So I'm not any different from any other man. I'm not any stronger or safer.'

'You're not quite so easy to kill. And now the runes are awake we can make you stronger still: the only way to use the runes is through you, through service to you.'

'But the other Yron, a thousand years ago, he died, didn't he? Or I wouldn't be here.'

MERRICKVILLE PUBLIC LIBRARY

'He was killed,' she admitted.

'How?'

'It was his sister, the sun. She too was made flesh in that age, and they fought, as you and she are always destined to fight. She defeated and murdered him.'

'And won't she be after me now?'

'No, she's gone. When she saw what her people had done in her name to her brother's followers, the hundreds of thousands of deaths, she chose to leave the world and she never returned. You're safe, Krishanjit – we'll make you safe.'

Safe from his sister, at least. When she turned from the boy, she saw that Dae Hyo had started a fire blazing as they spoke. 'Do you think that's wise?' she asked him.

'I'll douse it when the sun sets. My brother needs hot food.'

She couldn't argue with that and watched in silence as he plucked the two plump birds he'd shot during their walk. His expression suggested he thought she should take over the task, but she'd never learned menial work in Mirror Town and had seen no need to master it after leaving.

While the meat roasted over their fire, Dae Hyo and the boy talked quietly, nonsense about the right flowers to weave into your horse's bridle and the correct berries to bring when wooing a woman. Dae things, which should mean nothing to the moon's heir, but Krish had declared himself Dae with a brutality that still shocked Olufemi.

It was as they were eating that she heard the hoofbeats approaching. She looked up, alarmed, but it was already too late. The rider was less than a hundred yards away and staring in their direction. Dae Hyo's wretched fire had probably drawn his eye.

She looked to the warrior, expecting that he'd draw one of his many weapons, but he gulped down the haunch he'd been chewing, leaned back on his elbows and shouted, 'Be welcome, friend. There's meat to share if you want it.'

'What are you doing?' Olufemi hissed as Krish asked 'Why?', but the warrior only smiled at their questions.

The stranger's horse trotted closer and Olufemi forced her expression into calmness as she saw his face. He was Ashane, like Krish himself and like the men who were pursuing him. The newcomer wore no marks of allegiance, but then neither had the ragtag force that had invaded Smiler's Fair. And there was a sword slung at his side.

'You've ridden fast,' Dae Hyo said, eyeing the horse's lathered flank.

The man swung himself gracefully from the saddle. 'It's true, I've been pushing Unmol too hard.' He patted his mount and then pulled out a cloth and began drying her.

'In a hurry, then. I tell you what, it's hard to blame you in these troubled times. That place –' Dae Hyo nodded towards the smoke on the horizon '– fell apart like a wormy apple and all the maggots crawled out.'

The man raised an eyebrow, clearly wondering if the warrior meant to imply he was himself one of those maggots, but Dae Hyo's innocently friendly expression seemed to reassure him. 'Dangerous times indeed. You're citizens of Smiler's Fair yourselves, then?'

'Just passing through when the fire started,' Dae Hyo replied. 'And yourself?'

The man had a shipborn face, all clean lines and smooth skin. It barely wrinkled as he smiled. 'The same. I'm Ravindu of Fort Daybreak.'

'Dae Hyo and Dae Krish,' the warrior offered before Olufemi could prevent him. 'And this is Olufemi, a mage of Mirror Town.'

Ravindu nodded, seemingly unconcerned by the names, but did his eyes linger a moment too long on Krish as the boy rose to greet him? Olufemi had lived through three days of unrelieved tension, and no longer trusted her own judgement. Still, as she watched Dae Hyo hand a roasted bird leg to the stranger and then a flask of vodka, she was certain she didn't trust his judgement either.

'You're heading the wrong way if you mean to return to Ashanesland,' she said to the stranger as he stripped the bird's bones clean with his teeth.

'As are you,' he pointed out.

'But we're not Ashane.'

His eyes flicked again to Krish and then back to her. The hand not holding his meat had shifted to hover above the hilt of his sword and a cold wave shivered through her. But he merely pulled his blue-checked trousers straight.

'The truth is,' he said, 'I came to Smiler's Fair to escape . . . problems in Ashanesland. It wouldn't do to return there, not if I value my life.'

'I see.' It was plausible. The fair had always been a refuge.

The sun had sunk towards the western horizon as they spoke, and now only a sliver remained. The night was Krish's time, but the boy looked nervous as Dae Hyo quenched the fire with river water to let the concealing darkness grow.

'Afraid of who might see us?' Ravindu asked.

'Maggots,' Dae Hyo said and rolled on to his side, eyes shut in the instant sleep that Olufemi envied.

It took her far longer to escape consciousness. Age had brought that affliction and worry sharpened it. Krish's moon-silver eyes remained open a while too, but eventually his weakness overcame him and he began to gently snore. Ravindu's eyes had shut almost as quickly as Dae Hyo's and his chest moved gently; perhaps he was sleeping, or perhaps merely feigning it.

She reached down to hug Adofo, accustomed to warming him in the cold spring nights. But there was only a dent in the blankets where his body had briefly lain. She looked again at Krish and saw open silver eyes again – but they weren't the boy's. The lizard monkey blinked as he shifted against Krish's chest and then turned away from her to wrap his limbs round the boy.

She'd spent so long, so very many years imagining how it would be when Yron's heir was found. She'd never imagined this.

Krish woke to find a hand over his mouth and another pressed against his chest. He struggled for a frantic moment before something – maybe the elderflower-oil-and-whisky smell, or the rough feel of the palm – told him it was Dae Hyo. When he stilled, the other man released him.

The warrior grabbed his elbow to steady him as he rose and pointed to their left. Ravindu was sleeping there, turned on to his back with one arm curled against his chest and the other flung out towards them. He was very still. Krish's eyesight at night had always been strong, but he couldn't see the stranger's chest moving. And there was a smell too, one Krish had grown familiar with. The instant he recognised it he realised that the puddle of black around Ravindu's throat was blood and the dark slash across it a mortal wound.

He started back, heart pounding, only to see Dae Hyo's smile. The warrior showed his knife. He turned it in the moonlight to reveal the long stain along its blade before wiping it clean on the grass and sheathing it.

'You killed him?' Krish asked.

Dae Hyo frowned and put a finger to his lips, though Krish couldn't see any reason for stealth now: the man was dead. Dae Hyo hooked an arm under Ravindu's pack, gestured Krish to follow and strode away along the riverbank.

They walked for several minutes in silence, but Krish couldn't leave the question unanswered. He'd given Dae Hyo orders to kill – to murder – three days ago. Had his brother taken them as a general instruction? 'Why did you kill Ravindu?' he risked whispering when Dae Hyo stopped.

'I didn't like the look of him.' Dae Hyo dropped to his knees and opened the dead man's pack, pulling out clothes and food and cooking pots to strew them on the ground.

'Then why did you invite him to our fire?'

'It's simple, brother. I didn't want him to ride off and tell anyone else where we were and I couldn't be sure an arrow would kill him at that distance. But I know if I was hunting a man I'd want to identify him by more than his tracks. I didn't think he'd turn down the chance to study us up close, and he was safer where we could see him.'

'Unless he attacked us.'

'No cause for fear – he was only a little man. Didn't put up any sort of a fight when I slit his throat.'

'That's because you did it while he was sleeping.'

'Yes, but – ah!' Dae Hyo turned to Krish, grinning and waving a sheet of parchment he'd drawn from the stranger's pack. It was a drawing of a boy's face. It took Krish a moment to realise that it was his own: hollow-cheeked and wild-eyed. He'd seen his reflection so seldom that it jolted him how half-starved he looked. And he knew what the drawing meant: Ravindu *had* been hunting him.

'How did you know it was there?' he asked.

'I didn't. I was looking for coin or metal but this is good, isn't it? I always prefer to know I haven't killed a man for nothing. And look, three gold wheels, twelve feathers and a, well I'm not sure, to be honest with you. But it's metal and it has a man's face stamped on it, so it must be a coin. The horse as well: two more and we'll be able to make much better time. A good night's work.'

'But . . . if he was dead already, why were we whispering?'

'What? Oh.' Dae Hyo threw the parchment away and pocketed half the coins before handing the rest to Krish. 'I didn't want Olufemi to hear. Lion hunting isn't women's business. They're too kind: it hurts them to think of the death, and it's not a man's business to upset them.'

'Lion hunting?' Krish felt as if Dae Hyo had woken him halfway through a conversation he'd started with himself.

'I saw the tracks when I was scouting earlier. Big fucker.'

'Is lion good to eat?' Krish had killed one of the great cats once himself, but he'd only thought about taking its pelt, not its flesh.

'I don't know. The flesh is just flesh; it's the balls we want. That's where a beast's strength is. It's different with men – decent ones, anyway. They keep their strength along with their love in their stomachs. But animals only think about their cocks and the gods put all their power in that part of them. You're weak at the moment and not getting better quickly enough. I can see the mage thinking it. You may be this moon god she talks about, but you're in a man's body and that body needs healing. The lion's balls will do the trick.'

'But we need to kill the lion first.'

Dae Hyo grinned wolfishly. 'That's part of the fun.'

'Not when I'm so weak I can't draw a bowstring. Or – you're not expecting me to use my knife, are you?'

'Don't worry, brother, I'll do the killing. You just need to watch.'

It occurred to Krish to ask why he needed to be there at all, but he knew the answer. The murders Dae Hyo had done at his command, those blood-soaked moments he preferred not to dwell on, had bound them tight.

'How do we know where the lion is?' Krish asked. 'Did you find its lair?'

'Better – I found its food. Lions don't like to shift themselves when the sun's high. They hunt at night mostly, and they don't want to run too far even then. Lazy fuckers, but who can blame them? And they're clever, you can't deny that. They scout the land, just like I did, and find the places other animals are bound to go: watering places, mostly. Then they find a nice thick bush and hide in it until something juicy steps past.'

Krish looked at the river, rushing past to their left. Its banks were steep and rocky, offering no sure footing. The larger beasts wouldn't drink here if they had another choice.

Dae Hyo's expression was shadowed in the darkness but Krish thought he was smiling. 'You found the watering place,' he guessed.

'I found it,' Dae Hyo agreed.

They followed the course of the water downstream, the moon bright enough to guide their steps. Olufemi had told him they were heading for the coast and he'd always known that rivers led to the ocean eventually, though he'd never seen it. But the ocean that ate the rivers of his home was in the east. The one they now sought was to the west. It didn't seem possible he'd come so far, to the other side of the world.

Many things that had happened in the last few months didn't seem possible to him. His da's death was the least of it now, though sometimes he felt a shock of loathing when he remembered what he'd done. And then to find that he was heir to the Oak Wheel and, more than that, a god. But what did that really mean? His prow god still sat at the bottom of his pack, a fist-sized white stone whose name he hadn't yet dreamed. Was he that kind of god? Or was he more like the Five who shared a home with his true father the king?

As the water hissed over the rocks to his right and the night-time murmurings of the grasslands came from the left, he searched inside himself for what might make him different from other men. He couldn't think that there was anything. He needed food and water like anyone else, and pissed and shat it out again the same as them. Olufemi told him he'd brought power back to the runes, but he hadn't felt it. And runes were a sort of writing, which he knew nothing of.

He looked at Dae Hyo, who was scanning the landscape with his usual vigilance. The warrior had left his turban back at the camp, and the hair was flying loose from his topknot, curling in wisps round his pale face. His eyes were clearer than usual and his smell pleasanter. He'd drunk far less since they'd left Smiler's Fair.

Having a friend – a *brother* – was almost as strange to Krish as anything else. He wasn't sure he knew how to do it, but Dae Hyo seemed content enough. It was loyalty the other man valued and Krish could offer that, at least. And he'd learn the Dae ways too, if it pleased the warrior. His hair had already grown a little. It wouldn't be too much time before he was able to bind it into his own topknot.

Dae Hyo was slowing now, placing his feet more carefully and almost silently. That was one lesson Krish had learned well and he softened his own footfalls until Dae Hyo abruptly stopped, dropping to a crouch, and Krish knelt beside him.

The other man's breath was hot against his ear as he whispered, 'There, beyond that apple tree, do you see?'

The surface of the little lake was so still, its waters showed a perfect reflection of the flower-strewn shore. Their colours were lost to night, but their shapes were clear: big sprays of petals and stems covered in tiny bells and another, perched on the end of a long, tall stem, that looked like a goblet.

The animals took him a little longer to pick out, hidden among the plants. He heard their lapping at the water first, carried over the still night air. And then he saw the curved tooth of a boar and, further along, the branched antlers of a deer.

'Where is the lion waiting?' he asked Dae Hyo.

The warrior pointed to a clump of bushes only fifty paces from the water. The leaves were so thick nothing was visible within. It seemed strange that the creatures drinking at the lake didn't sense the predator waiting so very near, but the wind was heading from the water towards the lion's shelter and onward to Krish and Dae Hyo. The animals couldn't smell the lion – and the lion would be unable to scent him and Dae Hyo.

'Are we close enough?' he asked as the other man began to string his bow. It was a long shot, even for a good marksman.

Dae Hyo shrugged. 'I'd prefer the lion to eat the pig, and us to eat the lion, but if you fancy ending up in his belly yourself, go nearer.'

A deer wandered away from the water and Krish froze, but it galloped past the bushes and no attack came.

'Are you sure the lion's there?' he asked.

'He's there. A man gets a feeling for these things.'

'Then why didn't he kill the deer?'

'Well, do you prefer pork or venison?'

'Pig's better – more fat on it,' Krish said, though he'd only recently tried either.

'There you go then. Beasts have tastes like us and that lion knows what it wants.'

The hog was still snout-down in the water. Its tusks looked wickedly sharp and Krish wondered that the lion would choose that for its prey over the more fragile deer. But then he imagined Dae Hyo in the same situation and was quite sure his brother would have picked the harder challenge too. The thought made him smile, and then the boar moved.

Krish tensed, fingers gripping unconsciously at a bowstring he didn't have. But the boar was in no hurry, waddling away from the water with an easy gait.

The wind had stilled and the air felt thin and stretched, as if every animal at the lake and insect in the grass had paused to watch the outcome of the dual hunt. Krish realised he was holding his own breath and released it on a long, quiet sigh. Dae Hyo's usual restless fidgeting was gone. The warrior held himself with perfect, taut concentration as he studied the scene beneath them.

Even so, when the attack came it was almost too fast. The lion's coat looked grey in the moonlight. It growled low and lethal as it leapt, claws extended and mane floating behind it. The boar screamed and raised its tusks and, as the two met, Dae Hyo loosed his arrow.

The shaft struck the lion in its flank. The beast roared, stumbled and then rose to its feet with the arrow protruding from its side, rising and falling with the breath it still drew. Its head swung and its eye cut through the darkness with ease to fix on its attacker. And then it was charging towards Krish and Dae Hyo while Dae Hyo pulled a second arrow from the ground in front of him and the boar took its chance and fled.

Krish had forgotten how fast a lion could move, and this one was twice the size of the creature he'd once lured to its death. It was on them before Dae Hyo could draw the bowstring, and instead he was forced to grab the arrow in his fist and thrust it towards the great golden eye.

The lion twisted its head so that the arrow only grazed its cheek. It roared again, loudly and straight into Dae Hyo's face. The warrior flinched from the noise, the beast opened its massive jaws, and Krish didn't even realise that his knife was in his hand until he'd plunged it into the lion's breast.

The blade found the space between the creature's ribs by sheer chance. It was stopped a moment by the thick muscle of its heart, but Krish pressed forward, teeth gritted in a mirror of the lion's snarl, and then it was all the way in. The pommel quivered with the heart's last beats until the lion's breath rattled in its throat and it collapsed to the ground.

Dae Hyo stood stunned for a moment. The creature's claws had raked his face and his eyes were wild as he looked down at the corpse of the thing that had so nearly killed him. Then he looked at Krish and laughed.

Krish lay sprawled on the ground, his legs pinned beneath the dead lion. He could feel now how vastly it outweighed him. Its head was tilted to the side and it had died with its mouth open so that he could count every one of its sharp, blood-browned teeth.

'Are you hurt?' Dae Hyo asked, pushing against the beast's flank until Krish could pull his legs free.

'Only bruised. And tired.'

Dae Hyo sat beside him and sighed. 'I tell you what, you're not the only one. A fight takes it out of a man, no matter how few seconds it lasts. And you killed a lion, brother. A lion! You hardly need its balls.'

Krish grinned, suddenly giddy with more than blood loss. 'But only because you hurt it first. It didn't even see me.'

'That's why we hunt together. Look at it!' Dae Hyo ran a hand along the creature's jaw, almost gentle. 'Killing a lion isn't a one-man job.'

Krish's eyes filled with sudden and shaming tears. He didn't understand why he was crying and he swiped them away angrily.

'You *are* hurt,' Dae Hyo said, but Krish shook his head.

'What do you think it means, what Olufemi says about me?' he asked.

'That you're a god?'

'That I'm a god, that I brought the runes to life. Everything.'

Dae Hyo frowned fiercely and stared at his own fingers.

'Is it true?' Krish asked.

'About the runes, yes, I saw it happen. Something woke that mark of hers and it swallowed up the fire like water. We should have burned to death but we walked right through. I hear the best of the Maeng like to dance on coals to prove themselves, but that's nothing to striding through the flames themselves.'

'And being a god? I don't . . . I don't feel like a god. I don't know how a god's supposed to act.'

'However they like, it seems to me. Belbog and Bogdana enjoy doing good things, they're worth praying to, and Dana their daughter married her uncle Volos when she was asked, which was very dutiful. But then *he* turned against them and made all sorts of mischief and demons too. And as for the rest: Mladen only likes hunting and Svarog prefers to do nothing at all. They say that's why the Eom worship him, because he's the only god who loves idleness as much as them.'

'I suppose it's the same with the Five,' Krish said. 'The Lady makes storms and all sorts of weather – depending on what mood she's in. You can pray to her to make the sun shine, but she doesn't always listen. And the Fierce Child doesn't care for men at all. He only looks after the wild animals.'

'There you are, you see.'

It wasn't entirely clear what Krish was supposed to be seeing, but he smiled and leaned back against the lion's cooling corpse. The moon was sinking below the horizon, leaving almost total darkness behind, but he didn't miss it. He didn't have to be alone any longer; nothing else truly mattered.

3

She felt something she knew her sisters didn't share. The sunlight shattered into rainbows as it passed through the ice dome above, and the food was venison and pear, and everything was as it always had been by Mizhara's grace, and yet she was restless. Perhaps it was the child growing within her. She might have asked one of her sisters, but pregnancy was so rare among them, how was she to know what was normal and what unique to each mother?

It was the ninth day of her oroboros. She'd spent it in the great library, poring over the Perfect Law, as the Perfect Law itself dictated, but had written not a note in commentary. Her mind had been empty. No, worse: her mind had not been empty; it had been filled with thoughts of *him*. He was now in the care of others of her sisters, those in the early days of their own orobori, when work was to be done. But it didn't seem to her that caring for her husband was a form of labour.

She wasn't adept at reading those born of the dark lands. Still, she was sure Eric wasn't happy. Logic told her that he couldn't be, when he'd been so badly hurt. His nose had returned to health and his wounds hadn't festered, but there would be no regrowing his missing fingers and toes. Men were vain of their appearance, she'd been taught, and Eric had much to be vain about. What he'd seen in the mirror had pained him – that expression at least had been clear to her.

Mizhara hadn't meant for the thirteen husbands to be distressed. 'Treat them as you would that which is most dear to you,' it was written in the Perfect Law, 'for their flesh is as mine in my regard.' Was she truly obeying Mizhara's will by sitting here while Eric suffered?

Several of her sisters looked round as she stood. Mizhara hadn't left commandments concerning the appropriate length to sit at table, but by convention they all rose together. She avoided their gazes as she walked the length of the room to the exit, though if challenged, she felt confident she could justify her actions.

But she was puzzled to feel her breath shorten as she drew near to Eric's room. Maybe this too was a consequence of the baby growing inside her. It was very strange to feel her body out of her own control. She paused outside, staring at the hazy white outline of his bed and the fuzzy brown blot of his bedding. Was she wrong to come? Did something other than duty to Mizhara drive her? It was a worrying thought and she dismissed it. Her devotion to the Perfect Law remained absolute; it was merely her understanding of it that had changed. She wasn't ready to take the long walk into the white waste.

Eric lay with his back to her. She was sure he sensed her presence but his gaze remained fixed on the wall.

'Husband?' she said tentatively.

He had been sullen since the injury, but to her surprise he rolled on to his side to face her and even smiled a little. With his nose so much better the expression wasn't as twisted as it had been. His ear was ragged where the cold had torn away some of the tissue, but the rest of his face was as fair as it had always been, soft-featured and big-eyed. The world was filled with imperfect things and Mizhara had commanded her Servants to treasure them all the same. A focus on that which was deformed and damaged could only lead to harm. It was the path Yron had trodden to his ruin and the world's.

'You come to see me?' Eric asked.

'I came to see if you are well.'

'Well, ain't you a thoughtful one?'

Sometimes, she'd found, Eric said the opposite of what he truly meant, but she didn't believe this was such a time. 'Your welfare is my concern, husband.'

He sat up in bed, so that the thick furs fell away to reveal his thin chest. It was cold in the room, and his delicate white skin prickled into goosebumps, but he didn't attempt to cover himself.

'I ain't feeling too bad,' he said. 'Ear's not hurting and I can feel my fingers – the ones I got left.' She winced a little at his words but he laughed. 'It's all right, honest. I'm over my snit. Sorry if I was snappy before.'

'You behaved exactly as you ought.' She paused to consider her words, troubled by them. They weren't strictly true and Mizhara had commanded truth above all else, but she had surely only meant between her Servants. The truth was a sharp-edged thing and these sunless people might be too fragile for it.

'Nah, I was rotten to you – it weren't right.' He looked momentarily downcast, but he quickly seemed to shrug it off, rising from the bed to pull on his shirt. She watched his remaining fingers, nimble as they tied the ribbons at its front, slowly covering up the almost hairless skin of his chest. When he picked up his fur jacket and shrugged it on, she wrenched her eyes away.

'You wish to go outside?' she asked.

'Thought we could go for a walk. It gets boring, trapped in here. I know you got your studying, but these are long days when a boy ain't got nothing to fill them.'

The days weren't long but endless in Salvation, where the sun never set. And Eric too might have filled them with study: the oroboros was for him as much as any Servant. But she said neither of these things; she merely nodded and strode through the door after him.

He led her through the golden birches that grew in ordered ranks to one side of the city. The leaves filtered the constant sunlight, offering dapples of shade and a more gentle illumination. She often came here herself on the first day of her oroboros when she reflected on all that she hoped to achieve in the twelve days to come. Mizhara had caused the trees to grow where nature would have bred none and she felt the remnant of her mistress's magic beneath their boughs, a gift she'd left behind when she departed. It warmed her to think that Eric too found comfort here. There was little else that they shared.

'It's pretty, ain't it?' Eric said.

She nodded, gaze still on the trees. The breeze was icy but it moved the leaves in a pleasing dance.

'I grew up in a forest,' he said. 'Did you know that? Up in the Moon Forest, or down in the Moon Forest I ought to say now. But I left when I was twelve and I ain't spent much time near anything growing since.'

She tried to imagine what a forest might look like. Mizhara had spoken of them when she wrote of her campaign against Yron in the dark world, yet no living Servant but one had ever left Salvation. Its ice crept into all her imaginings and the woodland of her mind was more white than green.

'Do you miss your home?' she asked him.

'Best not to cry about what's past. It's only what's coming what matters.'

That was a very odd idea, as if all that had gone might be erased, leaving nothing but a white blankness like the snows in front of them. Mizhara's presence and words were all behind them and if they didn't look back, how would they see their mistress?

'I can see you don't agree,' her husband said, better at reading her expressions than she was at interpreting his. 'Maybe when you got more past to think about, there's more point thinking it.'

But that seemed wrong to her as well. Her oroboros stretched back many decades, as unchanging as the Perfect Law. Individual days blurred into a ceaseless cycle of devotion to Mizhara. She realised it wasn't so for him or any in the dark lands. How would it feel to have each day different from the last, and the events of the next undecided? But she was sure this was a thought she oughtn't to think.

'Or maybe you don't want to think about what you've done – at least, not what you've done what's different from what all the rest of your sisters did,' he added slowly. 'Being all exactly the same, that's what you lot aim for, ain't it? Never standing out, never even having names.'

She drew herself up, sensing disapproval in his words. 'We all strive to be as Mizhara wished us. She wished the same for all of us, and that we are alike is a sign that we, imperfect as we are, are obeying her will.'

'And she didn't want you to have names? Must have been awkward when she was still alive. "Oi, you – come here! Not you, the one with blonde hair. No, the other one with blonde hair." Can't have made giving orders easy. And it's not like you *are* all the same. You had different dads, right? It took me a while, but now I can tell you apart. I can definitely recognise *you*.'

'I am failing, then.' But the thought wasn't as disturbing as it should have been.

'Maybe I'm just clever. And I can't keep calling you *you*. It's rude.'

'You may call me wife, if you wish it.'

'But I've got dozens of wives. How will you know I'm talking to you?'

She backed away a step, towards the comfort and shade of the birch trees. She was suddenly sure this was a conversation she wasn't allowed.

'I'm going to call you Drut,' he said decisively.

'No, no you mustn't.'

'But it ain't even a name – it's just a word in my own language. That's all right, ain't it?'

'What does the word mean?' she asked cautiously.

'My darling,' he said. 'The kind of thing a husband says to his wife, at least where I come from.'

'You mustn't,' she repeated, backing away again.

'I'll see you later, Drut,' he shouted, heedless, as she fled beneath the shadow of the trees.

Eric found Rii where he'd arranged to meet her, in the lee of a monumental tower of snow, its peak curled into fantastical icy ramparts. Now that his time in Salvation had stretched into weeks, he'd begun to recognise the features of the landscape around it. Much like the Servants, it only seemed the same everywhere until you looked closer.

Rii had dug beneath the snow, hunching her huge body so

that it was hidden from the city. They weren't exactly meeting in secret, but that didn't mean they wanted an audience either.

She shivered as he approached, sending a small storm of flakes floating through the air around her.

'Don't know what you're complaining about,' he said. 'You've got fur.'

'And thou art wearing it, morsel.'

'Yeah, but you grew up round here, didn't you? You're used to it.'

'My master provided us warmth, molten rock to heat our home. It is the Servants who disdain comfort in their city of ice.'

That wasn't hard to believe. The Servants didn't seem to understand the concepts of pleasure or fun, but their innocence was useful in a way. They didn't lie and they didn't seem to understand that anyone else might.

'Thy wife grows closer to thee?' Rii asked.

'She's a peculiar cove. And I wouldn't want to say for certain she's falling, but she ain't cold neither. She's been coming to see me every day, and none of the others do. Yesterday she tried to give me the choicest cut off the shoulder, saved it for me special. But I got a bit too forward earlier, tried to give her a name. She weren't too keen on that.'

Rii gave her painful piping call, which Eric knew meant he'd displeased her. Well she'd have to grin and bear it, wouldn't she? It was a slender needle she'd asked him to thread.

'Thou must tread with care, morsel. Thy wife is young by the count of her people, but old still compared to thee. She is untutored in those things thou knowest best, but no fool. Have a care not to alert her to thy purpose.'

'I won't. Only . . . flirting and winking and flattery's a game I don't mind playing. Baiting a hook for her heart just don't seem right.'

'And was it right of them to bring thee here, so much against thy will? Was it right of them to bed with thee, so much against thy nature?'

He snatched a glance at her, shocked she'd figured that out.

'That's true I suppose,' he admitted.

'Then continue with thy smiles and thy flattery. Win her friendship if not her heart.'

'Don't you worry, I know what I'm doing.' He thumped a palm against her furry flank. It earned him a glare from her half-blind black eyes and a waft of the mouldy cinnamon scent that accompanied her everywhere. 'I'm not a boy who goes back on a deal what's been shook on. When my son comes, I'll get him from her, and then you'll fly us out of here.'

Her flank twitched beneath his hand. *'That I cannot do.'*

'What? Then what's the point of the whole plan? You were the one what wanted to save the lad.'

'And so I do, but I have been bound to this place by a magic stronger than steel. I may only depart with the Servants' leave, and why should they give it when I mean to betray them? But do not despair, morsel: there is another way. Mount and I will show thee.'

Her hair was greasy as he grabbed handfuls of it to pull himself on to the saddle on her back, but he was used to her now. He only gasped a little when her great wings beat downward and she sprang towards the sky.

Salvation was soon invisible beneath him, just a glitter of ice in this cold land. He huddled deeper in his furs and closed his eyes against the glare, only opening them when his stomach lurched unpleasantly and he knew that Rii was descending. Snow still covered the ground beneath them, but ahead there was a crisp blue expanse that gradually resolved into wave-ruffled water. As she landed, a gaggle of black-and-white flightless birds scattered, honking their displeasure.

The ice had risen into high cliffs against which the wild waters of the ocean broke. The ocean's force was so great that he could see great chunks of ice broken off and floating away, each bigger than Rii. But they weren't the only thing moving on the blue swell. As Rii settled on the cliff edge, he saw ships staggering across the huge waves.

Rii shrugged her shoulders irritably and he slithered from her back to stand beside her. The cliff was only thirty paces high and the ships ventured so close to the shore it seemed certain they'd be wrecked before they could reach the rough wooden harbour. But as Eric watched, two men leapt down from the ship's tall side, carrying a rope as thick as their arms between them, and made it fast to the dock as the salt spray of the sea drenched them. They were so near he could see their long white faces and the dark curls of their hair.

'They're Moon Forest folk,' he said in surprise. 'I never knew the folk to take to ships. I never even knew them to leave the forest, except for the Wanderers and us Smiler's Fair folk. What are they doing all the bloody way out here?'

'These are not thy countrymen.'

'Well, they ain't Ashane. Could be from the savannah, I suppose, though the shape of their faces don't look right.'

'They are thy precursors, the race from whom thine own sprang, before thy ancestors travelled to my master's forest.'

Eric stared at the men below him in fascination. Every Jorlith and Rhinanish child knew the story of how their peoples had wandered in exile from their old homes before the Hunter had guided them to their new one in exchange for a tithe of their children to fight the moon monsters.

The sailors had noticed their watchers on the cliff. He saw some stop to stare, and others rushed below deck, but most continued their work and he guessed they must have encountered Rii before.

'The cursed Servants trade with these men and others who travel the waterways,' she said. *'Coin will buy their service and passage for thee and thy son.'*

'Coin we don't have,' Eric pointed out.

Rii raised her claw and picked open the clasp of her saddlebag with unusual delicacy. *'Look inside if thou doubtest me, morsel.'*

He started to push her claw aside and then froze with his hand still against its sharp edge. Inside the bag, emeralds and sapphires and diamonds glittered in the sunlight.

'My master studied their making in a darker age of the world. In his wisdom, he fathomed how to form jewel from stone and filled our halls with them for our entertainment.'

'And the Servants don't know about the gems?'

'They know and use my master's jewels to buy their food, their furs and their husbands, but there is more hidden in his citadel than could ever be spent or found. The price of thy passage a hundred times over I can supply, but thou must do thy part.'

All those jewels could buy more than just his passage. He imagined taking a few diamonds back with him, many a ruby or an emerald or two. He'd only have to spend one diamond to build a shipfort grander than Lahiru's to float on the lake beside his, and an emerald for the mammoths to pull it. Lahiru's wife might not like it, but another diamond would pay for men to guard him and then let her try to hold a knife to his throat again. He'd come to Lahiru as an equal and they could start over.

If messing a little with his wife's heart was the price for that, well . . . Rii was right. He hadn't asked to be brought here and he didn't like what they made him do now he was here. If he figured out a way of escaping it, who could blame him?

4

In the twilight, the humped forms of the dead moon monsters were hard to see, and Cwen slowed as she approached them. The local merchants had eyed the hawks askance as they sliced the choicest cuts from the grotesque corpses, but they hadn't dared to speak with the Lion of the Forest herself, who was overseeing the work. Afterwards, the Hunter had ordered the gawping merchants to bury the remains.

Cwen passed one half-dug pit now. The work proceeded slowly; the refugees from the Spiral had friends and family to put to rest before they attended to their killers. Hawks had died too, but they wouldn't be buried here; their bodies would be taken back to the forest when the Hunt returned. Cwen was beginning to wonder when that would be. Her mistress hadn't said, but days had passed and no more monsters had emerged from the trees. Cwen didn't understand why they were lingering here.

Their mounts didn't seem to understand it either. They were restless, and grew more so with each day that passed. As she neared the paddock they whickered or hooted or bayed, depending on their type. Some growled and snarled, an aggressive sound that should have been trained out of them in the years of their captivity.

Her own trotted nearer as she approached, his clawed feet digging deep divots out of the grass. She removed her hawk mask and clucked in greeting but he didn't hiss back his usual reply. His long, forked tongue lolled from his mouth, a froth of saliva around it. Beneath the rune brand on his forehead, his eyes looked as wild as the day she'd first captured him. They flickered over her without a hint of recognition and then fixed themselves beyond her to glare at the setting sun.

She frowned. The tame monsters were protected from the sun's power by the Hunter's mark, but none of them had ever learned to love it and they hid from it when they could.

'Osgar,' she whispered. 'What's wrong?'

She'd been forbidden to name him, but she was too weak to feel nothing for the beast who'd carried her into a hundred fights and still bore the long red scar along his jaw where he'd risked his own life to save hers from a monster that might have been his sister. She thought the Hunter would forgive this one small disobedience in eighteen years of loyal service.

'Osgar,' she said again and he shuddered all over as something seemed to drain out of him, then turned to butt his scaled head against her chest. She rubbed him behind the green and yellow whorls of his ears where he was most sensitive, and he sighed in pleasure. Why *shouldn't* she name him, when he showed her such love? He didn't flinch away from her touch as the Moon Forest folk of the Spiral did. She'd spent so long with the Hunt, she'd almost forgotten what it felt like to be so shunned.

'He senses his master's presence,' the Hunter's voice said close behind her. 'They all do.'

Cwen couldn't repress a guilty start, but when she turned there was no sign of reproach in the goddess's expression. But then, her face had always been hard to read beneath its scars and its soft, inhuman glow. 'They did well enough, though,' Cwen said. 'They're just a little restless, that's all.'

'Now they are restless. Soon they will be unmanageable. My mark has Mizhara's virtue in it but Mizhara is gone and Yron has returned. His hold over the children of those he created cannot be broken.'

Cwen looked across the paddock at the hundred and more beasts the Hunt had brought with them. She knew them all. Those four sharp horns marked Godric's mount, and that high, arched back carried Mildburg on their hunts. Cwen had helped her clutch-mate capture the creature and her finger was still crooked from where he'd snapped it in his jaws. Now he licked her hands if she stroked him. Or he had, before the moon rose.

'It is time,' Bachur said gently, resting a hand against the wolf that sat at her feet.

'Time for what?'

'They must die, before they leave our service for their master's. We must kill them before they turn and kill us.'

Cwen bowed her head to hide her stricken expression. 'But eldest, they still obey us.'

'Do they?' Bachur's golden gaze swept the field, where the mounts stamped and shuffled when once they would have drifted into sleep. Cwen saw that the moon was already in the sky, and that the beasts were moving to face it, eyes glittering in the growing darkness. But when she held out her hand to Osgar, he nuzzled it.

'He knows me.' Cwen swallowed and made herself meet the goddess's bright gaze, never a comfortable thing. 'I'll kill him the moment he turns, I swear it.'

Bachur smiled and nodded. 'My trust in you is complete.' She turned her own eyes to the moon and stared at it for a long moment, until the reflected silver seemed to swallow the gold of her pupils. Then she sighed and turned back to Cwen. 'Come now, there is a boy we must question and I want you there.'

'A boy?'

'One whose journey has been the opposite to that of these creatures. Come.'

The Hunter led Cwen to her own tent. The inside smelled of the forest, as anywhere around the Hunter had a tendency to do. Two of her wolves lay curled asleep in one corner and the goddess stooped to caress them as she passed.

The boy was in the area set aside for eating, squatting on a pile of cushions. He was tearing into a haunch of meat as they entered, the fat smeared across his chin and lips. Cwen wondered if telling him that the joint came from one of the dead moon beasts would diminish his appetite.

He looked up as they both entered, scrambled to his feet and then bowed low, which struck Cwen as a waste of effort, but Bachur smiled and raised him with a hand beneath his chin. She looked into his eyes for a long moment and he met hers with obvious difficulty. His, Cwen saw, were a startling grass green. His gaze lingered on the four long scars marking the Hunter's cheek, as everyone's did.

'I'm sorry it's taken so long to come to you,' the boy said. 'I meant to come sooner, but my mother's not been well.'

'And now?' Bachur gestured the boy to sit and sank cross-legged on to the cushions opposite him.

Cwen remained standing and watchful, hidden behind her mask. She knew what her role was meant to be: the drawn knife, always sharp and ready.

'My mamma's better,' the boy said, 'and my news can't wait. The moon's returned.'

'We know that,' Cwen said. 'That's why we're here.'

'What is your name, child?' Bachur asked.

'Oh, I'm sorry.' He seemed shaken by his own forgetfulness, his confidence slipping for a moment to show the youth it hid. He couldn't have seen more than twelve summers. 'I'm Jinn, the son of Vordanna. We're Worshippers of Smiler's Fair.'

'And the god you worshipped was Yron,' the Hunter said. The boy looked shocked but he didn't deny it and she nodded. 'Some from the Spiral have heard you preach. They warned me of you, but I saw your face on the day the Hunt rode and heard your words and I knew you were not my enemy.'

'I'm not,' Jinn said fiercely. 'I ain't your enemy and I mean to be your friend. Power grows from knowledge, ain't that what they say? And I know a thing or two about the moon.'

'I would expect no less of one who once served him. But you must tell me why you serve him no longer.'

The boy dropped his gaze, watching his own hands work in his lap. 'He let me down, that's the long and short of it. I spent my whole cursed life in spreading the word about him, and what happened when he came back? Not a word, not a hint even, nothing to let me know of it. My mamma, she told me I had the moon's power, but that's a lie. She used me to earn coin and I don't know why else, but it wasn't for my benefit, that's as sure as frost in winter.

'And then my mamma got sick, and he didn't help her either despite all she'd done for him. But you did. You saved her, or leastways you saved everyone including her and me. So if I'm gonna give my loyalty to any god, and serving gods is all I know, I'd rather it was you.'

'Well, fuck,' Cwen said. 'That's a good answer.'

He smiled a little uncertainly at her masked face.

'And a true one,' Bachur said. 'Then tell me what you know of the moon.'

'He's come back. You knew that already, but maybe you don't know this: he was born the son of the King of Ashanesland.'

'He was?' Cwen took a step closer to him. 'Strange we never heard of him before.'

Jinn smiled bitterly. 'You think I don't know how you feel? He was born to the King but he wasn't raised by him. A prophecy said he'd kill his father and a nursemaid stole him away – snatched him out of his ma's own bleeding stomach, or so they say. He was raised a landborn goatherd in some mountain village where no one who mattered ever went.'

Inside the tent, the Hunter's golden skin looked the colour of leather and her eyes were dimmed. On anyone else, Cwen would have attributed the tightening of her lips to fear. 'What is his name?' Bachur asked.

'Krishanjit. Krishanjit of Ashfall, heir to the Oak Wheel if his father would have him, which of course he won't. There's a great big golden prize on his head and every scrub in Ashanesland is searching for him.'

'They will not find him,' the Hunter said. 'It begins so quickly and almost without a murmur, but it never finishes with such ease. When it ends, it only ever ends in blood.'

Cwen woke with the dawn, as she usually did. Her body felt tense and her mind clouded, although she'd slept the whole night through. The daylight sliding through a slit in the canvas was tentative, as if unsure of the welcome it would get from her. She flung back the flap and found it a grey day, gloomy with the promise of later rain.

She sniffed at her armpits and then shrugged into her jerkin. The smell wasn't rank enough to merit a wash. A hawk didn't want her prey scenting her before she approached, but a clean person didn't smell of nothing, just of clean person. Better to cover yourself with the scent of other animals and ignore the upturned noses of the folk of the Spiral.

A group of richly robed merchants watched her as she approached their wagons. They were Moon Forest thegns and she wondered for a brief moment if they knew her parents, if she might have met them herself in her youth. She studied their faces closely and their eyes dropped away from hers, perhaps fearing even so limited a contact would pollute them. Unseen, she sneered as she walked past. Maybe she had once known them, but what did it matter? All they saw was the bird mask over her face. It was all they'd ever seen, even before she wore it.

She recognised another mask approaching, a red and black striped thing that was meant to be a woodpecker but looked more like a horse. Aesc said his mother had carved it herself, and that his mother could barely carve a carrot and make it look like a vegetable. Cwen smiled at him, knowing he'd sense the expression in the way she held her body, but the smile dropped when he ripped the mask off in plain sight of the Moon Forest thegns. None but another hawk was meant to see his bare face.

His bare, crying face, she realised. His eyes were red-rimmed.

'What's wrong?' she asked, clasping his shoulders. His face was longer even than usual and the laugh lines by his mouth had been pulled into the service of a less cheerful expression.

'It's . . . go to the paddock, Cwen. I don't – she said . . . Just go and see.'

Cwen felt a twist of dread in her gut, a feeling she thought she'd left behind as a child. It was stupid. How bad could it be? She released him so abruptly he staggered back a step and strode towards the paddock.

The smell of blood hit her first, blood and the hint of cinnamon that always accompanied the moon's creatures. The field was awash with gore, the grass red and black where it had already begun to dry. This slaughter wasn't quite recent.

Every mount was dead. None of them had been left to suffer, there was that at least. The only sound was the muffled sobbing of a pair of the youngest hawks, crouched next to the corpses of their beasts.

Cwen found Osgar at the northern end of the paddock nearest the forest. He'd crawled forward a few paces with the mortal wound in his stomach, trying to reach his old home. She could see the smear of blood across the grass and the unwinding guts he'd left behind. She crouched by his corpse, leaning her head against his until the Hunter came to her.

'Cwen,' she said, and Cwen nodded but didn't turn round. Osgar's tongue was hanging out between his scaled lips. In death it had turned a dull grey and she thought about the way he used to lick her face and how it had reminded her of her father's hounds in the days when theirs was the only touch she'd known.

'Cwen,' Bachur said again. 'Look at me.'

Cwen obeyed; she always did. Bachur's face was as stern as she'd ever seen it, exactly like the image of the unbending goddess painted on the side of every Wanderer's wagon.

'You killed them,' Cwen said.

'Because you could not. Rest easy, child. I understand you were not ready, though I warned you long ago this day would come.'

'When the war was over.' Cwen heard the note of anger in her own voice and didn't try to suppress it.

'When it was necessary,' Bachur said with steely strength. 'They had to die before they disobeyed us, not after. War is hard, Cwen, and the choices it puts before us are between evil and greater evil. When the time comes again, will you do what you must? You are my blade, the sharpest and best of them. Can I trust you to cut out the gangrenous flesh of the world, however much pain it causes?'

Cwen nodded, the only reply she could give. But she looked at Osgar's corpse and doubted.

5

The Salt Road stretched ahead of Alfreda, fifty paces wide and so straight its far end met the horizon, its crystals sparkling brilliantly in the sun. It had been there when the Hunter first brought the folk to the forest and it had remained unchanged in all the years Alfreda had travelled it. Rain should have washed the salt away centuries ago, but some power kept it as it was, straight and perfect and free of all vegetation. To either side of the road, the tall trees kept their secrets in their shadows.

Algar dozed in the seat beside her, his thigh pressed against hers and his head resting on her shoulder. Awake, he was handsome enough to please any girl, his cheekbones high and delicate where hers were a little brutish, his fine curly hair the same chestnut as her own coarse mop and a wiry quickness against her raw strength. But right now a trickle of drool was seeping from the corner of his mouth. She smiled and wiped it away with her sleeve.

They were a week's travel from the edge of the forest and the Spiral where they'd spent the bulk of the winter. Alfreda hated the place. It was full of people, with nowhere to go for privacy. She should be glad to return to the Moon Forest, but perhaps the company of strangers, even such a great crowd of them, was to be preferred.

'You're thinking,' Algar mumbled against her shoulder. 'I can feel it.'

She shrugged, jostling his head so he lifted it off her. 'Not about anything important.'

'Contemplating our future and not liking what you see?'

She laughed, because he always knew her.

'It will be fine, Freda, you'll see.'

'Fine for you, with all the pretty girls to court.'

'Fine for both of us, with our new fire javelin to sell. We're going to change the whole forest, I know it – put the Jorlith out of a job!' His face was a little red with passion and she brushed a curl from his brow to calm him. He smiled, but still said, 'It's the Hunter's will. She always told the folk to use our minds as well as our muscles.'

'And a great lot of good it's done us,' she said gloomily, and to that he had no reply. The Maeng had been less than happy to find two Wanderers stealing the design of their fire javelins. Their departure from the settlement on the tribe's lands had been hurried and not entirely voluntary.

Algar scratched a hand through his curly hair as his eyes scanned the forest around them, always curious. In the quiet she could hear the meaningless chatter of the birds and the *crick* of smaller creatures in the undergrowth. Gradually, though, the noises died until the only sound was the rustle of the wind through the treetops.

'Have you noticed . . .?' Algar said.

'Aye. Something's scared them.'

His ears were keener than hers and he reacted first, leaping from his seat towards the covered back of the wagon. Then she heard it too: a rumbling that was half vibration and half sound. She cursed and followed her brother. Unguided, Edred whinnied and stopped to scan the barren road for vegetation.

'It sounds *huge*!' Algar whispered. 'But it won't break out of the forest, will it? The sun will kill it.'

'Not before it's run right over us.' Alfreda reached for her largest hammer, the one with the long handle and the hooked head, which she'd always thought could serve as a weapon – but she'd never really thought she'd need it to. She expected Algar to grab the sword she'd forged him, but instead he began frantically pushing against one of the wagon's side panels.

It took her a moment to realise what he was doing. 'Oh, no. We haven't tested it yet, Gar. The Hunt will be here soon, they'll take care of it.'

'Have you heard their horns? They're not coming, Freda! And this is what we made the fire javelin *for.*' With a final push the panel swung loose to slap against the wheel below. Algar's creation lay inside, the strong oak tube and the spear it was made to fire. But the device took time to prime, and the pounding footsteps grew louder every second. She could hear the rustle and snap as whatever beast was coming tore through the undergrowth.

'Where's the black powder?' Algar yelled.

'There's hardly enough for one spear cast!'

'So? Are you saving it for a special occasion?'

He was right. She pulled herself into the wagon and dropped to her knees beside the strongbox in its far corner. It was gloomy inside and it took her eyes crucial seconds to adjust while she fumbled for the container and turned the key to snap it open.

The powder was inside, hoarded in a sealed leather bag. She grabbed it just as something very fast and very heavy struck the side of the wagon. The impact flung her into the air and then into the thin wooden slats of the far wall. Tools and knives flew around her, slicing her skin, while loose clothes tangled her arms and legs as the wagon tipped, teetered and then fell on to its side.

The wind was thumped out of her; all she could do was gasp for breath while blood trickled into her eye from a cut on her brow. Then she heard a yell and a pained grunt and her mind emptied of any thought but one: *Algar.*

Her legs shook as she rose. The cramped space was filled with the smell of pickled eggs from shattered jars. The broken glass cut her as she stumbled from the back of the wagon into daylight.

The fall had cracked the wooden frame and the fire javelin was trapped between splinters and in folds of ripped cloth. Algar knelt, trying frantically to pull it free, but he'd only succeeded in wedging the long tube even deeper into the wreckage. Maybe it was because he wasn't watching his hands. His eyes were fixed on their attacker.

It was only twenty paces from him. There were scuff marks in the road where it had spun round after toppling the wagon.

Now it stood watching Algar, breath huffing out of its nostrils in puffs of steam, its front leg pawing at the ground like a bull getting ready to charge – but ten times the size of any bull Alfreda had ever seen. Her hands were sticky with sweat as she raised her hammer and faced it.

She could already see the gesture was futile. The creature was covered in grey overlapping scales as thick as her thumb. Twin horns stood out from its forehead, each bone white and wickedly sharp. The eyes beneath were silver and almost beautiful. It seemed to be assessing her just as much as she was studying it. Then it opened its mouth to reveal the double row of teeth inside, grey like its scales and cruelly serrated.

'It's standing right in the sunlight,' her brother said. 'How can that be?'

'The scales must protect it,' Alfreda said. 'I think they're lead. You need to unharness Edred and get away.'

'And what about you?'

She didn't answer, and he smiled tensely and looked back down at his contraption.

'Gar!' she yelled, yanking at his wrist.

'I'm not leaving you, Freda.' He shook her off, more strength in his thin arms than she had given him credit for. His fingers worked to a little more purpose now and the fire javelin pulled free of two of the broken slats surrounding it. 'I can do this. Just keep that thing away from me.'

She tore her eyes from him to face the beast. It had moved closer while they spoke, and now it lowered its head so that the bone spikes of its horns were level with her heart while its eyes looked into hers with a sort of brutish hate. Its flanks trembled, the heavy muscles beneath its scales bunched and Alfreda bolted left as the creature charged.

It was terrifyingly fast. Its massive head swung to watch her sprint down the Salt Road and its body swiftly followed. A deep growl grew in its chest as it galloped and she could smell its breath: fetid meat mixed with a strange hint of cinnamon.

She was running too fast to change direction. She flung herself to the side instead, falling on to her shoulder and rolling clumsily to her feet.

The creature was right behind her. She raised her hammer to her shoulder, braced her feet and then it was on her. The first snap of its teeth missed her shoulder by the breadth of a hair. She swung the hammer in return, catching the creature a glancing blow on the side of its jaw before the weapon skidded off its scales and thudded to the ground.

The beast shook its head, snorting, and then fixed its silver eyes on her again.

'Come on, you bastard!' she shouted, backing away. Fifty paces in front of her, Algar worked at the wagon. Did he have his invention free now? She thought maybe he did, but it would be too late for her. The creature opened its mouth wide enough to take in her whole body, as a strange high-pitched scream came from the back of its throat.

She braced her feet and her hammer and knew she wasn't ready to die. Her sacrifice might save Algar but how would he cope in this world without her? The creature lunged, drool dripping from its needle-sharp teeth. Her shoulder muscles wrenched as she lifted the hammer and swung it again, straight at the beast's mouth.

It cried out in pain and so did she as its teeth shattered and fragments flew out to score her cheeks. Saliva spattered her and burned like acid. She flung herself back, expecting the beast to follow, but it had retreated too, roaring its agony and rage.

'Alfreda!' Algar screamed. 'The black powder!'

It took her a moment to realise what he meant. She'd taken the powder and left him with a weapon that was useless without it. When the creature had finished with her it would turn on her brother and her death wouldn't even have a purpose. The monster glared at her, blood and drool oozing from its shattered teeth.

She raised the hammer again, swinging it high above her head. The creature screamed in fury but flinched back, and in the second of its fear she threw the hammer at its head and then dived between its splayed legs. It was so tall she only had to crouch a little to pass beneath its belly. But the monster knew where she was and was already turning, its thick neck craned down to see her.

She turned with it and looked up. Its belly was white and only thinly scaled, as she'd hoped. If she'd had a sword it might all have been over, but she only had a belt knife. She drew it and slashed upward. The pale flesh parted like butter and blood welled and fell from it, burning as it splashed her. Where it landed on the ground it hissed and a white froth turned the earth to mud and sucked at her feet as she tried to run from the beast and towards her brother.

Behind her she heard the scrabbling of the creature's claws as it turned. Then there was only the thump of its massive legs as it raced to catch her. It was very close and she was very tired.

But she was only thirty paces from Algar and he'd finally freed his invention. Its thick wooden nose pointed towards her as he crouched beside it, the spear in his hand ready to be inserted when the black powder was in. The creature roared behind her and she felt the heat of its breath on her neck. Its teeth were broken but its jaws were still strong. They snapped and she felt the sting in her scalp as it tore out a lock of her hair. She'd run out of time and Algar was still ten paces away. She pulled the pouch from beneath her shirt and flung it towards her brother, flinging herself to the ground at the same time.

The beast landed astride her. One of its massive feet stamped down towards her head and she rolled desperately away from it. She inhaled grains of earth with each breath and the salty tang of them dried her throat. The beast roared in her ear and she knew its head must be inches from hers. There was another roar, deeper than the first, and a sharp smell in her nose. Then a crushing weight dropped on top of her and everything was black.

She woke to the feeling of being shaken. It pushed needles of agony into her muscles and she muttered weakly in protest, but the shaking kept on and her name was repeated over and over in a voice that didn't sound quite like Algar's; too muffled and thick. She felt a droplet of water fall on her face, then another.

Oh, he was crying. That wasn't right. She groaned and forced her eyes open.

Sunlight glared down into them and shattered into crystalline fragments when she blinked away her own tears of pain. 'Gar,' she croaked.

He flung his arms round her, sobbing and squeezing hard. The pain in her bruised body was intense, but she didn't mind because he was alive. They both were.

'Is anything broken?' he asked. 'Can you move?'

Her joints felt as if they'd been welded together and her muscles unwound, all the tensile strength gone out of them. Algar had to slip his arm under her and heave before she could sit up.

The beast was dead. It lay sprawled across the Salt Road a few paces away, a carrion owl already perched pecking at the red wound round the spear in its throat. She wondered how Algar had lifted the corpse from her, then saw Edred near the creature's head, a rope trailing between them.

'The enlarged fire javelin worked,' she said.

Algar grinned. 'It did!'

She looked at what remained of it: a pile of splinters. Algar's face was scored with red marks from the destruction of his invention. The black powder must have shattered the tube even as it sent the javelin on its way. 'We won't be using it again, though.'

'We won't.'

'You saved my life.'

His smile softened into something more tender. 'Of course.'

She levered herself to her feet and staggered over to the dead beast. She could see now that the spear was buried in its neck to nearly half its length. It hadn't needed to penetrate iron, but the scales it had punched through were hard enough. Algar's modifications had given the fire javelin far more force than it had ever possessed before.

'You're a genius,' she told him.

'But I needed you to make it. We need each other.'

She hugged him, ignoring the agony of her bruised ribs. 'Always, Gar.'

He squeezed her back, then pulled away. 'We need to move. Best we get clear of this place before that thing's bigger sister turns up.'

She looked at the wreckage of their wagon. The wooden panels were splinters, shards of random colour where once there had been an image of the Hunter. Their possessions were scattered over the road, pottery shattered and clothes stained with mud and salt. 'We can't just leave the wagon behind.'

'It's only the panels are broken. The frame held and the base is solid. We can pile everything on it and fix it later when we're far away. There'll be more than birds coming for that carcass soon, and all the black powder is gone.'

'We should do some scavenging too, take some of its scales with us. They're metal. Lead, I think.'

'Lead's useless.'

'Maybe. But who knows what you'll invent next?'

He grinned at that and took her arm to support her as she limped round the beast's corpse. Her knife was still stuck in its belly, gore crusted round the hilt.

'Be careful,' she said as he reached for it. 'Its blood burns.'

He wrapped the sleeve of his tunic round his hand before pulling the blade free. The creature's head rested against the ground, pointing towards them, and Alfreda took the time to study it more closely. It looked like nothing she'd seen before. Its scales were reptilian but its head was furred. Its nose was as snub as a pig's and its eyes, even now they were glazed in death, seemed filled with hate.

Her brother circled the beast, intent on the thick scales that ridged its back. He grimaced as he forced the knife between them and sawed at whatever lay beneath. A smell of decay already hung in the air and it grew stronger when the knife popped free and the scale clattered to the ground at Algar's feet. Alfreda turned it this way and that with her foot and watched it gleam dully in the sunlight.

Algar knelt to bang the hilt of his knife against it, and it clanged, exactly like metal. 'You're right, I think. Lead. And look at where it came free – there's more scales beneath.'

She peered at the wound on the creature's back and saw that he was right. Beneath the grey of the metal was another layer, greener and more organic. These scales were smaller and where the knife had nicked one, black blood oozed from the cut. As sunlight hit it, the flesh began to bubble and steam. She frowned. 'That doesn't make sense. How can scales grow on scales?'

'I don't think they did. Look.' He used his knife to prise away another scale, exposing its underside. There was a thin growth on it – no, it was a hook that had been punched into it.

'It's armour,' Alfreda said. 'Someone put armour on this thing.'

'Because what you really want to do with a monstrous great creature like this is make it even harder to kill.'

She laughed, though it hurt her ribs. 'When I was little, Mum told me stories about the moon. She said he made the monsters in the forest and that's why the Hunter had to kill him.'

'You told me those stories too. But I thought that's all they were.'

Alfreda looked back down at the beast. The sunlight was slowly eating away at it and she realised that soon there'd be nothing but the grey metal left. 'Maybe not.'

'Then the Hunter's really going to love our fire javelin, isn't she?'

6

Dae Hyo had been right about the lion's testicles. Krish finally felt his strength returning. The horses they'd stolen had helped them to eat up the westward miles and three days ago, when the ground became too marshy for their mounts to find footing, he'd set them loose without a worry.

Both mounted and on foot, the lizard monkey chose to travel clinging to his shoulder, and the warmth of Adofo's body was an unpleasant addition to the growing heat as they travelled. The air seemed honey-thick and heavy with moisture. But the monkey's constant chatter was soothing in a way Krish couldn't quite explain. If he only half-listened, it almost sounded like words.

The vegetation had changed along with the temperature, the grass of the plains giving way to a wilder profusion of plants. They were filled with moisture too, many with thick leaves that squelched into green mulch if you squeezed them. Others had thorns and his hands and face were scored with scratches that the relentless buzzing insects were drawn to in thick black clusters.

Krish couldn't decide if this new landscape was loathsome or wonderful. His body dripped with a constant sweat and they'd all begun to smell awful, worse than any billy goat. There was a green moss creeping from his armpits down his arms and chest, persisting no matter how much he tried to scrape it off, and he thought there might be small beetles living in his hair. But the dense leaves hid them from pursuit and there were flowers everywhere. He'd never known the world could be so colourful.

He brushed aside a dangling red bloom, its petals bigger than his hands, and found himself standing on yet another riverbank. Though it seldom seemed to rain, there was water everywhere on the ground. At one point, from one of the higher hills, he'd had a startling overview of it: streams and rivers like a net cast over the greenery. He'd hoped for a glimpse of the ocean, but Olufemi said that was many miles away yet: the full breadth of Rah lands lay between them and it.

'I don't know why we're coming here,' Dae Hyo said as he studied a scratch on his arm, which looked as if it might soon begin to fester. 'The Rah can barely be counted among the Fourteen Tribes. They won't help us.'

'They *will* help us,' Olufemi told him impatiently. Krish didn't think she much liked the warrior. But then Krish wasn't sure she much liked him, despite her claim that finding Krish had been the whole purpose of her life.

'Where *are* they, though?' Krish asked. He'd seen fruit on many of the trees, and strange creatures in the waterways that lived within their own armour but were tender when roasted. There was plenty of food here. It was a more fertile land than the one he'd grown up in, and yet it seemed empty. They hadn't seen another person or any sign of them for the last four days.

'The Rah like to leave some clear space around their borders,' the mage told him. 'The other tribes haven't been the best neighbours to them.'

'When I was Ashane – when I *lived* with the Ashane,' Krish amended at Dae Hyo's scowl, 'they talked about the Fourteen Tribes the same way they talked about the Ashane shipforts. Like . . . like they were just different parts of the same people. But the tribes seem to hate each other more than they hate any outsiders.'

'The Fourteen Tribes are united by shared custom and shared history but that is all,' Olufemi said. 'After they crossed the ocean to come here, the Geum died in the desert, and the rest spread themselves from the sea to the mountains and from the Silent Sands to the Moon Forest. The new land changed them, as new things will. The Gyo, the Gung, the Nae and the Dogko made themselves stronger by forming the Four Together – the Five Together before the Yeum departed for colder climes and far stranger ways. The Seonu reappeared after their wanderings to make their home in the cold, high mountains, and the Ahn made a place and a living for themselves trading along the water of the New Misa and through the Silent Sands. And the Eom and the Rah chose to isolate themselves from the rest.

'But where the boundaries of tribal lands meet, there is sometimes conflict. As, I believe, there has been conflict between neighbouring shipfort lords. Such is the way of things: sharing is hard and taking is easier. The Gyo took from the Rah and so now they make provision to ensure they aren't stolen from again.'

Dae Hyo shrugged. 'The Gyo fought them once, but that was long ago. A man shouldn't hold a grudge that long.'

'So say you, who—' Olufemi began heatedly, and then cut herself off with a snap of teeth.

'If you think you'll compare what happened to the Rah with what the rat-fucking Chun did to the Dae . . .' Dae Hyo's face glowed red with rage and Olufemi held up her hand placatingly.

'No, no, you're right. It's not the same. The Chun went beyond the violence of any previous conflict. They did something no civilised people had ever done when they slaughtered the Dae. They turned themselves into something else, no longer a tribe but a band dedicated purely to war.'

'The Brotherband,' Krish said. 'But the Brotherband worship *me*.'

'Well,' she said, suddenly uncomfortable. 'Well indeed, young Jinn moved them to the moon's worship, but that wasn't what turned them into killers, I promise you. And as for the Rah, it's not so much a grudge they hold as simple wisdom. In the War of the Red Grass of which our warrior speaks, they were robbed of all their remaining pastureland. No doubt they'd prefer to keep what territory remains to them.'

'No one else would want it.' Dae Hyo gazed unlovingly at the humid landscape. 'You can't keep horses here, or rabbits, and corn would drown if you planted it.'

'The Rah thrive on other things. They're fisherfolk and farmers and they breed livestock more cunningly than any of the other tribes. That's how they guard their lands. And we're approaching the border: it's time for us to take some precautions. There!' she said to Dae Hyo, pointing at a purplish vine curling up a tree trunk and drooping violet blossoms above their head. 'Fetch those for me, will you?'

Dae Hyo looked dubious and Krish said, 'I'll do it,' finding handholds to pull himself up the thick trunk. Climbing, at least, was one thing he had more experience of than the warrior, and it felt good to use his newly regained strength.

Among the branches, the smell of the flowers was almost overpowering: cloying and not entirely pleasant. They were dripping too, an amber liquid that had smeared the bark and stung a little against his grazed palms.

'All of them,' Olufemi said. 'And hurry.'

But he couldn't resist climbing higher. The tree offered an easy upward route, almost a ladder of branches. The smell grew weaker as he pulled himself higher where a breeze was able to penetrate the leaves, and when he was near the top he could finally see through them. They'd scaled a hill to reach this tree and the view was sweeping: green in every direction, a far darker and denser colour than the grasses of the plains.

'Come down!' Olufemi shouted. 'It's dangerous!'

Krish ignored her. Heights had never made him dizzy and the tree was more sturdy than the cliffs he'd once scrambled up in search of goat feed in lean times. It was strange to think he'd never do that again.

'Brother!' Dae Hyo yelled. 'You must come down!'

'I'm fine,' Krish shouted back. 'I'm just looking around.'

'There are serpents in the trees, you fool!' Olufemi called and the instant her words registered he realised that the brown twig by his right hand was writhing, raising its small head to watch him with blank black eyes.

And once he'd seen that, he saw the rest: a thin green snake by his foot, and on a lower branch a monster as long as he was tall, its belly bulging grotesquely with the remains of its last meal. His eyes locked with those of the serpent near his hand as he slowly drew it away, expecting the plunge of fangs into flesh at any moment.

'Careful,' Dae Hyo warned, 'she says they're venomous.'

Sweat beaded his brow as he inched his hand back and the creature swayed, swayed – but didn't strike. The moment he was out of its reach he grabbed a branch and began to scramble down, refraining from going at full speed only out of fear that he'd tread on another snake in his haste.

'And don't forget the flowers!' Olufemi added, as if he didn't have more crucial things to concern himself with. Still, he found himself plucking the great violet blossoms from the branches as he climbed past and flinging them down to her. Then he heard a hiss and the wedge-shaped head of the huge creature twined round the lower branch turned towards him. He yelped and flung himself from the tree, falling the remaining fifteen paces to the ground to be caught by Dae Hyo. Olufemi frowned down as they both collapsed to the sodden earth, gasping.

'Listen to me next time,' she said and turned away to collect the blooms.

When they made camp that night, Dae Hyo and Krish trod down all the plants to leave no hiding places for the smallest serpent, while Olufemi hovered over her cooking pot, stirring in the purple blossoms and other flowers she'd sent them to pluck over the course of the day.

'No antivenom will save you from their bite entirely,' she said as she stirred. 'But this will prevent death from all except the scarlet adder. It might even prevent loss of the bitten limb, if you're lucky.'

Krish didn't think she was joking. He found his eyes constantly darting about, searching for the small, scaled bodies.

'Only the Rah would choose to live in a place so cursed as this,' Dae Hyo said.

'The Rah know what they're about,' Olufemi told him. 'And besides, Krishanjit, they're your people. They chose the worship of the moon years ago. You'll be safe among them, if you can resist the urge to slaughter them yourself.'

He couldn't find a reply to that and the rest of the evening passed in brewing her antivenoms and searching for fruit and tubers to make their supper.

In the morning, he found that she'd brewed an even less pleasant concoction: a soup of dark black mud and leaves.

'Smear this over you,' she said, although she made no move to spread the pungent mess over her own clothes.

'Why?' Dae Hyo dipped a finger in the pot and frowned as he smelled it. 'Will it frighten away the snakes?'

'Quite possibly.' She lifted out a ladleful and turned to Krish. 'But it's the crocodiles I'm more concerned about. We're less than a mile from the start of their range.'

'Crocodiles? Are they a form of serpent?'

'In a manner of speaking. They're relatives, at least.'

'And they're venomous, I'll wager.' Dae Hyo looked disgusted.

'They hardly need to be. They're twenty paces long and walk upon their legs, though they're quite happy to swim when that's required. They could have you in their stomachs in three swallows.'

'But they don't like the taste of mud?' Krish hazarded, though it seemed unlikely if they made their homes in the clogged rivers of this territory.

'They don't like bright clothing,' Olufemi said, smearing the mud across his beaded shirt. 'Or rather they like it too much: the Rah have trained them to see those wearing the clothing of their warlike neighbours as prey. The Rah themselves prefer to dress in darker colours but as we've brought no change of clothing, the mud will have to suffice to make you less appealing.'

When she was finished, they walked in a tense silence, but the land around them filled it. There was a deep barking that made Krish jump until Dae Hyo whispered 'toad' to him. The buzzing of insects was constant and a moist throaty roar that the warrior couldn't identify. Olufemi merely raised an eyebrow when Krish asked what it was and he knew it must be the sound these crocodiles made.

The water was everywhere, gurgling hidden behind dense bushes and running in plain sight in silvery runnels over the flat ground. In places, clumps of lilies floated on its surface, delicately beautiful. Krish was studying one of the flowers when the first head broke from the water and blinked in his direction.

Olufemi had seen it too. 'Keep going,' she said. 'Don't show it your fear.'

Krish didn't know how it could fail to smell the terror sweating out of his body. Even Dae Hyo looked alarmed. The thing's head was all teeth: jagged and sharp, they were still hung with the red remains of its last meal. It rose out of the water to waddle on to shore and he saw just how big it was: the size of a horse, but much lower to the ground.

'It's slow, at least,' Dae Hyo muttered.

'Don't be fooled,' Olufemi said. 'They can outrun a man when they need to.'

As she spoke, another head broke the water, and then another. Krish saw two more in a broad stream that ran to their left and then a third lying in the pond directly in front of them. Its head rose beneath a pad of lilies so that the flowers drooped absurdly over its heavy brow as it loped through the mud towards them. The muck covering it oozed back towards the ground to expose its moss-green scales, blunt leaf shapes that armoured the beasts all over.

The other crocodiles approached too, at least a dozen of them. They roared as they came and even Olufemi shivered and stopped in the face of their advance. Adofo galloped over the ground to fling himself into Krish's arms, his tail a tight noose round Krish's waist.

'They're no danger to you,' Olufemi said, though whether to Adofo or him, Krish couldn't be sure. 'The Rah feed them. They're hoping we'll do the same – they don't mean to eat us.'

'And when we *can't* feed them?' Dae Hyo asked. They'd had no meat for three days and these didn't look like beasts that would savour fruit or grain. 'I tell you what, I don't think they'll just walk away disappointed.'

One of the creatures roared again, an angrier sound, and Krish thought Dae Hyo was right. They wouldn't leave while they were still hungry. He backed away a step, only to feel Dae Hyo's hand on his shoulder.

'They're behind too, brother.'

Krish glanced at Olufemi, but her expression didn't offer much hope. She looked panicked.

'The runes, mage!' Dae Hyo hissed. 'Use the runes!'

She blinked as if the thought hadn't even occurred to her, and then flung her bag to the ground and began desperately rooting through it. 'I think there's a chalk, yes, I think . . .' She'd grasped it in her hand when the crocodiles charged.

Krish flung himself in front of her, a protective instinct he didn't fully intend. Dae Hyo tried to fling himself in front of Krish in turn, and they ended up shoulder to shoulder in front of the mage, a sword in Dae Hyo's hand and Krish still fumbling his knife from his belt. Dae Hyo's blade slashed at one of the beasts as it hurtled towards them, every bit as fast as Olufemi had warned. The blade bounced uselessly from the thick scales and then the creature was past and all the others with it, and not a single one had even snapped its long jaws at them.

Krish turned, shaking, to see that the crocodiles had found other prey. They were clustered in a horrible feeding frenzy over a victim who remained hidden by their massive bodies, only scraps of clothing and flesh visible as the predators tore them free. *Better him than us*, Krish thought, except he was sure it would be them next.

But then something else landed among the vicious jaws and for just a moment he saw it clearly: a hunk of meat wrapped in cloth. The crocodiles fell on it too and Krish looked beyond them to see the man who'd thrown them their food.

The man raised a lazy hand to wave when he saw them looking. 'Olufemi,' he said in lightly accented Ashane. 'A long time since you've visited us and a dangerous way to return. Could you not wait for a guide? We'd have sent a boy to bring you through safe if we'd known.' He threw the beasts another bloody chunk.

'I couldn't wait, Uin. I've news for you and enemies who'd stop me bringing it.'

Uin threw the last of his meat away and came towards them through the crocodiles, hopping over their tails with no sign of concern. He was shorter than Dae Hyo and perhaps a little darker, but his features were definitely those of a tribesman. Still, there was something about his face, the way he held himself, that seemed quite foreign. His eyes were cautious and narrowed as they flicked over Dae Hyo and Krish.

'You bring strangers to our lands, Olufemi, where no strangers are welcome.'

'I bring you your god,' Olufemi said. 'Will you let him pass?'

Uin's eyes settled on Krish, now wide and full of wonder.

Uin had given them mounts to ride, some relative of the crocodiles five times their size. Their backs were so broad Dae Hyo sat cross-legged on the saddle, and he wobbled uneasily as the monster waddled forward. Its splay-legged stride ate up the distance with ease and the crocodiles were soon lost to sight behind them, probably still squabbling over the last of their meal. He saw others lift their heads from streams and ponds as they went past, but when they realised no food was being offered, they quickly sank down again.

Gradually, the landscape changed, the water remaining but the drooping plants and dense trees diminishing until there was little but low grass on the riverbanks.

Soon the grass itself had been replaced by a patchwork of neat green squares. People laboured in these half-drowned fields, though Dae Hyo couldn't guess what crop they were tending. There'd be no game here, no deer roaming in this endless farmland.

The path their mounts followed broadened until their great clawed feet began to make a hollow sound with every step and Dae Hyo realised they were walking on wood. It was a road and all around was not wilderness but civilised land. He saw floating platforms with crops of brightly coloured flowers rooted on them. There was a field of red blooms, another of purple and then one of soft green ferns. Nothing here seemed to grow out of place or out of line. The orderliness of the Rah territory now being revealed was all the more startling for the veil of savagery behind which it hid.

Finally they came to the settlement and their mounts dawdled to a stop. Of course there were no tents here: the Rah thought themselves too good to live as the other tribes did. Instead they'd built houses, dark-stained wood like those of burnt Smiler's Fair, but to an entirely different design. Their homes were low and sprawling and widely separated. No, Dae Hyo realised, *entirely* separated. Each was constructed on its own floating raft of reeds. He saw two men hook up a crocodile to the far edges of one raft and drag it away through the water. Their houses were as mobile as any Ashane landborn caravan and far bigger. It was clever, in a Rah sort of way.

While he stared, Uin dismounted and crossed to Krish, bowing and reaching up a hand. 'Will you come with me, great lord? Your people wait to meet you.'

It was true. Groups of men and women were emerging from all the scattered houses, soberly dressed in the Rah style but with a bright excitement in their faces. Word had clearly travelled ahead and they poled their flat-bottomed boats towards Krish: close but not too close, as if they were afraid to touch him, or maybe afraid to offend him.

His brother looked baffled. Olufemi had said he was a god, but she hadn't said what kind. Dae Hyo loved Krish as well as any man loved his brother, but he didn't think anyone would mistake him for one of the more warriorlike of the pantheon. He seemed like a scribe for one of the greater gods, clever and necessary but hardly a figure of awe. Especially not smeared in mud as he was right now.

Except the Rah men and women clustered about did look awed. They smiled at Olufemi, barely even noticed Dae Hyo and kept their – well, he had to be honest – their worshipful gazes on Krish. It was almost insulting.

Uin didn't seem keen to share his prize with his brethren. He put a proprietorial arm round Krish's shoulders, which made both Krish and Dae Hyo stiffen, and ushered him inside the nearest house.

In their disappointment, the rest of the Rah finally turned to Dae Hyo and he smiled at them as he followed his brother and Olufemi indoors. The Rah were barely members of the Fourteen Tribes; they'd turned themselves into sit-still people just like the Ashane. But the Rah weren't currently trying to kill him, and that was good enough to be getting on with.

Inside, Uin let them wash at last and gave them fresh clothes – Rah clothes. Dae Hyo squirmed uncomfortably and followed his host to the dinner table. The mage had kept her own robes, muddy as they were, but Krish too was in borrowed brown. Dae Hyo didn't like the way his brother looked in the sombre hemp shirt and trousers. He didn't look Dae.

The food wasn't Dae either. There was a lot of it, but he suspected the meat was snake. It was pale yellow and dripping with grease and not at all something he wanted to put in his mouth. He did it anyway, determined to be courteous.

Uin talked expansively, telling Olufemi of the messages he'd sent out announcing Krish's arrival and the important men who'd be flocking to meet him. Olufemi nodded as if she believed him, but so far all he'd brought to the table were his wife and two daughters, the three of them so meek and quiet they barely added up to one person's worth of conversation between them. The girls were no older than Krish and the mother a beauty pared by time to unappealing boniness.

When Dae Hyo speared the last greasy chunk of meat from his plate, a woman drifted forward to serve him more. He saw Krish eyeing her askance and it was clear why: she was Ashane – a slave, although his brother probably didn't realise that. The Moon Forest boy who'd brought their clothes was a slave too, and the tribeswoman they'd glimpsed bent over the pots in the long, low kitchen. And all of them had the dreamy expressions and dead eyes of those that drug, bliss, had its hooks in. Krish didn't know what rat-fuckers these Rah really were.

And Uin was doing everything he could to stop Krish realising it. The man knew how to be charming and he had stuck to speaking Ashane the moment he realised his god had a shaky grasp of the tribe's own tongue. He smiled as he leaned across and refilled Krish's glass with the thick, sweet wine these Rah seemed to like.

Krish had already drunk two glasses and Dae Hyo knew he wasn't used to it. His cheeks were flushed and his eyes glazed. Not a state for good judgement, as Dae Hyo knew well enough. At the moment, Krish was staring rudely over his host's shoulder.

'Ah,' Uin said, following the direction of Krish's gaze. 'You're admiring our serpents. There's no need to fear, great lord. Even if they could get loose from their tanks, we've milked all the venom from them.'

'You milk snakes?' Dae Hyo asked. 'I can't imagine it's good drinking.'

Uin's smile thinned as his attention switched from Krish to Dae Hyo. 'Do you know the best antidote for venom, warrior?'

'Not being bitten.'

'The venom itself. Like any painful thing, our bodies grow calloused against it until it can no longer hurt us. When you people invaded us—'

'It was the Four Together, not the Dae!'

'When our cousin tribes decided to take our grazing lands, we let the wilderness claim our new border. And then we drank the venom of all the snakes that came to make their beds there, a little more every day from our youngest age, until the bite that would be death to any invaders was nothing to us. Now no one comes here uninvited.'

'You're saying we're safe here?' Krish asked.

'Great lord, we would spend our lives to protect you.'

'But you'd prefer the snakes to spend theirs.'

That surprised a laugh from Dae Hyo but Uin seemed affronted. His cheeks sucked in until his face looked as long and unfriendly as a snake.

'Krishanjit means no offence,' Olufemi said hastily.

'What? No!' Krish thumped a hand on the table with a little too much force, so that the clay plates jostled and clattered. 'I think it's . . . it's clever. Why fight when you don't have to?'

'But I've told your people,' Olufemi said carefully, 'that you'll lead them to victory against their enemies. That your ascendancy will mark the time of theirs too.'

'The Rah aren't his people!' Dae Hyo snapped. 'We've only come here to get away from those rat-fucking Ashane scum. My brother is Dae.'

'Krishanjit is of all peoples, and of none,' Olufemi said.

'But Lord Krishanjit has come to lead *us*,' Uin said. 'Isn't that true, great lord?'

Even the slaves turned their dazed eyes to watch as Krish looked between their host, Dae Hyo and Olufemi. Uin's wife seemed to be holding her breath and the oldest daughter twisted her hands in her lap. Dae Hyo realised he'd clenched his own fist and made himself loosen a finger at a time and rest them on the table. *He* didn't need to doubt his brother.

'Yes,' Krish said, 'I have come to lead the Rah.'

Uin nodded as if it was the answer he'd expected all along, and Krish never saw Dae Hyo's shock, because his eyes stubbornly refused to turn to his brother.

7

Marvaṇ woke coughing, as he had every morning since the fire that took Nethmi from him. He pulled himself upright and let the cough continue until he could spit out the gobbet of phlegm and soot that had been lodged in his lungs. The fire had taken his health from him too, but he found that he didn't much care. He'd known Nethmi only a few days and it seemed improbable and foolish that her absence could feel so vast to him, but there it was. There were so few people in the world who were unlike all the rest, and he'd lost the only other one he'd ever met.

Hunger gnawed at his stomach. He contemplated not eating, but starving to death wasn't the way he'd choose to go, and besides he was sure he'd feel less wretched soon. He'd never realised how useless love was. What was the point of a feeling so tenacious it could survive even the death of its object?

He'd salvaged nothing from the fire; his only possessions were the clothes on his back and his twin tridents. His cat Stalker had either burned or fled and he'd slept alone on the ground and left a damp hollow when he rose.

Work was an option, but not an attractive one. Robbery seemed preferable. He'd resorted to it only once before, when he'd purloined the mammoth from his family's stables that he had used to buy membership in the company of Drovers. Back then the risk had been slight. His family would rather have lost the mammoth than retrieve it and admit one of their scions was a thief.

This time he couldn't afford to get caught. Many more Jorlith than others had survived the fire, their enforced sobriety and gateway stations having placed them in the best positions to flee.

Now they earned their bread by keeping order among refugees who might otherwise descend into a rabble. Marvan had seen a boy hanged yesterday, and he'd only stolen a chicken. Any witnesses to Marvan's own crime must be eliminated.

He'd slept a little distance from the remnants of the fair and the walk back over a small hillock gave him a good view of it. It was a pitiful thing, barely a hundredth of its original size. The streets were laid out in an echo of their old arrangement, but there were buildings missing in each of them, like rotten teeth fallen from a diseased mouth, and those that remained were blackened with soot.

Animal pens sprawled to the left of the fair and nearby the survivors of the Merry Cooks had set up shop, a haze of smoke hanging over their stalls. His mouth watered and he spat again to clear it before sitting down. He didn't intend to snatch just a few crusts or one roasted bird, like the careless hanged boy. It was money he wanted, and the cooks were among the few residents of the fair who still had a way to earn it. They had bladders and guts too, and they'd need to empty them.

He watched the clouds drifting until he saw the first figure detach itself from the crowd. His stomach clenched in anticipation until he realised it was a woman. He'd killed a girl once but it had given him no satisfaction. It was like eating potatoes when you hungered for meat.

Another woman followed and then two men together, perhaps heading out for more than a piss. Then, finally, a man alone wandered from the safety of the rest. His path would take him behind the hillock Marvan occupied and no scream would carry from the lee of the mound to the other Merry Cooks.

Marvan waited until the other man was out of sight of the fair before descending to meet him. The cook looked up, his cock limp in his hand, as Marvan's shadow fell over him. 'Marvan!' he said. 'And here was me thinking you'd died in the flames along with all the rest. I shall have to tell Fat Pushpinder – she was asking after you only yesterday. So did you hear the chatter?'

It was Damith the baker. Damith, who'd first told Marvan of

Nethmi's crime and led him down the path that ended here. Marvan shifted the tridents in his hands, flipping them to sit along his forearms so they'd stay hidden as he approached.

'You know I don't listen to gossip, Damith.'

'Oh, you say that, but every man likes to know what every other man is doing and better yet when it's something disreputable. Isn't that right, Marvan?' Damith's voice remained calm as he spoke but he'd left his cock hanging loose, his hands trembling beside it.

He knew, Marvan realised. Damith didn't need to see the tridents to guess what was coming but Marvan showed them to him anyway. Just because this killing was from need didn't mean he couldn't enjoy it. 'I don't really care what anyone else does or thinks,' Marvan said.

A sudden spurt of piss came from the end of Damith's cock as fear made his bladder realise it had a little more to give. 'This is tasty fare, Marvan, I promise. I promise. Seonu Sang Ki has found his father's killer, and what do you say to that?'

Marvan was almost within striking distance. 'I wish him joy of his justice, whoever he is.'

'But there'll be no justice, not yet.' Damith was gabbling now. It was fitting, Marvan supposed, that he wanted to spend the last moments of his life as he'd spent so much of the rest of it: passing on meaningless gossip. 'The woman's pregnant with Lord Thilak's own child, or so they say, though I say they won't be certain till the baby pops out brown and noble-looking.' His smile was ghastly. 'This Nethmi was in Smiler's Fair long enough to find a thousand other fathers if she liked, and who doesn't like that sort of thing?'

The tridents landed on the grass with a thud softer than the sudden pounding of Marvan's heart. 'Nethmi? Nethmi is alive?'

Damith smiled tremulously. 'There, you see. I knew you only pretended not to care.'

It wasn't easy to enter the Ashane camp. Armed guards ringed it and they had the uneasy looks of men who felt themselves in enemy territory.

'I need to speak to Seonu Sang Ki,' Marvan told the nearest.

The man was skinnier than a landborn farmer's horse. 'Only Ashane get in to see the boss,' he said.

'I *am* Ashane,' Marvan pointed out.

'Proper, I meant, not Smiler's Fair scum.'

'I am Marvan of Fell's End, Lord Parmvir's son.'

The man frowned suspiciously at him. 'Then why aren't you in Fell's End?'

It was a reasonable enough question and not one whose answer Marvan felt like sharing. He'd meant to save his choicest morsels of information until he was in front of Seonu Sang Ki himself, but it was clear that wouldn't do. 'I come bearing news of your fugitive,' he told the guard.

'What fugitive?'

Marvan sighed and then regretted it as the soldier's knuckles whitened on his sword hilt. 'I mean this Krishanjit,' he said. 'King Nayan's long-lost son.'

'You know where he is?'

'I know where he *was*. Do you think that might be of interest to your lord?'

They brought him to the centre of the camp. Seonu Sang Ki was easy enough to spot, although Marvan had never met him, but if his mixed blood hadn't singled him out, his vast bulk most definitely would. Marvan had never seen a man so fat and he couldn't help marvelling at that grotesque stomach before his eyes rose to meet Sang Ki's. They were full of a shrewd intelligence that knew quite well what Marvan had been staring at. He realised he'd need to be careful.

'You bring me information about young Krishanjit, I gather,' Sang Ki said. 'How marvellous. And how very hard to prove its authenticity – unless you mean to produce him in person.'

'I hear you've found your father's killer,' Marvan replied. 'The Lady Nethmi of Whitewater.'

Sang Ki's expression, which had been amiable, became markedly less so. 'I thought you were here to impart information, not fish for it.'

Marvan shrugged as nonchalantly as he could. 'Like most things, information isn't free.'

'And you'd like to be told the location of Lady Nethmi in return for yours.'

'That would hardly be a fair exchange. Everyone in the fair knows where Nethmi is. What I want is . . .' But he hesitated. Nethmi *had* killed this man's father. No doubt he'd found that upsetting.

'You *know* Nethmi.' Sang Ki looked momentarily startled, then thoughtful. 'You met her after she came to the fair.'

'Yes. And we, she and I, we met your misplaced prince.'

'Ah.' The other man studied him. 'You love her.'

Marvan was shocked to realise he was blushing. 'I don't wish to see her killed, certainly. If I can help you find Krishanjit of Ashfall, will you let her go?'

'Perhaps you should tell me what you know.'

'We captured the prince.'

Sang Ki raised a disbelieving eyebrow.

'We didn't know who he was or that he was sought. We . . . I'll be honest with you, friend. We meant to rob him and we captured him to do it. We had him tied up when the fire started and we had to leave him there.'

'Tied up?'

Marvan nodded.

'Well, that's a most fascinating if not entirely salutary tale. I don't wish to appear rude, but I can't help returning to my earlier point. What evidence do you have?'

'The boy had the strangest eyes I've ever seen – moons where the pupils should be.'

'Indeed. Precisely the description I gave all the men who were searching for him. I believe it may even have been drawn up for me on a parchment or two.'

'He grew up in the White Heights, a landborn goatherd who killed his own father, or rather the man he believed to have sired him.'

Sang Ki's eyes narrowed. 'Now that's an interesting story and not one I've heard before.'

'He told me so himself. He probably meant it to impress me.'

'And of course the prophecy said that he would kill his father, without specifying which one.'

'Yes.'

'Which you knew.'

Marvan inclined his head and Sang Ki smiled. 'It's a very pretty little narrative and exceptionally neat. I'm not sure how it helps me, even if it is true.'

'What if I told you of a way to tell whether any of these blackened bones you've been digging up actually belong to the boy you want?'

Sang Ki leaned back, fist beneath his many chins. 'That would certainly be helpful.'

'He had manacles, one on each wrist. We used them to tie him up. The metal should have survived the fire, or left some remnant for you to identify. Tell me that isn't helpful to you.'

'It is – that information has been tremendously useful in my search, but I'm afraid you weren't the first to impart it. I'm beginning to think you may be telling the truth, but I've heard nothing to indicate that you know whether the boy actually survived the fire.'

Marvan's breath shortened and he pressed his nails into his palms hard enough to cut. 'I've told you more of the boy's history than anyone else. That must be worth something.'

Sang Ki leaned back, smiling, and of course the bastard saw that he cared too much. 'Your information certainly has some value.' He snapped his fingers at one of his men. 'Give this man five gold wheels and send him on his way.'

Marvan knew that arguing would be pointless, yet found he couldn't help himself. 'And Nethmi?'

'Will remain in the care of the physicians until she's given birth to the child.' His shrewd eyes scanned Marvan, clearly wondering if the child was his. Marvan wondered the same thing and didn't know how he should feel about it. 'Her worth is far higher than this nugget of news,' Sang Ki concluded. 'Now, if you'd brought me Krishanjit himself . . . But of course you didn't.'

*

Sang Ki found Nethmi in precisely the position he'd left her. She lay on her back, eyes shut and much of her face and body muffled in bandages. Only the slight movement of her chest betrayed that she was still alive.

The tent stank of urine, burnt flesh and unguent, though Min Soo had left the flaps open to air it out. Sang Ki shooed the physician through them and then took his place on the bedside stall. It creaked beneath his weight and Nethmi winced, as if even the vibration of his movement caused her pain. For a moment, looking at the cracked and weeping flesh around her bandages, he wondered if she'd been punished enough. But how could she have been, when she was still here and his father wasn't?

'I've just made the acquaintance of a friend of yours,' he told her closed eyes. 'A close friend, I think, although I may have been misreading the situation, in which case I can only beg your forgiveness for my crass assumptions. But he seemed willing to do a great deal to free you.'

He paused, looking down at her. He'd forgotten quite how *small* she was, a pitiful huddled shape beneath the sheets.

'It's curious to think that you might inspire that sort of loyalty,' he said at last. 'You were such a . . . cool woman. Cold, really. Just what did this Marvan see in you? But then, I asked the same question about my parents. You're quite like my mother. I hadn't considered that before.'

He looked around the tent. Min Soo had insisted he be allowed to bring his other patients with him to the Ashane encampment, but they'd died one by one. Now only their beds remained, and Nethmi. She clung tenaciously to life in a way that didn't entirely surprise Sang Ki. He'd never questioned the strength of her character, only its content.

'I wonder if he brings our lost prince to me whether I *will* let you go. I suspect that I might, but it would pain me. You've taught me just how much hate I'm capable of and I suppose I'm grateful for the lesson.'

Nethmi shifted and her mouth worked. 'Water,' she rasped.

Her bandaged hand rose an inch from the bed before falling weakly back again.

He found that his cruelty couldn't match his anger and filled a glass before trickling the liquid over her cracked lips.

'Thank you,' she whispered.

'You're quite welcome, Nethmi.'

He knew his smile was in his voice. He was looking forward to the moment when she realised her rescuer was also the man who would hang her. But when her eyes opened to bloodshot slits, her expression didn't change.

'Who's Nethmi?' she asked.

He sat back, startled. 'Come now, let's not play this game. A terrible trauma, a lost memory. It's the sort of stuff the King's Men performed in their cheaper melodramas, before the mage burned their fair down around them. I know full well that you're Nethmi, so your ignorance of your own identity – even if it's real – can't save you.'

She whimpered as she rolled over in the bed to face him, holding herself up on trembling arms. 'But I haven't forgotten who I am, sir. I'm Mahvesh of the Fine Fellows. I've never heard of any Nethmi.'

8

Their wagon was a sorry mess of hastily nailed-together planks and patchwork canvas, which rattled alarmingly as Edred pulled it over the ruts and potholes of the track. Ahead Alfreda could see the village high in the trees and the clearing where the corn crop was just beginning to venture above ground. They approached Deep Holt like ragged and destitute fugitives from some terrible battle.

'We could—' Alfreda said.

'We're not stopping,' Algar insisted. 'It's fine, Freda – they want to buy our wares, not admire our transport.'

'Wares' meant the fire javelin, all he'd been able to speak of since they'd proved its worth with the moon beast. It was rebuilt now, bigger and better, and Deep Holt was the first place he'd have a chance to show it off. Of course he couldn't wait.

Edred clopped a few paces closer and then Algar jumped down and tossed the reins to Alfreda before swaggering up to the gathered villagers. A Jorlith girl with yellow pigtails blushed at something he said and another scowled until he turned his smile on her. The boys looked on, envious, but Algar charmed them too.

Alfreda's stomach dropped as she saw one of the older men head towards the wagon. She turned her face away and dismounted, fussing with Edred's tack and hoping the man would take the hint.

'Alfreda Sonyasdochter, am I right?' the man said. 'I remember you and your brother when you barely reached your parents' knees. You used to carry water to cool the metal. Now it seems you work the forge yourself.' His eyes scanned her body, noting the disproportionate muscles of her right arm and the breadth of her shoulders.

When she didn't reply, he added, 'Well, anyhow, there's plenty of work for you here. The last time we saw a smith was when Wencis and his brood came by two full years past. There's horses need shod and blades to forge if you're after a day's labour, and much more if you've a mind to stay longer.'

He stared at her, and this time he was waiting for an answer. Alfreda's heart sped and her mouth dried. It was always this way when they were around other folk, ever since she'd been a bairn. Her mind just wouldn't keep quiet, showing her all the ways speaking could go wrong. What if she offended the churl? What if she made him laugh at her? What if she said something so stupid the whole village gathered round to laugh?

The man frowned at her, half angry at her rudeness, half puzzled by her lack of response. She knew she had to say something and opened her mouth to do it, but the words evaporated and left only a dry croak behind.

And now he was looking at her with pity. She felt a blush heat her cheeks and any words left leaked from her mind like water. Then a warm arm was slung round her waist, and she looked gratefully at her brother's smiling face.

'Freda's slow with her speech but fast with her fingers and the best smith this side of the mountains,' he said. 'Anything you need doing she'll do, and do it well.'

The churl turned to him, plainly relieved. 'Well then, be welcome. Your parents, may they have good rest, always gave fine service to us.'

'And so will we.' Algar grinned as he led the churl back to the other villagers. 'Bring us your metal and we'll shape it with fire. And if you care to come by later, we may have a little surprise. Our very latest invention, a weapon more powerful than any made before, and you'll be the first to see it.'

The charcoal at the heart of Alfreda's forge was cherry red when Algar returned with a flower in his curly hair. The petals were desiccated and a few had scattered over his scalp like snow. She wondered which of the village girls had placed it there.

'They've had three children born with the hawk mark this year and two more lost to Janggok raiders,' he said. 'And now some crazy person is putting armour on the moon beasts to make them even harder to kill. If anyone should want our advanced fire javelin, it's these folk.'

'But Gar, they're goddess-loving folk in these distant places, you know that. And you know how the Great Moot in Aethelgas reacted when you first spoke the idea. We need to go gentle with it.'

'But we're *right*, Freda, and those dimwits in Aethelgas and Ivarholme are wrong. Besides, last time we had no proof of the device. Now we've seen what it can do. One demonstration and the richest thegns and wergeld-wealthy Jorlith will be outbidding each other to own it. We just need to show them.'

'Maybe,' she said, meaning no, but he smiled at her as if it meant yes, and by the time he'd finished wheedling perhaps it would. 'Help me with the smithing now. I've a last few hoops to bind around the metal, or we'll have no javelin at all to show them. And the sooner this is done, the sooner you can go back to giving the eye to anyone in a skirt.'

'Can I help it if the world is full of beautiful women?'

She shook her head as he took up the bellows and began blowing on the coals through the tuyere, sending the glow from cherry through daffodil and finally to a pure, bright white. He flinched away from the heat of it, but Alfreda leaned forward, mesmerised as always by its intensity and astonishing power, to melt what nature meant to be solid.

Sparks flew from the forge and she felt them catch and burn in her skin, but she didn't flinch. She had scars enough already, white flecks like freckles all over her cheeks and arms. Algar hated the fire and what it could do to his handsome face. When he'd been only five, and their parents dying of the carrion fever, their father had urged Alfreda to teach Algar the craft she was already mastering. She didn't have the heart, though, to make him do something for which he was so ill-suited. Let him keep his unmarked skin and she'd do the work for the both of them.

It was different for her. People were hard, but this was easy.

Metal responded the same every time and just the way you expected: strike it hard enough and it bent, heat it and it softened. Metal did what you wanted and never asked anything in return.

'Come on, Freda,' Algar said. 'Stop dreaming and get working. I'm starting to fry.'

The concept was simple enough, making strong in metal what had been weak in wood. But metal was costly; she'd already melted down half their knives and one of her precious hammers to make this and even so she couldn't make it very long, yet length was needed if she wanted accuracy. Her only hope was to fashion it as round and smooth as possible. Except there was no way she could shape a tube that perfectly round, even with her smallest hammer – not if she wanted to leave its centre hollow. So clever Algar had come up with another way.

A drop of her sweat fell and sizzled into steam on the anvil. She'd prepared the rods already, made them as thin and smooth as she could and welded them together, but that alone wouldn't be strong enough to resist the explosive power of the black powder. It had driven that spear right through the moon beast's neck. It would certainly be enough to break this flimsy contraption apart.

The bands she'd fashioned lay on the anvil, based on the sort a cooper might use. She picked up the first, using the fire to soften it so that she could bend it round the ring of rods and hold them in place even against the explosion of the powder. Or at least so she hoped.

'It's looking good,' Algar said. 'I think this is going to work.'

She nodded, not lifting her attention from her work. She'd begun to share his enthusiasm, though. It was always this way when they made something new together. As the glow of the metal cooled from white to cherry and through to just the right shade of dark red, there was nothing to do but plunge it into the slack tub to quench it and hope that she'd made it right.

When they'd completed the device, the sun was close to its zenith and they settled onto a blanket as they ate the last of their cheese between slices of warm, fresh-baked village bread.

Algar leaned back on his elbows and looked up at the flat blue sky. 'It's the moon dark tonight, did you know? We can't miss the dance; they say the Deep Holt folk go crazy for the death of the moon.'

She smiled despite herself. 'Do they?'

'They do. There'll be mulled wine, and those little spiced cakes you can only get around here. The ones they make from the pods that grow on the featherfern trees.'

'Mum liked those cakes. Dad never wanted to stop between the Spiral and Greenstowe, but he used to because he knew Mum loved the featherfern cakes.'

The happy lines of his face dropped momentarily downward. 'Did she? I don't remember.'

'It doesn't matter.' She ran a soothing hand through his curls. 'It was a long time ago. But the cakes *are* good.'

As quick as mercury, his mood shifted again and he grinned at her. 'And the company too. Why don't you join in tonight, Freda? I've seen the boys looking at you.'

'Aye, looking at my muscles and envying them.'

'And your pretty face and envying *me* for getting to see it every day.'

'If you say so. You go, Gar. My anvil needs oiling and now we've stopped I want to give Edred a good brushing. Have you seen how shaggy he's looking? Just try not to break too many hearts.'

He smiled and crunched into a withered apple as a shadow fell over them. Alfreda twisted to face the newcomer. She hadn't heard his approach, silent as a wolf, and when she looked up she saw why. He was Jorlith: tall, muscular, golden-haired and grim-faced. There was gold round his neck and wrists, a man who'd killed enough to make himself wealthy from the wergeld.

'You're the smiths that Harold told me of?' he asked.

Algar rose and bowed smoothly. 'We are, sir. And he told you about our new weapon, I think – or do I guess wrong?'

Even the warrior's smile was grim. 'You don't. I'm Skuld Thrainson, spear-leader of Deep Holt.'

Algar bowed again, lower. 'Honoured. And you'll be wanting a demonstration, I think. That can be arranged.'

Alfreda clenched her fist. They hadn't tested the device yet; what if it didn't work? But she couldn't say anything and Algar wouldn't be stopped. He went into the wagon to fetch out the advanced fire javelin, leaving it wrapped in cloth all the better to intrigue the audience – and they had one now. A handful of Jorlith had come to watch, with a scattering of churls behind, standing on their tiptoes to see above the lanky warriors.

Algar was in his element. He took his time over unwrapping the fire javelin, enjoying drawing out the anticipation. But when the material was folded back and the rough metal tube revealed, Skuld frowned and there was a collective murmur of disappointment from the crowd.

'It's not a weapon,' Skuld said.

'It *is* a weapon.' Algar lifted it up and braced the bottom of the barrel against the wooden stand Alfreda had built for it. 'It's an advanced fire javelin. I've already used it to kill a Moon Forest monster ten times my height and a hundred times as ugly. A beast armoured in metal. Isn't that true, Alfreda?'

She could only nod, looking at the ground.

Skuld's hard face remained doubtful. 'You said a demonstration?'

'Of course. You see that tree over there, the twisted birch with a knot in it just like an eye? Fifty paces and I can—'

'No.' Skuld cut him off. 'I have a better target.' He made a sharp gesture at the other Jorlith, then folded his arms.

There was a commotion at the back of the crowd and when the movement ended it spat out two warriors with another man between them, his hands roped behind his back and his face bruised from a beating.

Algar's cheeks paled and Alfreda felt the blood drain from her own face.

'Oh no,' he said. 'No, I . . .' For once words seemed to fail him.

Skuld dragged the prisoner closer by the rope round his hands. He was a tribesman, round-faced and very young. 'He's marked to die with the moon,' Skuld said. 'You'll only be hurrying his death by a few hours.'

Algar's eyes looked everywhere but at the bound man. 'What did he do?'

'He's a raider.' Skuld had no difficulty looking at the prisoner. 'Filthy Janggok scum – his brothers carried off two women and a boy before we caught him. He told us where the others were hiding and now they won't be preying on decent folk again. It's time for him to join them where they've gone.'

Algar swallowed hard, but after a moment he nodded. 'Very well then. You'll need to position him some twenty paces away. And then stand well clear of him.'

'What if he tries to run away?' one of the churls asked.

'Tie his legs,' Skuld said impatiently.

There was an excited burble from the crowd. They'd thought they were here to see a demonstration, but instead they were about to witness an execution.

Algar pointed the advanced fire javelin towards the bound man. The brace should have steadied it, but Alfreda saw the muzzle wavering, pointing first up towards the sky and then sideways almost at the crowd. Algar's hands were shaking uncontrollably, and she clenched her jaw and moved to help him.

Together they got the device braced, and Alfreda put the small wad of black powder at the bottom of the tube by the touch hole before dropping in the lead ball above it. She'd fashioned it from the dead beast's armour and her skin flinched away from touching it; she packed straw around it to ensure it was wedged in tight.

After that, there was nothing to do but dribble a trail of black powder through the touch hole. The preparations complete, she and Algar looked at each other. They didn't need to speak. She knew what he was thinking: *we're about to murder a man.*

'Well?' Skuld said. 'Do you mean for him to age to death before you kill him?'

'Stand back, then,' Algar said, and took his flint to strike a spark at the end of the trail of black powder.

The flame gobbled the powder until it was inside the fire javelin and the rest ignited. There was no chance to watch the result. There was only a moment of light and force like nothing Alfreda had felt before. And then, without quite knowing how she'd got there, she was lying on her back on the grass, staring at the sky.

Her ears rang with a pure, clear note that blocked out any other sound. Her joints felt like they'd been loosened by the explosion and and her eyes seemed to lag behind her head as she rose and looked around. After blinking them a few times she could see that the figure standing to her right was Algar. She said his name, but she couldn't hear her own voice and doubted he could hear her either. He stared into the distance, brow furrowed as if he was picking at a problem without a solution, but when she touched his shoulder, he turned towards her.

'What happened?' he mouthed.

She shrugged.

Their audience, scattered by the explosion, began to regroup around the advanced fire javelin. The explosion had all but destroyed it. The hoops she'd bound round the barrel had torn and the welded rods had mostly fallen apart. The wooden support was nothing but splinters. It occurred to her that she and Algar were lucky to have survived their experiment.

'It broke,' she said to him as he approached, and for the first time was able to hear her own words.

He nodded, studying the wreckage of his creation. 'Oh well. It was loud, at least.'

'It certainly was that.' She looked for Skuld and saw him with another knot of people twenty paces away, staring at something on the ground. For the first time, she noticed the copper stink of blood on the wind. When Skuld turned to them, he was smiling.

'Algar,' she said, but he'd already seen. He took her hand in a vice-tight grip.

As they approached, Skuld waved back the Jorlith around him so that finally they could see what lay on the ground. The metal ball hadn't struck where they'd been aiming, but it had hit. The prisoner's legs were gone. Strings of skin and flesh hung from his thighs, and a shard of bone poked from his left stump. A wide pool of blood circled his waist. A few more drops fell to join it from the wrecked flesh, but it was clear the man's heart was no longer beating.

Algar made a strangled sound and fell to his knees, retching out a stream of bile. The sharp smell of it joined the stink of blood and shit.

'Well,' Skuld said, 'he's dead.'

Algar looked up, his eyes red-rimmed. 'That wasn't . . . that wasn't what I intended.'

Algar didn't go to the dance that night. He lay motionless in the bed beside Alfreda, looking up at the wagon's patched roof. It was too dark to see his expression but she ran her fingers over his face and felt the frown lines in his forehead and the downward tick of his mouth.

'You didn't know what would happen, Gar.'

He shifted beside her. 'I knew it would kill him. I wanted it to – that was the whole point.'

'You didn't want him dead, not really. You just wanted it to work.' But she couldn't quite put into words why Algar wasn't responsible, the way he could care so much about things that didn't matter and not even notice the things that did. 'I love you, Gar,' she said instead.

After a while he rolled over, his cheek resting on his hand as he faced her. 'It did work, didn't it?'

'Aye, it did. Of course, it also blew up.'

He shrugged, waving an airy hand. 'You can build another, can't you? We'll go and pick up what's left tomorrow. No need to waste good metal.'

'You know fine well if I build it that way again it will just break again. And it was pure chance we actually hit him. It's hard to aim when you're flying through the air.'

He laughed, and tickled her side until she did too. 'We used too much black powder, I think. That's all our stock gone again.'

'It is. And we don't have the funds to buy more.'

'We need to learn the formula for ourselves. Back on the plains, Maeng Kin's prettiest knife wife told me bat shit is one of the ingredients.'

'Was she drunk at the time?'

He waved his hand again, dismissing all practical problems as he always did, leaving it for her to find the solutions while his mind was already on the next big idea. 'We can find some and test it. It doesn't matter – we'll earn enough to buy the black powder if we need to. The real problem is how to make the barrel strong enough. Smooth, too, so the ball flies true, or we'll never aim it properly.'

'Well,' she said cautiously, 'I've heard of a way to cast metal. A mould formed of clay around wax would hold its shape, and I can melt bronze into it if I make a furnace hot enough. A barrel made that way should be smooth *and* strong.'

'Good, yes. And you could reuse the mould to make more. That black powder fuse will never do, though. It's far too dangerous to stand so near. Maybe we can have a long, slow fuse, to give us time to run.' He grinned at her excitedly and she nodded. She'd make the weapon again and make it better, if that was what it took to keep her brother smiling.

9

Uin kept his word, and the messengers he'd sent to spread news of Krish's arrival returned accompanied by men of substance from all the surrounding land. Their eyes alarmed Krish, so watchful and hopeful on him. And though Dae Hyo had been teaching him the language of the tribes, he found that these Rah twisted the words out of the shapes he'd learned. He left Olufemi to talk to them, and tried to ask Dae Hyo's advice, but his brother was sullen and unhelpful.

He understood why. He was Dae. He *was*. But he and Dae Hyo were a tribe of two and he needed more. If he was going to be a king, he needed to learn how to rule. And to take the Oak Wheel of Ashanesland from his father, he needed an army. The Rah seemed happy to provide a people for him to practise leadership with and soldiers to fight at his command, but Dae Hyo didn't listen when Krish tried to explain it. He just shrugged and drank more of the throat-burning wine the farmers brewed from their strange underwater crop.

On his third day in Rah lands, Uin took him beyond the cultivated fields, into the shadow of the jungle that ringed their territory, and showed Krish a string of reed rafts with neat wooden buildings on top of them. The wildlands were close enough that he could smell their wet decay, and hear the croak and chitter of a thousand hidden creatures. But those sounds were soon drowned out by the far louder noise coming from the buildings themselves. It was a constant, rhythmic clattering like nothing Krish had ever heard before.

Uin saw his expression and smiled. 'You wonder what it is, great lord? Merely the source of our wealth and the envy of the other tribes. It was my uncle's uncle who devised the singing spinner. Come, see for yourself.'

They entered the first house, a single long, low room so crowded that the warmth of all the human bodies added to the humidity of the surrounding swamp was almost unbearable – but Krish was too fascinated by what he saw to leave. All winter long, he'd watched his mother carding goat's wool and spinning it into yarn. It would take her weeks of work between her many other tasks just to make enough for one jacket.

Here, each man and woman sat behind a huge and complex wooden contraption, turning a wheel with one hand and moving a bar with the other. And somehow – Krish couldn't quite fathom how – this fed the raw fibre on to six different spindles as thread. None of the workers looked up at the newcomers; each was dully intent on their work.

'I saw no goats or sheep here,' Krish said to Uin.

'They don't thrive in our land.' Uin walked to the far side of the room, where another group of workers sat on low stools with plant stems clenched between their knees. 'We use vegetable fibres instead of wool and find it makes a stronger cloth, and cooler too. The best rope is made from hemp, and sails are strongest when they're fashioned from it, though our cousin tribes aren't much interested in that.'

There was more to see. Uin took him to visit five men working on the design of a loom that might take advantage of all the extra yarn they were producing. 'We'll power it with water,' he told Krish, 'but it would be best made of metal or, failing that, heart-wood of the Moon Forest oaks should be strong enough. They're costly though and we've yet to sell enough material to fund the building. When we do, though –' he grinned wolfishly '– we'll be the richest tribe on the plains, richer even than the Ashane.'

The Rah were so different from his own people: so angry and forward-looking. Krish realised that he understood them far better than he ever had his fellow villagers. Nothing had ever changed in the place of his birth and nothing new was ever made there. He hadn't known that things could be different, but a part of him had always yearned for some upending of all his youth's dull certainties. And now here was another way of doing things.

The next day, yet more men arrived from outlying settlements. Some of them brought their homes with them, towed by more tamed crocodiles, so that what had at first been no more than a small village became as crowded as Smiler's Fair.

Uin held a feast for them at noon on a floating platform on the water, with servants to wave palm leaves to keep off the insects and provide a cooling breeze. Crocodiles floated lazily in the water beside them, snapping at titbits of meat the men threw.

This time Krish didn't need Olufemi to speak for him, though he hesitated when they asked him questions about himself. What could he say? He'd begun to see that those Uin brought to meet him were all the wealthiest and most powerful of the tribe. The rest toiled at the singing spinner or in the waterlogged fields. Krish knew if he'd been born here it would have been to that work, not to lead, and he didn't want his followers to think less of him. But he was happy to ask *them* questions. He wanted to learn everything about them.

And as the meal progressed, he found another distraction. Uin's daughter Asook had been seated opposite him, beside the wife of a trader. He'd paid no attention to her that first night, and in the next days he was too busy. Now he had the leisure to look.

As Asook and the trader's wife talked Krish watched her mouth, trying to see if he could make out the words. He watched her lips and her tongue darting out to lick the fat from them. He no longer found the pale tribal skin strange and her body was pleasingly rounded and firm-fleshed. He'd noticed it before, without quite realising it. He imagined how it would feel to put his arms round her. She'd be solid but soft.

His shoulders twitched with the sudden discomfort of eyes on him and he turned to find Uin watching him watch his daughter. He flushed but the other man only smiled and said, 'You were impressed with our singing spinners, great lord?'

Krish nodded, too thick-throated to talk.

'But you've yet to see our greatest achievement. Asook?'

His daughter looked up from her conversation and Krish's blush deepened even though her eyes didn't touch him.

'When our meal is finished, will you take Lord Krish to see the reborn land?'

'Of course, Father.' She looked at Krish then and he couldn't read her expression.

She took him out in one of the narrow, flat boats the Rah seemed to favour, with a servant in the rear to pole them through the shallow waterways. No, not a servant: a *slave*. Dae Hyo had explained that to him and he tried to puzzle it out now, looking at the thin Ashane boy sweating as he pushed them along. His face didn't show the strain of his work. It didn't show anything much, except a dazed sort of happiness. Dae Hyo had explained that too. The Rah fed their slaves a drug they called bliss that took away their will and all their misery with it.

It seemed wrong, though Krish couldn't quite figure out why. If you were happy, did it matter if you were free? And how free was anyone, truly? Krish couldn't believe that his own boyhood had been much better than this slave's.

He thought of asking Asook, but when he looked at her face, the question dried up in his throat. They remained a while in awkward silence until she suddenly said, 'You come from the mountains, they say.'

Her Ashane was accented but otherwise perfect; he wondered if she'd learned it from her slave. When he didn't respond at once she lowered her eyes, watching her own fingers as they trailed through the water, picking up strands of reddish weed.

'Yes,' he said. 'The White Heights, which are tall, but not as tall as the Black Heights.'

She nodded, as if the answer didn't much matter to her, and they both watched the water passing by, the half-drowned fields of the grain he'd now eaten with every meal and knew was called rice.

'Is there much water in the mountains?' she asked after a little while.

'Streams. And snowmelt in the spring. Flash floods sometimes, but nothing like this. There's so much of it!'

She finally smiled at that, and then dipped her hand in the water and held out a cupped handful to him. She nodded at the quivering liquid and so he gently took her hand in his, his heart thudding at the contact, and put his lips to the water.

A moment later he spat it out again. 'It's salty!'

She laughed, but not cruelly. 'It's the sea! I guessed you must never have seen it.'

'The sea is full of salt?'

'All of it. It's . . . stronger than normal water too. I don't know how to say it. You float more easily in it than you do in a river.'

'So this is the sea,' he said, pointing at the winding waterways clogged with weed.

She laughed again. 'Not here. Not quite. You'll know it when we get to it, but first we'll pass the reborn lands. Soil we've taken back from the ocean.'

'You pushed the sea away from the land?'

'In a way of speaking, yes. Look – see over there?' On the left side of the stream they were being poled along, a tall earth bank had been constructed and faced with stone. 'That's to stop the water rising and drowning the fields. The rice is thirsty and doesn't mind growing with its feet drinking, but we wanted to grow other things as well, and now we can.'

The barrier that contained the river water was nothing to the walls that held the sea back. They were taller than him and stretched for miles in every direction, with gates where streams were allowed to trickle through under the command of those who'd built them. He'd never seen natural things so utterly controlled by people.

His own childhood had been lived at the mercy of rain and ice, but the Rah had told the greatest water in the world how it was to act. Their fields stretched for acres either way, planted with thriving green, red or yellow crops. This was the mastery he wanted to learn. This must be why Olufemi had brought him here.

Asook lifted a basket from the bottom of the boat. 'Do you want to eat?'

Krish's belly still felt stretched from lunch but he nodded. If they didn't eat, the slave would turn the boat round and his time with Asook would be over. The dreamy-faced Ashane boy held out his arm to help them both from the boat and then squatted back in his place, the pole across his lap.

Asook led him to a field of brilliant red flowers with a carefully managed stream trickling through it, and when she sat on the bank he gathered his courage and sat beside her. He wasn't close but she leaned a little away from him, an instinctive flinch. Then she smiled and shuffled forward instead, until her warm thigh was pressed against his. She was doing it deliberately, he could tell.

A jolt of lust went through him, and for a moment all he could do was breathe and try to keep his body from betraying his thoughts. She pulled out meat and bread from the basket and set them on a blanket in front of him, the same strain in her expression that was in his. Except, he realised with a far less pleasant jolt in his stomach, it had another cause.

He felt foolish for not recognising it sooner. Back home, Saman always had girls talking to him and laughing at his jokes, although he was a knobbly, bad-tempered youth with warts on all his fingers. But he was the son of Isuru the headman and whoever married him would one day live off a share of the other villagers' tithes in a big white tent.

And Uin had sent Asook to eat with him after he'd seen Krish's look. It wasn't even Asook who wanted the prestige of a union with him. That might have been bearable.

'Uin ordered you to spend time with me, didn't he?' Krish asked.

His voice was harsher than he meant it to be and he could see the effort it took her to keep her smile in place. 'He asked me to show you this place, yes.'

'But you didn't want to come.'

'No! Why would you—'

'Don't lie to me!' he snapped. Fury swept through him, and then a sudden understanding of how much power he had here. 'I command you to tell me the truth.'

She swallowed and looked away.

'I won't hurt you for it,' he said more gently. 'I just want to know.'

'I didn't . . . My father said you looked at me like a man who wants a wife, and that I should encourage it.'

Even though Krish had known it must be true, it still hurt to hear it. 'But you don't want me for a husband.'

She hesitated a long moment, and then shook her head.

He had all the power here. He could see her punished for this. He could *force* her to be with him. No, he wouldn't need force. Uin had already compelled her and Krish could look away from her face as he lay with her and never need to know what she truly felt. His cock hardened at the thought of having her round, firm body under him, but his stomach rebelled at it. He remembered his da, forcing his ma down to the bedding when he'd been drinking, ignoring her cry of pain when he pressed against the bruises he'd put on her.

'I don't want you if you don't want me,' he said, and was relieved to realise it was true.

She nodded, but didn't relax.

'Will your da be angry?'

'Not angry, no. There's my sister still.'

'I see.' He tried to smile at her. 'I wouldn't be such a terrible husband. I don't think so anyway.'

That won a very small return smile, but her eyes wouldn't stick to him. Krish realised that they kept drifting away to the slave boy in their boat.

'Oh,' he said. 'It's him you want to be with, is it?'

'What? No! Of course not!'

'I'm sorry, I don't know your ways yet. Is it forbidden to be with slaves?'

'No, it's not forbidden, but a woman would never . . . Only the men do it. My father—' She snapped her mouth shut on the rest of what she would have said.

'Your father lies with his slaves?' She was still looking at the slave by the boat and suddenly Krish understood. The boy looked like a full Ashane, but his skin was a little pale, his hair very straight. 'He's your brother.'

'No!' She looked appalled at the idea, but Krish didn't think he'd got it wrong.

'Not your brother, but your da's son,' he tried again.

She nodded reluctantly.

'And still a slave.'

'Of course.'

He thought he was beginning to understand. 'And when you look at me, you see him.' She squirmed uncomfortably, but he didn't really need an answer. 'Let's go back,' he said. 'I've seen enough.'

And what he'd seen, he couldn't unsee. Any man and woman here who wasn't Rah – any child – must be a slave. He was ashamed to realise that he'd been ignoring them, just as the Rah themselves did, the way a man would ignore a chair until he wanted to sit in it.

He made himself pay attention that night, at another dinner with more of Uin's wealthy friends. They'd all brought their slaves with them. They were a part of that wealth, Krish realised, and one these men were proud to show off. So they ate and drank and laughed and their slaves hovered around them, smiling their empty smiles.

The boy, Uin's son, served Krish his meal. 'What's your name?' Krish asked as he spooned vegetables onto Krish's dish.

The boy hesitated, head tipped sideways, as if this was a question he needed to consider carefully. 'It's Dinesh. My name, my name, my name is Dinesh.'

'Dinesh can show me,' Krish said the next day, when Uin suggested he might like to see the shipyards.

Uin glanced at Asook, sitting prim and upright in her chair. 'Perhaps my daughter . . .?'

'There's no need to disturb her,' Krish said.

Uin studied his face and then smiled knowingly, as if he'd seen something a little shameful there. 'Very well. Dinesh, you will take the great lord to the yards. The shipyards, do you understand? The place where the new ships are, not the fishing fleet.'

'The shipyard, yes, yes, yes,' Dinesh said, nodding happily.

Krish thought the boy would lead him seaward, but instead they turned inland and he wondered if Dinesh had truly understood Uin's instructions. Yet water was never far away in Rah territory and soon they came to the banks of the broadest river he'd yet seen, its waters flat and silver and stretching many hundreds of paces to the far bank. And here indeed were ships, dozens upon dozens of them in states of construction from simple wooden frames to high-masted, white-sailed completeness.

'Ships,' Dinesh said, as if Krish couldn't see them himself.

'For trading?'

'No, no, no, no.'

'Not trading?'

'Oh yes, trade and fishing but not these ships. These are to take back what's ours.'

The slave's face was as vacant as ever, and Krish knew he must be repeating Uin's words. 'The ships are for war?'

'To travel into the other lands. The other, the other, the other tribes, they see the water as a wall but we know it's a road. There are roads into all their lands and we can sail them. Only the Ahn use the rivers already and they can, they can, they can be bought.'

The Rah had money from their singing spinner to buy weapons and the crops from the reborn lands to feed the men to wield them. 'Was Uin waiting for me?' Krish asked Dinesh. 'Before he went to war, was he waiting for me?'

'You are the great lord.' Dinesh smiled even wider.

'And what do you think? About the war. About Uin.'

'I . . .' Dinesh shook his head, face slack with incomprehension.

'Is Uin good to you?'

'Uin, Uin, Uin gives me bliss.'

'And are you happy to . . . to be his slave?'

'Uin gives me bliss.'

Uin gave his slaves bliss. He gave Krish worship and shelter from his father's men. Uin would give Krish his daughter if he desired her, and all he wanted in exchange was his blessing on this conflict, for Krish to smile and wave off his people as they went to fight the other tribes. Krish looked at Dinesh's empty, smiling face and wondered if the bargains were fair: freedom for pleasure and security for war.

10

The attack came at moonrise. Sang Ki woke to screams, fire and the pounding of hooves.

Smoke billowed beneath the canvas and with it the smell of burning flesh. Muzzy with sleep, he thought he was back in the pyre of Smiler's Fair. He rolled to his side, coughing wretchedly and loose-bowelled with fear.

Sanity returned with his mother's entry into the tent. 'Control your bird!' she snapped before his gluey eyes had fully opened.

'What bird?' he asked. And then, more importantly, 'What's happening?'

'We're under attack.'

He forced his ungainly bulk upright with more haste than dignity. 'Who by? No, of course, the Brotherband.'

'Probably. At least a hundred mounted warriors. Our pickets gave warning but the sentries were overwhelmed. Come – the bird must be controlled.'

'The bird?' he said again, puzzled and frightened as he followed her out of the tent still wearing his nightgown. His bladder was early-morning full and in humiliating danger of leaking.

Outside was chaos. The Smiler's Fair refugees who'd attached themselves to his retinue like limpets ran about uselessly, and his soldiers pushed them aside as they sprinted from one side of the camp to the other. The fire at least was more limited than he'd feared. Two supply tents were aflame but a few of the refugees had found the sense to form a line and douse them with buckets of water. He saw riders circling the camp and arrows flying towards it, but none of the enemy appeared to have crossed the caltrop-strewn ditch that surrounded it.

And yet the noisiest commotion came from his left, well within the defended perimeter. There was a horrible inhuman shrieking and panicked human cries.

It was the carrion mount. Too big to take wing without her wheel perch to glide from and too stupid to understand what was happening, she was flapping her great wings and pecking with her viciously curved beak at anyone within reach. Sang Ki wobbled to a stop, a little impressed to see the elderly creature so warlike, and utterly unwilling to come within reach of her fury.

His mother pushed against him, forcing him forward a stumbling step. 'You must calm it – it's blocking the armoury.'

It was true: the bird had planted herself in front of the tent filled with spare arrows and a few precious metal swords, and was resisting all efforts to shift her. But Sang Ki failed to see why he might succeed where the strapping soldiers ringing her had failed. One was cradling his arm, which hung from his shoulder at a painfully unnatural angle. All were pecked and bleeding.

'It trusts you,' his mother said, pushing him again. 'Quick. Only our arrows are holding them back.'

At her words, the bird turned her beady black eyes on them. For a moment he thought the mount might have recognised him, and then she threw back her filthy grey head and screamed again.

'Laali.' He sidled forward a cautious step. 'Calm yourself, Laali: there's no danger to you here.'

'You can't *reason* with it,' his mother said, exasperated.

Well he certainly didn't want to *grapple* with her, but several of his soldiers had turned to watch him now, and some of the dollymops and merchants too. There was fear in their faces and not very much hope and he felt shamed by their lack of trust. He would do this. He must.

Speaking was clearly worthless. He tried a low cooing instead, a sound he'd heard Gurjot make when calming the creature. But there was no way she could hear him over the din of battle, and so he clenched his fists and eased nearer again.

Laali's ragged head turned, her wings fanned and he wanted

nothing more than to flee. But a fire arrow streaked through the sky, a tent blazed and more victims screamed, and so he held out his trembling hand and stepped within reach of the bird.

She reared, flapped her wings and then fell back to earth with a thud that shook the ground. Sang Ki bit through his lip, determined not to scream, and held his legs rigid so he wouldn't run. He accomplished his aims at the cost of a whimper, but no one was close enough to hear. Wiser than he, they'd retreated at the carrion mount's actions. And he felt them take a further pace back as Laali lowered her head, stared straight into his eyes and screeched her displeasure.

This was no good. He was achieving nothing. He drew in a breath, ready to move back – and the perverse creature chose that moment to bend her neck and rest her head against his still-raised hand. She made another sound, a soft caw that was almost like a cat's purr. Very cautiously, he stroked his fingers over her gullet and the purr deepened.

'Move the thing!' his mother said sharply.

The bird's eye rolled towards her in alarm but he cooed at her again, feeling ridiculous, and she calmed. 'Come with me then, Laali. Let's leave battle to those better suited to it.'

The fighting sputtered on for a short while, increasingly half-hearted attacks by the Brotherband driven off by increasingly heavy flights of arrows, until at last a force of Jorlith sortied from the vestiges of Smiler's Fair and the warriors were driven off.

Sang Ki ventured out when it seemed certain the danger was past. Laali accompanied him and he was grateful for her presence. Any surviving Brotherband warrior might think twice about attacking a man accompanied by the huge bird. And at least her stink was no worse than the smell of a battlefield.

There were Ashane corpses here and there, and the occasional blond Jorlith. Most were black-haired tribesmen, though, and Sang Ki frowned as he realised how few of them there truly were. He waited, his hand against Laali's back as scavengers both human and animal began to descend on the dead. Laali herself leaned down to peck out the eyes of one poor unfortunate and Sang Ki held down his heaving stomach and looked away. All must act according to their natures.

Very soon, the scavengers outnumbered the dead and his mind circled back round to examine that fact. Chung Cheol's band alone had comprised more than lay here, and the Brotherband in its entirety was said to number in the thousands. So where were they?

He was still pondering the question when he heard a loud moan and a curse simultaneously to his left. It was a thin Moon Forest man, swaying back from the body he'd been looting and paler than usual with fright. The man on the ground, the Brotherband warrior, was snarling up at him, his hands clutched tight against the wound in his belly.

A survivor. Well, that could be useful.

At Sang Ki's orders, they brought the warrior to the tent that held Nethmi. The man screamed when he was lifted and hurled abuse at the Ashane soldiers carrying him. He didn't sound like a person who intended to die any time soon.

Min Soo crossed his arms when he saw the warrior tied down to one of his cots. The physician's purple hair looked black in the dim light and the orange dye on his face was beginning to flake.

'This man is in need of your assistance,' Sang Ki said.

'This man is Brotherband,' Min Soo countered.

'I thought your kind aspired to help all those in need?'

'The Eom? I can't imagine where you heard such a thing.'

'Not the Eom – *physicians.*' As it often did when talking to this man, Sang Ki's patience began to fray. 'Are you not in the business of making the sick well? Or do you object to the fact that he's a prisoner?'

'I don't treat rapists or the murderers of children.'

'Oh. If it's any consolation, I want him alive so that I can question him.'

'Do you intend to torture him?' Min Soo asked.

'No!'

'Really? You have curious principles, Ashaneman. You refuse

to lay a hand on a man guilty of crimes that would turn any civilised person's stomach, and yet you intend to hang a woman so badly burnt you were able to mistake her for your father's killer.'

Sang Ki looked across at Nethmi, and was startled to see that her eyes were open and a few of the bandages on her face had been removed to reveal the ravaged skin beneath. She was propped half-sitting against her pillows and had clearly been listening to the entire exchange.

'This woman *is* Nethmi,' he told Min Soo. 'She may claim I'm mistaken, but she was wearing Nethmi's blade when I found her. It's easy to lie about your identity when your face looks like . . . that.'

'Yes, things must be very easy for her, with her body so burnt she may yet die and scars that might make her wish she had.'

'I . . . I could still die?' Nethmi asked.

Min Soo snapped his head toward her and – rather surprisingly – blushed. He clearly hadn't realised she was conscious. 'I apologise,' he said. 'The chance of death is slight. And the scarring . . . others have learned to live with worse.'

She shrugged and then whimpered at the pain the movement caused her. 'It doesn't matter. I'd rather know the truth.'

'The truth. Ha!' Sang Ki laughed, not entirely spontaneously.

'I *am* Mahvesh,' she said. 'I ran the Laughing Rabbit – an anchor for an ale, the cheapest in the fair. Ask anyone, they all know me.'

'I did ask,' Sang Ki admitted.

'And?' Min Soo glared at him.

He sighed. 'There was such a woman, but her establishment burned down with the rest of the fair.'

'I see. And did she resemble my patient?'

'She was Ashane and she was short. I brought one of Mahvesh's former customers in when Nethmi was sleeping to see if he recognised her, but the bandages were hardly helpful and why should I have believed him even if he'd claimed an acquaintance? The citizens of Smiler's Fair were never known for their honesty.'

'So it is impossible to know,' Min Soo said.

'Well, I suppose it's impossible to be entirely certain.'

'And yet you still mean to hang her after her babe comes out.' The disdain on the physician's face shone through the flaking orange dye. 'I stand by what I said. And if you don't have the stomach to torture this Brotherband scum, I don't have the time to heal him.'

'But . . .' The argument was so absurd, Sang Ki couldn't quite frame the words to refute it. And now he saw that the warrior was watching them too, eyes wide with his pain.

'*You* can torture him,' Nethmi said, looking at Min Soo.

The physician frowned. 'I may not care for him, but—'

'Not physically,' she said. She shifted, painfully slowly, until she was upright and facing him. Her tongue darted out to lick what had once been her lips. 'The Eom have . . . potions, medicines. I've heard about them. You can cause pain, or pleasure or—'

Sang Ki snapped his fingers. 'Or force the truth from a man unwilling to impart it. That is indeed said about your tribe, Min Soo. Or have we been misinformed about that too?'

The physician looked startled, and then he nodded.

The drug took two hours to work. Sang Ki returned to the tent when the time was up to find both Min Soo and Nethmi seated by the warrior's bedside. She was wrapped in a silk sheet, perhaps the only thing she could bear to have touching her cracked and bleeding skin. He didn't know why she wanted to be a part of this interrogation, but the physician's expression suggested it wouldn't be wise to ask.

The warrior was propped up in his bed. His bandaged stomach seeped red but his smiling face showed no pain. His eyes were wide and his pupils black pits. They tracked Sang Ki as he approached.

'Is he ready?' Sang Ki asked.

The warrior gurgled low in his throat like a baby laughing. 'Ready!' he said, as if he found the word ridiculous.

Sang Ki frowned. 'Clearly he'll speak, but is he rational?'

'There's nothing wrong with his mind,' Min Soo said snappishly. 'Haengbog doesn't affect what's thought, only the feelings that go with it. It's close in effect to bliss, though less evil.'

'I've never been so happy,' the warrior said, grinning up at the physician. 'Thank you.'

'And will you answer my questions?' Sang Ki asked.

'Will it make you happy?'

'It will.' He forced a smile of his own.

'Then ask.'

Nethmi was looking between them as they spoke, her mutilated face impossible to read. 'What's he saying?' she asked.

'Ah, you don't speak the language of the tribes,' Sang Ki said in Ashane. 'Curious for one raised in Smiler's Fair.'

'Ashane's the language of the fair. It was all I ever needed.'

'Ask your questions, shiplord,' Min Soo interrupted. 'The drug's effects won't last for ever.'

'It's so long since I was happy,' the warrior said. 'I remember the Spring festival when I was four . . . My father carried me on his shoulders to the top of Horse Skull Hill. I saw the Four Together. I saw all of them there below me. So many people, so many colours. And I was part of them. That moment, I felt . . . But never again. Never again. Then my father joined the ancestors and my mother married another. My brothers died of the carrion fever, and I was . . . I was just one. Just one, until the Brotherband came . . .'

'Why *did* you join the Brotherband?' Sang Ki asked, ignoring the physician's scowl. The opportunity to ask such a question might never arise again, and historians would want to know what had drawn so many to that savagery. Sang Ki knew how a segment of the Chun had seized control of the tribe and renamed themselves the Brotherband, and everyone knew what the Brotherband had done to the Dae, to the women and their children. But what had become of them after they'd retreated into the Rune Waste, why they'd emerged to raid the other tribes and draw recruits from among their worst young men . . . That was a story yet to be told.

'They came to our hearth last winter,' the warrior said. 'We thought we were ready for them, but they were so many. They were fine fighters. So strong. They killed the first men who opposed them. Not me . . . Not me . . . I'd eaten meat too old. I was behind my tent shitting when they came. Shitting my guts out and I felt like I'd die.' He giggled.

'I heard the screams and the metal. Blood and death. When I came out from behind my tent it was over. My cousins were dead, and three of them had Cho Hee on the ground. She was always the prettiest. I courted her with berries and bull blood but she wouldn't have me. Cho Hee on the ground and one of them saw me watching. He said, "Do you want this, brother?" I did. I did. Of course I did.'

'I don't want to hear this,' Min Soo growled.

Sang Ki wasn't sure he did either. 'You raped your own clanswoman?'

'They said the moon was rising. They said it was time for men to rise up and take what was theirs. They pulled off her dress. I saw her breasts and—'

'Stop!' Sang Ki snapped. 'Enough.'

'Is your curiosity satisfied, shiplord?' Min Soo asked, winding his purple hair round his fingers. 'May we get to our purpose now?'

'So you joined the Brotherband,' Sang Ki said to their captive, 'and the Brotherband serve the moon god.'

'The moon has risen,' the warrior said. 'Our time has come.'

Sang Ki nodded. 'Indeed, the moon's avatar is in the land. Would you know precisely where?'

The exaggerated sadness on the warrior's face was as extreme as his happiness had been before. 'No, he's lost. Lost and can't be found! Chung Cheol thought he'd be in the fair, but there wasn't a hair of him.'

'And yet you attack us still.'

'Don't leave an enemy to stab you in the back. Every man knows that!'

'In your back?' Sang Ki asked. He looked at the warrior,

slouched in his bed, smiling as his lifeblood leaked out of him. 'If we're to your rear, then what lies before you? Where is the Brotherband heading next?'

'The Hunter has left the Moon Forest,' Sang Ki told his mother. 'She's brought the Hunt from the shadow of the trees for the first time since she emerged to take revenge on the Eagle Band of the Dogko for slaughtering a party of her Wanderers.'

'And?' His mother had been sleeping, a crease of red on her face and her eyes moody with broken rest. She liked to have eight hours of sleep each night, precisely. She liked everything to be precise, the day cut into clean, even segments and everything within them orderly.

'She's come for the moon god, there can't be any doubt of it,' Sang Ki said. 'Or at least the Brotherband don't doubt it. The Hunter is called the Sun's Right Hand for a reason, and they believe she's their master's enemy. She'll gather the folk against him and bring an army of Jorlith from the forest to destroy him.'

His mother rubbed her creased cheek, her eyes narrowed in sudden interest. 'So the Brotherband will go to fight them first?'

'Precisely.'

'Good, then. Min Soo says Nethmi is well enough to travel. With the Brotherband gone, it's safe to return to the mountains.'

'Return? Oh, no. With the lost prince still loose on the plains and we with nothing to show for our troubles? That's not at all what I'm thinking.'

'You've no idea where the lost prince is.'

'I know where his *army* is.'

'There are thousands in the Brotherband. Tens of thousands! You're not fool enough to fight them. You're a child – not fit to make such a decision.'

He was stung despite himself. 'I learn the tribe's secrets on my twenty-eighth birthday – less than half a year's time. If you chose to you could tell me them now and the Seonu would take my orders without question.'

Her face told him what she thought of that suggestion. She'd always preferred making rules to breaking them.

'No? Well, it's no matter. Only *your* people would say I'm not yet a man – and it's the Ashane whose good opinion I've been courting. Whose good opinion you told me to court. My armsmen don't think me too young to lead them.'

She looked angry, as she always did when he crossed her. A soft part of him cringed at it. 'Your armsmen are wrong. You *must* return to the tribe.'

'Must I? The Brotherband mean to take the Hunter's forces by stealth. If they succeed there'll be no one west of the mountain who can oppose them. King Nayan's son will face King Nayan with half the world under his command, and how well do you think that news will be received in Ashanesland, when it's learned that I might have prevented it?'

'You *can't* prevent it. Sang Ki, please . . .' She grasped his plump forearm, the physical contact between them so rare he stared at her hand in bemusement until she took it away.

'I can,' he said. 'The Brotherband are being clever. They think they know a secret way to come to the Moon Forest and avoid detection, but their cleverness will defeat them. I *will* follow them, and I *will* destroy them and there'll be no more questions then about my fitness as an heir. Or as a man.'

11

The rain bath was high in the treetop, where the trunk was narrow enough to sway in the wind and the water slopped from side to side. Algar laughed as he dunked his head and then shook it to scatter droplets all over Alfreda and the three thegns and four other Wanderers in the bath beside her.

Aethelgas lay far below, a jumble of buildings clinging to the branches of the tallest ice oaks in the forest. Each dwelling was competing to outdo its neighbours, some with obscenely wasteful facings of metal, others with delicate ceramic tiles all the way from the Eternal Empire. One, quite close below, had covered its flat roof in statues of all the gods of the plains. The blasphemy was startling but Alfreda suspected it was the expense that would rile its neighbours more. She recognised the work of Dae Ji Won, a hundred years dead and the finest woodworker the tribes had ever produced.

There were other buildings lower still, the shacks of the poor come to live off the largess of the chief thegns of the Moon Forest. But they were hidden in the shadow of the great mansions.

Ivarholme, suspended in the trees to her left, was a far more sober affair. Its longhalls looked no different from those of any far-flung village. Only its gardens lent it colour, spring-filled with the bloodbells and bluebells from which the Jorlith healers made their beer. Of the folks' twin capitals, she'd always preferred Ivarholme and its warriors, who appreciated her wares and were too polite to stare at her over-muscled body. But Aethelgas was where Algar thrived and where he was sure their brass fire javelin would find its market.

Because the Hunt was coming to Aethelgas. It hardly seemed

possible. In all the centuries since the very first Folk Moot, when the people had sworn themselves to the Hunter, she'd never again showed her face to any but her own hawks.

Algar looked at Alfreda and winked as he rubbed the rainwater over his face. A Wanderer could be made pure enough to mix with thegns by the ritual bath, but what would make him fit to meet the Hunter? And he *meant* to meet her. He meant to show her the brass fire javelin.

The bath swayed even more fiercely as someone climbed the ladder that led to it. Alfreda could hear his breath all the way up, and when his face popped above the rim, it was red and sweating.

'She's coming!' the newcomer gasped. 'The Hunt will be here by sunset!'

Algar stood so quickly he threatened to overbalance the platform. 'Come on, Freda. We'd best get ready.'

Ready to show the Hunter the weapon Algar had once boasted would put her out of work. Alfreda shivered.

Whenever they came to Aethelgas, they stayed in the Grey House, a mansion that had been in Eadric Godricson's family for a dozen generations. Despite his wealth, Eadric kept a meagre house, but Algar had made him an ally in his work on the fire javelin and discovered other entertainment in the three unmarried daughters who still lived in the family home. Algar's favourite had always been the curly-haired eldest, and it was she who answered the door when they knocked – answered it with a babe in her arms not more than a few months old.

Her brother's expression was almost funny. He wasn't one to think much about consequences, and here was a little pink wailing one, squirming in its mother's arms. It had been almost exactly a year since they'd last lodged in Eadric's house and Algar had found a welcome with his daughter.

And then Eadric himself strode down the corridor towards them and suddenly it wasn't funny at all. His rust-coloured eyes blazed beneath curled hair almost as pale as a Jorlith's.

'So,' he said. 'I suppose you've come to offer for my daughter's hand, and only twelve months too late.'

'I . . .' Algar said, and then didn't say anything else.

'No?' Eadric sneered. 'You haven't even that much honour?'

'You wouldn't have me,' Algar muttered.

'You're right – no decent family would. Now get out.'

The door slammed, leaving a reverberating silence behind. Algar stood staring at it for a long moment, then turned to Alfreda. He looked lost. 'But I don't even know if it's a boy or a girl,' he said.

'It's a problem, is what it is.' Alfreda pulled on his arm to draw him away. There were eyes at surrounding windows, drawn by Eadric's heated words, and she didn't want to share their business with the world. It was probably best to get out of Aethelgas altogether. There was certainly no question of lodging with Eadric now, and who knew how many others he'd shared ill-word of them with?

The sky path between Aethelgas and Ivarholme was the broadest in the forest. Unlike Aethelgas, the Jorlith capital was a home for the wounded and the crippled. They'd paid in blood for the safety of the folk, and the Rhinannish – thegn and churl both – settled the debt with fruit and meat. She and Algar weaved between the wagons being pulled across the broad wooden planks of the sky path, one piled high with potatoes, another bloody with sheep carcasses. On a different occasion, Algar would have snagged an apple from the third, but her brother seemed in a daze. Alfreda kept hold of his arm and led him safely through.

The noise of the traffic cut out abruptly as they reached the far end of the half-mile span between the twin capitals. No noise was allowed in Ivarholme, nothing to disturb the tranquillity of the sick. The churls stepped sweating out of the traces of their wagons and carried the goods the rest of the way by hand. Even their voices quietened to whispers no louder than the shushing of the wind through the leaves above.

The scent of the flowers hit her as they climbed the wooden ladder to the strangers' longhall. The bluebells smelled sweet and the bloodbells spicy. The combination was curiously soothing, like a half-forgotten memory of childhood.

Algar didn't look soothed, though. He was whistling through his teeth, a nervous habit he'd had since he was seven. Alfreda ruffled his hair, which made his lips twitch into a brief smile, and led him inside the longhall. At least here there was some noise. The men and women seated at the wooden tables laughed and talked and drank and no one watched them enter.

Algar winked when he caught a pretty waitress's eye. Alfreda sighed as he held up two fingers for beers. Some instincts couldn't be suppressed, even by such recent evidence of what they led to.

When he looked back at her, his roguish smile had returned. 'Go on, Freda, say it.'

'Say what?'

'All those disapproving things balancing on the edge of your tongue. You won't enjoy your beer until you drop them out.'

'What's the point? It's done now.'

'Done and cooked and out of the oven. I *was* careful, you know. I didn't finish inside her.'

'I don't need the details!'

'All I'm saying is there shouldn't have been any bairn. Maybe it isn't mine.'

'Was anyone else courting her?'

He took a swig of his beer and licked the white froth from his lips. 'I never knew of her lying with another – but then she was obliging enough to have some fun with me, so she clearly wasn't averse to the idea.'

'She was a well-behaved lass before you got to her. I doubt she let anyone else take the liberties you did. You've got a special talent for seduction.'

'Others might mean that as a compliment.'

'Aye, but others don't have to deal with the results. We can't stay here, not now. Eadric has too loud a voice in the Great Moot. Who knows what he's been saying against us?'

Her brother looked genuinely bewildered. 'You can't mean that, Freda! Not show off our fire javelin? But this is the market for it, and with the Hunter coming – this is the moment, I feel it.'

'No, this isn't the time. We'll return when Eadric's found a man poor enough to raise another's bastard for the dowry and respectable enough to cleanse his daughter's reputation. We can make our living the way we always have. We've never gone hungry, have we? Everyone knows we're the best smiths in the forest. We'll come back when the Hunt's gone and you aren't in danger of offending our god. Or worse yet, flirting with her!'

He grinned at that and shrugged and she knew that she'd have her way. Algar had learned how she was: water on most things he cared about; iron when she was sure of herself.

She grabbed Algar's hand and pulled him from the table. Their wagon was beneath Aethelgas and the walk back to the sky path seemed to take far too long, now she knew escape lay at the end of it. Algar didn't seem to care. He looked around at the austere longhalls, the neat gardens and the cripples walking them, always endlessly curious, and smiled at the fair-haired Jorlith girls, as if there was no lesson at all to be learned from what had happened.

The way down from Aethelgas to the dirt below was a spiral stair suspended between three ice oaks by ropes thicker than her wrists. The treads were as deep and long as a man, and each was intricately carved, no two the same. There were pictures of villages from the long-lost Rhinanish homeland, and the three-masted boats on which the Jorlith had helped them to flee it. The stair was almost as old as the cities themselves and no one remembered who had made it or how.

She trod a horned owl, a dancing couple, a baker and a seascape beneath her feet without pausing to admire them. Algar's hand was still in hers and when they rounded the next curve in the stairs, it gripped her fingers convulsively.

Eadric was there with a cluster of churls, the burliest of his clients. Alfreda wished fiercely and futilely that she had her hammer with her. She noted that even the largest of the churls was shorter than her, and she clenched her fists and prepared to make the best fight of it she could, pushing Algar behind her.

And Eadric laughed and slapped her on the shoulder before flinging his arm around Algar's. 'Gave you a fright, did I? I suppose you don't expect to see a thegn so low on the stair, but

I had to make sure my men found the right wagon. Couldn't have them ransacking some stranger's home, could I? But they did find it for me – and it's just as impressive as I'd hoped.'

Behind him, the churls parted and she saw that four of them were straining under the weight of the bronze fire javelin, held in a canvas sling.

Eadric's arm squeezed tighter round Algar, until her brother winced. 'Couldn't let you leave without a demonstration,' he said. 'I've been looking forward to it all winter.'

Eadric took them to the square of the Great Moot, where Algar had originally intended to display their new device. When they arrived, Alfreda was shocked to see a crowd of dozens, maybe hundreds of thegns gathered. The churls placed the fire javelin at one end of the wooden platform and then moved back, positioning themselves so that one stood blocking each of the exits from the platform. The belt knives they wore were nearly as long as swords, and their hands hovered near them.

Algar hadn't noticed. He was staring round at the crowd with bemusement and a little satisfaction. She wanted to shake some sense into him. It didn't seem possible he could believe Eadric had forgiven him. And yet as she saw his stiff shoulders relax and his tense grin turn into a genuine smile, she knew that he did. He judged everyone by his own standards, and he would never hold a grudge against a man for courting a pretty girl.

She tried to move closer to him, to whisper a warning in his ear, but somehow she was surrounded by men, pressing against her from all sides and driving her back, away from Algar and the fire javelin. She tried to shoulder them aside and a hand grabbed her arm and twisted it behind her back until she gasped in pain and stopped struggling.

'No need to worry, lass,' the man holding her said pleasantly. 'It's just a little demonstration.'

She tried to call out to her brother, to warn him of . . . She didn't know what. Something. But there were so many people here. Whatever she shouted would be heard by them all and her words were too shy to emerge from her throat. She tried to force them to obey her. She *had* to. But her voice was gone and she couldn't recover it.

Algar watched as Eadric set up the fire javelin for him, drawing the fuse through the touch hole and dropping a heavy round ball into the other end.

'You need to put powder in first,' Algar said.

'I put it in earlier – you talked about it often enough. I know how it works. It's all ready. And look, there's your target.'

They'd set it up at the far end of the platform, nearly eighty paces away and far out of any realistic range for the fire javelin. Maybe this was what Eadric intended: a public humiliation and all hope of selling their costly invention gone.

The target was a simple wooden board, but someone had painted the outline of a man on it. They'd daubed two blue eyes and a wide, moronic smile. Alfreda remembered the man they'd killed back in Deep Holt. She couldn't recall the colour of his eyes. They couldn't have been blue, could they? He'd been a man of the tribes. But when she looked at the grinning outline she saw him.

Eadric stepped away from Algar and nodded at the fire javelin. 'Go on then. We're ready.'

Her brother's throat bobbed as he swallowed. The tension was back in his shoulders. 'I can't light it – I need my touch-stick.'

He and Alfreda had devised it after their experience in Deep Holt. It held the flame at its four-foot end and kept them safely away from the explosion.

Eadric shrugged apologetically and took another two steps back. 'I'm sorry, I didn't see it in the wagon. But you're not going to let that stop you, are you? Not with all these people waiting. Or are you afraid of your own weapon? That's hardly much of a recommendation for it.'

Her brother stood in isolation beside their weapon. He looked small and young, his cheeks rosy in the fresh spring breeze. His hair needed combing and there was a smear of black on the shoulder of his shirt. It was the mark of Eadric's hand, grimy with black powder.

Alfreda struggled again, gritting her teeth against the pain, and more hands grasped her. 'Quiet,' the same thegn said. 'This isn't your show.'

A hush fell on the crowd as Algar pulled out his flint and kindling. The flame flickered as he held it, shaking along with his hand.

'Go ahead,' Eadric said. 'Show us what you've made.'

Algar's eyes found hers in the crowd. She renewed her struggles and her arm was twisted until the pain forced her to her knees. Her brother took a step towards her.

'Now!' Eadric barked.

Algar stared at her and she shook her head but he didn't understand. He thought they were threatening her to make him do as Eadric demanded. She gasped when he turned his back on her and knelt beside the fire javelin. He made a few adjustments, sighting down the barrel as if there was any chance of hitting the target. As if it mattered.

When he was finished he leaned back as far as he could. The kindling had gone out and it took his shaking hand three attempts to relight it. As he lowered it against the touch hole, she finally managed to speak, but her shout was drowned out in the roar of the explosion.

Cwen's horse reared as the huge noise echoed down the line of march, breaking the waiting silence that fell wherever Bachur walked. She looked at Aethelgas, sunlight-dappled in the treetops ahead. It was clearly the source of the sound, but she could see no evidence of battle or disaster.

'Black powder,' Bachur said beside her. 'I believe it must be an accident and therefore nothing to concern us.'

It was so strange to see the Hunter mounted on her bay gelding. It was fucking strange to see the whole Hunt riding like a raiding party of the tribes. Cwen's own horse shifted beneath her, made nervous by the wolves that loped behind Bachur, and she pulled on its reins in irritation. At least hers *was* a horse. More than two-thirds of the rest were sitting uncomfortably on black deer.

With their own mounts slaughtered, they'd had to take what was available, and the Maeng favoured the slope-backed creatures for reasons Cwen had never understood.

The column stretched back a long way down the Salt Road. Cwen had never seen the Hunt gathered in one place before. She hadn't realised they were so many, a vast flock of hawks. The forest had been stripped bare to bring them here, leaving hundreds of villages near defenceless against the monsters. Cwen didn't understand why. There were many places the returned moon god might be, but Aethelgas surely wasn't one of them.

As they approached the city, Cwen saw figures begin to descend the monumental stairway at its heart. Further away, the Jorlith were pouring from Ivarholme and the churls from their fields. The Hunter watched them with her eyes narrowed. Then she nodded once and pulled her reins sharply left, weaving her horse through the column to the far side of the Salt Road. Her golden skin and hair looked like a flame amidst the leaf-green and mud-brown clothing of the hawks. Like a forest fire sweeping through them.

Cwen dragged her own mount to follow. Some of her fellow hawks raised their brows at her as she passed, and she shrugged and waved them on. If Bachur had wanted the whole column to stop, she would have said so.

When Cwen approached her, the Hunter dismounted, raising a hand to help Cwen from her own horse. Her mistress's flesh burned with a strange cold fire and Cwen held the touch a moment longer than she needed, drawn to it as always.

'I am leaving you,' Bachur said, watching the long column as it rode slowly past.

'Leaving?' Cwen studied her scarred face, trying to read expression where there was seldom anything but calm. 'Have you found the moon god? But leaving without the Hunt? Isn't that bloody dangerous?'

'Where I go, I must travel alone.'

'I . . . I see.'

Baruch smiled fondly. 'No, you do not. I will explain. The

moon god remains lost and his forces free. I name you my deputy to rouse the people of the Moon Forest against him. For all their vows to me, I know the Rhinannish will be unwilling to release the Jorlith to fight, but perhaps the full force of the Hunt will help to persuade them. You will speak to the Great Moot on my behalf and make my will known to them. You will speak as if *I* speak – I want no doubt of it.'

Her hand dropped Cwen's and reached up to her mask, untying it from round her head and flinging it carelessly into the forest. 'My hawks will no longer hide their faces from them. Tell the rest. It is these people's daughters and sons who have shed blood to protect them. I will not allow them to hide from that truth any longer, not now all must make the same sacrifices you have.'

Cwen felt naked without her mask. The people of Aethelgas and Ivarholme were swarming over the front of the column. Some of them must surely be able to see her. One of them might even be her mother.

'And be careful, my Cwen,' the Hunter said. 'Not all dangers here can be seen; others too wear masks or hide in shadows. The people of the moon did not all die in the last war and I fear some of them work against us still, here in the forest that once was his.'

'What about you?' Cwen asked. 'If you don't know where the moon god is, where are you going?'

'I am returning to my people.'

'The other gods?' The Hunter had never once spoken of them.

'No,' Bachur said. 'No.' She drew in a deep, shuddering breath and Cwen realised in shock that her mistress was unsure of herself. Her ageless face looked suddenly young. 'They are not gods, Cwen, for neither am I.'

'But you're a thousand years old! You haven't aged a day in all the time I've been with you. You haven't died from injuries that would kill anyone. I've seen your guts when a beast gored you and a day later you were healed right up! And the animals of the forest – the wolves flock to you like sheep. They eat from your hand like hounds. If you aren't a god, I don't know what the fuck a god is!'

'Something else,' Bachur said.

'Then you lied to us. You lied to *me*.'

'I never claimed to be other than I am, but it is true I accepted the names your people threw at me, as you accepted the mask they put on you. Now you see me bare.' She touched her own cheek, running her fingers down the grooves of the long, white scars, the only blemishes on her perfect body despite all the wounds it had taken. 'These marks that you and all your brethren have so wondered at, *these* are what a god does. Do not worship gods, Cwen – they are not worthy of it. You and I are something better. Do you understand?'

Cwen fought back tears for the first time since the night she'd left her village to join the Hunt. 'No. No, I don't.'

Bachur sighed. 'I fear you will, before this ends. It matters little now. Will you obey me?'

Cwen nodded. God or not, the Hunter was her mistress and Cwen had loved her with the same fierce passion for more than half her life.

'Then go. My wolves will guard the forest while you take its people to war. We both have much work ahead of us, and none of it easy.

12

The grey light of an overcast dawn seemed to blur into the grey formless dreams that had troubled Krish all night and his chest itched with a hundred red bites. He scratched at them with his nails and then let his hand drift lower, into the tangle of hair and on to the hardness beneath. His hand tightened, his stomach with it—

And as his head cleared, he realised he wasn't alone. Dinesh was in the room, on the bed with him. He had his hand round Krish's penis.

Krish jerked back, shocked. 'What are you doing?'

The boy's eyes were clouded. 'You don't, you don't, you don't like it?'

'I don't!' He snatched up the thin sheet and pulled it over his wilting member. 'I don't want you to come into my room unless I ask.'

Dinesh looked as sad as he was capable of in his drugged state. 'I'm sorry. Master Uin said you wanted me to.'

Suddenly, Uin's knowing smile made sense. 'That isn't true.'

'Master Uin likes it,' Dinesh said. 'He says I do it well.'

'I'm not him!' Krish snapped before the full horror struck him. 'You're his *son* – how *could* he?'

'I like to do it,' Dinesh said, but he liked to do everything he was asked.

Krish imagined Uin sending the boy to all his friends, a favour for anyone who'd pleased him. 'Have you done this for anyone else?' he asked, not sure he wanted to hear the answer.

'I offered Dae Hyo, but he asked if I still had my balls.' Dinesh's hand reached beneath him, as if he wasn't quite sure of the answer. He nodded at what he found. 'I told him I did and he said, he said, he said no. Have I done wrong, great lord? Is it wrong to do this?'

'Yes – if you don't want to. *Do* you? If nobody asked you, would you want to?'

Dinesh frowned, just one line on his perfectly smooth forehead. Krish realised it was a sign that he was being forced to think about something he didn't really understand, but felt compelled to answer because Krish had asked it of him. He felt a sudden swell of tenderness for the boy, the same he'd felt for his goats when they were hurt. Dinesh was as helpless and ignorant as them.

'The way to tell,' Krish said patiently, 'is when your – your member – when it gets hard. Was it hard when you looked at me sleeping, or at Dae Hyo?'

Dinesh shook his head, still seeming puzzled.

'Is it ever hard?'

'I saw, I saw, I saw Asook and Ensee naked, since they were little. When they were little, then it made me feel soft inside.' He touched his stomach and Krish felt his own clench. It was hard to imagine that Dinesh had any feelings beside a dazed happiness. 'But when they were bigger, with breasts, it was nice. I touched myself until Uin saw me and beat me for it. Why did he beat me, great master?'

Krish couldn't bear to think of Uin and what he'd done any longer. It filled him with the same helpless anger he'd once felt for his own father. 'If you want to lie with someone, do it,' Krish told Dinesh firmly. 'But not . . . not because Uin tells you to. And not with Uin – never again. Now please go – I need to dress.'

'Good, good, good,' the slave said, reassured to have clear instructions, and left the room through its reed door.

Olufemi's fourth experiment was almost complete when Krish entered her laboratory. Her mind was clear, the rune forming within it, and she was poised to channel the power of the moon when he pushed open the door and broke her concentration. The rune and all her work faded away into nothing. She huffed in irritation and opened her mouth to order him out, but when she saw his expression she put down her tongs instead. The boy was clearly distressed.

'Is Uin a good man?' he asked before he'd shut the door.

She laughed, startling him. He took a step back and then paused to study the room. She supposed it must look peculiar to one who'd grown close to manhood as a primitive goatherd in the mountains of Ashanesland. To her the laboratory itself was distressingly primitive. She could hardly recreate the workrooms of Mirror Town here, but Uin had given her everything she'd asked for, including this house. It floated on the ocean's border, where she could watch the waves beating against the sand in the moon's rhythm.

Krish's gaze lingered over the glass bottles of spirits and acid and mordant and venom, the piles of paper with her careful notes – and later angry scribbles – and the pottery and rock and precious metal fragments etched with symbols he couldn't possibly understand.

'Uin is a useful man,' she told Krish. 'That's all. Why is this question troubling you now?'

He sighed and pushed aside her papers to sit on the table. 'Why does Uin follow me? Dae Hyo told me the moon isn't a god of any tribe, and the Rah were followers of Marwit, the god of nightmares. Why would they start worshipping *me* instead?'

'Why does it matter? I've preached the news of your return for years and they listened.'

'But they keep slaves.'

'Indeed they do, though very few of them. Their work isn't hard, if that's what worries you. Unlike the poor, they don't break their backs labouring over the looms or ruin their joints in the water of the rice fields.'

'But they . . . the Rah use them in their beds. And Uin's slave, the Ashane boy, that's his own son. Even if the rest is right, that can't be. To use your own blood that way, it's – it's monstrous.'

'Is it? No child can come of it and with the bliss inside him, I'm sure the slave enjoys it. Besides, the Rah have little choice but to enslave the children of their slaves. The babes drink bliss through nine months of growing in their mother's womb. By the time they're born, they need it as much as they do their mother's breast milk, which is also rich with bliss. They've never known what it is to be free or to have their own will, so how can they miss it?'

'Then they should stop feeding the mothers bliss! How could Uin want his own son to be so, so empty?'

'No doubt he hopes his wife will give him a better one now she's finished with daughters.'

He smashed his fist against the wooden bench. 'I don't understand how you can make a joke of this!'

And suddenly her own anger was spilling over: old rage and new and most of all at *him*, for everything he'd cost her. 'You think I find it funny? You asked how Uin came to the moon. I'll tell you. He came to Smiler's Fair because one of his slaves had fled there: Vordanna, with his son Jinn growing inside her.'

Krish frowned, not frightened by her rage but puzzled. 'If she was fed bliss, how did she have the will to escape?'

'Because Uin takes the drug away from his female slaves when he rapes them! He says it's better that way, that a woman's more enjoyable when she knows what's happening to her. And so Vordanna came to me and *we* raised Jinn, and when Uin came seeking her I spoke to him about the moon while I made plans to kill him, but for some reason I've never understood he *listened* to me.

'He became your follower when you had precious few and I knew that as one of the wealthiest of the Rah he could lead others to you. And so I let him walk away, this man who'd hurt Vordanna and made Jinn from her rape, because it would serve your cause. It was all for you!'

'Oh. I . . . I see. I . . . thank you.' He paused a long time, perhaps gathering courage to ask the next question. 'Where are Vordanna and Jinn now? Were they in Smiler's Fair when—'

'They're dead.' He hung his head and she trembled in silence for a moment. 'Go now,' she said when she could say it calmly. 'Your questions are answered.'

When the boy was gone, she looked back down at her ruined experiment. It didn't really matter. It would have been the third time of trying, and she couldn't believe she'd get a different result now than she'd seen before.

It was one of the simplest of all conjurations: a breathing of life back into a plant many months dead. The brown, wilted thing sat on a bench inside a bath of water, sugar and warmleaf sap, which Morayo Abiola's 900-year-old notes suggested was the perfect nourishment. Olufemi had formed the glyphs of being, Hoy and May and Hähes, Blood and Leaf and Spirit, and linked them with two glyphs of becoming: Yag for growth and Yaw for joining. The rune she'd built from them and held in her mind had been perfect.

And it had accomplished nothing. The plant was as dead as it had ever been. The glass she'd marked for strength had shattered when she dropped it and remained clear even when she graved it with Yi, the glyph of obscurity. For three days she'd tried every rune she'd ever found in her years of research and not a single one had worked.

Whatever had happened back in Smiler's Fair, when Yron's rune had seemed to eat the flames, it was unrepeatable. Krish was here, right by her and growing in power, and yet the runes remained as dead as they had ever been, her rituals incapable of wakening them.

The discipline required was hard, not just to hold the shape of the rune in her mind but to call on the powers needed to quicken it: the sun and the moon, which was both a rock in the sky and the poor and ignorant goatherd she'd hunted for so long. Only the priests of sun and moon were permitted use of their powers, and so that was what she'd made herself, over all her long and lonely years of travel. She'd preached Yron's worship to a thousand strangers and now she asked just this in return.

But perhaps the fault wasn't in her; perhaps it was in him. If he was Yron returned, then it seemed the moon had come back without any of his virtue.

That evening, they invited Krish to another feast. In this humid land the air didn't cool as the light faded and so it was again held outdoors. Huge insects emerged to flutter round the guests in a knot of gangly limbs and smaller ones darted in to bite. At a sharp gesture from Uin, slaves moved to stand at each corner of the table, holding candles whose scent seemed irresistible to the insects.

Krish took his place at the long table's head, with Uin at his right and Asook at his left. She darted looks between him and her father, perhaps wondering what they'd said to each other. Uin in his turn looked probingly between Asook and Krish, and then between Krish and Dinesh.

Everyone was talking about war. The man who owned the second largest loomworks after Uin suggested a winter campaign. Another man, round-faced and narrow-eyed, wanted to challenge the Ahn for mastery of the inland waterways. Uin preferred to head north and wrest back their ancient grazing lands from the Four Together.

The fact of war was never in question; only the details were discussed. Olufemi sat silent further down the table, Dae Hyo drank and drank at its base, and no one suggested that Krish should be asked for his opinion. He hadn't thought being a ruler would be like this, but perhaps it was his fault. If a ruler wanted to be obeyed, he must issue commands. And if there was a deal to be made – if Uin wanted this war, then he must offer Krish something in return.

'Listen,' Krish said, and said it again, louder, when it didn't seem that anyone would.

'Great Lord?' Uin asked.

'I rule here, is that right?' Krish asked Uin and beyond him all the men at the table.

'You are our god.'

'I am,' Krish said, with a certainty he didn't feel. He looked around the table, at the slaves holding the candles, swarmed with insects and mottled red where they'd already been bitten. 'Keeping these slaves – all slaves – it's wrong, and I want you to end it.'

There was shocked silence and then the rumble of a growing wave of protest.

'End it,' Krish said again, loud enough to drown the other voices. 'You want me to be your god? You want me to lead you to war? Then obey me and free your slaves.'

13

For the first time in her life, she was unsure of what to do. The sunlight shone pure through the ice, illuminating the white, unadorned cube of her room, and she wished her mind had the same clarity.

There were so few lacunae in the Perfect Law. Mizhara had told her Servants all they needed to know but, imperfect as they were, they had failed to record every word. They had failed to record what was to be done on this night of her oroboros, when she should be with her husband, although her husband's services were no longer required.

The Perfect Law didn't say but her sisters decreed that, when pregnant, a Servant would abstain from congress with her husband. The act was for procreation, and as procreation had already occurred it was needless. 'Do nothing that has no purpose,' Mizhara had said. But *did* it have no purpose?

She was too restless to remain still. Her sisters suggested the time be used for meditation on her coming child. Mizhara said, 'Think on what will be done so that it may be better done.' She would meditate while she moved, an active body being the best home for a quiescent mind.

She let her body guide her, and it took her to the chamber of statues. Her own was here among the thousands, an icy image of their mistress as imperfect as all the rest and yet, she hoped, acceptable in its striving towards perfection. She passed other such strivings and tried to regard them with an uncritical eye.

It was difficult. Surely Mizhara's nose had not been so narrow as that one suggested. She knew the Servant who had sculpted it was younger than she. And the eyes on the statue ahead were crooked, though its creator was only one generation removed from the time of Mizhara herself.

But none of them had met their goddess. Only one Servant still lived who had, and she was lost in sacrilege so profound it was dangerous even to think of her. For the very first time, she wondered if it was truly possible for any of them to know Mizhara. A word spoken might have a dozen meanings, a word written a thousand. 'Do not stray,' Mizhara had commanded them, but how could they obey when none of them could see the path?

She walked on, threading between the cold, silent forms. It was too warm. The high domed ceiling was melting. Water dripped everywhere and the thousand faces of Mizhara were slick with it. Could they be melting too? It shouldn't be possible, but each one she passed seemed a little less defined. The sculptures were deforming into a perfect sameness very different from the one their creators had intended.

The meltwater fell on her like rain until she came to a sculpture she knew had been created by one of her sister wives. The warmth hadn't yet penetrated to this corner of the vast chamber and the sculptures were still pristine. This one seemed to her to more closely resemble her sister wife than their goddess. It was very like her, to see a reflection of herself in what was most good.

And at this moment her sister wife was with Eric. All of her sister wives were with him. She realised with shock that this thought, this image had lurked in the back of her meditations all along. Now she could think of nothing else. She pictured Eric smiling as he coupled with them. She could see every curve of his face, every downy hair on his cheek. Mizhara had gifted her Servants with excellent memories, but it didn't feel like such a blessing now. She could see Eric's hands running over flesh that wasn't hers. He had called her Drut: beloved. He had said it as if he meant it just for her, forbidden as that was. At this moment, was he calling her sisters by the same name?

'You're angry,' a voice said at her side.

She turned, startled, to see one of her sisters beside her. It was troubling that she'd failed to hear the footsteps approaching. 'Mizhara told us that anger is the fourth least desirable of the emotions,' she said.

'Nevertheless.'

She studied the face studying hers so intently. It was almost a mirror of her own. It had occurred to her before that this might be the sister who had given birth to her. She'd never cared before; now it seemed very important.

'I am . . . I have lost control of myself,' she confessed.

'You're pregnant.'

'Yes.'

Her sister smiled and touched her own stomach. 'I remember when I was in the same state. The body is a curious thing. Blessed Mizhara didn't make us, has anyone ever told you this? She used her power to transform the first Servants in their own mothers' wombs. It is why we were imperfect and must remain so. During pregnancy our bodies concern themselves only with the nurturing of the child: our minds become subordinate to them.'

She touched herself in the same place her sister had. Was it possible the child was the cause of all this unsafe thought? 'And if I still feel the same after the birth?' she asked.

'Then you must take the long walk into the ice, but it's a vain question. You can't know now how you'll feel then.'

'Thank you, sister,' she said, and watched the other Servant walk away. It was true, she supposed, that she couldn't know how she'd feel once the child was born. But she knew how she felt *now*. And as she stood in the great domed chamber surrounded by a thousand melting figures of her goddess, she knew what she'd do about it.

Drut found Eric at midnight in the pear orchard. The boiling orange sun was touching the horizon so that the limbs and leaves of the trees were as golden as their fruit.

Eric's skin looked golden too and his hair bright. She knew that he often came here after the seventh night of his oroboros, when the Tears of Mizhara still slid through his veins and he couldn't yet sleep. Her sisters would be abed, though, as the Perfect Law dictated. There would be no one to witness this.

He didn't seem entirely surprised to see her. Drut felt the curious sensation of her heart speeding at his warm smile.

'Missed you earlier,' he said.

'There . . . there was no need for me there. I am already with child.'

'Yeah.' He ran his hand over the swell of her belly. The feeling was entirely different from when Drut had touched it herself. 'But that ain't the only reason for a bit of slap and tickle. If we weren't meant to do it so often, why was it made so fun?'

'Would you like to do it now?' She flushed the moment she asked, shocked at the impulse that had pulled the words from her.

'Feeling a bit randy, are we? That's all right – I'm a boy who's always happy to oblige.' He reached out with his hands to take hers. Encased in furs as his were, it felt a little like being held by a bear.

'I shouldn't,' she said, but they both knew that she nevertheless would. 'And anyway,' she added, more sincerely, 'it's far too cold out here. And . . .'

'And a bit public inside. Well, don't blame me. It weren't my idea to build the whole bloody place out of ice. But I know somewhere more private – better suited to our needs. I ain't saying it's romantic, but your sisters don't never go there.'

His gloved hand kept hold of hers as he drew her back towards Salvation, over the sparkling, sun-stained snow. She couldn't guess where he was leading her and was afraid to ask. If she started to speak, she wasn't sure what she would say.

He pulled her through the grand entrance arch and along deeper corridors, quiet always and silent at this time of night. Their feet pattered softly on the ice and they could have been the only people in the world.

When they came to the staircase leading down, she pulled back, but he just took her hand in both of his and drew her downward. They passed the floor holding her own cell and then the great machine that kept Salvation always in sunlight. Drut was sure he'd halt then, perhaps thinking the bone-deep thrumming of the device would hide the sound of their own activities, but he only walked deeper, until suddenly there was rock and not ice beneath her feet.

At that she finally did stop. He pulled against her, but he was no match for her strength when she chose to use it. 'You can't come here,' she told him.

He pulled off his gloves so that he could rest the bare, pale skin of his hands against hers. 'But I already have.'

'This is an evil place. *His* place. The moon's.'

'Yeah, I know. But he's dead, ain't he? Mizhara killed him before she left you lot all on your lonesome. And she made you build your city here, right on top of his. She can't have thought it was too bad, right? Or else she'd just have, I don't know, whatever it is gods do. Burned it into ash, probably.'

He walked down a dozen of the steps and turned to face her, holding out his hand. This time when she took it, it was warm and soft, flesh against flesh. He drew her down into the darkness, until only a glimmer of her mistress's light remained to guide their way.

She felt when they reached the bottom. The air was heavy and she knew the chamber they'd entered was vast, but she could see none of it. She could barely see Eric as he turned to her and smiled and shrugged his shoulders to allow his sealskin jacket to slip to the floor. Underneath he wore a shirt sewn with seed pearls. She felt their texture beneath her fingers as she reached for the buttons, and then that too was gone, and his trousers with it.

When he was naked, he went to work on her clothes. She watched the floor as his mutilated fingers slipped beneath her robe and slid it from her shoulders. She shivered whenever his bare skin touched hers, although his fingers weren't cold.

Then they were both naked and he took her hand and guided it on to his penis. 'Give it a stroke, then,' he said. 'Get it good and hard.'

She'd never had to do this before. The Tears of Mizhara ensured continuous arousal from anyone who took them, and the act wasn't meant to be about his pleasure. But she caressed him as he'd instructed, softly at first and then much more firmly when he wrapped his hand round hers and showed her how.

His eyelids drooped and he grunted a little with each thrust into her palm. 'Enough now, gorgeous,' he said, finally pushing her hand away. 'Don't want to waste it, do you?'

She didn't. She desired it. Mizhara had commanded them to treasure every piece of their husbands, and she wanted the feeling that came when it was inside her.

'You ready for me?' He looked for the first time a little uncertain of himself. 'Want me to give you a tonguing first?'

She wasn't sure what that meant but it sounded like a delay and she didn't want to wait. She felt as if she was walking along the edge of an ice cliff that, if she ever stopped, would crumble beneath her and send her plummeting down. She laid herself on their shed clothing, and he eased himself down on top of her, resting his slight weight on his elbows. His penis prodded her thigh and he looked down at it.

'Go on then,' he said. 'Show him where to go.'

She reached more confidently for it this time. He closed his eyes as she held it against herself.

'Ready?' he asked and he must have felt her hair brush against his arms as she nodded, because he pressed in.

It didn't hurt. That surprised her. Usually during the coupling there was pain, but now there was only pressure, building into pleasure as he moved. He kept his eyes closed. She watched him the whole time. His mouth worked, muttering words she couldn't hear. She reached up a finger to trace his lips and he sucked it into his mouth and ran his tongue round it. She gasped at the sensation and he began to move faster and faster until she felt an intense clenching and then an intense release. He carried on, the stimulation now *too* much, *too* intense, until he reached his climax too.

He collapsed on top of her and then muttered an apology and

rolled to the side, but kept an arm flung round her. It rested, warm and sweaty, across her breasts.

Now the act was over, every thought she hadn't allowed herself to think before filled her head. This was wrong. Mizhara might not have spoken on the issue, but Drut knew it. She knew it from the guilt gnawing at her. His semen felt sticky and unpleasant on her thighs, his sweat was smeared across her skin and she didn't want anyone to know what they'd done.

He must have felt her tensing, because he turned to face her, propping himself on an elbow and studying her face.

'Ah, you got the guilts,' he said. 'Don't you worry – it ain't unusual. Don't mean nothing.'

'I shouldn't have done this.'

'Give me one good reason why not.'

'It was not what Mizhara intended. It mustn't happen again.'

He was silent for a long moment. She knew she should pull away, but she didn't. She watched as emotions she didn't understand, as fleeting as a mortal's life, flickered across his face. He seemed at war with himself but finally he smiled and lowered his forehead until it was pressed against hers.

'All right then, Drut. I'll give you one good reason why it should. Because I . . . I love you. I love you, Drut.'

And then she knew that it would happen again. It would keep on happening, because she had never been taught what love was, but she knew that she loved him too.

14

The slave pounded on the door to Krish's room, as he had every day for a week. Krish suspected Uin had given him this room deliberately so that the slaves he'd freed could have easy access to him. He lay in his bed a moment longer, still tangled in nightmares of the Brotherband, not the men he'd ordered Dae Hyo to kill but others like them. In his dream they'd been so angry. Krish could feel their anger trying to pull him back down into sleep, but the pounding on the door continued and he threw aside the sheet and went to open it, careless of his nudity.

It was Dinesh. It was always Dinesh. He'd diminished since he stopped taking bliss. The skin of his face had tightened over its bones and his eyes were no longer tranquil. Now they were too bright and never still. They darted across Krish's face to his ears and down to his chest and bare feet before restlessly circling back up again.

'You can't come back here,' Krish said, less patiently than he had the first ten times. 'You don't live here now. I gave you your own home.' When he realised the slaves would no longer be allowed to remain in their former masters' homes, Krish had ordered the Rah to gift them a portion of the newly drained land. And when he'd realised the slaves were incapable of building their own houses, he'd ordered that done too.

Now everywhere he walked, he felt hostile eyes on him. The same people who'd cheered his arrival muttered behind his back and the slaves had sat in their new homes, weak and sweating. But Olufemi had told him how to grow the plant she needed to make the powder she'd devised for her lover, Vordanna, to keep her healthy without bliss. They'd harvested one small crop already and another, far larger, was on the way. Krish hated that the slaves needed drugging at all, but the mage said that without her yellow powder they would die in agony. And on it – well, if they weren't the people they'd been before enslavement, at least they were free. Many of them were well enough to work in their new fields themselves.

Many of them, but not Dinesh, the son Uin had fed bliss to from the moment he was born – from before it, even, while he was still in his mother's womb. He came to Krish every day and begged to be allowed to take it again.

'You'll get used to it,' Krish told him hopelessly. 'The others have. It's . . . it's better this way. You can't live here – you're not a slave any more.'

'No no no no no no,' the boy said. 'No no no. Not that. No.'

He pulled at Krish's arm, his grip weak but his ragged nails like claws.

Krish tried to gently prise his fingers free. 'You *can't stay here*.'

'No, no. No. *Not* that. Look!' He grabbed Krish's shoulders and spun him until he was facing away from Uin's house towards the sea and the slaves' new fields.

There was a churning cloud of black smoke above them.

By the time he got to the field, it was too late. The smell was vile, choking and over-sweet, and the entire crop was gone. A line of slaves stood and watched the destruction. They might have tried to quench the fire, bringing buckets from the nearby sea, but none of them had thought to. Some had tried to smother the flames with their own hands. Krish could see the burns bubbled on their skin and their incredulous expressions as they screamed or wept. When they'd lived on bliss, they'd never known what pain was.

Some of the Rah had gathered to see the conflagration, but not Uin and not any of his friends. Instead, after a short while, Krish saw Olufemi half-running, half-hobbling over the wooden walkway towards him.

'It's all gone,' he told her needlessly.

She stared in silence at the ashes, panting. There were strange black smears over the field, patches where the flames still burned even though there seemed to be nothing left for them to consume. He knew this was no accident. The fire had been set.

'We'll have to plant more,' he said. 'It's fast-growing.'

She shook her head. 'We planted at the right time, and with seed from the first crop. That's all used up now and there's no point planting the little we have left, not this late in the season. By the time it grows, *if* it grows, it will be too late.'

'Then what can we do?'

She turned her back on the burnt field and the wounded people. 'Tell them to go back to their masters.'

'But Uin did this, or one of his friends! I don't want to let him win.'

'That is the nature of defeat. It's seldom voluntary.'

'No, I won't do it. We'll ration what's left and plant again. This time we'll put guards on it.'

'*We?*'

He glared at her, suddenly furious. 'Yes, you'll plant the crop.'

'That's your command, is it? And I'm to obey it?'

'I'm a god – you told me that!'

'A god.' She laughed, a crackling sound like thin ice breaking. 'Well, I'll do as you say. It's probably best not to let Uin believe you're too easily cowed.'

He oversaw the planting the next day, and the day after that. On the third day, only half the slaves came to tend the fields, and on the fourth day none. Krish spent the morning studying the Rah alphabet, trying to pretend he didn't care. He ate a lunch of roasted lizards and rice, and when afterwards Uin invited him to view more of the Rah lands, Krish agreed. He wouldn't allow the other man to believe he'd won.

Their party rode north, until they reached the place where the marsh began its slow mutation into the badlands Krish had been told separated the tribe's lands from the Moon Forest. The trees were stunted, branches reaching out along the ground rather than up, and heavy with ragged cloaks of moss. The decayed stench was stronger and the birds and insects drabber. Everything was greenish grey or a faded bluish green so that his eye constantly wandered, searching in vain for something interesting to light on.

He rode in a silence that Uin and his cronies were happy to fill. Krish heard their laughter, saw their smiles and knew they were triumphing in the failure of his orders. It was almost unbearable, but he refused to let them see his anger.

'There,' Uin said, still with that gloating grin twitching on his lips. 'Can you see – the smoke on the horizon.'

The day was grey and overcast anyway and at first it looked like little more than a bank of clouds. But as they drew nearer Krish could see flecks of ash within it. It reminded him unpleasantly of the funeral pyre of Smiler's Fair. Their lizard mounts plodded over the ground, leaving no imprint behind now that marsh had turned to earth, dry and cracked into a thousand mismatched pieces. The air, which had been thick with moisture, was now almost desert-dry. Krish swigged from his waterskin, but it couldn't get rid of the acrid taste of whatever was burning far ahead.

Then the trees parted and a lake lay before them. Krish shielded his eyes from the sudden glare of the flames dancing above the water. No, not above, *on* it. The lake itself was aflame. Its water wasn't blue but a dull black, sluggish ripples crawling over its surface.

'Impressive, isn't it?' Uin said. 'It doesn't burn all the time. The rock-juice seeps up through the water and when enough has gathered and the sun catches it right, up it goes.'

Krish tried to look unmoved. 'It's interesting. You could spread the black stuff over some of the waterways at the borders and light it if invaders come. Although that might kill the crocodiles.'

'Yes, we'd considered that. But Yejun is sure it must have other uses and we'll discover them in time. We're good at that, we Rah. You don't know us yet, great lord, not in the short time you've been here, but you'll find there's a reason we do things as we do.'

Krish understood exactly what he was being told. He needed to accept the Rah way of doing things; that was Uin's message.

But there was another crueller one hidden inside it, because he recognised the rock-juice now. He'd seen it splashed over the burning fields four days ago. Anything he tried to build that wasn't Rah, Uin and his kind would burn down.

As soon as he was back in sight of Uin's home, he flung himself from his mount and ran towards the freed slaves' quarters. He felt Uin's eyes on him. He felt the other man's scorn and knew he deserved it, though not for the reasons Uin thought.

The sun was near setting, sinking over the water and staining it orange-pink. He poled a boat to Dinesh's reed-born hut first, but the boy wasn't in it. There was only the stench of vomit and sweat-soaked sheets tangled on the floor.

Uin's son was in the next hut. He looked like he'd shed half his weight in a few days; his cheeks curved in beneath their bones and the outline of his ribs was visible under his thin shirt. The stench of him was worse up close, but he wasn't the sickest person there. That was the woman on the cot, full Ashane and glaze-eyed with pain. Her suffering was so fierce it was difficult to read anything else in her face, but Krish thought she might be Dinesh's mother.

She was almost certainly the baby's mother too. Dinesh held it cradled against his thin chest, though he must know the futility of the gesture. The babe wasn't recently dead. Its flesh had softened a little, sagging from the bones, and even from the doorway Krish could smell the putrefaction. The flies swarmed around it while others clustered at the lips and eyes of the woman on the bed. She would be next and the vermin knew it.

When Dinesh turned to look at Krish, his gaze was the clearest it had ever been. 'Please,' he whispered, 'we need bliss. Please.'

Krish turned his back on the boy and the dying woman and the decaying baby and fled.

He found Dae Hyo surrounded by empty bottles and the harsh smell of what had been in them. The warrior had stripped to his trousers and his bare chest was a red mess of insect bites. His face was little better, one eye half closed from an oozing lump on his brow.

He raised the one full bottle in greeting when he saw Krish. 'Lovely place you've found for us to live, brother.'

Krish sank to the ground beside him, beneath the broad leaves of a marsh palm. The tree offered shelter from the sun but no respite from the humid warmth.

The warrior took two more long swallows and then lay back, the bottle resting against his chest and his eyes closed.

'The slaves are dying,' Krish told him.

'Are they?'

'It's my fault.'

Dae Hyo's eyes cracked open at that. He squinted at Krish. 'Don't concern yourself, brother. You tried to help them.'

'Yes, and I just made it worse.'

The warrior shrugged. 'The Rah will do what the Rah will do – I told you that. And the slaves aren't our people.'

'They're Ashane.'

With obvious effort, Dae Hyo pushed himself into a sitting position. 'Some of them. And what are *you*, brother? You once told me you were Dae.'

'I *am*. That doesn't mean I can't care about anyone who isn't.'

'I tell you what, that's exactly what it means.'

His eyes when they locked with Krish's were bleary but fierce. And there was a temptation to nod and remain beside Dae Hyo and accept that this wasn't his concern. But behind Dae Hyo's eyes he saw Dinesh's. He felt the accusation and knew that it was just.

'Keep drinking,' he told the warrior bitterly. 'I'll sort this out.' He knew he needed to talk to Uin, but he couldn't bear to do it yet. He turned his back on the houses and on Dae Hyo and headed west.

The ocean had no clear beginning. The tangle of streams broadened imperceptibly as they flowed and the earth paths shrank until after a while you realised that all the walkways were floating and there was no land left.

Krish stared at the horizon where the grey sea met the grey sky. He thought it might be raining, there in the distance. The wind blew towards him and the rain would arrive soon, but what did it matter? The air could hardly be any more full of water.

He heard the footsteps clattering on the wooden planks behind him. They were too light to be Dae Hyo's and too swift for Olufemi. When they stopped beside him he saw that it was Ensee, Uin's other daughter.

'There's a storm coming,' she said.

He nodded.

'We should go back. It'll come fast, they always do.'

'I don't mind getting wet.'

She laughed, a surprisingly joyful sound. Her face was gentle with youth, unmarked by any care or woe. Even her hair had the wispy fineness of a baby's, untidy above soft brown eyes and strong black brows, the only definite part of her.

He felt suddenly furious with her. 'Go back in if it bothers you.'

'It should bother *you*. It's not just a little rain. There – did you see the lightning?'

He had, a flash of blue that seemed to fill the whole sky.

'A storm like that can kill you.'

He shrugged again, a sullen gesture he couldn't seem to restrain. 'I'm sure your father wouldn't mind.'

'*I* would.'

He turned to face her fully, surprised. 'Why?'

She blushed and looked down.

'Oh. Oh, I . . . Oh.' He'd hardly spoken to her. Uin had seemed to lose interest in matchmaking when Krish wasn't hooked by Asook and this girl was so silent at the family dinners, barely a presence at all.

The leading edge of the storm saved him from finding a reply. She was right: it had moved far more quickly than he'd anticipated and was far more powerful than he'd guessed. The wind plucked at his clothes and the rain began to fall in big fat drops. He shivered, startled to be so cold when moments before he'd been far too hot.

It startled him again when she took his hand. His palm where it touched hers was the only warm part of him. 'This way,' she said. 'There's a house – a friend's house. We can shelter there.'

They ran through the storm together, hand in hand. The rain was so heavy he could see nothing through it, and he feared moment by moment that they'd plunge off the edge of the bucking wooden platform and into the sea. The sudden violence of the waves terrified him. He'd had no idea, looking out over the untroubled water of the last few days, that it was capable of such wildness. It rose in white-capped peaks and profound troughs that seemed to be waiting for him to stumble into them.

She knew where she was going, though. By the end they were holding each other upright against the wind's force as she banged on the door of a wooden hut whose raft had been roped to the side of the boardwalk. 'We're coming in!' she yelled. 'It's Ensee!'

The storm tore the door out of her hand as she opened it. It slammed against the wooden wall of the hut and cracked, a jagged black line running all the way through it. Krish tumbled inside after Ensee and tried to pull the door shut behind him, unable to overcome the wind's grip until another pair of hands joined his and they forced it into place.

The inside was little calmer than the outside. The storm churned the waters beneath the hut and the sides of the building seemed to bulge and contract, as if the house itself was breathing in time with the wind. The wood creaked and there was another, more rhythmic thumping. It was a device, a big wooden thing that rose and fell, pounding out a deep bass beat as it did. Krish didn't think it was another singing spinner.

The man who'd helped him close the door was a little older than Ensee, but thin-faced where hers was rounded, and far more solemn. His expression lightened when he looked at Krish. 'You brought him!' he said.

'Lord Krish,' Ensee said, 'this is Dongun.'

Krish's hair had grown long enough for him to wring out the ends, dripping water onto the wooden floor. 'Thank you for sheltering us, Dongun.'

'Of course, I – a cloth. A cloth for Lord Krish to dry himself!'

Another man shuffled out of the shadows, three times Dongun's age and half his height. He was mumbling as he walked and he mumbled still as he held out a black-splotched rag.

Krish smiled his thanks, but the old man had already begun to shuffle back to his device, stumbling when the floor lurched on the waves.

'Please excuse him,' Dongun said. 'He's a little . . . Yes, but we're all so glad to see you, Lord Krish. That you came here, it's . . .' He seemed bewildered that his words were failing him.

In his time with Uin, Krish had almost forgotten that he was a god to these people, his arrival long awaited. Ensee's father had never treated him as more than a useful ally. Not even that: a totem. The way these people looked at him was something else. It made him feel awkward in his own skin, and terribly false.

'My father's been showing you things, hasn't he?' Ensee said. There was friendliness but much less deference in her voice than in Dongun's.

It was a relief and he relaxed as he turned back to her. 'The flood defences, the burning lake. It's impressive.'

'Yes, he likes impressive things. But he never showed you this.' She took his hand again to draw him closer to the noisy device. She had to shout to be heard over its clattering. 'This is an automated quill – a word-maker. My father doesn't see the value of it.'

Krish watched, fascinated, as a sheet of parchment slid through the machine and the old man pulled a lever, bringing down a wooden block to thump against it. When he lifted it again, it had left behind black writing, covering the whole page. And then another sheet came through and was marked in turn. Krish looked closer and realised there was more than writing on the sheet: there was a picture too. It was crudely done, but not so crude that he couldn't recognise his own gaunt face.

'What *is* this?' he asked Ensee.

'Of course, you can't read it, can you? I thought among your people it might be different.'

'Among the Dae, reading is a woman's right,' he said stiffly.

'Even the Rah remember that much of the old ways. Writing is a woman's skill. But we read *for* the men, the rich men. No one else has the coin for books. Until now.' She smiled and gestured at the device.

'But words are no use to those who can't read them,' Krish said.

'That's why I'm teaching the poorer men and women, and they've been teaching the rest.' He realised she was shaking, but her expression was determined.

'Uin doesn't know,' he guessed.

'You won't tell him,' she said uncertainly.

'No. But why are you doing this?'

'Because words, written words, they're *everything.* Knowledge dies in the mouth but lives on the page, that's an old saying of the mages and they know more than anyone. For years here the rich have grown richer and the poor poorer. The rich have all the knowledge. They're using it to push back the sea and they'll keep the new land that's born of it. They use it to buy slaves the poor can't afford. They buy people to make their food while the poor starve because they don't have enough of it. The poor will farm for the rich on land the rich own and they'll never make their lives better. Not unless they *know* better. That's why some of us are teaching them to read. They can learn and they can talk to other poor people all over Rah lands.'

She pulled one of the sheets from the tray and handed it to him. It was warm, and the ink smudged beneath his fingers.

'We have people who'll carry these all over Rah lands. We're telling them what you've done, freeing the slaves.'

Up close, he could see that they'd drawn his nose too large and the crescents of his pupils seemed to take up all of his eyes. 'Freed them to die.'

'It doesn't matter,' she said fervently.

'How can you say that? There are, there are babies . . .'

She blushed and bowed her head. When she raised it again, her expression was calmer but no less determined. 'These slaves will die, but there won't be any more. No more captives taken from their home. My father won't lie with any more women who don't have a choice. He won't make me any more slave brothers.'

She took his hand and squeezed it between both of hers, cream, brown, cream, his rough fingers tangled with her soft ones. 'Don't back down. Don't let my father win. What you're doing is right.'

15

Sang Ki had read quite a number of rousing speeches over the years, their transcriptions more or less accurate, but he'd never previously been called upon to deliver one. He was surprised to find his palms sweating and his mouth dry. He was also surprised to find that he'd sought the company of the carrion mount for comfort. It was absurd. The bird smelled horrendous and was highly unlikely to give him any useful advice.

'I'm a fool, Laali,' he said, patting her matted feathers, 'and apparently also a sentimentalist.'

She cocked her head to regard him through one fogged black eye. Since they'd started their travels she'd become more restless, sometimes flapping her wings as if she longed to take to the crisp, clear air of the northern plains. It was said Ashane the Founder had stolen the carrion mounts from the ice of the Great Nothing, so perhaps this seemed like home to her. It felt very far from it to him.

He looked back at the train of his followers. They stretched over the grasslands behind him in a long column, gradually congealing as he watched into a sweating knot at the heart of the campsite his mother had selected with her usual eye for detail: near to fresh water and with a clear view in all directions. They were close now, close enough that their next march would need to be in battle formation. He'd brought all the fair's refugees with him, unwilling to leave them unguarded on the great plain, but he'd leave them here with a few Jorlith, safe from the fighting.

The plains seemed featureless but they were far from it. Sang Ki had brought half the maps his father's library possessed on his travels, and he was glad of it now. Two days ago they'd passed by the Diamonds of Iskra, a ring of small but deep lakes, icy even in summer. Those were marked on every map and showed that they'd veered a little to the east of their destination. Yesterday they'd turned west to walk through the Deulpan Gae, the Field of Dogs. Sang Ki had hoped his trip might shed light on why it had been given that name, but he'd seen nothing except a jumble of boulders scattered for a mile in every direction over the silver-green grass.

Today they would finally reach their destination, a place shown on only one of his maps. Perhaps the other cartographers had chosen to omit it, sensing something of its provenance.

The deep paths, the night roads, nameless but everywhere, or so his one map said. It was a strange, bare thing, without other topographical features, only a fine tracery of lines criss-crossing the continent from the Eternal Empire – whose southern coast was marked on it, as it was nowhere else – to the Great Nothing. Sang Ki reckoned the map to be nearly a thousand years old, but the hand that had marked other features on it was more recent. In blue ink, and at only eleven points, this unknown geographer had added another feature: the places where the night roads were exposed to the air.

Sang Ki had seen one for himself, in the depths of the Rune Waste. And there was another, only a few miles ahead of them now. The Brotherband were using the night roads to travel from the Rune Waste to the Moon Forest, he was sure of it. How else could they hope to fall upon the Hunt without warning? Sensible people shunned the unlit ways and the worm men who used them. But the oldest texts in his father's library called the worm men the moon's servants. Sang Ki thought that alone among the tribes, the Brotherband might not fear them.

He looked again at the force he'd brought, gathering to hear him speak, to hear the words he must find that would explain why and how they could defeat a force greater, more disciplined, more *savage* than themselves.

'Wish me luck, Laali,' he said.

*

An hour later, he looked at the crowd of upturned faces in front of him and knew that luck alone wouldn't be enough. 'We'll find them,' he said in what he'd planned to be a spirit-lifting conclusion, 'and we'll defeat them. My confidence in you is absolute.'

There was a half-hearted cheer, its message clear. He might have confidence in them, but they had very little in him. He'd seen it in their eyes, trailing over his rolls of fat as he spoke and wondering what he knew of war.

At least the Jorlith in the vanguard looked ready for battle. Sang Ki pulled on the rein of his mammoth and led it in among the steel-tipped sea of spears as they began the march. The fair could afford metal for its guards and his own were also so armed, but the Ashane levies and all the citizens of the fair he'd pressed into service were armed with flint.

Surprise, at least, was possible. Walking beneath the ground, the Brotherband couldn't know what awaited them. Sang Ki meant to plant an ambush and wait for them to stride straight into it. It seemed a foolproof plan, but many a fool had felt the same and suffered the consequences.

He had fewer than a thousand men. The Brotherband boasted at least five times that, maybe more. Their captive had been vague on the numbers and Min Soo's drugs had worn off before Sang Ki could press him. Still, they had surprise and they'd have the higher ground. This morning, when a distinctive rock formation had left him sure of the direction, he'd sent scouts ahead to the place where the roof of the deep way had collapsed and – so his map claimed – exposed it to the air.

And there was one of them returning now. No, more than one – at least a dozen, sprinting through the tall grass. Sang Ki frowned. He was no seasoned military commander, but he strongly suspected they weren't bringing him good news.

He'd become more adept if not more elegant at dismounting from his mammoth. His mother watched in silence as he slid down the beast's hairy flank.

The Jorlith spears shifted like stalks of wheat in a high wind to let the scouts pass. By the time Sang Ki had found his feet and his balance, the first of them was before him. He was Jorlith too and was usually as blank-faced as all his kin, but his expression now wasn't hard to read. He was horrified.

A terrible squawking distracted Sang Ki from the sight as Laali pecked a path through the warriors to rush to his side. She cawed disapprovingly and he rested his hand against her great grey wing, more for his support than for her comfort.

'They're already here?' Sang Ki guessed. An army massed to meet them was a far different prospect from one marching oblivious into an ambush.

The scout shook his head.

'They *aren't* here? Then some other problem?'

Two other scouts had joined the first, gasping for breath. 'They *were* here,' the shorter of them said. 'They're gone now.'

'How can you be sure?'

'Come and see for yourself,' the first said grimly.

The tribespeople had camped near the entrance to the night roads, at least a dozen packs of the Four Together. Perhaps they hadn't realised where the entrance led. And even if they had, why should it have worried them? They knew the worm men couldn't emerge into the light of day. But the Brotherband had.

The men were merely dead. Sang Ki had seen enough corpses in Smiler's Fair to have become inured to the look and stench of them.

It was different with the women. He'd known – he'd heard it from his captive's own mouth – what the Brotherband did with those they caught. But hearing and seeing were very different things. That, he supposed, was one of the more important lessons of the last few months.

The Brotherband hadn't even tried to hide what they'd done. They hadn't granted their victims that dignity. The women lay where they'd been ravished and then stabbed, or strangled, or killed by the act itself, by the things those savages had used to do it.

They hadn't spared the children, not if they were girls. One of them had left his spear behind, the butt dug into the ground and a baby fresh from its mother's womb impaled on the point, a glint of metal piercing – but Sang Ki had to look away.

It almost would have been easier to bear if he thought this was a message for him, a warning not to follow. But, deep beneath the earth, the Brotherband couldn't have known that he was tracking them. This wasn't any kind of message, it was only an ordinary day's endeavour.

Sang Ki walked through it, making himself look at the least mutilated of the corpses, forcing himself to reckon how long ago the slaughter had been done: at least two days, he thought. The flies had begun to feast.

Finally, he found the source of the attack. The roof of the deep way had caved in, a very long way down. He thought he could hear water down there; it was too dark to see. The cleft was narrow but the walls of the chasm weren't steep. The collapse must have happened years ago, and over time the rain had worn one side away, leaving a ramp that must have been very easy for the Brotherband to climb. He could see their shoe-prints in the soft earth. They'd probably grown tired of the dark after days below ground. They must have welcomed the chance for some fresh air and slaughter.

And now they were back out of sight and out of reach, marching towards the Moon Forest and the unprepared folk. They had two days' lead, maybe more. He could send his fastest horsemen to try to outpace them, but it was unlikely they'd succeed. The land in this part of the plains was rough. There were ravines, rivers, fields of poison-thorn not even a horse's hoof could risk. His men would have to go a roundabout way, while the Brotherband forged ahead on their straight, underground path.

He had been right, and it had done him no good at all.

He told his army to stand down. What else could he do? They set up camp, only a few miles from their previous one, and he retreated to his tent. But his tent was empty, and the last thing he felt in need of was his own company.

He wasn't entirely surprised to find himself heading to the hospital tent instead and its one inhabitant: the woman who still claimed not to be Nethmi.

She was awake, but her eyes stayed fixed on the canvas above her, so his were free to study her face. The burns had begun the process of healing. They were no less red but somewhat less inflamed. The scarring would never be gone, though. Her beauty had been taken by the fire. *Nethmi*'s beauty, he was – no, he wasn't quite sure of it. That was the problem. He wasn't sure, and he wanted to be.

'I have a problem,' he said.

Why should it trouble me? Nethmi might have said. This woman didn't. 'What is it?' she asked.

'My plan has failed. The Brotherband have outpaced us and now the Moon Forest awaits their ravages. If the lost prince's forces triumph there, the plains will be next, and after that Ashanesland, and with each victory their forces grow. You heard our captive too. That's how they recruit: offering life to any man they capture in return for his service. The beast they have let loose lurks in the heart of many men – or so they believe, and the evidence would seem to support it.'

'Then you've got to stop them.'

'Would that it were so simple.'

'You've got a carrion mount. Min Soo told me.'

He'd thought of this too, of course. But, 'An ancient carrion mount, barely capable of flight. And she'll let no one but me near her.'

'Then you'll have to ride her, won't you?'

He laughed at the absurdity of the idea, and the bulk of his stomach jiggled as if to make his point for him, but her mutilated face wasn't smiling. He wasn't sure it was capable of the expression any longer.

It was strange to find himself being advised by this woman. Of course, if she *was* Nethmi, the advice could be meant to kill him. 'I'm far too fat for the bird to carry,' he told her. 'Besides having no idea how to fly or guide the beast.'

'If you want to stop them,' she said, 'you're going to have to try.'

The wheel perch was a perilous looking thing. Wood was scarce on the plains, and they'd constructed it from saplings and planks scavenged from wagons that were themselves scavenged from the wreckage of Smiler's Fair. No one looked too confident about the venture, Laali least of all.

The bird's head twisted between the wheel perch and Sang Ki, her expression – if she could be said to have one – dubious. In her heyday as a carrion mount she would have climbed many such a contraption to launch herself airward on her patrols of Ashanesland. It had been many years, though, since she had performed that service and she and her rider had been retired to the White Heights. There they'd had real cliffs to fling themselves from. She didn't seem keen to return to her earlier methods.

Sang Ki wasn't too fond of the idea either. Along with the wheel perch they'd had to make him a riding suit. Among the refugees of Smiler's Fair was a man who'd once been the paramour of a carrion rider. He'd flown on the mount and he told Sang Ki the high air was colder than he could imagine. Leather was a necessity. It had taken the coats from three men of normal size to construct it and now it creaked and chafed as he reluctantly walked to the foot of the wheel perch.

His mother was waiting there for him, as he'd expected. 'This is lunacy,' she said. 'You've done your duty as an Ashane – more than your duty. King Nayan will see that. Now it's time to return home and tell him what you've learned.'

'Mother,' he said, and paused. He knew there was no argument that would convince her. Her face was set and angry, an expression that experience had taught him could only be shifted by complete capitulation. She had never trusted anyone's judgement but her own, not even his father's.

'You're far too heavy for her. You could die.' She still looked angry but she sounded anguished. It was easy to forget that she loved him.

'Oh, I think I'll survive the endeavour,' he said, though he thought no such thing. 'The carrion mounts are able to carry two fully armoured men to battle. She may not like it, but she can lift even my weight if she tries.'

'Please, Sang Ki. These Moon Forest folk are nothing to us.'

He was glad she'd said it. It helped his certainty to harden. 'Nothing? Truly, Mother? Do they mean so little to us that we can watch what was done here be done to them? You're right, I suppose. King Nayan won't be grateful if I save the Moon Forest folk from the Brotherband. They *are* nothing to him. But I won't let the Brotherband slaughter them if I can prevent it. I couldn't live with myself if I did.'

It was curious that it was true. Sang Ki had always thought of himself as a pragmatist, not a moralist. But it seemed there were some limits to his detachment. Unfortunately, the Brotherband had tested them. He stooped to kiss his mother's cheek, then rested his hand on Laali's new saddle and led her up the steps of the wheel perch.

Laali seemed to perk up as they climbed. The grubby feathers of her neck stood up in a proud ruff and she looked at the faces below and cawed in triumph or challenge. Then she turned her head to Sang Ki and butted it against his chest.

He stroked the oily feathers when they reached the flat top of the perch. 'We can do this together, can't we?' he said, looking into her eye.

They'd fitted her out in the best approximation of a flying rig that the carrion rider's paramour could remember. They'd even provided stirrups to help him up the side, but it was still a difficult and undignified process. Laali turned a disapproving eye on him as he heaved his bulk on top of her.

But then, almost unbelievably, he was in the saddle and she hadn't collapsed beneath his weight. He could feel the tension throughout her body as she strained to hold it, but when he flicked the reins, she took two wobbling steps forward until her talons were gripping the edge of the wheel perch.

It really was a very long way down. If she fell rather than flew it would kill them both. He made himself remember in unpleasant detail the corpses of the slaughtered tribeswomen. It didn't really help, so instead he made himself think about all the people below, and how they'd laugh at him and lose what little respect they had for him if he came back down again. He thought about his mother, who would never accept his defiance again, if he let her win now. And then he kicked his heels against Laali's flanks.

She stretched out her wings to their full extent and *tipped* over the edge of the perch. His stomach lurched as she fell and fell and kept on falling. The ground wasn't so very far below them after all. It was close and getting terrifyingly closer. He could see the low, yellow-flowered bushes. He could see each blade of grass. Until, with an effort he could feel in the stringy muscles beneath him, Laali raised her wings and flapped.

She did it once, weakly, then again more powerfully. And again. Until, unbelievably, the grassland beneath them became something they were travelling over, not towards. And suddenly they were rising, the air blowing furiously against his leather coat and an exhilaration he'd never known pumping heat through his blood.

16

Krish made himself go to the slaves' huts every day. Ensee said it was like picking at a scab, and he thought that was right. If you picked a scab long enough, it left a scar behind. A scar helped you remember and he didn't think he should forget what he'd done here.

Every day he went there were fewer slaves. The fields they'd begun to sow with such hope were turning back to swamp now. He'd heard muttering, and not just from Uin's friends, that the land should be given back to those who could work it. He knew he'd have to do that, eventually. When all the slaves were dead.

The few remaining had congregated in the largest house. The air stank of their vomit and Krish gagged but forced himself to enter. There were only eleven left: five men and six women. There were no children, and no one old; they'd been the first to go. The rasping breath of those still clinging to life seemed to rise and fall in time with the shushing of the waves against a shore he'd meant for them to call their own. As he listened, one of the breaths faltered, rattled and then stopped. Ten left.

Dinesh was one of them. That had surprised Krish. The boy had seemed so weak and needy. He'd begged for bliss as if he couldn't live without it, but alone among them it almost looked as if he might. His mother had died two days ago. Krish didn't know if the man he was tending now was some other relative of his. It didn't look likely – the former slave had the pale skin and strange yellow hair of the Moon Forest. It was stuck to his forehead with sweat and he moaned constantly as Dinesh smoothed a damp cloth over his face. The man turned his head painfully until he could see Krish. Astonishingly, he smiled.

'I'm sorry,' Krish whispered.

Though Dinesh didn't speak, Krish understood his look. *If you were truly sorry, you'd end this.* But Ensee had explained why he couldn't. These people suffered so others didn't. It had sounded so right when she'd said it, sitting among her friends beside their automated quill. But she hadn't said a word to him since, just kept her eyes as downcast and demure as they'd always been at her father's table. And it was far harder to believe her here.

'You freed us,' the dying man said.

Krish nodded, knowing he should come closer but unable to make himself.

'I'd forgotten what it feels like to be me,' the man said. 'I was twelve when they took me. I . . . I can hardly remember all the years. I don't even know how old I am.'

'I wish I could take the pain away,' Krish said.

The man's eyes closed wearily. 'I remember my mother's face now. I wonder if she remembers mine.'

It was too much. Krish turned his back on them and left.

Uin and his friends were sitting on the broad garden platform outside his house, maps spread out on the ground between them.

'Come, Lord Krish,' Uin said cheerfully. 'We're making plans. Your input would be valuable.' He knew Krish had been visiting the dying slaves. His own good mood seemed a consequence of Krish's despair.

'Plans for what?' Krish asked, kneeling beside the map.

'For war, of course. The Four Together have gone unpunished too long, and our people are hungry for land. It's time we took back what was ours. The men are being told to prepare themselves; weapons are being issued. Our cousin tribes like the cloth we make very much: so much better than any they can weave. They've bought from us for years and never thought that we'd use the coin to buy metal. When they meet us on the field of war this time, they won't find us so easily defeated.'

'Not with our god to lead us,' another of them said, staring fiercely at Krish.

Unlike Uin's gaze, his seemed filled with genuine dedication, not mere calculation. Krish found its fervency unnerving and dropped his eyes to the map. It showed all the lands of the tribes, the Rah huddled in this marshy seaside area. Theirs was by far the smallest territory. He could understand why they wanted to increase it.

'The people will be glad of more fields to till,' Krish said, running his fingers over the territory that Uin had marked in red: the territory to be won by force of arms. 'How will you share out the land when you have it?'

Uin smiled. 'Fairly, of course. Those who contributed the most – who bought the weapons, organised the war – will get the most. This is the Rah way.'

'The Rah way. Yes, I understand.' Krish nodded to them all and headed past them, into the house. He felt their eyes on him all the way, curious or angry or maybe even admiring. None of it felt comfortable or right.

He hadn't asked the other question: what will you do with those you defeat? In the past they would have been taken for slaves. And if he let Uin win this battle now, they'd be made slaves again. It wouldn't matter if he forbade it. If they saw him surrender in this, they'd know he could be made to surrender again. He *couldn't* order the slaves to be given bliss. Ensee was right. They suffered so others wouldn't.

But there was Dinesh. He looked as if he might survive, even without any help. If Dinesh did survive, just Dinesh, that wouldn't really matter, would it? It wouldn't mean Uin had won.

Krish had seen where Uin kept the bliss he fed to his slaves. Krish had watched the ritual each morning and evening, when the slaves came in turn to kneel at Uin's feet and be given what they needed. He stored it in a box beneath his bed. In those early days, he'd seen no need to hide that fact from Krish.

Uin had replaced the lost slaves with servants. Ensee said the servants were cheaper: their labour cost less than the bliss used to feed the slaves. But Uin didn't trust servants, who weren't wholly his. They weren't allowed inside the house in his absence, and there was no one to see as Krish crept into Uin's room.

It was richly decorated: ivory from Ashanesland, silk hangings from the Eternal Empire, beadwork of the Four Together. Uin had taught Krish to recognise these things. Everything Uin owned was the best. The slaves had been the same. It occurred to Krish that they'd always been more decorative than useful. Uin valued them for what they said about his status, not for what they could do. And when Krish had taken them away from him, he hadn't robbed Uin – he'd demeaned him.

It didn't surprise Krish to find that the trunk under the bed was locked. Olufemi had told him that, given the chance, bliss addicts would dose themselves to death. Uin kept the key on a chain round his neck.

Krish's da had had a locked box too. He'd kept their meagre store of coin inside, doling it out to Krish and his ma if he felt inclined. One time, when his ma was ill with a sickness they'd feared might be the carrion fever, his da had said it wasn't worth the expense of medicine from the headman's store. If it was the carrion fever, no herbs would cure her. His da had stalked out to hunt and Krish had been left to stare at his mother, writhing with pain in her furs. He'd stared at his mother and he'd stared at the lockbox and after a while he'd realised something: a box was only as strong as its hinges.

Uin could afford a better class of lock than his da, but the hinges were the same brass with the same small screws holding them on. Krish's stomach jumped uncomfortably as he shut the wooden door, wedging one of Uin's spare sandals beneath.

When the first screw fell out, he heard the outside door open: a distinctive creak and click. There were footsteps on the floor, too light to be Uin, but too heavy for Asook. They came towards the door and he froze, but they stopped just shy of it. To its left, he realised, where Uin kept the jars of candied fruit he'd paid some Ahn trader a small fortune for. There was a rustling and Krish guessed that someone was rooting in the jars. It must be one of the new servants and he smiled, glad that they'd proven as untrustworthy as Uin feared.

A moment later the servant had gone and Krish returned to

his task, more surely this time. The last screw fell free and he levered the box open.

There must have been two hundred or more tablets inside, cherry red and smaller than he expected. The slaves were given one in the morning and one in the evening. If Krish took twenty, they wouldn't last Dinesh much longer than a week. But if he took more Uin would certainly notice what was missing. He scooped out thirty and began hurriedly reattaching the hinges.

Later he sat on the riverbank, watching the sluggish water seep towards the sea and wondering if he should find Dae Hyo and leave. Perhaps he'd bring Olufemi, perhaps not. Aside from healing his wounds, she hadn't proven much use to him since they'd met. She'd only told him things it did him no good to know.

Just below the surface of the water, a school of fish hovered. He leaned forward to look more closely and as his shadow fell over them they darted away, all in formation. He watched them until the green of the water masked their jewel-like blue. It was strange how many things in this land were brightly coloured. He'd seen insects in virulent shades of green and red, the purple-and-yellow banded snakes he'd learned to avoid, and the multicoloured, raucous birds.

It had been so different in his home. When he remembered it now, he remembered shades of grey and brown. No one and nothing had wanted to stand out. In the mountains, the only attention you were likely to attract was unwelcome. But here everything wanted to be noticed. He supposed it was the same with Uin. He had gold, luxury, position. He had everything he could need, but he wanted more. This war he meant to use Krish to lead, he said it was to avenge old wrongs, but why should he care about them? The shame of his ancestors' defeat wasn't his shame. When Krish had spoken of taking revenge on his father, Uin had seemed to understand: he said it would be the next battle after the defeat of the Four Together. Maybe he even meant it. But if Uin conquered Ashanesland it would be for his own glory. He'd make a slave of all the Ashane, and there would be nothing Krish could do to stop him.

Was that the price Krish must pay for revenge?

Another school of fish had settled into the hollow that had been occupied by the first. These were orange, like tiny flames in the water. He was thinking of the burning lake and his own helplessness when another shadow fell on the water and these fish fled just like the first.

'You look unhappy,' Ensee said.

'I've not got much to be happy about,' he admitted, turning to face her. She barely seemed to have heard him. Her round face was flushed and her lower lip raw where she'd gnawed it between her teeth. 'Is something wrong?' he asked.

'No. No, everything's all right. We're ready.'

'With the sheets you were printing, the message?'

'More than that. Will you come with me?'

Dae Hyo was drunk, Olufemi distant and his own thoughts painful. Ensee at least seemed to take some pleasure in his company. She thought the best of him and he needed that. She smiled when he rose and gestured him towards the pens where the lizard mounts were kept.

Riding beside her, he thought about Dinesh. Krish had feared the boy might be reluctant to take a cure that was only for him, but he hadn't understood what bliss meant, what it did to a person. Dinesh had looked at the pill the way a baby looked at its mother. He would have done anything to be given it. Leaving the other slaves to a death he'd no longer share was nothing compared to his desire for the drug. Krish felt soiled by both what he'd done and what he hadn't, for saving Dinesh and condemning the rest.

Ensee didn't seem to notice his distraction. Her body was almost vibrating with tension and she kept snatching quick glances at him, her eyes as darting and nervous as the fish. It was very different from how she'd been when she'd shown him the writing device. She'd been sunny and confident then.

'Where are you taking me?' he finally asked her.

She scanned the country all around instead of replying, as if she thought listeners might be hiding among the green stalks of rice. Perhaps they were. Uin had no trust left for Krish and it wouldn't surprise him to learn he was being followed. But it seemed unlikely he'd doubt his own daughter: it would be an admission of weakness, that he couldn't control his own family.

'There's a meeting,' Ensee said. 'Everyone from all over Rah lands. We sent out the notice the day after you came to the scribing house, when I knew you'd stand against my father. I haven't even met a tenth of the people coming, but they're all yours. They're your followers – your true followers. You'll see.'

He realised they weren't travelling alone. Most of those they passed ignored them, absorbed in their labour. Others paused to watch and mutter among themselves. But some put down their tools and followed on the wooden walkways, or in boats, or with ropes across their shoulders, towing their own hovels behind them.

Soon they were at the centre of a crowd: hundreds at first and then thousands. The people watched him and walked and some smiled at each other, but few spoke. The loudest sound was the high laughing calls of the birds.

'They're very serious,' he said to Ensee.

'They've been waiting for this day a long time.'

By the time they halted, the crowd was so large he couldn't see an edge to it. They stood, waist-deep in the water, their faces turned towards the low platform Ensee was leading him to. Others waited there: Rah men and a few women, all older than himself and Ensee, most stooped or scarred by age and work. Their eyes brightened when they saw him and one stepped forward, a silver-haired, bushy-browed man.

'You came,' he said to Krish. His smile was full of rotten teeth.

'Ensee asked me,' Krish replied.

But the man didn't seem to be listening. He turned to the crowd and shouted, 'Lord Krish has come to us,' and they roared in reply, a sudden shocking outpouring of sound.

The speeches began, the young man he'd met in the scribing room going first. They were in the tribe's tongue, which he still spoke only haltingly, but he understood the sense of them. A time for change had come. Krish had shown them the way. He would lead them. The eyes of the crowd moved between him and the speakers and he tried to stand tall and look resolute.

After the young man there was an old woman, and then an old man. Finally, the silver-haired man moved to the front. The crowd was in tumult, riled by the other speakers and, Krish thought, by their own existence. He'd begun to see how people found strength and purpose in numbers. Maybe that's why the villagers of his home had been so weak. They'd been too few.

When the crowd was silent, the man smiled his rotten smile and turned to Krish, beckoning him forward. 'Will you speak to them, my lord?' the man asked him.

'I can only speak Ashane,' Krish said. He tried to step away, but the man flung his arm round Krish's shoulders, holding him in place.

'Enough of them will understand. And even for those who don't, they'll hear the voice of their god. The great families thought to keep it for themselves, but they couldn't. Show them, great lord!'

Krish looked over the crowd, thousands and thousands of faces, almond-eyed and pale and foreign, all fixed on him. He could see the legs of those nearest, submerged in the dirty water of the fields, strong-muscled. They had the bodies of those who made a hard living from the land, just like the men and women he'd grown up among.

'What shall I say?' he asked. Uin had never suggested that he talk to such a multitude. And because Uin hadn't, he would do it.

'It's not for me to choose your words, Lord Krish. Tell them what seems right to you.'

He almost laughed because he'd never been less sure. 'Brothers,' he said, 'and sisters.'

The crowd let out a ragged cheer. He let it build and die, glad of the chance to figure out what came next. 'Brothers and sisters,' he said again when they were quiet. 'I've come a long way to be with you – halfway across the world.'

His voice wasn't as strong as the other speakers'. He'd never had enough breath in his chest and he could hear his words echoing and re-echoing as those at the front of the crowd repeated them to those further back, those who understood translating for those who didn't.

'I've been beaten down all my life,' he shouted. 'My da – he told me that I'm nothing. I think people tell you that too. But you aren't. No one's nothing. The slaves I freed weren't nothing. You can be what you want, if you want. You can be anything. That's . . . I think that's all.'

The crowd roared. It was a frightening sound, the sound of a beast about to charge. He didn't think his words had earned it, but the old man smiled at him and let him retreat so he could hold the stage himself.

'You see – the god the rich brought us tells us we're as good as them,' he said, still in Ashane, as if he wanted to be sure Krish understood. 'And we can be as free as them. We can be as free as the slaves. If we have to pay the same price as them, we'll pay it. That's what Lord Krish has shown us: death before surrender!'

He looked at Krish for confirmation and Krish could only nod, numbly. Was that really the lesson he'd taught? The slaves hadn't chosen death; he'd picked it for them.

'We won't work in their fields any longer,' the old man said. 'We won't be second in every line, last at every table. Their crops will rot in the ground and our blood will water them. Uin said that Lord Krish would bring change. He has! The old Rah are no more. The new Rah are born today!'

The roar was continuous now, the thousands of faces in front of Krish ecstatic. This wasn't what he'd meant when he told them to be free, but he knew it didn't matter. And if their deaths helped defeat Uin he should be glad of it. He tried to be, looking out over the men and women and children preparing to tear apart their land and their own lives in his name.

17

Sang Ki was exhausted. The sun had set and risen again while Laali flew and still he'd kept on, pulling up on her reins every time she set her head downward. He was bleary-eyed and foggy-headed, but the journey had taken its greatest toll on her. Her feathers had never been glossy, but now they were falling out. When he reached to pat her shoulder in comfort a great clump of them came loose, fluttering downward on the freezing wind towards the ground she longed for. The skin beneath was pink and delicate, absurdly vulnerable-looking.

'Good girl,' he crooned. 'You're doing so well.'

At the start of the journey her head would swivel to watch him at those words, but now she just looked forward. Her massive wings had pushed them on, until at last he'd seen the border of the Moon Forest beneath them and the Salt Road cutting a straight line to its heart. His maps had led him true, but the journey wasn't over. Aethelgas and Ivarholme lay in the trees. And so he'd led her on, for mile after wearying mile of unending green below and blue above.

There was an unhealthy sound in Laali's breathing, a wet rasping as if something had broken inside her. She was an old bird, and even a young one might have balked at this journey. His mother had told him he was too heavy for her, as he'd been too heavy for most things men were meant to do, but he hadn't listened. He hadn't wanted to believe it.

If he stopped now, they could both rest. An hour, even a full night, it shouldn't matter. They must surely have overtaken the Brotherband by now. But if they landed, how would they take to the air again? There was no wheel perch here. No, they must go on.

If they could. The sky seemed limitless and they were in its centre. But gradually he noticed that the trees below were clearer, no longer a green blur but each branch distinct. A wagon rumbled below them and he could make out the form of its driver. Then the broad trefoil leaves themselves were visible. They were dropping fast.

'Laali, Laali,' he crooned, 'a little quicker, my girl. Beat those wings a little harder.'

And though he could barely credit it, she tried. He felt the ingathering of her breath, the groan that went with it, and the tensing all through her body as she pushed the air away in a mighty beat of her wings. There was a waft of carrion stink and he realised that he no longer minded it. The smell was hers.

The trees retreated and the wagon with them and for a moment his chest felt hollow with joy. But it couldn't last. She began to drop again, much faster this time. That last effort must have burned out what reserves of strength she had. He stroked her grimy feathers and spoke to her but this time there was no response. They were no more than a hundred paces above the trees. Fifty.

He clutched his legs round her middle and pulled the reins desperately rightward, towards the nearest track. If she fell in the treetops, it would be the death of both of them.

She didn't respond, still falling. Forty feet. Thirty. He sawed on the leather viciously, cutting into her neck. She cried out in pain but at last she moved, veering towards the compacted brown of the road. Ten feet from the treetops, and then they were nearly four hundred feet high again, above the track. And ahead, he saw their destination at last: Aethelgas and Ivarholme. The folks' twin capitals hung improbably from the branches of the great ice oaks, mansions with brightly tiled roofs and solid, dour longhalls and walkways and shacks, all far above the shadowed ground. They had made it.

But it was the end of Laali's strength. Her wings were barely beating. The moist rasp of her chest had become a terrible, wet gurgling and the ground rushed up to meet them, far too fast.

The impact jarred through his whole body. His spine bent and for a terrible moment it felt as if it might break. There was the cracking sound of bones snapping and two screams: his own and Laali's. After that, there was blackness. And when he woke it was to pain and the smell of blood.

Laali's body was beautifully soft beneath him. He wanted to lie still and never move but he knew that he couldn't. His legs wouldn't obey him and he had to use his hands to grab handfuls of her feathers and drag himself off her. He could hear a commotion in the distance, the sound of voices.

'I'm sorry, Laali. I'm sorry,' he said at the pain he knew he must be causing her. The agony when his knees touched the ground was terrible, and he fell forward onto his stomach, floundered like a landed fish, then finally righted himself.

He was on the ground by Laali's head. 'I'm sorry,' he said again, but this time he knew she wouldn't hear him. Her eyes were glazed and empty. Her body had cushioned his and she'd saved his life, but at the cost of her own.

He stroked his fingers through the grubby grey feathers of her face, pushing them back into order. Then, for the first time since his childhood, he bent his head and wept.

Cwen lowered her bow and eyed the target. Two in its centre, a hundred paces away, and one in the outer ring. She watched the last arrow tremble as she heard footsteps racing towards her and frowned. Though the aim was good, the power was lacking. Most things a woman could do as well as a man or better, but this was not one of them. The strength needed to penetrate the armour of the greatest moon beasts still eluded her.

'Mistress Cwen,' the approaching churl said. 'You're needed, Mistress Cwen!'

She turned to face him and he took a step back. She hadn't made herself popular in the weeks since Bachur's departure. She'd demanded the mustering of the Jorlith for war and they'd found every excuse to delay. The villagers needed their protection; Janggok raiders were everywhere; moon beasts too, now the

Hunt had abandoned their patrols. So many excuses, you might almost take them for cowards.

'What the fuck are you interrupting me for?' she asked.

The boy flinched, and she felt bad. He was younger than she'd been when she was taken for a hawk.

'What is it?' she asked more gently.

'A visitor – a carrion rider from Ashanesland. He's asking for you.'

'For me?' It seemed unlikely. She'd never once left the Moon Forest. They said she had Ashane blood in her, but she'd never met an Ashaneman.

'He asked to speak to our leader,' the boy said. 'And the thegns thought – they think he means you. He's talking war.'

The boy ran ahead, leading the way. Other hawks had seen the conversation and she nodded at Wine and Wingard as they trotted up to walk on either side of her.

'Trouble, I hear?' Wine said.

'Big trouble, they say,' Wingard agreed. A savage mauling by a vulture-beaked moon beast had destroyed for ever his resemblance to his twin, but they still seemed to have only one thought between them.

'A carrion rider from Ashanesland,' Cwen told them. 'I can't think he's come to discuss the weather.'

'What's war in Ashanesland to us?' Wine asked as they began to climb the long stair.

'We've war enough of our own,' Wingard agreed.

But Jinn had told her that the reborn moon was the son of the Ashanesland king. 'Maybe it's the same war,' she said.

They'd brought the carrion rider to one of the Jorlith healing halls. He lay on a broad bed, surrounded by concentric rings: healers, then thegns, behind them the chief Jorlith spears and loitering on the rim a few of the richest churls.

Cwen halted when she saw the carrion rider himself. He was huge, bigger than she'd imagined even his mount being. Pale too, not just from sickness but from some mixing in his blood. His blond hair was matted with gore and his back had been propped against a mass of pillows. His narrow, shrewd eyes met hers as she approached.

'You're their leader?' he asked.

She shrugged. 'I'll do.'

His face flushed with sudden anger. It made him look a little healthier. 'For the love of the gods! I've ridden my poor Laali to death to reach you. Can you not at least find the courtesy to grant me an audience with those who need to hear my message?'

'A message of war?' she asked, and at his nod, 'Then I'm the woman to speak to, myself and the Jorlith spears. I'm Cwen, the – the leader of the Hunt.'

The rider – Sang Ki, he named himself – was too injured to leave his bed. He gave Cwen his map instead, and they both grimaced as they studied it.

The Hunt knew of the night roads, of course. The moon beasts sometimes used the underground routes to evade them. But the monsters seldom came so close to Aethelgas and Ivarholme, surrounded as they were by sunlit fields, and so the Hunt seldom came either. She never would have guessed so many of the deep paths led here.

With Wine and Wingard beside her, she went to view the largest, which lay hidden in a copse of trees left standing between three cornfields. If the Brotherband were coming – and why would Sang Ki lie? – then there was no time to waste. They could reach Aethelgas in less than a week.

Brambles caught at her clothes and scored her face. It was slow, sweaty going, but she could see a lightness ahead, a clearing between the trees.

'Sunlight,' Wingard said. 'That's good. That'll stop them.'

'These are men,' Cwen reminded him, 'not monsters.' Though from what Sang Ki had told her, the monsters were preferable.

No deep way she'd seen before had an entrance so broad. Most were merely pits where the ground had fallen in to reveal the secrets hidden in its guts. This place, though, was no accident. There was an arch tall enough for any moon beast to pass through and for five of them to walk side by side. There were carvings on the arch, intricate lines and whorls that she was sure must be letters, but in no language she'd ever seen. Bachur might have been able to read them, but Bachur wasn't here. There was only Cwen.

This wouldn't be an easy place to defend if the Brotherband emerged in force. Sang Ki reckoned they weren't expecting resistance, so she could set an ambush that might shock them. But retreat would be easy for them: into the inky darkness under the earth. None of Cwen's fighters would dare follow them there. And if they met resistance here, there were a dozen other exits they could use, scattered all around Aethelgas and Ivarholme. If Cwen split her force to blockade them all, any one group would crumble at a strong blow from the Brotherband.

It wasn't good. It was very fucking bad. At least the Jorlith would have to listen to her now; they'd have to muster for war. It wasn't much consolation.

When she returned to Aethelgas, she called a guor moot, a battle meeting of all the leaders of the folk. The Rhinanish wanted to hold it on the platform of the Great Moot, the Jorlith in their Hjaldr Longhall. She told them all it would be on the ground.

'The ground!' a thegn leader protested. She didn't know which one; she hadn't bothered to learn their names. 'But we can't touch the ground. We're thegns!'

As if she might have forgotten. 'You'll be fighting on the ground, might as well get used to it now,' she told him, and used his stunned silence to walk away.

In the end, the thegns found a way to please themselves, like they always did. They had the churls build a platform for them above a fallow field, so their purity wouldn't be polluted by the earth their lessers touched every day. Cwen thought of ordering them to tear it down, but restrained herself. She needed these people. She needed them all.

The thegns had sent four representatives, the richest men among them, as if wealth was a qualification for war-planning. The thirteen spear-leaders of the Jorlith sat in a stiff row, as upright and unbending as their weapons. The hawks outnumbered them all, as she'd intended.

The carrion rider, Sang-Ki, sat propped on cushions beside her. He looked a little further from death than he had when he arrived, but still sickly pale. 'Tell them what you told me,' she said to him, adding, 'briefly,' because she'd already learned how he liked to talk.

'The Brotherband are coming here,' he said, 'to wipe out the Hunt if they can and slaughter as many of you as possible while they're about it.'

He looked at her, and she smiled her thanks. That was just as short and brutal as she'd wanted.

'We have guards on the Salt Road, and the Maeng to get through before they reach it,' a flame-haired thegn said. 'I see no reason to panic.'

'They're using the night roads,' Sang Ki said. 'They're coming straight here.'

Cwen nodded. 'My people have scouted them. There's one entrance bigger than you can bloody believe, and at least a dozen more smaller ones. Don't know why there's so many round here.'

'I think I might,' Sang Ki said. 'The Moon Forest must once have been a stronghold of the moon god. It explains why so many of his monsters make their home here. I believe that's why your Hunter brought you here, all those years ago: to act as a bulwark against his beasts and his return.'

'Aye,' Cwen said, 'that was her covenant with us. A home in return for our fighting strength. For hundreds of years only us hawks kept the bargain. Now it's time for everyone else to do the same.'

'But we're not fighters,' another thegn protested. 'We're merchants.'

'The Brotherband won't care,' Sang Ki said. 'I've seen their work. You can't let them through. Whatever the cost, you have to stop them.'

'But how?' That was one of the Jorlith, as thin and golden as a stalk of wheat. 'A dozen entrances, and there's barely two hundred healthy warriors here. We've sent out a summoning for more—'

'*Now* you've sent it,' Wingard said bitterly.

'We've sent it, and we might get another two hundred more in time. There's less than a thousand of you hawks, and even if the thegns fight . . .' He looked around at them, his expression so contemptuous that Cwen smiled. 'Even if they fight, all they can do is provide more targets. We'll never keep the Brotherband from emerging. It's better to prepare Aethelgas and Ivarholme for siege. We bring up food, break the walkways. If they follow, we fight them in the treetops, the Jorlith way. Up here, the advantage is ours. We can hold for weeks and whittle their strength away.'

'If you hide up there,' Sang Ki said, 'I don't believe you'll have yourself the siege you want. The Brotherband are savages but they aren't fools. They'll scatter through the forest and visit their barbarity on all your villages.'

'Will they?' That was the second thegn again, the one with curly hair so fair it might almost have been Jorlith. 'What's your interest in this, Ashaneman? You've come a long way to bring a warning to a folk who aren't your own.'

'If you'd seen the Brotherband's work for yourselves, you wouldn't ask that question,' Sang Ki said quietly.

'Really? I amn't so sure it's our poor innocent bairns you're here to protect. We may be distant, but news flies over the mountains eventually. The moon returned is the son of the king of Ashanesland, isn't that so?'

'He's the moon, the source of evil. It doesn't matter what flesh he was born in,' Cwen snapped.

'But he *is* the Ashane prince, all the same.'

'He is,' Sang Ki admitted.

'Then forgive me, but I can see another reason why you've come here to us, and not just from the good nature of your heart. The Ashane king wants his son dead, we've all heard the stories. The Brotherband are his son's men. Do I need to spell out every letter of the sentence?'

'Spell it how you want,' Cwen said. 'And think what you want of our carrion rider. The truth won't be changed by it. The Brotherband are coming here and if we don't fight them, they'll kill us. Are you fucking stupid? It's death or battle. Which will you choose?'

'Battle,' the Jorlith spear-leaders said fiercely, in a chorus.

'We'll fight,' the flame-haired thegn said, making it sound like more of a question than a statement.

'We'll do what we must,' the argumentative one added, ambiguously.

'I'll fight to protect my daughters,' the youngest said loudly and firmly, glaring at the others.

'Well,' the last said hesitantly. He'd yet to speak and his pale skin flamed red when everyone turned to look at him. 'There's maybe another way. There's a woman – a Wanderer. Alfreda Sonyasdochter, I think she can help.'

'Enough of that!' the blond thegn snapped.

'No, listen. There is, Mistress Cwen. There's a weapon.'

18

Krish woke to find Dinesh's hand on his shoulder, shaking him. 'It's time to break your fast,' he said.

His eyes were glazed and his expression vacantly happy. Krish knew what he really wanted. He reached inside his shirt, where he kept the pills safe, and handed one to the boy. He had to look away as Dinesh swallowed it; it was horrible to see the boy's joy at being given the thing that enslaved him. And he truly was a slave again. He'd returned to his father's house to wait at his table and take his orders, to be nothing more than a possession. He *needed* orders, now that bliss once again had hold of him. And Krish could hardly blame him for returning here. Was he meant to return to the empty huts where all his fellow slaves had died? Krish didn't blame Dinesh; he blamed himself.

'Your meal,' the boy said again, and Krish realised that he would have to rise and face the morning and Uin's self-satisfied eyes over the table. Uin had never asked why Dinesh had returned to him, but Krish was sure he knew.

The others were already seated when he arrived: Ensee, Asook and their mother, with Uin at the head of the table. Olufemi wasn't there. She'd been around very little since the slaves' fields had burned. Krish had tried to talk to her, but she'd shrugged him away impatiently.

Dae Hyo was missing as well, probably drinking already. He'd done little else since they'd arrived in Rah lands.

It was only as Krish sat down that he saw the table was empty. He felt Uin's eyes on him, noticing him notice. The other man's expression was carefully blank. 'Aren't we eating this morning?' Krish asked.

'There's no food.' Uin looked back at Krish, refusing to give him more, forcing him to ask. But Ensee spoke before he had to.

'There *is* food, Father. The cupboards are stocked.'

Uin glared at her. 'We must preserve what we have for needier times. Haven't you heard? The workers in the fields have put down their hoes. They say they won't farm until they're given an equal share of the land.' He paused a calculated moment before adding, 'They say this is your command, Lord Krish.'

'It's what they want!' Ensee said hotly.

'You support the starvation of your family and loss of all their wealth?' Uin asked.

'We can share the wealth without losing it,' she said, but it was a mumble, directed at her empty plate.

'My daughter doesn't understand how money works,' Uin said to Krish.

'What will we do, Father?' Asook asked, as meek and dutiful as ever.

Uin's gaze didn't waver from Krish. 'What *will* we do, great lord?'

'I didn't tell them to leave their fields,' Krish said, and saw the betrayal on Ensee's down-turned face. 'I didn't tell them to, but they were right to do it. This is Rah land, the whole tribe's. What comes from it should belong to you all.'

'I never heard that was the Ashane way. Or does your father the king share all he has with his goatherds?'

'It's the Dae way,' Krish said, with more conviction than he felt. 'And the Rah can change. Isn't that what my coming means, a time for change? Perhaps you thought it would only change for other people, but you were wrong!'

Krish rose abruptly from the table, upset by the anger in his own voice. It wasn't wise to show it to Uin. The other man was always in control. He could only see Krish's loss of it as a victory.

'Excuse me,' Krish said as calmly as he could, 'if there's nothing to eat, I think I'll go outside.'

But once he'd closed the door behind him, he didn't know what to do. He should find Olufemi, he supposed. The mage needed to know what was happening. She needed to help, though she'd laughed at him when he'd suggested using her runes to cure the slaves. He'd been so angry with her then that he hadn't sought her out since. But he couldn't afford to be angry with everyone.

Her hut lay at the end of a narrow walkway between a cornfield and another lying fallow. He was halfway along it when he heard footsteps on the wood behind him. *Uin*, he thought, *waiting until he could catch me alone*. He felt foolish and afraid as he turned to face his pursuer, but it was only Dinesh.

'No more for now,' Krish told him. 'You can have another pill before you go to bed.'

But the boy just stood in front of him, arms loose and eyes vacant.

'What is it?' Krish asked. 'Did Uin send you?'

Dinesh shook his head. 'I'm not Uin's.'

'No, you're not.'

'I'm yours.'

'You're not anyone's, Dinesh. You're free.'

'I'm *yours*. Uin thinks I came back to him. I came, I came, I came back for you. And he doesn't, he doesn't see me. He speaks in front of me.' Dinesh grasped Krish's arm, his grip surprisingly hard. 'He speaks in front of me. Do you see?'

Krish thought he did. 'What has he said? And who has he said it to?'

'A man like you. Like my mother.' There was no sadness in Dinesh's face when he mentioned her. Perhaps he'd forgotten her death.

'An Ashane?' Krish asked.

Dinesh shrugged. 'A man from another land. Uin will, he will, he will sell you to their king and let him kill you.'

Dae Hyo's eyes didn't seem to be working properly. He opened them when he heard Krish's voice, but someone had made the sun much brighter than it was meant to be. It stabbed painfully into his head and he shut them again and groaned.

'Get up,' Krish said. 'I need you.'

'I'm sleeping, brother,' Dae Hyo told him.

'You're lying in the middle of a rice field. Your feet are wet.'

He opened his eyes again, placing his fingers over them so that he could see stripes of Krish, stripes of sky and blessed stripes of darkness. 'It's comfortable.'

'Get up, please. This is important.'

Even from the bits and pieces he could see of him, Dae Hyo could tell that his brother was upset. He sighed and rolled into a sitting position, cradling his head in his hands until it stopped whirling.

'It's Uin,' Krish said, crouching beside him. 'He's planning to sell me to my father – my real father, the King.'

Anger instantly flared. 'I tell you what, he won't live to do it!' Dae Hyo said, but Krish grabbed his arm and kept him from rising.

'No. We can't just kill him. He's got an ally, an Ashaneman. We need to find out who that is. We need to stop him telling my father where I am.'

'Ah, that's simple then. We'll track him like the animal he is. Those two must meet and once we catch them at it we can kill them both.'

Krish's eyes were shadowed. They'd always been too full of thoughts, which never did a man any good. 'Do you think this is my fault?'

'Well . . .' Dae Hyo sighed and slung an arm about his shoulder. 'You might not have chosen the smoothest path, but you're not to blame for the rocks on it. That Uin was a rat-fucker before you came here and he'll be one to his grave. Now remember what I've taught you. Move slow, move silent, breathe with the wind and listen with your body.'

They kept off the walkways, moving through the fields on either side. The crops were blooming with summer and the cover was good. It was easy, easier than it should have been, even though his head was still so heavy with drink his legs didn't always move in precisely the way he told them to.

'Those Rah are a lazy bunch,' Dae Hyo whispered to Krish when he realised that every field they'd passed through had been empty. 'These crops won't tend themselves.'

'They're Uin's fields,' Krish said. 'His workers have decided they won't harvest another man's grain any more. They'll only return when they're given a share of the fields.'

His brother looked guilty and Dae Hyo asked, 'Your idea?'

Krish shook his head and then shrugged. 'In a way.'

'Good. It's the Dae way: the land is the tribe's, not any woman or man's. Only the things that move on it can be owned and the things you grow from it yourself.'

'It's the right way. I should have listened to you. I am Dae.'

'So you are, brother,' Dae Hyo said, ruffling his hair. He felt a hope that he hadn't since they came to this ugly, water-clogged land. So Krish had walked in a wrong direction for a while. It was Olufemi's fault for leading him astray and Dae Hyo's duty to show him the right path.

They came to the field bordering Uin's house without any troubles. It was filled with tall, purple flowers. Dae Hyo didn't know what crop would one day come from them and didn't care. He crouched low and pulled Krish down with him. They were only just in time – here was that shit-eater Uin now, pausing by his lizard stables as if considering whether to saddle one, and then setting off on foot instead.

'You were right – he's up to no good,' Dae Hyo whispered to Krish. 'Afraid he'll be too visible mounted.'

The other man certainly seemed to be trying to move stealthily, but he was making a shockingly bad job of it. He placed his feet slowly and carefully, lifting each one too high like a horse picking its way through rocks. Thanks to that, the imprint each left behind was as clear as day. A child could have followed his tracks. And he kept glancing back over his shoulder, a sure way to show anyone who cared to notice that he was afraid of being followed.

But however often Uin looked, he didn't truly see. Dae Hyo and Krish moved like distant shadows, twenty paces back in the fields, and the Rah man's eyes never hooked on them. Dae Hyo nodded approvingly at Krish. His brother was a little late to the skills of a man, but he was a fast learner.

Uin was walking a bloody long way, though. He led them both beyond any place Dae Hyo had travelled to, far inland. The fields became more ragged and less fertile, the plots assigned to the poor. Their huts lay scattered about and here the people were at last, sitting outside, laughing and singing as if they were all having a party.

Then they were out of the fields altogether and into a wilder land. Here the Rah had allowed fingers from the jungle that enclosed them to poke into their territory in a messy way that seemed unlike them. Perhaps its presence made them feel safer. It was one of these fingers that Uin entered; Dae Hyo and Krish had to follow. This was where the snakes were and all the other nasty things the Rah chose to live alongside. Vines trailed from the trees to grab them as they passed, or crawled on the ground to snare their feet. Birds turned beady eyes on them and shrieked.

Luckily for them, Uin didn't go too deep in. Ahead appeared a clearing like a piece of Rah land within the wild. The trees half-hid the little house that sat on stilts in its centre and the man perched on a stool outside the house. He looked up when Uin approached and smiled.

As they crouched among the big-leafed plants that ringed the clearing, Krish stared at the man, shocked. 'That's Marvan,' he whispered to Dae Hyo.

Dae Hyo shrugged.

'The man who tried to kill me in Smiler's Fair.'

Dae Hyo growled low in his throat. He could picture the deep cuts all over Krish's legs, still half-healed. Those had been the gift of a man who liked giving pain and Dae Hyo would be delighted to return the favour. He put his hand on his knife hilt, but Krish clasped his own over it.

'Wait,' he said. 'We should hear what they say.'

The two men were talking quietly, but this was a watery land and sound travelled well over water.

'. . . stay here?' the one called Marvan said.

Uin smiled, a savage expression Dae Hyo had never seen on his face before. 'Not long now. Not long at all.'

'And word has gone out to Sang Ki in what's left of Smiler's Fair?'

'Better than that,' Uin said.

Even from their hiding place, Dae Hyo could read the expression of dismay on the murderer's face. 'There's nothing better. I told you to tell Sang Ki!'

'You came to *my* lands, Ashaneman, asking favours of me. You don't tell me what to do.'

'I'm sorry, friend.' Marvan did a good job of sounding like he meant it. 'It's only that Sang Ki's forces are the nearest. You don't want to let this troublesome lad slip your net, do you?'

'I won't. I've sent to tell his own father of his whereabouts. Though if I can, I'd rather present him a corpse than a living boy. But we can't be seen to do the deed ourselves – too many here love the fool, even among the better men.'

'I don't want to tell you your business,' the Ashaneman said, clearly intending to do just that, 'but it sounds to me like your opposition to the boy is known. When he goes missing or turns up dead, there are sure to be suspicions.'

'Yes, that's why I've taken some good clothes from the store we use to feed the crocodiles. We feed them meat dressed like the men of the Four Together. I'll tell the men I've selected to dress in those clothes when they take Krish, and they'll be sure to let a few people see them at it. I'll throw the Four Together as Krish's killers to the common people like red meat, and they'll devour it. The war will be fought even more fiercely with Lord Krish as its victim than it would be with him as its leader. And our workers will be fighting for the right to return to their fields and looms and sow and weave in Lord Krish's name.'

'Well,' the other man said, 'you *have* thought it through. And no qualms about killing your own god?'

His tone was playful. Everything he said he made sound a bit of a joke, but Uin answered him seriously. 'Gods sometimes die for their people's sake. If you knew more of the ways of the tribes, you'd know that.'

Beside Dae Hyo, Krish had grown more and more tense with every word spoken. 'Have we heard enough now, brother?' Dae Hyo asked him.

'They've sent word to my father already,' Krish said. 'It's too late.'

'Too late for that maybe. Not too late to stop the nearer half of their plan.' Dae Hyo took his brother's hand and placed it on the pommel of his belt knife. 'I'll take the Ashaneman and you take that scum Uin.' The Ashaneman had a dangerous look about him, but Uin was no fighter; he was one who liked to order other men to get their blades wet.

When he knew his brother was ready, in his mind as well as his body, Dae Hyo held up three fingers, two, one and then he sprang from cover and his brother was running beside him – just how it was meant to be.

For the first moments of their charge, their targets were frozen in shock. An instant later they acted – in exactly the opposite way from that Dae Hyo had predicted. The Ashaneman took one look at them, turned on his heel and fled, while Uin snarled and drew his own belt knife.

Dae Hyo hated to leave Krish facing that steady blade. But the Ashaneman was already at the border of the clearing and they had their targets. Changing a plan mid-skirmish only ever made a bad situation worse. He flung himself after the fleeing Marvan and left his brother to fight his own fight.

The Ashaneman was very fucking fast. He ran like a deer fleeing a wolf and Dae Hyo charged after like a bull in heat. The underbrush parted for the fugitive and was crushed beneath Dae Hyo's feet and for a short while that's how it was, the distance between them neither opening nor closing.

But Dae Hyo was a warrior, and his brother's life was the wager here. He could throw more money on the table. His legs burned with it but he forced them faster, and though the

Ashaneman tried to do the same, he was shorter and weaker and Dae Hyo was going to have him.

Only Dae Hyo was still drunk, and the Ashaneman wasn't. The root caught under his foot and tipped him straight over and he didn't have enough of his wits about him to put out his hands and stop the fall. Belbog's malice put a rock right where his head landed and for a short while all he knew was pain.

When he returned to himself, he realised he was lucky the Ashaneman had been too frightened to come back and finish him off. He followed the other man's trail to the edge of the wilderness, but there was no hope now of finding him. In open Rah land he could have gone anywhere, and if he'd used the wooden walkways that criss-crossed it, there'd be no way of tracking him. Dae Hyo was trying all the same when he remembered what he should have thought of immediately: Krish facing Uin with nothing but a knife and his own not too impressive training.

Dae Hyo followed his own trail back through the undergrowth, uncaring when it ripped his clothing and cut his skin. If Krish was dead, his brother, his only brother . . . He couldn't bear to think of it.

He burst back into the clearing, throat dry with fear – and saw Uin on his back, blood on his face and Krish's knife at his throat, with Krish crouched on top of him. Dae Hyo bent over, hands on his knees, and gasped out his relief.

'Marvan?' Krish asked.

'I tell you what, he got clean away.'

'It doesn't matter,' Krish said after a moment. 'There's no use lamenting the arrow that missed.'

'This one found its target true.' Dae Hyo strode over to the two of them. 'Well fought, brother.'

'It was easy,' Krish said contemptuously, though there were cuts on his arms oozing blood.

Dae Hyo looked down at Uin. 'No need to prolong the moment, brother. He plotted to kill you. The elder mothers would say you had a right to kill him in return.'

Dae Hyo could see Uin's hands shaking, but he managed to look straight in Krish's face and say, 'You can't kill me. You need me to bring my people to your side. Your peasants alone can't protect you, not from what's coming.'

'From what *you've* summoned,' Krish said, and Dae Hyo sighed. Once a man started talking he found it much harder to go back to killing.

'I can unsummon it,' Uin said.

'And why would you do that?' Dae Hyo asked.

'To save my life.' He eyed the hand holding a knife to his throat. 'There's no point pretending I've discovered a sudden love of you.'

'He'll *promise* he'll do it to save his life,' Dae Hyo told Krish. 'Saying and doing have never been the same, or poor men would eat deer liver every day.'

Krish nodded, but he didn't slide the knife to spill all Uin's blood. 'I know. There's a way to make them the same, though.' He eased himself off the other man's chest and gestured for him to stand.

Dae Hyo pressed his own knife against Uin's back, right where it could slip in under a rib and find his heart. 'Are you certain, brother? I wouldn't trust this one if he swore the rain was wet.'

'I wouldn't either. That's why I'm giving him this.' Krish reached beneath his shirt to pull out a pouch, and from the pouch a red pill.

It took Dae Hyo a moment to realise what it was, but not Uin. The man jerked in shock and despite the knife pressing against his back, tensed as though he meant to try to get up and run.

'Hold him,' Krish said.

Dae Hyo tried, sheathing the knife to hook his arms under the other man's and lift him off the ground. His legs still kicked, even when Krish pressed his knife against Uin's jugular. He struggled until Krish said, 'Swallow it or die,' with a firmness Dae Hyo wouldn't have thought him capable of.

Even so, Uin seemed to take a moment to decide which he preferred before wilting all at once in Dae Hyo's arms. Krish hooked a finger in his mouth to open it, put the pill in and then held it closed along with his nose, stroking his throat until he was sure he'd swallowed. It looked like something he might once have done for his goats, forcing down medicine they didn't want.

When it was done, Dae Hyo released Uin. All the fight had gone out of him, though the bliss couldn't be working quite that fast. He let them push him ahead, through the undergrowth, back along the wooden walkway and past the huts where his workers turned unfriendly eyes on him.

He let them push him nearly all the way back to his home. His steps began to stumble as they drew closer and Dae Hyo thought the drug must be taking effect. He stopped a moment to look in the Rah man's eyes and Uin grinned back at him.

'It's done, brother,' he said and Uin laughed.

'Done, done, done,' he giggled. 'Yes you are.'

A man who'd heard battle didn't forget the sound of it. But the sound Dae Hyo heard now was worse than anything he'd been a part of. The death of the Dae might have sounded like this, if he'd been there to witness it. There were shouts and screams and the clash of weapons everywhere.

While Dae Hyo looked frantically around, trying to find the source of it, Uin pulled away from him, still smiling and laughing like this was all some joke. Dae Hyo could see a little of what was happening. There were men mounted on lizards fighting men on foot. Men with metal against men with flint, but there were far more of the men with flint and women among them too. The whole of the Rah tribe seemed to have chosen this moment to go to war with each other and it looked like they didn't mean to stop until most of them were dead.

Dae Hyo looked back at Uin and found him already fifty paces away and staggering further, towards the mounted men. Krish made a move towards him, but Dae Hyo took his arm. 'Let him go, brother. We've got worse problems.'

19

It wasn't that tupping a woman was horrible, precisely. Eric had plenty of practice at it with his wives, although the Tears of Mizhara made the whole thing a bit of a dream. It was just that Drut wanted him to do it so very much, and he had to keep seeming enthusiastic. But if there wasn't another cock involved in proceedings, his enthusiasm waned along with his member. At first when he was with her he'd thought about Lahiru, but after a while that had started to seem like a betrayal. Daft, really, when his whole time with her was a sort of treachery, but a boy felt what a boy felt, so now he thought only of her.

Drut was close to spending, and he could keep his interest up just a little longer. She had his face between her hands, her lips on his, motionless now that she was so close. He kissed her anyway and muttered the sort of sweet nothings his time at Madam Aeronwenn's had given him a fair store of. They seemed to do the trick, as Drut soon gasped, shuddered and stilled.

He made the right noises for finishing too, though the truth was he was nowhere near it. Still, his prick wilted appropriately and he pulled it out of her, using his arms to hold himself above the growing swell of her belly.

She liked to be held after, unlike most of his clients. He curled an arm round her and swept the sweat-soaked golden hair away from her neck. The ice above them was softening, dripping on to his bare skin. He'd have been happy doing this down below, in Rii's realm, but it had seemed to make Drut uncomfortable. She built them little round ice houses instead, which lasted just long enough for the deed to be done and then melted away all the evidence. He had to be impressed with her cunning. He hadn't thought she had it in her.

'We should stop this,' she said. She said it quite often, but sounded less convincing every time.

'I'd die if you left me,' he said.

She sat up abruptly and he thought he might have laid it on too thick, but then she took him in her arms, squeezing far too tightly, and said, 'I will never leave you, Eric. You're my husband.'

'But you ain't just my wife to me, Drut. You're more than that.'

She loosened her grip so she could lean back and look him in the face. Her own was flushed from their bed-sports. 'You mustn't say these things, Eric.'

He darted forward to peck her on the lips. 'I'll only think 'em if that will make you happier.'

That surprised a laugh out of her, a rarity. But her expression quickly shifted into shock.

'You all right?' he asked.

She touched her stomach. 'I think she moved.'

'Our baby?'

'Yes. Yes! I felt it again. She's quickened!'

'Oh.' It had to happen, of course. He wanted this child, or at least Rii did and he wanted Rii to get him out of there. But it still gave him a nasty jolt. Suddenly it went from 'Drut's pregnant' to 'Drut's having my baby', and those weren't words he'd ever once imagined thinking.

'Here,' she said, taking his hand and pressing it against her belly, 'can you feel?'

They stayed that way a long while, but there was nothing except the warmth of her tight-stretched skin. 'No,' he said eventually. She looked terribly downcast, so he added, 'But it don't matter. I'll feel it another time. I got months and months.'

'Three months,' she said, and he frowned. He hadn't got her in the family way all that long ago. 'We don't carry our children as long as your kind,' she explained. 'Usually they are within us for no more than half a year. One of my sisters told me it's because our infants can't wait to see the sun with their own eyes.'

'Only three more months.' He tried to keep the alarm out of his voice. Rii must have known it, he supposed, but he'd thought they'd have far longer to put their plans in place.

Drut dropped her eyes and pulled away from him a little. 'Eric, I've been told the way it is in the wider world. But among us, daughters are raised by all the sisters. We aren't told who bore us – our only attachment should be to Mizhara, and after that all our sisters equally. She won't be told that you're her father either.'

'Won't be told . . .?' He was surprised at the genuine outrage in his voice. He hadn't thought he cared a whit for this child, except for the freedom it could buy him. But he *was* the father. He'd made this life.

'I'm sorry,' she said. 'But *you'll* know *her*. I've thought about this, and read such passages in the Perfect Law that relate. There's nothing to forbid us taking an interest in our daughter, in watching her, as long as we don't make any claim on her that's different from the claim of sisterhood we all make on each other.'

She looked pained, and as his irrational anger died he knew it was a good thing. It was useful that she cared about this child. He'd hoped for longer to talk her round, but this seemed a good opening to broach it.

'Our daughter,' he said. 'You always say that. But what if it's a boy?'

'Why would you say that?'

'Well, I've wondered. You must have thought I would. You lot are all women, so what happens to the boys? I ain't been a father before, but I know this much: half come out with dangles and half without.'

'Not among us,' she said. 'The Servants of Mizhara are all as she: female. It wouldn't be . . . It *could not be* that I'm carrying a boy.'

'Yeah, but what if you were? I'm a boy, ain't I? Stands to reason I might produce one. And there's a first time for everything.'

'No there isn't – not for that!' She rose and made to stride past him.

'Hey now, I didn't mean nothing by it.' He reached for her hand.

She shook him off. 'Never speak of that again, Eric. It's unthinkable. Abomination! Our daughter will be perfect in Mizhara.' And with that she was gone, ducking under the low lintel of their little ice hut.

He rolled back onto the fur bedding and sighed. Only three months, and that was how she felt. He needed to talk to Rii.

Except, as he realised a while later, Rii was nowhere to be found. He'd visited the furthest sun-pear orchard, where she sometimes liked to loiter, but there was no sign of her, not even the imprint of her huge clawed feet in the snow. There was another place she'd showed Eric, where the snow was sculpted into wonderful whorls and spikes. He'd thought it a natural thing, until she'd flown him above it and he'd realised the design was actually writing, in a language he didn't know. 'My master's work,' she'd said proudly, but today she wasn't there either.

Finally, he descended to the ancient city beneath the Servants' quarters. He'd decided not to go there too often. He didn't want his wives getting funny ideas about where his loyalties lay. But it was early in the day – Drut always came to him early – and there were few of them about. He nodded and smiled at those he saw and made his way to the staircase of ice leading down.

He remembered how the transition from ice to stone, light to darkness had once scared him. Now he took comfort from the old place, the moon's place, still whole even if clearly conquered. The moon would rise again and Eric would rise with him, that's what Rii had said. Staring into the darkness of the vast rock chamber, with its ranks of silver-skinned statues, Eric could believe that.

Only Rii wasn't there either. It had been days since he'd seen her, he realised. That wasn't so unusual. She came and went as she liked, despite being bound to obey the Servants. But he really did need to speak to her. Three months and Drut appalled at the mere thought of bearing a boy? He needed to speak to Rii today.

'Rii?' he called out quietly, and then more loudly, 'Rii!'

The echoes chased themselves around the cavern, but there was no reply.

Perhaps she was deeper than his voice could reach, walking or flying the streets of her dead lord's city. Eric had never been further than the bottom of the stair. He didn't know what else lay beneath Salvation and he'd never felt much urge to find out. Was afraid to, if he was honest with himself, and what was the point of lying inside your own head? This wouldn't wait, though.

He'd discovered, after a while in Salvation, that the light suffusing even its lowest rooms didn't come straight from the sun. The ice walls were inlaid with some substance, ivory maybe, that gave out the glow. He'd missed it at first, because it was all white like the rest. But now he knew what to look for he only had to ascend the stairs four flights and he found it: a panel carved in the likeness of Mizhara, with yellow glowing gems for eyes. When he was sure he wasn't being watched, he dug his fingers into the ice to either side of the panel and pulled.

It came out easy as you like. It wasn't a big thing. It fit in his palm quite neatly, with the yellow glowing eyes looking up at him. He shivered. It was like Mizhara herself was watching him, and he knew what he was doing now must be breaking one of her many rules. But then, he meant to break a great many more before this was over.

At the bottom of the stone stairs, he held the panel up and swept it around. The light came from its eyes like a yellow beam, piercing the darkness. He saw more statues, a line of them stretching all the way from the foot of the stair to the distant wall. Their silver eyes reflected back the light, rejecting it.

The statues led, he could see now, to a gateway in the cavern wall. He walked along the line of them, darting the beam of light here and there to see what else he could uncover. To his left the light picked out another carving in brief, mismatched glimpses, so that it took Eric a while to realise it was just one figure, as immense as the chamber itself: a gaunt, tip-eyed man. Was that the moon god? He didn't have a very comforting face.

Halfway to the door Eric passed five wells, hooded over with silver. One had red stones in it, rubies probably; others were sapphire, amethyst, emerald and a bright orange gem he'd never seen before. He took a quick detour to look over them, but when he shone his beam downward he couldn't see the bottom, though he could hear the distant sound of waves lapping. Was it water below? It seemed strange to have these five separate wells where just one would do. Anyway, there was no chance Rii would fit down there, so he moved on.

The gateway when he came to it was carved with the same writing as the ice outside and the stone stair: curved and twisted and hard to follow. There was writing like it on the great machine at the heart of Salvation too, but he could see now that it had been changed, overwritten with Mizhara's words when she'd taken the power of the machine for herself. Her writing was all straight lines and angles, as unbending as the Servants.

Then he was through the gates, and there it all was in front of him: the moon's city. He'd somehow thought it would be just like the cavern at the bottom of the stairs, large and empty and rough. It wasn't. It was beautiful. The buildings were all curved, just like the moon's writing. And they fit together in odd ways that bent the eye. He'd be following the line of a wall and suddenly it would seem to become another house's roof. The structure on top of the tallest tower looked like a dome one minute and a bowl the next. As he stared at it in bafflement it flicked between the two – dome, bowl, dome, bowl – until he had to tear his gaze away.

The place was vast. He'd thought the cavern beneath the stairs was big, but it would have fitted under here a hundred times. The top of it was so high even the light from Mizhara's lamp couldn't reach it. It might almost have been in the open air. A flight of stairs led down to a broad way that he guessed must be the main street. He hesitated before descending. If Rii was hiding in the city there wasn't much chance he'd find her. But he'd come this far and a boy didn't get anywhere by just giving up.

His footsteps in the cavern above had been muffled by dust.

Here they rang loudly on every tread. It was as if the long-deserted city had been thirsty for sound and pulled every drop of it out of him. He tried to walk on his tiptoes but it did no good. Well, not to worry. He wanted Rii to hear him, didn't he?

Then he was at street level with the round-walled houses on either side. At first they were plain, little more than churl huts made from stone rather than wood. But as he walked deeper, navigating the curving streets by instinct alone, they began to get bigger and grander and decorated all over. The carvings were wonderful to look at. There were beasts like the monsters of the Moon Forest, but walking side by side with men and women as if they were all great friends.

On the next house there was a carving of the underground city itself. Eric leaned closer to look and saw that the very house he was looking at was part of the carving; and had a carving of the city on its side. It was as he looked closer, leaning right in to see if the carving of a carving had a carving too, that he heard the footstep.

He jerked upright and spun round, but the beam of his light showed only more walls and more carvings. Just his nerves, he decided, but his pace was quicker as he walked on and he didn't stop to look at any more decorations.

When he came to a crossroads, he heard it again: not just one footstep this time, but many. He stopped and they halted just a beat after he did, as if he'd caught them by surprise. His breath hitched and his heart pounded once, hard, and then raced like it wanted to break out of his chest.

He needed to leave – right now. But the footsteps had been behind him. If he turned round he'd be heading straight for them. He hurried on instead, finding streets that curved towards the exit, his stride growing quicker and quicker until he was almost running.

The footsteps behind him matched his pace. They weren't trying to hide now; they must have realised he'd heard them. And he could hear breathing too, a rough rasping that wasn't quite human.

He did run then, too fast. He turned left, left again, but the streets curved and twisted and soon he'd lost all sense of direction. After that it was just panic. He was gasping for breath, his legs burned and the footsteps were still with him. They were to the left of him, so he turned right, and then they were to the right of him and he turned left, and when he finally heard them in front of him and his lungs just couldn't drag in air fast enough, he fell to his knees in the centre of a hexagonal plaza.

They approached from every one of the six streets, moving slower now, their footsteps a steady *tap-tap-tap*. They must have realised that he'd stopped, that there was no escape for him.

When the first of them emerged from between two narrow, orange-painted buildings, he couldn't stop a whimper. It was a worm man. He'd never seen one before but there was no mistaking it: ashen-skinned, black-eyed and viciously clawed. He swung the light towards it, though why he wanted to see it more clearly he wasn't sure. But the instant the beam approached it fled, fading back into the darkness with a high scream.

There was another footstep behind him. He stumbled to his feet and spun towards it, spinning the beam too, and it fled. They feared the light. Of course they did: it was Mizhara's. The worm men couldn't abide the sunlight, every child knew that. He swung the light all around, making himself dizzy with it. The worm men fled it and he smelled the stink of burnt flesh. The light could hurt them.

But there were so many of them. They ducked and weaved and came on, and didn't seem to mind that their grey flesh was scored with black scorch marks – until one got close enough to strike his arm and knock the lamp from his hand.

It fell face-up on the cobbles, slightly tilted so that the beam of light shone upward and leftward, falling on the top of a distant building and illuminating a winged shape. For a moment of fierce hope he thought that it was Rii, come to rescue him. But it was only a sculpture of her, or something like her, and now the worm men were between him and the light.

He shivered, knowing he was staring at his death. It didn't

seem possible that it could end this way and he felt almost more angry than afraid. What a stupid way to go. Unburied and unmourned. Would his body even rot, in this dry place so far beneath the ground?

A worm man stepped forward, his raggedly clawed hand held out. Eric closed his eyes and took one breath, three, ten, until his chest was so tight you could have played it like a drum.

But the blow never came and on the eleventh breath he opened his eyes.

The worm man was right in front of him. Its thin cheek and thinner arm were striped with scorch marks and its big black eyes were studying him, running up and down the length of his body. Close up, he saw that its eyes weren't entirely dark: there was a sliver of silver curving up one side of them, like the crescent moon. And all of a sudden the fear left him. These were the moon's Servants, that's what Rii had told him. These were what his son would be, the son whose very first movement Drut had felt today. He ventured a tremulous smile.

The worm man tilted its head and blinked. He was glad it didn't try to smile back. He wasn't sure he wanted to see what its teeth looked like. Then it lowered its hand and pressed it against Eric's stomach.

He had to tense every muscle to stop himself flinching away from those long, bony fingers. But the worm man didn't try to hurt him. It just kept its hand against him, surprisingly warm, and frowned.

And suddenly Eric realised what it was trying to do. He was the father of a worm man and somehow this one knew, but it didn't quite understand.

'It ain't inside me,' he told it. 'I ain't the mum – I'm the dad.'

It watched his mouth move as he spoke, but it didn't seem to understand words either.

'It's all right,' he said anyway. Filling the eerie silence made it easier to ignore the press of that inhuman hand against him. 'The baby's safe. I won't let no harm come to it.'

And maybe the worm man did understand that. It nodded

once, sharply, and every single one of them turned away. Their footsteps pattered against the cobbles and then they were all gone.

The instant the last footstep faded, he picked up his light and fled.

He woke, an uncountable amount of time later, sweaty and disoriented. He didn't remember going to bed. He didn't remember much after he'd fled the worm men. He must have found his way back to Salvation somehow. He was in his own room in his own bed, with his own furs tangled around him. His dreams had been filled with grey faces and black eyes, but they hadn't been nightmares. In his dreams he'd held his newborn son, and those black and silver eyes had looked up at him so trustingly.

Some of the whores of Smiler's Fair, the ones whose lack of care landed them in the family way, had spoken about loving their child even before it was born, when it was nothing but a swelling of their stomach. Eric had thought it was daft then, but he didn't now. The promise he'd made to the worm men to save his child wasn't just air. He wouldn't let his son die.

He went to his basin to splash water on his face and finally noticed the distant racket that had been going on since he woke, a sound unlike any he'd heard in Salvation before. It was women's voices. It must be the Servants, though it wasn't much like them. He was pretty sure getting all agitated like that went against the Perfect Law.

He wandered the halls a while, finding them empty, before he realised the noise was coming from outside. Could it be an attack, the moon's forces against the sun's? But it didn't seem likely they could have come all the way here to strike in secret.

It might be safer just to stay in his room, all the same. He stopped in the middle of a wide white hall, considering it, but found that he couldn't. He'd always hated games of hide-and-seek when he was a boy. Cowering in a hole waiting to be caught was worse than just facing it. It wasn't bravery, just a different form of cowardice.

As he approached the arched entranceway of Salvation, he could see a blurry golden crowd through the ice and another form, big and black, that could only be Rii. Outside he found that the Servants were all ringed around her, anger in every stiff line of their bodies. And that's what the shouting had been: they were shouting at Rii.

Or – no. As he pushed his way forward he could see more clearly. They were shouting at the person riding on Rii's back. It was another Servant, with the same golden skin and hair and ears that weren't quite right. She was the spit of the Hunter, the Lion of the Forest. Her hair was a tightly curled bush standing up from her head, her nose broad and her lips full. She would have been beautiful, if it hadn't been for the four long scars running the length of her face.

And she was just as angry as the Servants. Their faces were twisted with the emotion, but it didn't sit comfortably there. They weren't used to feeling strong things. This newcomer was, he could tell it immediately. Her face looked deeper than all the others, in a way he couldn't quite explain, and there seemed to be a golden light glowing from it, a little like the light that came from the ivory images of Mizhara herself. He thought, suddenly, that despite her unageing face she showed all the years she'd lived in it.

'Sisters,' she said, more calm than everyone around her. 'Let me dismount. You must listen.'

'They do not heed thee,' Rii said.

'Anathema!' one of the Servants hissed. 'Don't bring your blasphemy to Salvation.'

'Take the long walk into the snow, as you should have done centuries ago,' another said. She spoke gently, as if she meant it as advice, but there was venom beneath the seeming concern.

'You have nothing to say to us,' a third told the newcomer.

At that, her patience seemed to snap. 'I have this to tell to you,' she said, suddenly fierce. 'And you *will* listen, sisters. You will listen and you will act, because the moon has risen, and the great war is come again.'

It was amazing how so big and noisy a crowd could go silent so quickly.

'You lie,' one of the others said eventually, but she didn't sound as if she meant it.

'The moon has returned,' the newcomer said. She swung her leg over Rii's hairy flank and slid down to the ground into a space that had finally been made for her. 'We must fight him. It is our duty to Mizhara; on that at least, I think we can agree.'

She strode towards Salvation as if the place was her home and the other Servants her guests. There was still muttering from among them, but they followed after obediently enough. Eric watched them all troop through the arched entrance and down the straight cold corridors, watching until enough icy walls lay between them that they were all hidden from view. Then he turned to Rii.

'So that's where you've been,' he said.

She shifted in the snow to face him, leaving a smear of grease on the pure white. *'I was summoned, morsel, and had no choice but to depart.'*

'Well you're back now, that's what matters. And we got trouble. The babe's coming in only three months. Why didn't you tell me that?'

She lifted the upper joints of her wings until they touched her large, cupped ears, shrugging in her own way. *'I am not thy teacher.'*

'But listen, Rii, I talked to Drut yesterday about what if –' he lowered his voice to a whisper '– what if it's a boy.'

'That was foolish, morsel.'

'We only got three months. I had to raise it sooner or later. Anyway, I didn't precisely get the response I wanted. I don't reckon there's any way she's gonna help us steal the kid. We'll have to pinch it somehow, and then it's you and me on our lonesome.'

'Then the news is doubly bad,' she said. *'It is an ill wind that blew me here, with that one on my back. She brings the tidings we hoped to keep from the sun's cursed Servants, that my master has*

returned. And it is worse than that, also. Long ago, in the last days of the great war, I was a leader among my master's forces. And that one found me, and caught me, and placed her rune upon my flesh and commanded me through its power. I owe my captivity to Bachur, whom thy people named the Hunter and worship as a god.'

'*That's* the Hunter? But she can't be. She can't be only a Servant!'

'The eldest and most powerful of them, but a Servant still, though she hid that truth from thy people for the centuries of their service to her. She alone among her kind continued to battle my master's forces after the war was won.'

'And now she's back here. And she's the one what caught you?'

'And holds me still, morsel. I must obey her. While she remains in Salvation, I cannot aid thee. Thy son is doomed, unless thou alone canst aid him.'

20

It was strange how grief changed the colour of the world. The trees Alfreda could see through the windows of her cell seemed grey and the sky that met them at the horizon just a darker shade of it. Even the sun burned with a pale light. The hours passed, empty and unendurably slow. She hadn't realised how many hours there were in a day, and every one was filled with thoughts of Algar. They hadn't allowed her out to see his burial, but she could picture it anyway, and his beautiful face decaying beneath its shroud.

Hunger gnawed at her, but she ignored it. When they pushed food through a flap in the cell door she let it rot on the plate. One corner of her room was a pile of mouldy bread and congealed gruel and the flies that came through the bars on her window to feed on it. Sometimes there was noise outside, voices she chose not to hear and yells of alarm she didn't care about.

Her mind kept presenting images to her, pictures of her brother's face. Sometimes it was his expression as he died, sometimes the look in his eyes as he laughed at one of his own jokes. They were equally painful. Other times she heard his voice as he talked about the advanced fire javelin, how it could save the folk from the monsters. The only bright thing in the world was the fury in her head, but she couldn't find a way to express it.

She had to stop herself from thinking about Eadric. The rage was too much; it felt like a hole in her chest that might suck her in entirely, until there was nothing left. She thought about the fire javelin instead. The path from Algar's first dream of it to his body blown to pieces seemed entirely straight seen from this direction. The fire javelin had killed him as surely as Eadric had.

She was studying the wall of her cell dully, wondering if she had the strength to break it, to find Eadric and make him pay, when she realised that someone was watching her through the slot in the door. She could see nothing of the face, only the very pale blue eyes and a hint of lines around them. She watched the eyes watching her, but whoever it was left without entering her cell and she was surprised to feel an ache of disappointment. After the days trapped inside her silence, she found herself longing for conversation.

An hour or so later, the eyes returned, but this time when they left off their watching Alfreda heard the scratch of a key in the door's lock. She clutched the spoon they'd left her convulsively, and then dropped it. She'd thought she wanted company but now the prospect of it horrified her and she retreated to the furthest corner of the small room.

It was a woman. Her skin was almost as dark as an Ashane's, her hair fire-red and her face filled with a liveliness that instantly made Alfreda feel her own grief more. 'I'm Cwen,' she said. 'Leader of the Hunter's hawks.'

Alfreda could see the birthmark on her cheek, a darker blot against the brown. The Hunt had been coming to Aethelgas, she remembered that now. Algar had wanted to meet the Hunter and Alfreda had joked that he meant to flirt with her. She could picture his smile when she said it, the crooked curve of his lips.

'You're Alfreda Sonyasdochter,' Cwen said, when Alfreda didn't supply the name herself. 'Have you heard what's happened outside your cell? There's to be war. The Brotherband are coming to the Moon Forest and we're near defenceless against them. Barely more than a thousand spears and hawks against their thousands.'

The Brotherband were butchers, everyone whose wagons had crossed the plains knew that. If they were coming to Aethelgas there would be blood spilled. All those people who'd stood and watched as Algar died. Eadric, his throat slit by a Brotherband blade, his daughters despoiled by far, far worse than Algar. Alfreda smiled.

Cwen frowned at the smile. 'You're pleased that war is coming here? Is what they say about you true, then? You're a killer like your brother was?'

Alfreda turned away to face the wall. The other woman's presence had already exhausted her. She felt, for the first time, the hollowness of her stomach. Her head was pounding. She thought the pain might have been with her for a while, but she only now noticed it.

Cwen's step sounded on the wooden boards, moving nearer. There was a waft of air against her and she thought the hawk might have reached out her hand, but there was no contact. The hawks were polluted by their contact with the moon monsters, yet it was Alfreda who felt untouchable. There was a wall around her, higher than an ice oak and stronger than steel.

'You have a weapon,' Cwen said from close behind. Her voice was less friendly now. 'It's the reason you're in here. They tell me the one you used is broken, but we need you to make more.'

More fire javelins. Alfreda laughed at that, a soundless exhalation of air.

'You think that's funny? The Brotherband won't spare you. Do you know what they like to do? If you're lucky they'll kill you before they fuck you. They might cut off a few pieces of you first. Or maybe you'll get really lucky and they'll have their fill of raping before they reach you. They like fire too. Have you ever seen a woman burned to death? I have – some of the monsters of the forest breathe fire. The pain is like a knife through a foreskin, I'm told. And you're a very long time dying.'

But fire just made her think of Algar. There had been flames in the explosion that killed him. It horrified her to think of his face ruined. The image of it overlaid her memories of him, so that she saw him as a boy with red and bubbling blisters on his cheeks, as a young man with his mouth burned down to the brittle white of his teeth.

'Shit,' Cwen said. 'You're not talkative, are you? Think about what I've said then. If you don't care about our lives, think about your freedom. You can have it in exchange for more of those weapons.' Then she was gone and Alfreda could slip back into her silence.

She didn't think about her freedom. Why should she care? She found it impossible to think much beyond the next hour. Considering her future made her painfully aware of Algar's absence from it. She did think about the fire javelin. She couldn't help herself. If an attack was coming soon, there wouldn't be much time to make new ones. Cwen didn't understand that. The hawk probably imagined a row of blacksmiths at a row of forges turning out dozens of the thing. Maybe Algar could have thought of a way to make that possible. But Algar was dead and Alfreda wouldn't make a weapon to defend his killers.

She thought she might be left in peace after that. She'd done nothing to let Cwen think she'd relent. But a few hours later there was another set of eyes at the slit in her cell door, green this time.

These ones didn't watch her for long. A moment's fixed stare, a blink, and then the key was sounding in the lock again. Alfreda didn't retreat this time. She clenched her fists, wondering if she might hit Cwen. Not her probably, but any Rhinanish man who dared to come through.

But it wasn't a man. It was a boy. His skin was almost as pale as hers, his cheekbones sharply slanted. His was a face from the far south, from the savannah where even Smiler's Fair didn't venture, and he had the narrow eyes of the tribes.

He was holding two bowls of stew in his hands. They'd provided her with no table, so he set them on the floor. As he did, she saw his eyes caught by the piles of mouldering bread and meat. 'They told me you weren't eating,' he said. 'I can see they weren't joking.'

The smell brought water to her mouth but her stomach was too knotted to eat.

He shrugged and picked up one of the bowls. 'Well I'm hungry anyhow. Hope you don't mind if I start without you.' He smiled at her, briefly turning his long, solemn face into something brighter and younger, then sat cross-legged on the floor in front of her.

She watched him eat, looming above him. He did seem to be hungry. He was too thin for a boy his age, not quite yet flowered into manhood. She remembered when Algar had been that age and it had been a daily fight to get food inside him. *Cooking is a waste of a good day*, he'd told her, and so she'd cooked for him and sat and watched him as he ate, just as she was doing with the boy now.

'I'm Jinn,' he said between mouthfuls. 'Don't worry, I know your name. Alfreda, ain't it? It's a pretty name. And I know you don't much care to talk. I been asking around. The folk here think you're simple, but I don't see how that can be. You're a blacksmith, ain't you? That ain't a stupid person's job. But if you don't like flapping your mouth the way I do – Mamma says I talk enough for ten – I'll just leave this here.' He pulled out a sheaf of parchments from beneath his jacket and quill and ink to go with them and set them down in front of her. 'A person ought to be able to have their say.'

She didn't touch the parchment, but she sat down beside it, bringing her eyes nearer to his level. Her stomach grumbled and she was surprised to find herself reaching for the stew.

'It's good,' he said. 'Those Jorlith know how to cook. I heard what happened to you,' he added, as if it was just a continuation of the same thought. 'They said your brother killed a man while he was pretending to demonstrate some new weapon, botched it up and got himself killed in the process. They say he made you go along with it, because you ain't quite right in the head.'

The clay bowl cracked in her suddenly clenched hands and the stew dribbled warm and sticky through her fingers.

'See,' the boy said. 'That right there is why I ain't so sure what they say is the truth. They said your brother – Algar, wasn't it? – they said he was a head shorter than you and built light, not like you. Now I've seen you with my own eyes, I don't reckon there's a man in the whole Moon Forest could make you do something you didn't want. And as for killing someone with an exploding weapon in full view of all the folk . . . They said your brother was cunning, but that don't sound like a cunning man's plan.'

Alfreda felt the flowering of something she couldn't identify. Was it rage or gratitude? She skittered backwards along the floor, away from the boy, but he just smiled and chewed another mouthful of stew.

His almond eyes were very green, bright and far too clever as he looked at her and waited to see if she'd reply. There were so many things she wanted to say, they crowded her throat and blocked it so that none of them came out.

'Well,' the boy said, 'shame for you not to eat anything. You're nothing but skin and bones. Very big bones. I'll just set the rest of my meal down here and leave you in peace.'

She sat, motionless, and watched him rise and lock the door behind him. The smell of the stew permeated the cell, masking the fouler odours of rotten food and her own waste in the corner bucket.

She *was* hungry. She pulled the stew bowl towards her and scraped it clean. Afterwards, her stomach felt swollen, full after too long empty.

She looked at the parchment, blankly yellow and right beside her left leg. Jinn hadn't believed Algar was a killer, but he hadn't known the full story. And Jinn had been sent by Cwen, that was clear. The truth felt like a physical thing inside her: a weight and a sickness like sour meat, impossible to digest. She wanted it out of her. She wanted others to know it.

Her hand shook as she wrote, but the words came easily when she didn't have to speak them. She wrote until it was all out, and then she banged on her cell door until someone came to take it.

Cwen frowned at the parchment. It wasn't what she'd hoped: it wasn't information about how to build the weapon it had become increasingly clear they'd need, but it was something.

Wine and Wingard were reading over her shoulders. 'Reckon it's true?' one of them asked. With them behind her she didn't know which; their voices were exactly alike.

'I'm as sure as shit stinks.' She knew who Eadric was now: the proud thegn with hair the colour of a Jorlith warrior's. He was also, she recalled, the one who'd protested most strongly at the idea of using the imprisoned blacksmith's weapon. 'Bring Eadric to the moot court. I'll fetch this Alfreda.'

'And then?' Wingard asked.

'Bring the other thegns too,' she told his twin, 'and the Jorlith spear-leaders while you're at it. It will do them all good to be there.'

The cells were on one of the lowest platforms, not quite in permanent shadow – the folk wouldn't risk that, even for prisoners, not when a fortnight without sun might be enough for the worm men to come – but they were gloomy and constantly under the *drip-drip-drip* of dank water from the grander homes above. When Cwen had visited Alfreda earlier, she'd thought the sound might have driven the woman mad. She still thought her a little crazed, but now she understood what had made her that way.

The blacksmith was standing in the centre of the small cell when Cwen entered it, her looming form seeming almost to fill the place. She'd been huddled away before, trying to make herself small. Now her anger was evident. Cwen smiled at her. Anger she understood.

'You don't like to speak,' she said to the other woman. 'That's fine. Hilda's the same – lost her tongue when a moon beast put its beak inside her mouth and ripped it out, root and all. She can't speak but it doesn't mean she's got nothing to say. Come with me now and I'll do your talking for you.'

Alfreda wasn't a well-looking woman. Her face was drawn, as though she'd eaten little or nothing since the moment they locked her up, and hers wasn't a body that could do without food. It was as solid and strong as a stallion's cock, not the sort of body you usually saw on a woman. Her face wouldn't be hardening any man's prick, either. It wasn't a stupid face, though, and after a moment she nodded.

They walked out onto the platform and up the steps in silence. But she felt the eyes on them, peering from behind curtains and around tree boles. The good folk of Aethelgas were no doubt wondering what she was doing letting their dangerous prisoner out, and no chain on her. Well, they'd see.

The hawks had gathered all the leaders as she'd asked. A big muttering crowd of them stood outside the moot hall, mostly thegns and a few churls on the rise.

Bachur had left her in charge and told Cwen to do whatever it took. Cwen thought about Osgar, lying with his guts in a trail behind him. She thought about that a lot. Sometimes she woke with the image in her mind, from dreams she didn't remember but which left her shaking and miserable. Osgar's death had been necessary, a price that had to be paid. And she'd cared for Osgar a great deal more than she'd ever care for anyone here.

She didn't speak to the thegns, just walked into the moot hall with Alfreda a very tall shadow behind her. The thegns grumbled but followed after. They didn't like her rudeness, she knew that. Well, they could put spikes on her manners and shove them up their arses. She wasn't here to make friends.

There was a round table, a ring of wood that took up almost the whole hall. It was meant to show that all were equal among the folk, as the Hunter had told them they should be. But the thegns liked to put everything in order, purest to filthiest and best to worst. There was one big chair at the end of the table, carved with owls and broad enough that three men could have sat there. The chairs running round the table diminished in size from that one, so that those opposite were little more than footstools: a perfect hierarchy.

Cwen walked up to the biggest chair, feeling the thegns bristle and watch her every step. She put her foot on it, used it as a step to climb onto the table, and then gestured for Alfreda to sit there. The blacksmith obeyed, her drawn face blank as if the symbolism of the gesture was meaningless to her. Maybe she thought Cwen had chosen it because it was the only one that fitted her brawny bulk.

The thegns understood well enough, though. The discontented murmurs grew into outright rebellion. 'What's the meaning of this?' asked a thick-necked thegn with prideful eyes.

'The meaning is I want you all to sit down,' Cwen said. 'Well? What are you waiting for?'

It was satisfying looming above them on the table as they reluctantly took their places. She wasn't sure who she'd usurped at the head, but they all spent a while shuffling around, making sure they were still ranked as they ought to be. One poor man, wearing the only tunic without a thread of gold in it, was left standing at the far end of the table.

Eadric was only three chairs down from her, a place of honour for a man high in the Great Moot. His eyes barely left her the whole time the little dance was going on, and then it was only to look at the blacksmith.

Alfreda didn't return his gaze. This was a woman, Cwen thought, with a lot of feeling dammed up inside her. A dangerous woman, if the dam broke.

'You have us here, hawk,' Eadric said, when the shuffling of feet and chairs was finally over. 'There's work to be done. You know this better than us, but you've dragged us away from it, so better explain yourself.'

She looked at him for a long, cold moment. She'd been clutch leader since she was fifteen, the Hunter's second for the last four years, ever since Hrodgar had taken a tusk in the gut. She knew that honey drew flies just as well as shit. But sometimes shit was what you needed.

He wasn't weak though. He didn't yield. 'And that killer you've brought,' he said. 'I heard she refused us her weapon, so I cannot think why you've brought her among us, and unrestrained too.'

'Unrestrained. A killer.' Cwen's eyes swept around the table. They were all watching and her guts knotted. This wasn't the same as leading her clutch, bringing down a moon beast with their arrows and spears and blades. 'Tell me again what happened that day.'

'It's simple enough,' Eadric said. 'That villain Algar's weapon killed two good men and himself with it.'

'And he *meant* for that to happen?'

'Aye, he was an ill-favoured sort.'

'But a handsome man, I hear?'

He shrugged with an impressive display of indifference. 'I wouldn't know. I don't eye a man with that in mind. Perhaps it's different among the Hunt.'

'But your bonny daughter saw him with little else in mind, or so I'm told.'

His face went red with rage and although no one else spoke, she felt it: the interest, and from a few men further down the table, the suppressed laughter. So it *was* true. She hadn't been quite sure until that moment.

'That's a lie!' Eadric said.

She enjoyed keeping her calm while his ire rose, and seeing how that made it rise further. 'Is it? She's a bairn bouncing on her knee these days, I've seen his rosy face myself. And no husband to claim the making of it.'

She wondered if there'd ever been such a conversation with her own dad. There might have been whispers about her mum, as her belly grew with Cwen. There must have been a reason they'd prayed to the Hunter to take this bastard child away from them. But Eadric's grandson had no hawk mark on him. Whatever Eadric might have wanted, his daughter loved the child. She'd probably loved this Algar too.

'I don't know how it goes among you thegns,' she said, 'but among most people I know of, babies don't come unless a cock gets put inside a woman's cunt. Did this Algar put his cock in your daughter?'

Her words drew shocked gasps from the thegns and finally drove the blankness from even Alfreda's face.

'The truth of the matter is you had hands on that weapon of Algar's more recently than he did,' Cwen told Eadric. 'He and Alfreda were ready to leave Aethelgas, but it was you who bade them stay. It was you made them demonstrate that weapon in front of all those folk. I think it was *you* that messed things up, meaning to sabotage the weapon so only its user died and getting it wrong and killing two other innocents along with him. How right am I, tell me? But tell me true – we hawks know a lie when we hear it.'

That itself was a lie, but they weren't to guess it. The folk liked to know as little as possible about the lives of the children they sent off to kill and die for them. Eadric's face was an interesting thing: a visible struggle on it between rage and fear and the temptation to try to squirm out of it.

It was rage that won. 'So what if I did want him dead? He

lay with my daughter, and him some filthy Wanderer, took what wasn't his to take nor hers to give. He ruined her and if I killed him it was no less than he deserved!'

There was a frozen second after that, everyone too shocked to act. Then Alfreda leapt to her feet, murder in her eyes. Cwen clasped a hand on her shoulder, firm as she could but still not strong enough if the blacksmith really meant to break it. 'No,' Cwen said. 'This is my task.'

She leapt from the table, over Eadric's head and behind him, so that she was penning him in. 'You owe Alfreda wergeld for her brother,' she told him. 'We'll take it from the death-reckoning of your estate.'

She'd never killed a man before. She had to think carefully about where she'd place the knife, under the ribs and up. She held it there as blood spilled from his mouth and his eyes went wild, and then screaming, and then just blank.

It felt very different, killing a man, from killing a beast. The thing that had fled from him – that she'd driven from him – was so much greater than what a creature lost in its dying. She'd thought she had been anticipating this moment, but she realised now she'd been dreading it. His blood felt filthy against her hands. But it had to be done. That's what Bachur had commanded her: to do what was needed.

His body fell backwards, off her knife. It made a messy shape on the floor, the spreading pool of his blood a messier one all around it. The death had bought her more silence from the thegns, and no protests. It had achieved that much, but it needed to achieve more. She sheathed her knife, gory still, and wiped her hands on her tunic before she turned to Alfreda.

'That's justice,' Cwen said. 'Your brother's avenged and you'll have his blood money and his bairn too, if you want to take his lover into your family and have the raising of it. Enough moping. Your people have done right by you. Now it's time you did right by them.'

21

It wasn't clear who was winning. Krish cowered in the doorway of an abandoned slave hut with Dae Hyo in front of him and Dinesh behind and decided that it looked like everyone was losing.

'I'll tell you what, brother,' Dae Hyo said, 'I've had better days.'

Krish had never seen battle before, but once or twice a year taletellers had come to his village and shared stories of them. They always sounded so . . . orderly. Each side lined up, perhaps the greatest warriors duelled, a charge straight at each other and then it was all over.

This, though, was such a mess. There seemed to be no armies, just individuals out for blood. Rich men on lizardback swung swords as they galloped past. Poor men on foot tried to pull them down and stab them with their flint knives. Sometimes gangs would wait in ambush. He'd seen a woman leap from a breadfruit tree on to a rider's mount and stab him where he sat. And he'd seen three lizard-riders corner a man and take a very long time about killing him.

But not all those mounted were Uin's men and not all those on foot favoured Krish. Early in the conflict, Krish and Dae Hyo had found a group of farmers to shelter them. But their home had been attacked, the farmers had scattered and when Krish had seen another huddle of men in poor clothes, he'd approached them – only to have one pull a knife and try to stick it in his gut. Dae Hyo had killed him, but now Krish didn't know who to trust.

The weather had worsened with the conflict. On the first day there was rain, which seemed to congeal into fat drops out of the moist air. Krish felt as if he might drown in it. The third day there was thunder and lightning. Now a storm was brewing, driving them to this slave hut, bobbing on its raft. A small battle raged in the burnt fields all around as the powerful wind grew.

'We need to find Olufemi,' Krish said. He'd said it before.

'We need to *leave*, brother,' Dae Hyo replied. He'd said that more than once too. 'Besides, she's probably dead.'

She probably was. They'd tried to make their way to her hut more than once, but fighting had turned them back every time. And each side knew Olufemi was allied with him. She couldn't be safe.

'We'll try to find her one more time,' Krish said stubbornly.

'I can, I can, I can fetch her for you,' Dinesh said brightly. He'd found them early on the first day and stuck like a burr ever since. Dae Hyo cast frequent, irate glances at the boy, who seemed to have no instinct for self-preservation and a tendency to speak out at the worst moments, but Krish couldn't abandon him. Krish owed Dinesh a debt and he couldn't repay it that way.

'We'll all go together,' Krish said. Dae Hyo scowled but didn't complain.

The hut that Uin had given Olufemi was by the sea. At first the route was easy, walking between rafts packed so close together there was no water to be seen. The Rah often travelled with their homes towed behind their mounts, each group of allies like a clot of earth that split and fled when enemy rafts came near. It made it seem as if the whole land was at war with itself. But whatever fight had raged here seemed to have long passed. There were scorch marks on the wood-plank walls and silence from within. If anyone remained, they didn't want to be noticed.

The building nearest to the sea was a wreck, but Krish thought its ruin might have come before the fighting. Moss coated the shattered woodwork and some species of insect had made its nest inside, an improbable cone-shaped structure as tall as a man and made entirely of withered leaves. The little creatures seemed to sense the humans crouching beneath them. Krish saw a line of them leave the nest, antennae twitching and mandibles wide as they marched towards them.

Beyond lay only waterlogged fields, a jetty holding the sailing boats of Rah fishermen and, in the distance, Olufemi's hut. This was the nearest they'd yet come, but the remaining distance was the most dangerous. The sea was wild today, stirred up by the salt-filled wind. The tide was in and it curled and dashed itself against the raft holding Olufemi's home. They'd have to wade to reach it and they'd be exposed the whole time. Krish knew that his dark skin made him easy to recognise. With Dae Hyo beside him too, taller than any man among the tribe, he'd be hard for unfriendly eyes to mistake.

'She's probably dead,' Dae Hyo said again as the first of the insects reached and bit them.

'Probably,' Krish agreed, and ran forward.

Dinesh came straight after and Dae Hyo only a little behind. Their loyalty warmed him. He'd seen so little of it since the day he'd left his home.

The clean smell of salt water battled the stink of rotten vegetation, which swirled on the water's surface. It made each step a struggle as the roots and vines below tangled their feet.

A hundred paces out, and the water was to Krish's knees. The wind had picked up too, or perhaps his strength was failing. It was hard to stay upright as it pushed and pushed against his back, trying to blow him over. He leaned forward and it snatched up the sea and flung it into his face in eye-stinging gusts.

'Look, Krish, look!' Dinesh shouted, as cheerful as if they were drinking fermented goat's milk in their tents. 'Look – there she is.'

He was right. The door of Olufemi's hut had opened a crack and the mage's head poked out of it. She seemed to be looking away from them, at the peaks and troughs of the waves.

'Olufemi!' Krish shouted, but the wind stole his words.

'She should be careful she doesn't—' Dae Hyo said, and didn't need to finish the thought as a sudden blast of wind ripped the door from her hands and pulled her out with it. She hung a moment, legs kicking, and then fell into the water.

'Can she swim?' Dinesh asked.

Krish didn't know. He knew he couldn't, but he kept walking towards her all the same. His feet were swept out from under him once, twice, and then Dae Hyo grabbed his arm to pull him up, half-dragging him towards the hut.

Olufemi's head had disappeared beneath the waves. He didn't know how deep the water was there. The mage wasn't a tall woman and the waves were towering now. Even if she could swim, she'd have to fight their power. He saw her face surface for a moment, gagging and gasping for air. It sank again and an arm broke the surface, a foot.

Dae Hyo pulled them on grimly, another three dragging paces through water that was now waist-deep. The wind drowned out all sound but Krish could imagine Olufemi's cries as he saw her mouth open desperately again above the water before filling with it and sinking.

'Leave me,' he yelled to Dae Hyo. 'Save her.'

The bruising grip on his arm loosened and the full force of the waves snatched at him again. He leaned into it, gritted his teeth and kept his feet. Dinesh did less well. Krish saw the boy fall and rushed to pull him up. They clung to each other as they watched Dae Hyo half-run towards Olufemi with a strength that seemed incredible.

'Can he, can he, can he save her?' Dinesh asked.

'I don't know,' Krish said. 'She's . . . I don't know.'

Dae Hyo had reached the point where they'd last seen Olufemi, but there was nothing except water and white foam seething round his chest. His face was set in a grimace of effort and Krish realised he hadn't thought to ask if Dae Hyo himself could swim. The warrior's eyes met his for a moment, and then he shrugged and ducked his head beneath the waves. He emerged thirty heartbeats later, gasping, and barely waited before plunging back down again.

'Will he die?' Dinesh asked and Krish hissed, 'Shut up!' and kept watching the waves for Dae Hyo's head to appear again. He waited and he watched and for long, agonising moments there was only the water – until at last Dae Hyo came to the surface, and this time there was something in his arms, a robe-wrapped bundle.

The mage looked so small clasped there, but Krish could see the effort it was costing Dae Hyo to hold her. Her robe was waterlogged and her form entirely motionless. It was impossible to tell if her chest still rose and fell. She seemed like an inanimate thing, jetsam Dae Hyo had dragged from beneath the waves.

'To shore!' Dae Hyo shouted.

Now they were opposing the wind, fighting it for every step. It pounded against their chests, trying to force them over, to push them under. Krish held grimly to Dinesh, helping the boy up when he stumbled. It was strange to find himself the stronger one.

Dae Hyo pushed through the water as if it was air. His massive thighs carried him far more swiftly than Krish could travel, even with Olufemi in his arms, and he'd made it to the weed-strewn sand while Krish and Dinesh were still hip-deep. The instant he was above the tideline, Dae Hyo flung Olufemi to the ground and began pressing brutally on her chest. Krish couldn't understand what he was doing until the mage suddenly rolled on to her side and coughed a fountain of seawater out on to the shore. She was still retching when Krish reached her.

'She died,' Dae Hyo said with some satisfaction. 'But there's ways to bring them back, if it's soon enough. The elder mothers taught us that.'

'I wasn't dead,' Olufemi croaked, in her usual irascible way. 'Merely unconscious.'

'Your heart wasn't beating,' Dae Hyo insisted.

'The cold slows it.'

'Have it your way. And you're welcome.' He turned his back on the mage and began wringing out his clothes as she shucked her sodden robe.

Her dress beneath was thin cotton, almost transparent now that it was soaked. It showed the outline of her belly, the dark shadow at the juncture of her thighs and the sagging sacks of her breasts. Krish caught himself staring and looked away, his cheeks flaming.

There seemed little point in trying to dry themselves. The wind had slackened but the rain worsened. It fell in sheets that seemed almost solid. The sky was so grey it might have been night, the sun hidden beneath layers of cloud. The only illumination came with the lightning, blue sheets of it that spread uncannily over the breadth of the ocean. And the tide was still coming in. Tendrils of seawater were already creeping towards the dune where Olufemi sat.

'We need to get away from here,' Krish said. And then he looked up, away from the sea, and wondered if they'd be able to. There was one small figure, racing through the rice fields towards them. Behind were far more, a line of them at the horizon and closing fast. Krish thought they must be mounted.

'Krish?' the nearest figure shouted, her voice reedy over the wind, and he realised that it was Ensee. 'Lord Krish, what are you doing here? This is a terrible place to be!'

'Olufemi!' he shouted back, pointing at the mage still sitting at their feet.

Ensee lowered her head to sprint the remaining distance between them. She was gasping when she stopped, her face running with rain and her hair lank with it. 'I came for her,' she said. 'I came to warn her.'

'Warn me of what?' Olufemi asked, holding out her hand imperiously to Dae Hyo until he helped pull her to her feet.

'My father,' Ensee said, looking landward, where the line of men had drawn closer. 'He'll kill you if he catches you.'

But Krish didn't see any way that he *wouldn't* catch them. He'd brought a hundred men and spread them out like a net along the shore.

'The boats,' Olufemi said. 'They're our only chance.'

'Can you manage one?' Dae Hyo asked.

'I can manage it better than a sword in the gut,' the mage snapped.

The jetty lay east along the shore, a good distance away. Krish wasn't sure they could reach it in time, but Olufemi was right: he didn't see any other hope. They turned towards it and began struggling through the sand.

Krish kept his eyes on the boats. He didn't want to see how close Uin had come, though the boats were alarming enough on their own. They were tossed on the waves like leaves on the wind. As he watched, one turned over entirely and another snapped the rope holding it and was dashed and splintered against the wooden walkway.

'Is it safe?' he yelled. As another boat capsized, the question answered itself.

'Faster, brother,' Dae Hyo said. He *was* watching the lizard-riders approaching. Krish gritted his teeth and pushed on as Dae Hyo half-carried Olufemi beside him.

Only Ensee wasn't struggling. She ran ahead on the sand, her footsteps as light as a bird's, saying, 'Hurry. Oh, please, hurry.'

By the time they reached the boats only two remained whole and Uin's men were within bowshot. As they sprinted towards the jetty, arrows thunked into the sandy shore, throwing up fountains of spray, and stuck quivering in the wooden planks of the boats.

The further boat was bigger and clearly better built, but they'd be dead before they reached it. The nearer had only one sail and planks that were warped and stained. In wordless consent they all threw themselves over its side and into the cramped interior.

Someone else was already there. Half-blinded by salt spray and his own panicked sweat, Krish saw only the blurred outline of a man, his hands at work on the knotted ropes holding the boat to the jetty. Dae Hyo huffed and pulled out his sword, clearly meaning to cut through them, but the man shouted, 'No! We'll need them!' just as an arrow struck the deck only an inch from his fingers. Shocked, he stared at it for a moment, then went back to his frantic unknotting.

Krish chose another knot and started picking at it. Salt had crusted over the rope and bound it into something solid, but fear gave him strength. He could hear the voices of Uin's men, urging each other to close the distance and finish them off. Finally, the knot came free and the tension in the rope released, pulling it through his hands so rapidly it burned and he cried out and dropped it.

'Don't let it go!' the man shouted at him, and he grabbed for it, catching the very end before it could fall into the sea and hauling it in. The others had chosen their own ropes to work on and now the boat was free. It bounced on the swell with a sickening back-to-front and side-to-side motion. The man was at the sail, doing something Krish couldn't fathom that was somehow raising it up the tall pole in the boat's centre.

A few more inches and the wind caught it, pulling the cloth taut and dragging the boat forward, away from the shore. The man was still busy at the ropes, pulling some, tying off others. The sail moved, lowered. The boat began to run a little more smoothly – until another rope untied itself, flapping loose, and they'd lost all their forward motion.

The wind, which had become their tool, was once again their enemy. The boat bucked like a frightened horse. Arrows rained down and Krish heard a sound he thought might be the lizard mounts wading out into the waves.

'Grab that line and bring it here!' the man shouted at Krish.

Krish looked at him to see which rope he meant and, in the instant their eyes met, he knew him. It was Marvan.

'Do it or we'll all die!' Marvan shouted. The boat shook, the arrows fell and Krish knew he'd be a fool not to obey him. He grabbed the rope, gritting his teeth as he held it against the might of the wind.

'Tie it there,' Marvan instructed, pointing to a knob of wood on one of the boat's flanks. 'Wind it twice round and then pull and hold. I might need you to release it later.'

Krish did as he asked and Marvan continued snapping out instructions. Ensee obeyed them quickly and competently, Dae Hyo and Dinesh looking to Krish and waiting for his nod before they did the same. The sails shifted again and the boat steadied, still plunging up and down the huge waves yet holding a recognisable course, away from the shore. Flights of arrows darkened the sky behind them but they fell into the waves, and the shouts of the pursuing men grew angry and despairing before they were lost in the wind entirely.

Krish smiled in triumph, then gasped as the wind rose again with startling unpredictability. The rope in his hand pulled tight, the boat jolted and he wrapped his hand round it, leaned back and thought only about the present moment.

The whole day passed that way. It was hard to tell the hours apart, all filled with rain and salt spray, the caprices of the wind and Marvan's firm, shouted orders. The sun set, leaving them in a lonely, moonlit darkness. The wind finally calmed and the boat could run smoothly over the waves without constant tending.

Krish tied off the final rope the way Marvan instructed him and collapsed to the boards beneath, more exhausted than he'd ever been. Dinesh and Ensee did the same, settling down amidst the clutter of ropes and fishing pots and nets, but when Dae Hyo had finished his task he drew his sword and turned to Marvan.

'I tell you what,' he said, 'we've unfinished business with you.'

Marvan didn't reach for the twin tridents hanging from his own belt. 'You can kill me if you like, friend, but who'll sail your boat?'

'I can manage well enough,' Dae Hyo said, stepping forward and then staggering as the boat rocked unexpectedly.

'In that case, be my guest.' Marvan spread his arms as if inviting the blade into his chest. His own legs were braced with relaxed ease and he stood comfortably upright while Dae Hyo staggered again and dropped his sword. 'I should mention,' he added, 'that I grew up sailing boats such as this. If you mean to make a long voyage – where *do* you mean to go?'

The question was directed at Krish. Dae Hyo looked at him uncertainly as he stooped to pick up his weapon.

'He's right, we can't kill him yet,' Krish said and Dae Hyo reluctantly sheathed the sword.

Marvan showed no sign of relief. He just smiled and nodded. 'So what course shall I set?'

'I need to go back,' Ensee said. 'You can put ashore further south, where there aren't many people, and I'll make my own way home.'

'You can't,' Krish said. 'Your father—'

'Won't hurt me. He doesn't even know I'm part of this. He thinks I'm at home with my mother.'

'But—'

'I have to. I helped to start this war. I can't run away from it.'

She looked at Krish intensely, and he knew what she was thinking. He thought it too. He'd also been responsible for the bloodshed that had torn the Rah people apart. But she hadn't said that her side would win. And even if they did, what remained for him there? Only to wait helplessly for the arrival of his father's army.

He'd seen Uin's maps, the ones he'd used to plan the war *he* wanted. There was one place this boat could take him where he didn't think his enemies would follow. 'We'll put you ashore if you want,' he told Ensee, and looked away from her wounded expression. 'But we're sailing south – to Mirror Town.'

22

Laali's corpse was rotting by the time Sang Ki found men willing to help him carry her away. There were no people to spare from the battle preparations, Cwen had told him with one of her fierce smiles. But the stink of the carrion mount had probably become too much for the people living above it, and so a group of grumbling churls were sent with a blanket to carry her corpse away. They wrinkled their noses as they rolled her on to it and a shower of maggots fell out of her.

'Just chuck it in the trees, aye?' one of the churls said.

'I've found a spot,' Sang Ki told him, struggling to keep his voice pleasant. 'We'll take her there and bury her.'

The looks he got were daggers, but they lifted her up and followed where he led without complaint. He'd found the place the first day he'd been able to rise from his sickbed: a small wild patch between neat fields, it was filled with late-blooming bluebells. He'd imagined their seeds drifting down from the gardens of Ivarholme above, and the image had made him smile. It was a tranquil place where Laali could lie in peace.

It was also far enough away that the churls were sweaty and complaining by the time they reached it. 'This will do,' he said, and they dropped the body straight on the ground. Feathers fell out all around it and the smell worsened.

'A shallow grave will suffice,' Sang Ki said but they just laughed at him and dropped their spades beside her body.

'Dig it yourself then,' one of them said. 'We've more important work to do. Or haven't you heard there's a war coming?'

They walked away and there was nothing he could do to stop them. His back spasmed when he bent. His whole body was agony when he did nothing at all with it and mottled all over with bruises. The Jorlith medics told him he'd done damage to his insides that only time could repair, if it chose to. The soil at least was loose and he wouldn't just let Laali rot away. Perhaps burying her would stop her death nagging at him so. He couldn't bear to look at her decayed form as he dug.

And dug and dug as the spasms in his back worsened, to the point where he feared he was making the damage far worse, and yet the hole seemed to get no bigger. After less than an hour he was running with sweat and had made a grave only deep enough for a dog.

He heard the footsteps behind him and hoped it was the churls returning, having relented their callousness. But it was a woman's voice that said, 'You'd do better to burn her. A pyre.'

At first he couldn't think why he knew her, only that he did, and that the memory was an awful one. Then all at once he knew: the preacher boy and his sickly mother, the pair who'd disappeared with Nethmi after they'd murdered his father.

She looked far healthier now. Her brown hair was glossy and if her cheeks were sunken beneath her high cheekbones, at least they weren't flushed with fever. He stared at her, at a loss for what to do or say. Why was she here? Why, of all things, was she speaking to him?

'Here,' she said, when the silence had stretched quite thin. 'Let me.'

She began collecting fallen branches from the nearby trees, dragging them towards Laali's corpse. If the smell or the maggots bothered her, she didn't show it.

He watched her work until he'd put his mind back in better order. Now that the illness had left her he could see that she was a very beautiful woman, and not much older than him. 'I'm surprised to find you here,' he said eventually.

'Oh. Have we met before?' She turned to look at him over her shoulder.

'You came to Winter's Hammer,' he said carefully, 'with your son.'

She'd resumed her pyre-making, as if she didn't believe their current conversation to be of much moment. 'I wasn't well then. Jinn tells me we were captured. Men snatched us from Smiler's Fair, I remember that. Afterwards . . .' she shrugged.

'My father's men captured you,' he said stiffly.

'Did they?' Her intonation was curiously flat. 'Jinn didn't say. I know we got away.'

'By killing my father.'

She turned, a branch still in her hands, its shadow across her face. 'My little boy killed your father?'

She sounded so horrified that he found himself saying, 'He probably didn't do it in person. There was another woman with you, Nethmi of Whitewater. I strongly suspect her of being the culprit.'

'An Ashane?'

He nodded.

'I remember her, perhaps. A small woman. So small, and not happy. My Jinn spoke to her and then she left us. Yes, she left us on the great plains.' Her face glowed; she was clearly delighted to have remembered.

Sang Ki felt the last of his anger leaving him. It was very easy to believe she'd had no part in his father's death. It was possible her son was innocent too. Probable, even. The blame lay with Nethmi, as his heart had known all along.

The woman returned to piling branches round poor Laali's corpse. He joined her, hunting further afield now that the nearby ground was bare.

When they both bent over the same branch together, he asked, 'What are you doing here?'

'Helping you.'

'No, in the Moon Forest,' he explained patiently. 'Your boy preached the moon's message, but these are the sun's people.'

She picked the branch up before he could and carried it to Laali. He limped after, grunting as the too-fast motion twisted his back. She could move quickly when she chose. 'Will you not answer me?'

She dropped the branch and her head. 'It was Jinn's choice.'

'And you always do as your young son says?'

'I was . . . unwell. When I woke we were here.'

'And why did Jinn bring you here, among your enemies?'

She shrugged and turned to look at Laali. The decaying, maggot-ridden bird wasn't a pretty sight, but she stared at it a long time. 'It was my woman, Olufemi, who taught him the moon's ways. Before he was born she told me that's what he was meant to do.'

'Olufemi? That's a mage's name, if I don't mistake my etymology, and I seldom do.' He remembered the woman he'd met as he'd hunted for Krishanjit in Smiler's Fair, the one who'd been responsible for burning the whole place down.

'A mage, yes, a mage of Mirror Town. I went to her when I came to Smiler's Fair. I was dying, and she made me better, and she made it so my son wouldn't suffer the same illness. That was when she told me he'd be the moon's. The first word he ever said was "Yron".' She laughed. 'Olufemi was so pleased. I don't know why he came here. He doesn't talk about the moon any more. When I ask him he just smiles and tells me there's no need to worry.' She looked at Sang Ki, as if she expected him to offer her some kind of explanation.

'There comes an age when children must go their own way,' he tried.

The woman nodded, then looked back at Laali. 'Olufemi told me carrion mounts were the moon's once. She said he made far more of the world than we know.'

Laali no longer looked like she belonged to any god. They probably had enough branches now to burn what was left of her. She was held in a lattice of wood, brown leaves and grubby grey feathers poking out at intervals. He hadn't brought kindling, though. He turned to the woman, thinking to ask her if she had, when the first bell rang, loud and clanging and desperate. A moment later it was joined by a second, then a third, and then so many they were all just one clamorous noise.

The woman hugged her arms round herself, looking troubled for the first time. 'It's started,' she said. 'The battle's started.'

*

Cwen had drifted into half-sleep tangled between Wine and Wingard when the alarm rang. She had a moment of confusion and then one of fear: the reactions of childhood, when everyone knew the bells meant an attack, warriors of the tribes come to steal them away. And then she scrambled upright and knew: an attack *had* come, but it was no longer her place to cower while others did the fighting.

Hawks learned how to wake fast and fight soon. She buckled on her knife and quiver, took her bow and spears and was out of her tent with the twins beside her while the echoes of the first peal were still sounding.

'To me!' she shouted and the two score of her clutch gathered around her in a fighting order they'd had years to learn. She looked them over: weapons ready, grins or grimaces or stern blank faces, however each of them looked when battle was near. They stank of unwashed bodies and leather armour worn constantly over many days of waiting for this moment. Nearby, every clutch she'd ordered to camp by the entrance to the deep paths was forming up with the same haste.

The sun was almost overhead, a good sign. It warmed her as she ran towards the battle and she wondered why the Brotherband had chosen to attack now. They'd been underground for weeks; perhaps the passing of the days had lost all meaning to them.

The gateway loomed ahead of her. Ivy had climbed it and crystals in the stone arch twinkled in the sunlight. For a moment her eyes misunderstood the scale, so that the gate seemed the size of a normal door and the warriors emerging from it only toys. Then her perspective shifted and she saw it for what it was: an opening a hundred feet tall and fifty broad and a river of men, a flood of them pouring out of it.

The Brotherband wore black trousers, black shirts and silver turbans. They rushed out unopposed but fierce, men accustomed to fighting and always ready for it. She remembered what Sang Ki had told her about their massacre on the plains and thought she could see its reflection in their faces. They were men with the hearts of moon beasts.

There were already hundreds of them free of the deep way. Her stomach clenched. There were far too many, but her people were only just now mustering, the hawks and the Jorlith and the churls and thegns pressed into service. At least those few already in position had obeyed her orders and were waiting for her command. They couldn't afford to drive the Brotherband away unbloodied, to re-emerge and fight elsewhere. The invaders had to be killed here.

The warriors had seen her people. They couldn't have expected to encounter resistance so soon, but they screamed their rage and their defiance, and perhaps their contempt too. Cwen knew how thin her fighters were spread; she barely had two hundred here to stem this tide.

'Drive them back!' she shouted, and threw her long spear. It found its mark in a warrior's chest and the force of it threw him to the ground. Before he could rise, the rest trampled over him, blood fury driving them to meet the enemy.

Two clutches of her hawks stayed back and drew their bows. The range was short and she saw Arth, the strongest of them all, loose one arrow that went right through a man clear to the fletching. The flint tip pierced the chest of the warrior close behind and he yelled and pushed it away and the dead man with it.

Then she and her own clutch charged. Two of her hawks fell, three, a half-dozen from the Brotherband's own short bows and throwing-knives, until they met in a great clash with grunts and screams, the ground beneath them rocky with corpses.

'Push them back!' she yelled, but it was impossible to follow her own command. She'd never been in a fight like this. The moon beasts were huge and dangerous but the Hunt fought them one by one. Today's battle was chaos. To her left, she saw the stern-faced Jorlith keeping a line, shoulder to shoulder with shields high and spears out. The tide of the Brotherband crashed and curled and fell back against that barrier, but the rest of her force were suffering from their lack of the same discipline.

The thegns and churls seemed to do little but die. They were armed with swords and knives and axes and cudgels, but few knew how to wield them. She saw a thegn deflect the blow of a sabre with his sword, only for the man beside him to stand aside and let a spear thrust pierce his flank. Half of them lay dead or wounded and a dozen dropped their weapons and fled the battle, chased by the screams of those they'd abandoned.

Her own hawks suffered too. They fought in clumps now, back to back. Hers was to Wine and Wingard. She heard a yell from one of the twins and knew that he'd been wounded, but he didn't fall. She had her own wounds, but she barely felt them. Battle heated the blood so hot it burned out all other sensation.

The Brotherband warrior she faced was afire with it. She could see the lust for killing in his face as he swept his sword towards her guts. Her spear shaft deflected it, but he had the better weapon for this close-quarters fighting. His sword swung again and this time she wasn't quite fast enough. Her spear only half-turned the blade and an inch of steel bit into her side.

The warrior grinned and swung again and this time she was even slower, receiving a deeper cut on her other flank to match the first. She was bleeding heavily now and a bleeding animal didn't last long.

Her mind felt hazed and the haze helped. The warrior's face blurred until it could have been a beast's. She'd never fought men before but she'd killed a thousand monsters. His silver claw swung for her and she ducked the blow with ease. His teeth bared, he pressed forward and she saw the opening in his defences, the soft spot in the underbelly. She fought as well with left hand as with right; it was her greatest skill. Her spear in one hand, she drew her knife with the other and plunged it in, just where she'd struck Eadric and with the same effect.

Another warrior came, another beast and she pulled her blade free and turned on him. She was little more than an animal herself now, fighting with instincts that her years as a hawk had honed to a fine edge. She saw others of her clutch fall and didn't feel it. The Brotherband were fierce and they were numerous but they couldn't stand against her. She took a step forward, then another. Wingard and Wine moved with her, still alive. The Jorlith line pressed forward too, trampling the dead churls and thegns beneath them.

'Cwen!' someone shouted, Wingard or Wine at her shoulder. 'Cwen, look!'

She took a wound to her cheek from a knife, pressed her own into a throat.

'Cwen!' Louder and more insistent this time. 'Cwen, we're far enough!'

She deflected another blow, blinked and came back to herself. The battlefield expanded from this one moment, this one enemy, to a wider thing of which she had charge. The Brotherband had been pressed back. They were bunched at the mouth of the deep way now. But so many of her own were fallen. A single line of Jorlith stood between the tribesmen and the freedom of the forest. There were more Brotherband still within the vast tunnel and they were pressing forward, trying to force the Moon Forest folk back. She had to do it now, or it would never be done.

'Retreat!' she yelled. She was surprised to find her voice hoarse, as if she'd been shouting for hours. She didn't remember saying anything. 'Retreat!' But the rest were caught in their own battle fever and only a few hawks struggled to obey. The Jorlith line held, dropped a man, closed up and held again, wavering but not breaking and not moving.

'Retreat!' Wingard and Wine's voices joined hers. 'Retreat!' Now all the hawks were calling it, and finally the Jorlith and the few surviving thegns and churls heard. They'd planned for this moment for days, but plans were never forged strong enough to stay unbroken in the heat of battle. The Jorlith did it too slow, retreating one careful step at a time, spears still forward, as they'd spent years training to do. Her hawks tried their best but they were too locked into the battle, caught among the Brotherband with no hope of winning free.

'Get down!' she shouted instead, and Wine and Wingard echoed it, 'Get down!'

She fell on her face, the twins beside her, and as she fell she yelled, 'Set fire!', put her hands over her head and hoped that all the rest had done the same.

There was a moment when nothing happened. Another moment when the Brotherband yelled their victory, and then a sound like nothing she'd ever heard. It filled her head to the brim, driving every thought out of it. It seemed to last for ever; her ears rang with it long after the detonation itself was past.

She felt the wind of the weapon's discharge, the rush of many tiny things above her, as small as insects but far harder. Some of them were too low: they skimmed her skin and took it off. But the Brotherband were standing directly in the path of that deadly assault. Their screams were loud enough to replace the sound of the weapon.

She lay still and shocked for longer than she should have. Her body finally decided it was time to tell her all the damage it had suffered and she groaned in pain from a score of wounds. Her muscles shook with an exhaustion so extreme it was astonishing she'd managed to fight through it. Lifting herself to her knees felt like rolling a boulder up a mountain. It would be a while before she was able to rise to her feet.

But the vantage point from her knees was good enough. All the Brotherband warriors she could see nearby were dead or dying. The survivors were fleeing back into the deep ways, and she knew that in their place she would have done the same.

Alfreda's weapons, hidden in the trees around the battlefield, had reaped a terrible harvest. There'd been no time to make them from metal as the smith's design called for; they'd used the hollow bones of one of the great winged moon beasts instead. The screams of the dying were all over the battlefield, but Cwen could also hear them from one of the places where the weapons lay. She thought it might have exploded and killed its users.

But enough had worked. The small, round shot with which they'd packed the barrels had travelled through the Brotherband like a scythe. She thought there were Jorlith among the dead too, and hawks who hadn't heard or heeded her command. It wasn't always easy to tell; some of the bodies were so torn apart they were nothing more than meat and others had lost arms or legs or half their faces, chunks of flesh from their thighs.

She'd won this battle. In the quieter aftermath of the slaughter she could hear the sound of others drifting in. There were a score more entrances to the deep ways that they'd found and probably others they hadn't. The distant clash of weapons was proof that the Brotherband had divided their forces as she'd feared. Here they'd fought to victory. She didn't feel so confident about the rest.

Sang Ki had missed the battle entirely. If he were to be honest – and fortunately, no one asked him to be – he'd hardly hurried to the site of it once he realised the violence had begun.

He came to see the aftermath, though. His back ached and his feet were blistered, but he didn't complain as he walked beside Cwen and those of her commanders who'd survived. They began at the site of the biggest battle, where the work of sorting the bodies was under way, churls sifting through the human debris to find those parts that might belong to friends and scavenge those things that once belonged to enemies.

It was a terrible slaughter, yet Sang Ki found himself unmoved by it. The smell of blood and shit and the buzzing of flies was foul, but he'd seen worse in the wreckage of Smiler's Fair. He'd read that a man could become hardened to death. It was curious to find that it was happening to him.

That place was an unequivocal victory, and there were others. At the next site they visited – a sunken hole in the earth where the night roads came close to the surface – there were only Brotherband corpses. They'd found themselves unable to scale the steep earth sides with a force above sending arrows and spears down at them. One had tried to climb the vine lining the side of the chasm and died tangled in it along with his own guts.

The next site told the same story, but then the narrative began to change. They came to one place where the Jorlith dead were piled two high. The Brotherband had emerged in force from a rocky tunnel mouth and there hadn't been enough Moon Forest folk to turn them back. The warriors overpowered their foes and disappeared among the trees.

There were nineteen battle sites all told and at eleven of them the tribesmen had been repelled. He saw Cwen's expression harden as they visited place after place where the warriors had broken through. Even those who'd retreated from her own resounding victory might have found their way out elsewhere. And there could still be other entrances to the deep ways that they hadn't found, places where the Brotherband had simply strolled from the earth and into the trees.

Could they call it a victory? Aethelgas and Ivarholme were safe, but the Moon Forest was now dense with their enemies. There would be more and bloodier battles and there could be no more simple ambushes. Every future fight would be on even terms, terms that favoured the hardened and ruthless warriors of the Brotherband.

When he and Cwen finished their tour, they returned to the hawks' encampment. He saw that the Hunter's people had gathered their own dead, a very great many of them.

'A terrible loss,' Sang Ki said to Cwen.

She nodded. Her eyes lingered on two of the corpses, girls barely flowered, with long blonde hair matted with blood.

'You paid a painful price, but you saved many lives,' he tried awkwardly.

She nodded again. He thought she might be weeping, but when she turned her face to him her eyes were clear and her expression stern. 'The Hunter told me the fight would be hard. I didn't understand, but I do now. Whatever it takes, whatever it costs.' She looked again at the bodies of her dead hawks and then into the forest. 'They can't hide from me, them or their master. I'll hunt down every last one of them in the Moon Forest, and then we'll gather our army and hunt him down too.'

23

Surrounded by water, they were dying of thirst. Krish lay on the wooden deck, his face turned downward to press against the wood. A wave had soaked it and it was cool, soothing against his sunburnt skin.

'Get up, brother,' Dae Hyo said.

'I don't think I can,' Krish told him, but the warrior put his hands in Krish's armpits and hauled him to his feet.

'Land,' Dae Hyo said. 'Look.'

Land wasn't the problem, though. For the last week of their voyage they'd hugged the coast; they'd put to shore five times, but there'd been no rivers or springs, no fresh water at all. There was nothing but rock and sand, a shimmering pale yellow stretching to the horizon. He'd never seen a land like it, stripped of anything living. Even the rocks were as pale as bleached bones.

'We're here.' Olufemi's voice was no more than a dry croak and her lips cracked and bled as they stretched into a smile. 'We've reached Mirror Town.'

But Krish could see only rock, rising into sheer white cliffs on the shore and scattered in twisted outcrops through the water. 'There's nothing here.'

'It's the Wracked Shore,' Marvan said. The other man usually avoided speaking, as if he thought even on such a small boat they might forget he was there. But now he stood at Krish's shoulder, peering not outward but down, into the sea.

They were sailing above a graveyard of ships. The water was so clear, Krish could see the rocky bottom a hundred paces below and the scores of wrecks that littered it. The ship beneath them was huge, its wooden sides gaping open like cracked ribs and its mast casting a long shadow across the ocean floor. Seaweed swathed it and Krish saw the skeletons of its dead crew.

'I've read about this,' Marvan said. 'These are the vessels that brought the Fourteen Tribes to our land. The legend says they journeyed here in fourteen ships, but I suppose a little inaccuracy is to be expected.'

There were far more than fourteen. Krish lost count as they sailed above them, some as large as mammoths and others little bigger than their own boat.

Dae Hyo stared silently at the ocean floor and Krish remembered that this was the second mass grave of his people that he'd seen. But when Krish reached out a hand to rest against Dae Hyo's shoulder, his brother laughed. 'I tell you what, now I know why we never tried to return from our exile. Those aren't boats I'd want to sail.'

'But they mean we've reached Mirror Town?' Krish asked. He could see nothing beyond the white rocks on which the ships must have been driven to their destruction.

Olufemi's bloodshot eyes strained forward. 'Another mile, maybe a little more.'

Krish took his place back at the tiller to steer between the rocks as Marvan pulled the ropes that moved the sails. Dae Hyo remained in the bow, looking at the ships on the ocean floor below. And Krish watched Olufemi watching the shore until he saw her smile again. A thin trickle of blood ran from her cracked lip across her dark skin and she licked it up as her eyes stayed fixed on land.

'There,' she said, and pointed to a small deserted dock at the foot of the cliff. Krish pulled the tiller so that the boat curved through the water to reach it as Marvan spilled the wind from its sails to slow it to a stop. He leapt from the side to tie it fast and Dae Hyo lowered a plank to let them walk to land. It seemed to sway beneath Krish, as restless as the ocean.

Ahead a path wound up the cliff. The steps were even but steep and the group paused often on the climb. Krish felt his thirst more keenly now he knew he might soon slake it, and he was shaking and gasping for breath when they were only halfway up. The last fifty steps were smoother, running up the side of what was clearly a man-made wall – a defence, perhaps, though it was hard to imagine who might launch an attack here.

Then finally they reached its top. The sun blazed brilliantly down and shards of light lanced back, like a thousand fireflies hovering above the ground. Krish looked down, dazzled, and when he blinked the blaze away he saw Mirror Town.

At first he thought of Smiler's Fair. It was the only other place so large he'd ever seen. But Smiler's Fair had been made to move and, in the end, to burn. No fire could destroy Mirror Town's huge, sprawling houses of marble and granite and every type of stone. Krish couldn't see the city's boundary, only broad street after broad street lined with vast buildings and narrower ways threading through green parkland. There were people everywhere, many dark-skinned and curly-haired like Olufemi and many more from all the nations of the world. All were dressed in flowing robes, but those of the dark-skinned folk were embroidered and brightly coloured. And they talked as they walked, or laughed, or gestured wildly with their hands. The others drifted along, smiling blankly, wearing simple white.

'They're slaves,' Krish said. 'All those people are slaves.'

Olufemi looked at him sharply and then away. 'My people invented bliss and sell it to the Rah. Mirror Town is the womb of all slavery and grows fat from its fruits. Will you scorn your last refuge because of it?'

Krish felt his face heat with shame, because of course he couldn't. He could see the wealth she spoke of in every building, no two fashioned in the same style. One sprawled low and long, its walls rounded likes enormous wormcasts and faced with amber tiles. Another had built upward rather than outward, spiked towers reaching towards the pale blue sky. Some had a profusion of chimneys and others none, and the nearest had been painted with abstract swirls that drew the eye into infinite loops.

'But how does it all stand? How do people live here?' he asked.

'Why don't the worm men . . . Why don't my servants come to all those places kept in shadow?'

'Why do you think you outlanders have named this city Mirror Town? Sunlight poisons the land against your servants: anywhere it has touched is safe from them until the moon is born again each month. When we first came to this place, my people fashioned a thousand mirrors and a thousand thousand more have been made over the centuries since. They are on every roof and street corner and in every building, and in no building are there any doors. The mirrors catch the light and send it into rooms and corners that would otherwise be dark.'

'Cunning,' Dae Hyo said. 'If a people are going to sit still in one place, that's the way to do it. Although this wouldn't be the place I'd choose to sit. The sun's hotter than a blacksmith's forge. How does anything grow?'

'The power of the runes is faded, warrior, and gone from the rest of the world, but some of it lingers here still. There are orchards and fields that would put the farmland of Ashnesland to shame, and around them nothing but sand.' Olufemi's eyes swept the city and her expression was hard to read. Krish wasn't sure if she was glad to be home. 'My people chose this desolate place precisely for its remoteness and no one visits Mirror Town except by their invitation.'

'But *we've* come here,' Krish said. 'Will they let us stay?'

'My family will welcome me.' Olufemi croaked out a laugh. 'Or at least they will make room for me. Long ago, the Fourteen Tribes washed up on this shore and my people fed and clothed them and sent them on their way. As for you – you're nothing to them. For as long as they think of you as nothing, they'll tolerate you.'

'And what if they know who I really am?' Krish asked.

'The Brotherband knew who you were, and you killed them. The Rah treated you as their king and you betrayed them. Now no one who knows who you truly are will ever welcome you again. Be grateful that here at least there's no one who wants you dead – for now.' Olufemi stared at him a moment longer, then turned and began her descent into Mirror Town.

PART 2
Loyalty

24

Sang Ki approached the treetop village, as he'd learned to do, with trepidation. The small force around him were alert: some of his own Ashane, a few pressed Smiler's Fair men and two hawks to lead them. Their weapons were drawn and they moved as silently as such a force could down the weed-choked track. The paths were ill-tended this far from the Moon Forest's heart.

'Don't see anything,' the lead hawk hissed to Sang Ki on his suffering carthorse. His mammoth had fled into the plains never to be seen again while his mother had led his forces on the long journey to the Moon Forest. The horse he'd found to replace it struggled beneath his weight and jostled an aching body that was proving appallingly slow to heal from the damage he'd done it.

'Go then,' Sang Ki whispered. 'And good luck to you.'

He watched his men separate to ring the village, creeping through the fields that covered the ground below. This company was well-trained now. They'd had a good long while to practise their skills. The leaves had darkened over summer, the fruit and flowers swollen and bloomed and now the colours all around were red and gold and brown as summer had surrendered to autumn in the time they'd spent pursuing the Brotherband through the forest.

The nearest field was filled with wheat, tall and golden with fat, ripe seed pods. It worried Sang Ki that it remained unharvested, but he reminded himself that the sun shone less bright this far north, and the crops grew ready late. Still, he pictured what his troops might be finding. He'd seen it too often before: the slaughter and the mutilated corpses.

The Brotherband seemed to have a destination in mind. As

he and Cwen had tracked them, they'd swept in a broad swathe south and west through the forest. But wherever they were going, they weren't in such a hurry to arrive that they wouldn't stop for a little sport along the way.

The horse shifted restlessly beneath him and he dismounted, groaning as he landed. His back hadn't yet recovered from Laali's final, fatal plunge. Perhaps it never would. Ah well, none of them could remain unchanged by this business, and the price he'd paid was far lower than some. Far lower than that Laali had paid. What did it truly matter if he could no longer bend his back more than a handspan, if he slept barely an hour straight before the pain in his joints woke him? At least he lived to wake.

He heard a rustle in the corn, his stomach clenched with fear, and then the Jorlith spear-leader Eyjolf walked out from between the stalks, a broad smile on a face that didn't often hold one.

'Nothing,' Eyjolf said. 'The village is whole, not even Janggok raids to trouble them in the last few weeks. I'll give those bastards this: they've scared every other tribesman out of the forest.'

'But they didn't pass by here? Not even livestock gone?'

Eyjolf laughed a little wildly. He was drunk on unspent battle fury. Sang Ki had learned to recognise the signs. 'Nothing, I tell you. They didn't even know there was a war on, can you believe it? The thegns sit up there, untravelling, and the churls have their faces to the dirt. No Wanderers by and as far as they know it's all as it's ever been in the Moon Forest.'

'I thought Cwen asked you spear-leaders to send out messages to every Jorlith outpost?'

It was the wrong thing to say. The other man bristled. 'And so we tried, but do you know how many villages there are in the forest?'

'I'm afraid I don't.'

'Nor does any man. The Hunter commanded us, no place except Aethelgas or Ivarholme to hold more than 169 hearts. She wanted us spread over the whole forest and that's what's occurred, each village budding others and them budding in turn until there was a treeful of them. Too many to count.'

'And this one was unharmed.' Sang Ki took a moment to savour it. He wouldn't have to watch as his force built a pyre for the mutilated corpses, though as far as he and Cwen had been able to figure, this village lay in the direct path of the Brotherband's march. 'Well, it's good news. I dare say if they've not been attacked they can spare us lunch. There's time to eat before we move on.'

Cwen had never been so far from the heart of the Moon Forest, though other hawks had. Sometimes the monsters fled here, though the trees were barely tall enough to shelter them from the sun and so widely spaced that clearings were common. But Cwen had been stuck close to Bachur's side almost from her hawk day. She missed the Hunter fiercely. She would often turn to speak to her only to remember when she saw a plain and human face beside her that her mistress had gone. There'd been no word from her in more than three months.

Most often, the face beside her was that of the blacksmith, Alfreda. The tall, silent woman had become her shadow as she led her forces through the forest, sweeping the Brotherband before them. No, curse it. There was no need to lie to herself, though she'd told the soothing untruth to more than one panicked villager. Cwen was merely following in the Brotherband's footsteps as they walked where they chose, always one pace ahead.

She approached the village, her towering shadow beside her, but she didn't believe she'd see anything. This would be the third village now that the Brotherband had passed but hadn't attacked. She'd like to believe it was because their numbers were falling. The Moon Forest's villages weren't undefended and Cwen had found the bodies of tribesmen along with their victims in most places. But as she looked through the thinning trees, she thought it was something else. The Brotherband weren't fleeing *from* the Moon Forest, they were rushing *to* somewhere else.

'So where are those gut maggots going?' she asked.

There was no answer from Alfreda. The smith had yet to utter a word to her or anyone else, but she'd write her answer on a piece of parchment if it was important enough. And apparently she *could* talk; she'd been heard talking to her dead brother. Cwen didn't understand it. She couldn't imagine choosing to lock herself in silence. When she had an opinion, she wanted it heard.

'No point hanging around here,' she said. 'We may as well see if your fire javelin is finished.'

It never looked as if Alfreda was listening, but she matched Cwen pace for pace, though her long, heavily muscled legs were clearly accustomed to striding out more. Maybe not now, though; she was still barely eating and would only ever take food when the boy Jinn gave it to her.

And there he was now, at the edge of the campsite waiting for their return, almost as if he'd sensed it. Cwen could see his smile, whiter in the white of his face, as he jogged to meet them.

'No Brotherband?' he asked.

'No sign of them,' Cwen confirmed, to him and the hawks who were guarding their campsite, beyond the ring of stake-lined ditches they dug every night. That had been Sang Ki's suggestion. He was a strange man. Strange but clever, though he never used ten words when he'd a store of a hundred longer ones. It was a relief whenever their campaign to clear the forest split their forces and she didn't have to share his camp at night.

'Are you ready, Alfreda?' Jinn asked. 'I've been checking every hour and I reckon the clay's done, but I ain't sure. You don't know how I've been tempted to crack open the oven and have a look-see myself. It's only out of respect for you and your work that I ain't done it, which I hope you appreciate.'

The boy never seemed to have a problem chattering on to Alfreda, despite her lack of response. And Alfreda had a soft spot for him, Cwen could tell. The expression on her face right now couldn't be called a smile, but the smith looked less lemon-sucking than normal. She nodded at Jinn and turned towards the heart of the camp, where her forge lay.

It had taken them a long time to gather enough metal for this project. There were no copper or tin mines in the forest; the Hunter forbade it. Bachur didn't like the thought of her people crawling up the earth's arse where the worm men were. And few weapons were forged of brass when iron was so much stronger. They'd had to raid the homes of every rich thegn they'd passed for ornaments made out of the metal. It hadn't made them popular, and even less so when they'd stripped each village bare of its defending Jorlith.

But Cwen's force had grown into something respectable. Now if they met the full muster of the Brotherband, it would be the tribesmen who were outnumbered. She looked over her encampment, spreading far across the fields, and thought that Bachur would be pleased.

Alfreda's wagon wasn't far from Cwen's tent. It had the Hunter painted on its side as most such wagons did. The Wanderers travelled under her protection and didn't forget it. But Bachur's face had been painted perfect and unscarred. That was fucking typical too. The folk looked away from any ugly thing, especially if they were the cause of it.

Alfreda strode eagerly to her forge. Making the weapon was the one thing that seemed to bring any life to her.

'It's exciting, ain't it?' Jinn said. 'I've never been much for fighting myself. Too little for it, and too cowardly too. I ain't afraid to admit it. I see the knives out and the blood flowing and I just want to make myself scarce. But this thing here, this could change all that. Even more than any arrow, it could mean a man don't have to face his enemies to finish them.' He looked suddenly thoughtful. 'I ain't so sure that's a good thing, now I come to think about it. But I guess it's a necessary one.'

Alfreda tended her kiln while Jinn spoke. Cwen didn't understand the blacksmith's craft, but she could tell the woman was an expert from the way she worked. There was no uncertainty in her movements as she broke open the outer clay and revealed the mould within.

It looked whole and Cwen grinned, but the smith was cautious. She touched it first with a thick, water-soaked cloth and, when that made no steam, lightly with her fingers. Then she lifted the whole thing out and placed it by her forge.

'Did it work?' Cwen asked.

Alfreda didn't answer; she was too busy prodding and poking at the insides of the mould.

'She's got to make sure all the wax has melted away,' Jinn told her. The boy had paid far more attention to the preparation of the weapon than Cwen had. She was only interested in the result.

'And has it?' she asked.

The mould cracked open, its two halves separating as neatly as a walnut. Alfreda cradled them like a mother with her baby, smiling.

'Reckon it has,' Jinn said.

It wasn't easy to tell when the forest ended. The trees had been growing shorter for days, ordinary beeches and oaks and elms, not the vast moon pines and ice oaks Sang Ki had grown accustomed to. But that morning as they rode, he realised that grass was now a more common sight, the trees lonely sentinels in it.

His mother rode beside him, staring at the scenery disapprovingly. Too straggly for her, no doubt: too disorderly. It occurred to him that Seonu Hana had been born in exactly the right land, a place where snow reduced everything to the same neat blankness.

'I believe,' he said to her, 'that we have entered the badlands.

And the Brotherband had too. His knowledge of this area was scant: it looked to him to be merely an infertile wilderness between the Moon Forest and the lands of the Rah. It was hard to imagine what the warriors sought here, but he was sure it must be something. They were savage, but not unreasoning.

'King Nayan won't thank you for this, you know,' she said.

'As the tale of Jaspal and the five gold seeds tells us, work should be its own reward. Besides, I think he might. We are, after all, helping to diminish his rebel son's forces.'

'The Brotherband do as they please. They aren't this Krishanjit's men.'

She'd made this claim before, but Sang Ki didn't believe it. He'd seen enough Brotherband corpses over the last few months to know that each of them carried a mark Cwen had told him was the moon's rune. Some only wore it on pendants round their necks, but many had it tattooed or branded over their hearts.

'What about Winter's Hammer?' she asked, when that got no response. 'There's no one to rule there with you gone.' With *her* gone was what she truly meant. He had a sudden, vivid memory of her sitting in her study, neat stacks of paper all around listing the food stores in the shipfort, the hunting parties and what they'd brought, the income from tithes and the outlay in taxes to the King. Perhaps she always had ruled Winter's Hammer, even when his father was still alive.

'And what of Thilak?' she said. 'And Thilak's murderer?'

There it was again, the subject they'd hovered above or landed awkwardly on since the moment she'd first seen the preacher Jinn and his mother Vordanna among Cwen's followers. 'He's a *boy*,' Sang Ki said.

'And Nethmi's pregnant,' his mother said bitterly. 'Is that reason enough for Thilak's death to go unavenged all these months? I'd almost think you didn't care!'

'How can you—?' Sang Ki began, then clamped down on his anger. It flared up far more often now, the flames fanned by his sleepness nights and pain-filled days. 'We don't know that Jinn had any part in it,' he pointed out stiffly, 'only that he disappeared shortly afterwards. Which, given that we intended to execute him, one can hardly blame him for.'

'But we know that he's a traitor,' his mother said fiercely.

He stared at her, surprised by her venom. 'Well, yes, but since he betrayed our enemies to join our cause, I don't think we should complain.'

'You've read enough history in your father's books. A man who's betrayed once will betray again – betrayal is in his nature.'

'But Cwen has taken him under her protection, and we can ill afford to alienate her. Her forces—' He broke off gratefully at the sight of the bird winging its way towards them. He'd learned to recognise the tuft-eared little messenger owls. They were clever creatures; he was considering taking some east with him when he eventually returned home.

'Word from Cwen herself, I hope,' he said, holding out his arm for the bird to alight. They were trained to carry messages between two particular people, and this one had a fold of parchment in a hoop round its leg. It tilted its head to eye him quizzically as he pulled it out and read it.

'Ah,' he said. 'It appears Cwen has found our enemies' trail. And that they have regrouped – they seem to be moving en masse.'

'Don't look so pleased. All that you've won against them so far are skirmishes and ambushes. They won't be easy prey in a pitched battle with their full numbers.'

'Perhaps not, but Cwen has told me her own force is much expanded. No doubt we'll see for ourselves when we rendezvous. The bird will lead me to her encampment.'

The owl seemed to take that as permission. It fluttered from his arm and to a tree ahead, alighting in its branches and turning to see that they were following.

'Remarkable,' he said.

The little bird led them on what turned out to be quite a short journey. Sang Ki supposed it wasn't surprising. Both his force and hers had been following after different contingents of the Brotherband and as the warriors had converged, so had they.

Cwen was waiting for him at the edge of the camp, peering into the scrub with an impatient frown on her face. The instant she saw his horse she waved him on and then walked away, towards the far side of the huge camp.

'She has no manners,' his mother said, and it was hard to argue, but he liked Cwen nonetheless. Perhaps he liked her precisely because of how much she irritated his mother.

'You can get yourself settled here,' he said. 'I'll pass along anything she says that's worth knowing.'

His mother harrumphed, but after a last glare at Cwen's retreating form she moved to do as he'd said. She'd been such a powerful force throughout his life; but she wasn't a young woman any more and a full day in the saddle tired her.

He was exhausted himself and his back was agony, but he

knew that whatever Cwen wished to show him, it would be important. 'Dismount then,' she said when he drew near and looked away as he did it. She seemed to find the inelegant procedure as distasteful as he found it humiliating.

'Well?' he asked. 'What have you found to dazzle me with?'

'The Brotherband.' She gestured at the ground.

It was a trail even he could have followed. In the forest the warriors had made some effort to disguise their movements but that no longer seemed to trouble them. Or perhaps they knew that such a large force couldn't be disguised. Despite his blithe words to his mother, the sight of so broad a swathe trodden through the underbrush alarmed him.

'Looks like there's more of them than lice in a whore's pubes,' Cwen said, in her charming way.

'Thousands, I'd guess, though I'm no judge.'

'Thousands, you're right. I've sent scouts. They've spotted them, less than a day's march ahead. We've caught them up.'

'That's welcome news,' Sang Ki said, and tried to mean it.

'There's better, for us anyway. The Brotherband are on the hunt for larger prey than they found in the forest. There's another army here, or the remnants of one. Our scouts saw the Brotherband scouting it.'

'And they weren't seen?'

'It's not like they don't know we're after them. But they seem a mite more interested in this other gang – they're tribesmen as well, but who knows what tribe?'

'They didn't come from the forest?'

'Not unless they're Janggok raiders, and they aren't.'

'Then how did the Brotherband know their location?'

'I told you. They've been scouting.'

'But they've been heading in this direction for weeks. That's far longer than they could have known this other force was here.'

She shrugged. 'Listen to what I'm trying to tell you, Ashane. There's going to be a battle – tomorrow or the day after. The Brotherband will attack them, and we'll attack the Brotherband.

I didn't think we'd get another chance to catch them with their cocks hanging out, but this looks like it.'

'And you think our force and whoever these others are can truly defeat so many?' He looked again at the trail, a swathe of crushed brown grass and bent thistles leading towards the horizon.

'Well, as to that.' She strode a few paces to her left where a linen-wrapped lump sat on the ground, and pulled the cloth away with a showman's flourish. Beneath, golden metal gleamed.

'The fire javelin!' he said. 'She finished it.'

'This and one other. That's all we had the metal for. But these can fire more than once and they'll throw those killing balls a good distance. Even better, the Brotherband have faced this once before. The memory of that will be as big a weapon as the weapons themselves.'

It was true. The sound alone had scared him, and he'd been a good distance away. The sight of the slaughter and the dismembered bodies afterwards had been impossible to forget. Still, he looked at the Brotherband's trail, so very wide, and he thought of what his mother had said. Whatever Cwen claimed, he couldn't believe that the coming battle would be easy. He wasn't even confident it could be won.

25

Krish didn't know where he was, but he knew that he didn't belong there. The grass was too brown, the trees too many and too stunted, the air too hot. He came from a cooler place, but this was where he'd been drawn. It was his rage that had drawn him on.

He used to do his fighting on horseback, but they'd left their horses behind when they entered the deep ways. He remembered for a moment the terror of that endless darkness. He'd seen the worm men, their unnatural eyes watching from between cracks in the rocks. The eyes had their own light, a silver glow that was the only illumination below.

There were no worm men here, beneath the open sky. But *that man* was here, that man and all the men with him that he hated so much. He couldn't remember what the man had done to him, but he knew that he needed to die. Those murderers from the Moon Forest were closing in too, but that didn't matter. They weren't important now. Revenge was.

He lay in the long grass, hidden. The enemy encampment was large, yet ill-defended. These people were armed, but they weren't fighters, not like him and his brothers. There'd be a slaughter tomorrow and a reckoning. The mark of the moon burned on his chest, a good pain.

He rolled over so that he could place his hand on it, over his heart. But the clouded sky above was now clear, the sun too bright. The light stabbed into his eyes – and he woke in another place entirely. For a moment the dream clung to him, tangling him in memories he wasn't sure were real. A moment more and he knew himself and this place: Mirror Town. The marble walls, the open arch in place of a door, the slave stationed outside it: all these had grown familiar to him over his months here.

Krish had been provided with local dress when he arrived, though Dae Hyo said he ought to keep his Dae clothes. The warrior had done so and sweated through the crippling heat, but Krish could only endure one day of it before he tore them off and slipped into the loose, long-sleeved cotton robes that all the mages wore. He chose one from his wardrobe now, plain white without the complex embroidery Olufemi had told him marked each mage's place in their family and each family's place in the city. Krish had no family here. He was no one and they'd dressed him like a slave.

His room was in one wing of the mansion Olufemi said had been her family's since the city was founded. Its heart was made out of a smooth rock veined with red and blue and sometimes green. Krish had seen the rock before, in some of the ruins he and Dae Hyo had passed as they travelled the plains. He couldn't imagine how they'd been brought all the way here.

He passed the first mirror as he walked the long corridor that led from his room to one of the main courtyards of the house. It was lined with carvings and paintings and complex objects whose use he didn't know. It was the same everywhere he went. Olufemi's home was huge and sprawling, and Krish still hadn't seen a tenth of it. He hadn't been invited to.

Olufemi had told him that the mansion had been deliberately built to confuse. Few of the rooms were simple squares, like those of the Rah, or circles like the tent he'd lived in his whole life. Most were built on more than one level, so you entered on one and left on another. Corridors sloped and twined above and below each other. You'd enter at ground level and find yourself looking out of a window high above the city and never be quite sure how you got there. Olufemi's family were map-makers, and they'd found it amusing to design their home to elude their own craft.

When she was a child, she'd told him back when she still seemed to have time to speak to him, they used to tell stories of visitors who'd wandered off and never returned. One of her cousins swore she'd found the skeleton of an unlucky traveller in a distant room. Krish suspected it wasn't true, but he stuck to the few routes he'd memorised whenever he walked through the place. His reflection followed him everywhere he went, multiplied in every mirror so that he seemed constantly accompanied by a crowd of sombre-faced young Ashane men.

When he stepped outside, the sun hit him like a blow. He thought he'd been hot in Rah lands, but he hadn't understood what true heat was. That had been damp and cloying, like a sticky embrace. This was all the sun's work. It shone brighter than he'd known it could in a clear blue sky and seemed to suck the moisture and the energy straight out of him.

The Etze Mansion lay on the seaward edge of Mirror Town. The ocean was a stark blue too, and as reflective as a mirror itself. When Krish looked at it from the high wall that bordered the city, he found it hard to remember the storm-racked journey that had brought them there. Everything in this place seemed still, leached of the ability to move by the searing heat. The slaves crept along the broad streets and the mages drifted through them and no one seemed in a hurry to be anywhere.

Krish didn't know where he was going, but his feet led him inward, towards the heart of the city with its scores of sprawling, stone-built complexes in as many different styles. It was a hard place to walk, with the mirrors on every roof and street corner. The sunlight reflected in them stabbed at him whichever way he looked and his own reflection haunted him.

The slaves were everywhere, outnumbering their masters a hundred to one, working while the mages played. They reminded him a little of the residents of Smiler's Fair, a mix of people from all over the world. But Smiler's Fair had been filled with people living lives at full speed – lives they'd chosen, however rough. Here the mages had no need to rush and slaves had no energy for rushing and no choice, only the bliss that left them blank-eyed and compliant. The loudest sound was the shouts of the mirror masters, a cacophony that lasted all day. 'Turn one, turn, turn two, turn!'

It was odd being so easily able to understand what they said. Learning the tribes' language from Dae Hyo had been hard. For every two words that stuck in his memory, four more slipped out of it. But the warrior hadn't let up and Krish had got better. He hadn't even tried to learn the mages' tongue, but as if his earlier studies had worn a smooth groove downward in his mind, the knowledge slid in regardless.

'Turn east!' the mirror master nearest to him croaked, as a stooped woman by the mirror on the roof above cried, 'Turn west!' The piercing sunlight streamed between them and swept through the building opposite.

Krish realised that he'd reached his destination, though he hadn't known he intended to come here. The streets of Mirror Town were paved in a score of different ways: cobbles, glass, stone, wood. Here, though, there was only dusty yellow earth. It blew up in clouds around his feet as he walked towards the centre of the square.

There were fewer slaves here and more mages. Some had brought small, folding wooden tables and sat hunched over complex circular boards, the game called Night and Day that the mages seemed to take more seriously than anything. Others stood in rings around the eleven huge pillars that lay scattered around the square. Only five of them were currently occupied, and four of those occupants were the focus of the mages' attention.

It was impossible to speak to the men and women standing on the pillars. The lowest was almost a hundred paces in the air. But the mages came to watch, every day. Krish didn't know why. To draw inspiration from them, or to mock? He'd learned that standing on those pillars was a thing mages did when they needed to think deeply. They let themselves be taken to the narrow tops and they stayed there under the blazing sun, and slept there in the surprising chill of night. And they had visions, if they did it long enough, visions that had inspired some of Mirror Town's greatest inventions.

The pillar nearest him held a young man, swaying on his feet. On the ground below, four slaves worked the winches of a complex wooden platform. Its zigzag supports slowly straightened until it was teetering at the same height as the pillar. They'd put a flagon of water and a bowl of fruit and meat on it, but the young man ignored them. With his face turned to the sun, his eyes must be closed. Apparently, he'd been up there nearly a year. The same buckets that took up his food and water brought his waste products down. He'd said he wouldn't come down himself until he understood why sugar was sweet. 'The Bakari family,' Krish heard one of the watching mages say. 'They're all crazy.'

The tallest pillar, in the centre of the square, was made of a glass so clear there were angles from which you could barely see it. It was empty. He'd been told it was always left empty, in honour of its last resident. Ayo Abiola had climbed up there when she was seventeen and stayed until she was seventy-three. No one knew what she'd told her family when she came back down, but they'd been the richest of the great houses of Mirror Town ever since.

The pillar he wanted was in the far corner of the square and unattended. The mages weren't interested in the man who sat on its broad platform, sheltering underneath a white cotton tent. Krish grabbed a passing slave and said, 'I need to get up there,' and the woman drifted off to make it happen. It sent a twinge of guilt through him every time he commanded one of the slaves, but a little less each time. Nothing happened in Mirror Town if a slave didn't do it.

A few moments later, a platform was wheeled up. It was broader than the one they'd used to feed the other mage but not conspicuously more steady. 'I'll need food and water for him too,' Krish said. When they brought it, he had no more excuses not to step on to the rickety thing.

It creaked as the slaves below worked the winches. He sat and tried to brace himself against the rocking motion until he was at the same height as the top of the pillar. It was one of the broadest, nearly fifteen paces square. He unloaded the water and the food and lastly himself, and then waved at the slaves below to winch it down. It left him trapped but he wasn't afraid. Here he was the one with all the power. He was also the one with the knife, and Dae Hyo had spent months making sure he knew how to use it.

Marvan appeared to be asleep. He was lying on his back beneath the linen tent, his eyes closed. Despite the shade, the skin of his face and hands had darkened in the sun to almost the same colour as the mages'. Krish didn't know why he'd come here. He wasn't sure why Marvan was still alive. Once they'd arrived in Mirror Town they could have killed Marvan. He deserved it. But killing was hard when the blood was cold, unless you were Marvan.

'A visit,' Marvan said, his eyes still closed. 'You honour me.'

It was mocking. Nearly everything he said was mocking.

'Maybe I just like the view,' Krish replied and Marvan smiled and rolled up to sit beside him.

Below, the ten thousand mirrors glittered like jewels. 'Turn, turn, turn.' He could hear it faintly even up here as they moved the mirrors in the complex, pre-planned motions that kept their city safe.The sunlight blazed down and was passed between, each movement carefully calculated so that it swept through every window of every house and down every corridor into every corner.

Mirror Town seemed both more orderly and more chaotic from this height. The original seven great mansions of the seven great families spread in a ring around the fragile glass tower at the city's centre. They were curiously bulbous structures that looked more grown than built. But each had been added to and then added to again over the years, no addition the same, none made to be in harmony with each other. In fact, it looked like the exact reverse: that each great house was competing to outdo its neighbours, to build the tallest tower, or the broadest or the most ornamented.

The lesser houses squatted in the shadows of that vast, futile endeavour. And through it all the slaves crawled, doing anything that needed to be done so that the mages could devote all effort to their petty, meaningless competitions with each other.

'Behold the great city of Nkankan-lati-Ohunkohun,' Marvan said. 'I believe that's what they call it – it roughly translates as Something from Nothing. It's claimed that there was nothing but sand here when the mages came and there was a city surrounded by lush fields when they'd finished their magic. Perhaps it's true. They're a clever bunch, though I could wish they were more hospitable.'

The mages kept no prisoners that Krish could see and Olufemi's family had refused to lock Marvan in their house. Krish refused to let him go free, and so here he was.

'What can I do for you today?' Marvan asked after a moment's silence.

Krish shrugged, still looking out over the sprawl of the city, the straight blue line of the sea to the west and the greenery ringing its landward sides.

'You know I can be more use to you down below,' Marvan said. 'If you don't think the Ashane will come for you eventually, even here, you're a fool.'

'King Nayan won't come here. People are afraid of the mages. And it's a long way from Ashanesland. I've seen the maps.'

'And then,' Marvan continued, as if Krish hadn't spoken, 'there are all those new friends you made among the Rah. But I know your enemies. I can help you understand them, which is the first step towards defeating them.'

'I'll never trust you.'

'You can trust my self-interest. As Mirror Town is your last refuge, you're mine.'

'You're staying up here,' Krish insisted. 'You're lucky to be alive.'

'As are you. It seemed unlikely you'd make it out of Rah territory once you had Uin for an enemy. Why *did* you turn him against you? I understand he welcomed you as his god when you first came. That's quite an impressive reversal of feelings.'

'He was a monster,' Krish said. 'He enslaved his son. He . . . he mistreated him.'

'Ah.' Marvan leaned back on his elbows, smiling in satisfaction.

'What?' Krish snapped, and instantly regretted it. The other man took pleasure in baiting him.

'I was thinking,' Marvan said cordially, 'that you must have seen your own father's reflection in him. Of course I mean the goatherd who brought you up, not our King.'

Krish knew his face betrayed him as he said, 'What do you know about that?'

'Quite a lot. But perhaps you don't remember telling me. You weren't very well at the time.'

Krish realised what he meant. When Marvan and his woman had been slowly draining the blood out of his body, he'd tried everything to make them stop. He'd told them everything. His memory of that day was hazy now, but it was possible he'd told Marvan about his da.

'A violent man, this goatherd,' Marvan said. 'Beat you and your mother. Do you know what my father did?'

'Let me guess: he beat you too. You and me are alike really, and we should be friends.'

'My father did nothing. When I was six years old and my brother began to rape me, he did nothing. And when I told him, he said nothing. And so it carried on, for years, until I got strong enough. I killed my brother, but looking back on it, I should have killed my father. I wasn't thinking clearly at the time.'

The mocking tone was still in his voice. It could all have been a lie. It probably was a lie, but Krish thought about Dinesh and realised he believed it.

'Perhaps you wonder why I am what I am,' Marvan continued. 'Maybe you don't care, but I suspect you'd like to know. Perhaps that's your answer.'

'Is it?' Krish was suddenly angry. He didn't want Marvan to use this excuse because he didn't want it for himself. 'I cared for goats, but you know that. You know everything apparently. I studied how they passed down what they were from sire and dam to kids. It always got passed down, one way or another. No kid just came out the way it chose for itself. So your da was a terrible man, from what you say. And your brother too. Then maybe it's just in your blood – bad blood. Maybe if your brother had never touched you, you'd still be this way, exactly as evil as them.'

Marvan's face twisted briefly with rage. Krish's hand went to his belt knife and Marvan saw the movement and bared his teeth in what was almost a smile. 'And what blood have you got?' he asked.

'I've never beaten a woman or a child!'

'No? But then the goatherd wasn't truly your sire, was he? King Nayan didn't try to beat you as a child. He tried to kill you before you could grow to be one. He imprisoned his own wife for seven months. He didn't want any of this spoken about, of course. He wanted the details kept quiet, but servants and soldiers gossip and the shipborn like to listen. He didn't want any doubt that you were dead, that's the rumour the servants spread. He'd given his soldiers instructions, the moment you were born, to dash your head against the wall. After that they were to burn the body. Just to be quite sure.'

Marvan smiled at Krish's expression. 'That's the blood that's in you. And that's the man who's after you. I'm glad you feel so safe here. If I were your father's son, I'd have found a far more distant corner of the world to cower in.'

When the sun was sinking, the air rapidly cooling in a way he wasn't yet used to, he finally found Olufemi. She was in a building the mages called the Graveyard. Not for the dead, he'd been told, but for dead ideas.

There were mirror masters inside. They were inside every house, ceaselessly turning the glass in a pattern they'd long ago memorised. Echoes of sunlight from far above flashed into his eyes and then over the contents of the long, long hall. It shone on a thousand objects in cases, some hanging suspended from the ceiling, some dusty and discarded in corners. And, at the end of the hall, it flashed on Olufemi as she turned her back on him and walked into the next room.

He followed her into it, but she was already gone. There was only one thing there: a huge device hanging seemingly unsupported in space, a collection of cogs and wheels and marks he recognised as runes. The device looked as if it was meant to move but he could see rust on the cogs. Tiny heads poked out and chirped from a nest at its centre.

He followed Olufemi through room after room. The mirror masters in each turned to watch him pass and the light of the setting sun shone red on him through high windows or reflected from the glass. Every room was full, often overfull, wooden carvings piled on metalwork piled on devices that seemed to be made of bone. Half of the things he saw were broken, or he thought they were. It was hard to tell when he hadn't any idea of their purpose.

He found the mage – or maybe cornered her – in one of the deepest rooms. The light had been reflected by half a dozen mirrors to reach it and shone wan on her broad face. She was at the far end, and between them was a chasm in the floor, deep and dark.

'Yron's servants made that,' she said. 'It must have taken them months, years even to claw their way through the stone.'

'But how can they come here? Wherever sunlight has touched is poisoned against them, isn't it? At least for a few weeks. The mirrors—'

'The mirrors require masters, and two failed in their duty here. For months Tosin and Toyin Yejida sat and gamed and drank when they should have been turning. There are many duties you can shirk, but guardianship of the mirrors isn't one. Each of my people must give three years in the twilight of their lives to that service. Tosin and Toyin couldn't be punished, of course. They were the first to be eaten. But the Yejida name died with them. That was more than three hundred years ago, and now no one in all of Mirror Town will claim it. Their mansion lies rotting at the edge of the city; perhaps you've seen it.'

It took him a moment to realise she required an answer. 'I think I walked past it. It's half-eaten by the desert.'

'Eaten. Yes. What do you want, Krishanjit?'

'I came to talk to you about – about the runes. Every time I've asked you about them you've brushed me away. But Marvan thinks—'

'You've been speaking to that killer?'

'At least he *will* speak to me. I've been talking to him, and he says my father will come after me, even here. I want to know if your people's magic is strong enough to protect us against his army.'

'Protect *us*? Protect you, you mean.'

He didn't understand her hostility, though he knew it had been growing through the long slow weeks they'd been here. 'What is this place?' he asked. Not the question he wanted answered, but he thought it might lower the temperature of the conversation.

'The place where we put all the things whose purpose we've forgotten. We're great experimenters, *my people*. We like to discover new things, but we don't always choose to share them. And sometimes we like to explore old things. I did. I chose the runes, which few took even the slightest interest in.'

'Because they didn't work without the moon – without me – in the world?'

'Yes, very good. You *do* listen.'

'Then why did you study them?'

'The runes were neglected, but not abandoned, not entirely. Contemplating them has long been an exercise among my people, a way to still the mind when it's . . . troubled. When I was younger than you, I learned to contemplate them in that way.'

'Because your mind was troubled?' He studied her stern, seamed face, unable to imagine her young and unsure.

She pulled back the sleeves of her robe to bare her wrists to him. Long, pale scars crossed them, very like those he bore on his own thighs: the marks left by a blade. 'Yes, I was troubled. The runes helped me to find peace but when the feelings of – when the feelings had passed I was left with nothing. Only the runes, and the runes were meaningless. And if they meant nothing, what did *I* mean – what had all my suffering been for?

'I couldn't give my life meaning unless I gave the runes

meaning – gave it back to them. We were Mizhara's people once, her priests. But when her battle with Yron swallowed this land, our magic was used to slaughter his people. A terrible slaughter, the worst the world has ever seen. The rest of our people blamed us, though the guilt was everyone's. They drove us from our homes to this distant and lifeless place. We made the desert bloom with our magic and thought that this would suffice, but then Mizhara's guilt drove her to depart the world and our magic went with her. In its absence we made an empty exercise of the runes for ourselves and a pantomime for outsiders, a show we put on to convince them of our power. And so we lived for centuries with a shame we didn't admit in an exile we didn't choose.'

'But you found a way to bring the magic back,' Krish said. 'You brought me back.'

'Yes.' She sat down abruptly on a complex wooden device that had probably been designed for something else. 'Yes. I thought perhaps I could use Mizhara's magic alone, the sun's power that flows through the world as long as she lives, however distant she might be. But the runes remained powerless and I knew that their strength must be in their duality. Without the moon they're nothing, so I chose to call on Yron. Do you know how I did it? I caught a worm man. It wasn't easy; I nearly died in my attempts, but the third time I succeeded. I carved runes into his flesh that I'd taken years to devise and then I burned him and I took the ashes and I mixed them into your mother's food.'

'She didn't know?' Krish asked, horrified.

Olufemi laughed harshly. 'It wasn't a request I could see being well received. But I needed Yron to be born into power. The role he occupied, the position, it was a part of who he was. So I ingratiated myself into King Nayan's court, fed her and waited. And then, of course – well, you know what happened next. Those cursed truthtellers. For years they'd told anything but, and yet they sensed something about you, even when you were no more than a tiny pulse in your mother's womb.

'I thought I'd lost you and so I went to Smiler's Fair and I found another woman with a child in her, an escaped slave.

I had a little of the worm man's ash left with me, and I thought, why not? So I fed her that same meal. I told her it was medicine to save her son from the bliss pills. There's no such medicine, but why would she doubt me? My own lover! My own lover's son!'

Krish wished he could leave. He didn't want to hear this, and yet found himself asking, 'And did it work? Did he come out like me?'

'Oh no. He was something else, a strange thing, but not you. I trained him to be your priest instead, in the hope that it was your continuing presence in the world that prevented his own assumption of Yron's godhood. Do you know the first word he spoke? It was "Yron". His mother was so pleased. She was very beautiful and so easily persuaded. The bliss never really leaves a slave, you know. That's why, among we mages, it's forbidden to lie with them – it's as demeaning as lying with a mindless beast. But I broke that law as I'd broken so many others, and Vordanna believed everything I told her. I did all this and for what? For nothing.'

'It wasn't for nothing. It worked.'

She put her face into her hands. For a long time, the only sound was their breathing and the distant calls of the mirror masters. She looked very old and very weak. If he'd been told that she was dying, it wouldn't have surprised him.

'It didn't work,' she said finally, looking up at him hollow-eyed. 'I thought it had, but that one moment in Smiler's Fair was . . . I don't know. Luck perhaps. I've tried and tried since, with every rune I know, every combination of glyphs. I've searched here for old devices that might help, but none of it has worked. The runes are as dead as they've ever been. And you're – I don't know what you are. Just another failed experiment.'

He sank down opposite her on to a stool carved from ivory and inlaid with silver. It was worth more than any man in his village could have earned in a lifetime, and yet he suddenly wished that he was back there. 'What will we do when they attack?' he asked.

'Mirror Town's defences were all magical. Without magic, there are none. The choice will be yours in the end, Krishanjit. I burned Smiler's Fair for you, and the Rah tore themselves apart in your name. You could bring the same death here, I'm sure. But if you have any kindness in you, then you'll give yourself up when they come. I've ruined so much else in my making of you. I'd prefer—' She wasn't laughing, he realised. She was sobbing. 'Please don't destroy my home too.'

26

Drut was gone, flown off to the coast to collect a cargo for her sisters. Eric had pleaded to be allowed to join her, but she'd told him it wasn't proper. When he'd tried to use his tearful face on her, she'd looked so upset that he'd relented and just kissed her goodbye, then watched her ride off on a sled drawn by wolves, of all things.

It would have been useful to get another look at the docks from which he hoped to sail away, but having her gone was useful too; it gave him the chance to explore the city below, where she was reluctant to tread. Rii told him the place extended for miles and had many exits. Perhaps one might aid in his escape.

He hadn't quite lost his fear of the worm men, but he'd grown used to their soft footsteps padding after him as he explored the buried city. Sometimes he thought they might even be herding him, pushing him towards certain buildings or paths, but he couldn't guess why they wanted him to see those places, or what they hoped he'd find there.

One time they pushed him towards a small building composed of a series of nested round rooms, very cosy. The innermost chamber was covered in paintings of a woman – a Servant who looked a great deal like the Hunter. Who was she and why was she painted there? There was no clue in the room and Eric could hardly ask the worm men.

In another place he found what seemed to be stables, but the stalls were too long and thin for horses and on the floor he saw what seemed to be big, black feathers. He picked one up and found that it was made out of metal. When he ran his fingers down its tines, it played a tune so eerie he dropped it and hurried away.

On the second day of Drut's absence, he discovered the grandest building he'd yet seen. Its door was so high that ten Erics could have stood on each other's shoulders and walked straight through, and when he entered he saw that the floor was paved with intricately moulded silver.

The silver rang beneath his feet as he began to cross the broad expanse of the floor, but he stopped before he was halfway there. At the far end he could see a grand chair and above it a perfect model of the moon. He suddenly felt sure that this was Yron's palace, and as soon as he thought it he began to feel the moon god's power hanging over the place the way the moon hung over his throne. He didn't think Yron had any cause to hurt him, but a dead god couldn't be too pleased with the world. Eric nodded politely to the throne, then turned on his heel and left.

And now, on the third day without Drut, he'd found a long, long passage with plain walls and the drip of water somewhere above, though the stone itself was dry. After he'd walked a little way and found no rooms or doorways off it he would have gone back, but when he turned he saw a cluster of the worm men behind him, and they didn't seem inclined to move. He took a swig of his water and strode on instead.

His legs were aching before he finally saw a glint of light in the distance: the distinctive white glimmer of sun on snow. Suddenly desperate to be out, he sprinted up the rough steps at the corridor's end and into the sweet, cold air of the outside world. When he looked about him he found Salvation nowhere in sight, only the wild peaks and troughs of the snow from horizon to horizon.

It bothered him that he was starting to find this land beautiful. Sometimes, when he tried to imagine Smiler's Fair, he pictured it with snow drifted in its jumbled streets. His childhood memories of the Moon Forest had all the trees rimed with frost.

But that was the point of this, wasn't it? He meant to get out before all he could remember was snow. The boat Rii had arranged was still waiting on the coast. He could hitch a ride on that, if only he could reach it, and this was a pretty good first step. It would get him well away from Salvation without the Servants any the wiser about where he'd gone. He was feeling pretty good about everything, as a matter of fact, with the sun shining, the sky blue and, when he spun round, a big building right behind him that would do very nicely for shelter when he made his escape.

It was a shame the building had no walls, just a peaked roof and pillars at every corner, carved into spirals that foxed the eye if you tried to follow them. Or – no, not carved. When he went right up to the place and got a good look at the dull grey gleam of it he realised it was made out of lead. The metal was icy cold; it snatched a bit of the skin from the tips of his fingers when he made the mistake of touching it.

Apart from the twisty pillars, from the outside the building had seemed pretty plain. Inside, it was a different story. He glanced up casually at the high roof and then stopped for a long time and gawped.

It was painted all over, as fresh and clear as if it had just been done yesterday. It showed a hundred different creatures of a hundred different species all twining round each other. After Eric had spent a while looking, he realised that some of them were shagging and some of them were tearing into each other, in portions of the painting that were red and not so pretty to look at. He saw wolves snarling and cats curled into balls, rats eating and rabbits being eaten and all kinds of other things he couldn't put a name to.

And there was a man's face in the centre of it all. It was a face he'd seen before, carved on the walls of the city below: the moon god Yron. His face was long and thin, hollow-cheeked and very dark. Eric couldn't decide if it was handsome or ugly.

The temple in Smiler's Fair had been painted too, and some of the rooms at Madam Aeronwenn's. And there'd been stalls that sold little drawings to visitors who wanted more to remember the fair by than a case of the clap. It occurred to Eric that the moon would have fit right into his old home: he and the folk of Smiler's Fair seemed to have a similar way of looking at the world.

Even Rii might find a welcome there, if she could just shrink herself down a bit.

When he heard the growl and snapped his head round, it almost seemed like a section of the painting had come to life. But then he smelled the beast's rank breath and heard its growl and knew that it was real.

It was a bear, but bigger than he knew any bear could be, even the great brown bears of the Moon Forest. This one was white, a grubby yellow-white that would have disappeared against the background of snow that was probably its natural home. But here it was, inside this building. Its claws skittered against the metal floor as it paced towards him, and then reared up on its hind legs to roar. It was taller than him. It was taller than any man and that roar had given him much too close a look at its teeth.

He hadn't been afraid at first. It was all too sudden and a little too much like a dream. That roar did it though. His guts clenched and he wanted nothing more than to turn and run, but he couldn't show it his fear. Beasts knew what to do with prey that feared them. He backed away instead, his legs trembling so hard they threatened to tip him on his arse.

The bear's beady black eyes watched him as its front legs settled back down on the ground. It left its mouth hanging half open, ready to bite, as it swung its great hairy body across the ground towards him. Maybe he should run. It didn't look like it could move too fast. He drew a breath, trying to coil up his courage for it.

Then the bear swung closer, he backed away on instinct – and skidded and fell on to the smooth metal floor. The animal roared again, opening its huge arms wide, its black-clawed paws readying a crushing embrace. He tried to crawl away, but his mittened hands could find no purchase on the floor. The bear was right above him, jaws open, teeth bared – and a blot of blood on its throat where an arrow tip poked out of it.

He only moved when the bear started to topple and he realised it was going to fall right on top of him. He crawled just far enough away that only the bear's blood hit him, and sat panting beside the big corpse.

When the archer entered the building, he wasn't entirely surprised to see golden skin. It was only as she came closer to the massive body that he knew precisely which of the Servants it was. The Hunter's face was unmistakable.

'Thank you,' he said hoarsely.

She rested her hand on the dead bear's head, her skin a purer, glowing gold against the yellowish white fur. 'This is a dangerous land for those who do not know it.'

He laughed a little wildly. 'You're telling me!'

'Come then, I need your assistance.'

'Don't look to me like you need anyone's help.'

She drew out a hook-bladed knife from her belt and handed it to him. 'Some tasks are easier alone. Butchery is not one of them.'

'Butchery?'

'There is meat here in a land that is short of it. We shall not waste it.'

He watched, astonished, as she took hold of the bear by one outstretched paw and dragged it over the metal as if it weighed less than a cat. The body left a smear of blood behind it, dark on the floor and then a startling bright red when she reached the snow outside. She carried on for another fifty paces until she seemed satisfied and finally let the corpse drop. After that she drew her own knife, and he guessed it was time to work.

It was a hideously messy business, skinning and gutting and carving up that huge bear. It did give him a little satisfaction, though, to be doing to it what it had meant to do to him. Or so he told himself while he was elbow-deep in its intestines.

The Hunter made a very neat job of it. Stood to reason, he supposed. She wasn't a talkative sort, though, and after a while he felt obliged to fill the silence. 'I used to pray to you, you know,' he said.

She didn't respond but he thought that she tensed.

'All us Moon Forest folk did. But now your sisters, these other

Servants, they say you ain't no god. You ain't nothing but another one of them. Is that true?'

'I am no god,' she confirmed, gutting knife in one hand and the bear's huge, purple heart in the other. She threw the heart on to the pile of jointed meat and got back to work with the knife.

'But you told us you was. Ain't that a touch dishonest?'

That got her attention. She had the liver in her hand now. 'Attend me well, mortal,' she said and he thought for sure he was going to get some kind of stern answer, a warning not to be so cheeky. But all she said was, 'The flesh of the snow bears is good to eat, all but one part of it. The liver is poison, tucked inside the good meat though it is. You must cut all of it out before you feast, or suffer the consequences.'

He wasn't born yesterday. There was a message in that for him, though he wasn't quite sure what it was.

She let him brood on it in silence for a while, starting a fire from kindling she drew from a pack on her back and then setting a haunch of the bear to roast on it. He hadn't thought he'd have any appetite for the thing that had nearly killed him, but the smell of the cooking meat grew increasingly tempting and when she pulled the haunch from the fire, he tucked into it with a will.

She took a little of the meat herself, but only looked at it as it dripped fat on to the snow. 'This is the moon's place,' she said when he was nearly finished.

He looked up at her, hoping his face didn't betray him. 'Mizhara's enemy, you mean.'

'Yes. Yron's servants fear the sun, but lead shields them from it and is poison to my own kind.'

'It was dangerous for you in there? But you walked in easy as you please.'

'I could not have remained long.' She seemed to understand his doubting look and lifted her foot across her knee to show him the heel. It was scorched black all the way through to her skin, which was burnt and blistered where it had touched the metal.

'Thank you,' he said again, realising more of what it had cost her to save him.

'Why have you come here, Eric?' she asked.

It gave him such a shiver to hear her say his name that he almost replied. But he couldn't admit he'd found this place by following a path in the city below, and by the time he'd thought of what he could say, it was too late. His silence had stretched to a guilty length.

'I am not like my sisters,' she said. 'I was born among your kind ten hundred years ago, and I sought them out again when the folk wandered lost over the ice. I led your people to the forest and I have lived among them since. My sisters think they treasure their husbands but they do not understand you.'

'And you do?' It came out sounding halfway between hostile and fearful.

'I know your thoughts.'

It was the worst answer possible, leaving him to wonder just what she did know. 'I can tell you ain't like them,' he said. 'You're talking to me about something that ain't Mizhara.'

Her face, normally impassive, showed some expression then. He couldn't read it, though, and it was quickly gone. 'My sisters spend their bright days thinking of our mistress, but mine are occupied with her brother's legacy.'

'The monsters of the Moon Forest.'

'Not all Yron's servants are monstrous,' she said. 'I knew him in his youth, before he became that which he was. There was much joy in him, more joy than in my mistress. One cannot always know what a person is or will become. One cannot always judge a liver, or a heart, by the body in which it is housed.'

'I don't know nothing about that. I'm just a servant to the Servants, ain't I? The affairs of gods ain't my problem. My job's to service Drut—' He caught himself the moment he said it, but it was too late.

'Drut?' she asked.

He shrugged and made himself meet her eye. 'One of my wives. It only means—'

'I know quite well what it means.' She lapsed into a long silence, her eyes on the distant horizon. Then she sighed and dropped her meat on the snow uneaten. Still warm, it melted the crust of ice and grease and blood spread through it, messing up the whiteness.

'You have no idea of the danger of your path,' she told him, sounding sad rather than angry. 'I had hoped that no person would have to concern themselves with the affairs of gods again, but it was not to be. Yron has returned and the world must face him. I do not wish for this battle. I sought above all to avoid it. But I *will* fight it and I am not accustomed to defeat. Do you understand?'

Drut had never been so far from Salvation. Mizhara had drawn no illustrations in her Perfect Law and therefore there were no paintings in any book the Servants possessed, no pictures of anywhere in the wide, dark world. Drut had imagined the sea, but her imagination had been entirely wrong.

She stood on the icy cliff and watched it hurl itself against the rocks and wondered at the power of it. This was what her goddess possessed: this untameable strength. She'd never imagined that correctly before either. She'd seen it as something orderly and contained, like the Servants' lives in Salvation. But if such a thing as the sea existed in a world over which Mizhara once ruled, then Mizhara must be more powerful and terrifying even than this.

The ships were already docked. Drut saw small figures below, the ovals of their faces turned up to her. She returned to her sled and clicked her tongue at the wolves, urging them to take the winding path down to the shore. Once she might have walked it herself, just for the pleasure of the motion, but her pregnancy had rendered her ungainly. She still found herself startled, on waking, to feel the round bulk of her belly. But then she'd remember that Eric's daughter sheltered inside it and the burden seemed light.

The ships bucked on the waves, struggling to be free. She

watched the men at work unloading the crates, sure-footed on the walkways despite the wild motion. They were wrapped in furs that showed only their eyes, yet she found herself imagining what was beneath, the muscles straining in their arms and legs as they worked. This was what Eric had done to her. She sometimes felt as if her entire life before him had been a hazy dream and he'd woken her to the sharp-edged realities of the world.

Finally, the ship's captain saw her and crossed the deck to greet her. 'Gold?' he asked. His accent was thick and his eyes narrow and caged in wrinkles.

As she handed him the payment crate, she wondered what he saw when he looked at her. She was clad in furs too, but they left her hands and face bare. She felt the cold as the darklanders did, but it couldn't wound her as it had her beloved Eric. Her belly, full with child, was concealed from the captain. She fought the urge to pull back her furs and display it, to show him the new life that was growing inside her.

'There,' he said, when he'd counted and bitten every coin. The crates were piled haphazardly on the dock, far more of them than she'd anticipated. She and her sisters weren't many; she hadn't thought the shipment would be so large and her sled was too small to carry even a tenth of it.

'Do you have—' she asked, but the man had already turned from her. He shouted an order and the sailors swarmed up the beams and ropes of their ships. The lines were freed and the sails raised in a flurry of movement and then the wind was caught and the ships were drawing away, plunging up and over each wave and spraying salt-filled water in their wake.

Drut watched them as they headed for the horizon. She knew nothing of their land of origin, which wasn't a part of the land below where Eric and all the husbands had once made their home. She knew little of that land either, only what the husbands told, and they seldom spoke of the time before they came to Salvation. Even Eric, normally so ready to smile and speak, gave her little when she asked about his years before. Maybe he felt the same way she did: as if the part of his life that mattered had begun when they met. The thought pleased her.

But she would like to know more of the world. She'd like to see more, to know more than the ice of Salvation and the snow of the land on which it sat. If this war came, she knew she would get her wish. One thousand years after their ancestors had departed the darklands, she and her sisters would finally travel south once again.

The crates had been nailed shut. She looked at them, at the profligate use of metal just to secure them. There was no shortage of iron in the other lands, where the worm men never ventured and mining carried no risk of death. She'd brought no tools, so she set her nails into a narrow crack on one side and tore. Mizhara had given her Servants more strength than any darklander.

The swords spilled out onto the wooden dock with a clatter that set the circling seabirds scattering. Their cries echoed from the cliffs, a lonely sound.

Drut bent to the weapons and lifted the nearest. She grasped the leather sheath and pulled the blade free, holding it wavering in her right hand. Her left tested the edge of the blade and blood beaded along her thumb. This was a thing meant to kill. She swung it gently – and then more wildly as she heard the footsteps behind her and spun to face the newcomer.

Her sister smiled and stepped back. It was the one the darklanders called the Hunter, her skin glowing with a golden light that surely couldn't be Mizhara's. She'd allowed herself to be given a name and, even worse, to be worshipped as a god in the lands below. The other Servants called her 'Abomination', but Drut had a name too and she'd broken her oroboros to be with Eric.

'What are you doing here?' Drut asked.

'I came to assist in the transport of the weapons,' the Hunter said. She gestured behind her and Drut saw that the beast Rii was perched at the top of the cliff, a black hill against the blue sky.

'I'm surprised you trust her with this,' Drut said.

'I trust my control of her, as it was I who bound her.'

'But she hurt you when you did.' Drut gestured at the terrible scars on her sister's face.

The Hunter looked startled, moving her hand to touch them as if she'd forgotten they were there. 'Who told you this?'

'When you came, I read my sisters' accounts of you in the library, from when you were still among us. You told them that Rii lashed out when you bound her and gave you those wounds.'

'Indeed,' the Hunter said, calm once again, 'I did tell them that.' She moved to the shattered crate, stooped to find a sword of her own and drew it with far more grace than had Drut. The long steel looked natural in her hands. Drut saw that she was holding it in both and shifted her own grip on the pommel. The weapon immediately felt more comfortable.

'Well-made weapons,' the Hunter said. 'Do you believe they will ever see use?'

'Why else would we buy them?' Drut asked, but she understood her sister's question: the call for war hadn't yet been made, despite the bitter news the Hunter had brought them. 'Such a decision must be debated,' she said. 'It can't be made in haste. We have no choice but to search the Perfect Law for guidance.'

'No choice?' The Hunter frowned, and stepped forward suddenly, swinging the sword in short, strong arcs. She raised a brow and Drut realised she was expected to do the same. Her own movement was less sure, and her feet stumbled as she moved. The uncentred weight of her belly made it more awkward still.

'Thus,' the Hunter said, and showed her again.

'We are the Servants of Mizhara,' Drut said, repeating the motion.

'So we are.' Now her sister was demonstrating a more complex attack. It felt right to imitate her, the two of them moving together almost like the dance that Eric had secretly taught her to do with him.

'We are the Servants of Mizhara,' the Hunter said as she led their motions. 'Mizhara's enemy has returned to this world, and yet we do nothing.'

'Seeking the right path isn't doing nothing.'

'Spending days and weeks and months poring over the pages of books whose words you already know is worse than nothing. The Perfect Law will not tell my sisters how to act, because Mizhara did not know that Yron would return. But Mizhara spoke of the evil he brought to the world and her duty – and ours, as her Servants – to protect against it. My sisters believe that Mizhara would have counselled caution but she was far fiercer than they think. They buy weapons for a battle they will never find the resolve to fight, and in the meantime it is my hawks who are left to shoulder the burden that should be ours.'

Her hawks. Her darklanders, the ones she'd guided to their new lands and in return accepted worship from. Drut dropped her sword to the wooden dock.

The Hunter sheathed her own but kept it in her hand. 'My hawks call me Bachur.'

'Names are forbidden,' Drut said stiffly.

'You are mistaken. Our sisters have forgotten that once we all had names given us by Mizhara. One of our sisters, long ago, decided that to take on our mistress's task ourselves would be sacrilege, but I do not think it so.'

Bachur had known Mizhara. It was a shocking thought. The Hunter had breathed the same air as their goddess, heard her speak, knew how her voice had sounded. 'But Mizhara left us long before I was born,' Drut said. 'She left us the Perfect Law and it's all we have to guide us.'

'And yet,' the Hunter said, 'you have also taken a name.'

Drut felt her face move against her will, her expression betraying her. This was another way in which Eric had changed her, an unwanted one. She could no longer shield her thoughts from the world. 'It's not a name,' she said. 'Drut means "beloved" in my husband's tongue.'

'*Your* husband? But Bachur means merely "eldest". We are the same in this: others have chosen to name us and we have accepted it. The difference is, my name came from a goddess and yours from a man.'

'Eric meant nothing bad by it.'

'I have met and spoken to your husband. A strong heart beats in him, for all that he still looks little more than a boy. He is one of my nation, did he tell you that? Had events and human hearts shifted differently, he might have been born with the hawk mark on him, and you would never have met.'

The thought pained Drut more than she would have thought possible. 'Eric is where he was meant to be,' she said heatedly.

The Hunter said nothing, only turned to Rii, crouching on the cliffs, and clicked her fingers to summon her. The beast flew down, wafting a rank, spicy smell ahead of her.

'Come,' the Hunter said. 'We must bring our sisters the weapons they fear to use. Perhaps when they see the steel they will remember that they too were once made for a purpose.'

It was difficult work, loading the crates on to the beast, and the Hunter made no allowance for Drut's pregnancy. Rii assisted, grasping the wood of the crates with her long, sharp claws. The sight of them made Drut think of the scars on Bachur's face and she looked away from the beast's small, half-blind eyes towards the Hunter. White flecks of snow had settled in her sister's golden hair and lashes. She shone in the sunlight, far brighter than any of the other Servants. Drut felt dull and weak by comparison.

'Eric is very handsome,' Bachur said. 'He is very charming and he is very dangerous.'

'Dangerous?' Drut paused in her loading to stare in astonishment at her sister. Of all the things she might have expected her to say – that Drut was betraying Mizhara, that she must cease her secret trysts with her husband, that she would feel differently when the child was born – this was the very last.

'What do you know of him?' the Hunter asked. 'Of who he was before he came to you?'

'It doesn't matter – our husbands are reborn here. We never ask them about the time before.'

'Perhaps you should.' Bachur rested her hand against Rii's flank, her fingers curled in the grubby fur. 'They change us, these darklanders. My hawks have altered me in ways that I never intended. But this Eric *means* to change you; I have seen his intent in his eyes and its result in your face. Be very sure, my sister, that you know what he wishes you to become.'

When Drut returned to Salvation, she should have taken her place in the sun-pear orchards, helping to tend the trees. But there were many things she should have done these last few months and hadn't, and many more she shouldn't have done and had. She sat cross-legged on the floor of her room, facing the sun symbol on its wall, and prayed.

No answer came to her, perhaps because she wasn't sure what question she was asking. Did she want to be forgiven or permitted? She feared it was the latter and that could never be. Mizhara told those who broke her laws not to regret but to make amends. And if that couldn't be done . . .

After long hours when the only voice within her head was her own, she sought out Eric. He was wandering the outer reaches of Salvation as he often did. Though she'd once believed it was due to restlessness because of her absence, now she doubted that.

'Hello, lovely,' he said when he saw her.

He was smiling in a way that made it look like there were too many teeth in his mouth. She'd meant to approach the subject gradually, but she found herself blurting, 'Eric, where are you from?'

She wasn't sure if his expression showed alarm or surprise. 'The Moon Forest – I told you that before.'

'But you told me nothing *about* the Moon Forest. Nothing about your family.'

'There ain't nothing to say – they weren't no different from anyone else.'

Yet she knew he found the Servants' denial of difference strange. She was suddenly sure he didn't mean what he was saying. And then she knew what question to ask him. It was the question she should have asked long ago. 'Then why did you come to Salvation?'

'What do you mean?' He reached out for her as if he meant to take her in his arms, but she stepped away from him.

'Why did you choose to come here? To leave your family and your home behind?'

'Well, it was an honour to be asked, weren't it? Being a husband to you lot's about the highest honour there is.'

He was lying. She regretted that she'd come to know him well enough to see it. He'd tried to run away from Salvation and his life here. They'd never discussed it but she knew why he'd walked out into the snow and nearly died. So how could what he said be true? And if it wasn't, what did it mean? What did his attentions to her mean? A horrible coldness took hold of her as she remembered that he'd only confessed his love to her after his attempt to escape failed. He hadn't been able to get away on his own; had he thought he could persuade her to help him?

'Tell me the truth,' she begged him.

'That is the truth or Eric ain't my name. What's come over you today, Drut? I know a woman sometimes gets to feeling moody with a baby inside her. It's all right – you know I love you.'

But she didn't know it. She didn't know it at all, and so she turned her back on him and walked away.

She returned to her cell, where prayer seemed more impossible than ever. In front of her, blocking her imagine of divine Mizhara, stood Eric and all the things she'd done for his sake. When she'd believed he loved her, she'd justified them all. But even if he *had* loved her, they wouldn't have been justifiable. And now that she feared he didn't, they appeared as abhorrent as they'd always been. She was abhorrent and her continued existence unbearable.

If you have fallen into irredeemable error . . . She knew what her sisters would say; what the sister who might also be her mother had said. She must take the long walk into the ice from which there would be no return. It would kill the child inside her too, and that was unforgiveable, but she couldn't bring herself to care. If Eric didn't love her, *because* Eric didn't love her, there was only one path left open to her.

27

Cwen had grown used to this feeling, the morning before a battle. It was a little like the feeling she'd known as the Hunt prepared to track down its prey. Back then, what seemed years ago but was really only months, her gut had churned with the fear of what might happen: the prey escaped, a hawk hurt. These days it was heavy with the knowledge of what *would* happen. Hawks would die – the only question was how many. On this day, with this battle, she knew it would be hundreds.

She looked over her shoulder, expecting to see Wingard and Wine, and saw Hilda instead. She'd sent the twins to captain other wings of the attack. It wasn't a natural way for a hawk to think – commanders and soldiers, orders of battle – but she'd had to learn it, or see even more of her people die.

Some way behind her a big horse stood uneasily, Sang Ki on its back. The shiplord had a good head for tactics and she trusted him to command the battle if she fell. He watched her intently, waiting for the signal that it was all to begin.

The terrain here favoured her tactics. The tangled, browning grass, the scattered rocks that ranged from mammoth- to hand-sized, the low, bent trees: it was all good cover for a force that planned a sneak attack. The colours were dustier than those of the forest, but the greens and browns the hawks wore to hide them among the trees would serve well enough here.

She missed the trees, though. She wasn't used to so much sky. It stretched from horizon to horizon looking as dusty as the plants. It made her feel watched, though she didn't think the Brotherband knew they were coming.

There'd been no spies and no scouts captured from their enemy in the last day. She couldn't see many of the warriors now, even from her position so close to their encampment; just a few guards and no visible pickets. Maybe they thought no force would be strong or bold enough to attack them. That seemed like their kind of arrogance.

They'd certainly made no effort to defend their camp or disguise it. It sat to one side of a sluggish river, an untidy jumble of tents and other lumpy shapes that were hard to make out at this distance. Probably men sleeping on ground trampled to mud by the thousands of warriors who'd spent more than a week stopped here, for a reason Cwen had yet to fathom. The force they seemed to be following was only one valley over and was far weaker than they were. And yet they hadn't attacked. She wished she knew why.

But there was no easy way to find out and nothing to be gained by continuing to watch. Besides, with so many living off such barren land, the forage was nearly all gone. Cwen had to attack now, or her people would starve.

She took one last look back at her own force, ranged behind her in untidy ranks. The archers stood forward, arrows in the ground before them like the spines of a hedgehog. There, at least, they bettered the Brotherband. The tribesmen didn't favour the longbow and their range was far lower than the hawks'. The signalman was behind her, different flags in hand. That was something else Sang Ki had worked out, a way to communicate between their forces. He said that he'd read it in a history book. She nodded, and the blue flag was raised: bowmen attack.

Her people knew their business. They waited a count of three, until the signal had time to pass all round the perimeter. Then they all reached forward to grasp their first arrow, the yew bent and the arrows flew.

She watched the lethal arc of them. The distance was great but not too great for the longbow. The arrows fell where they were intended – into the heart of the camp – and as they fell another flight was loosed, and then another.

She had her own spears ready and loosened her knife in its

sheath. Her back prickled with sweat and every muscle in her body was taut, waiting for the Brotherband to scream in pain and rouse themselves, and then scream in anger and charge.

But the charge never came. There were a few screams, more groans. She could see the distant silhouettes of men rising, spilling out of tents. But no counter-attack came and her people kept bending their bows and the Brotherband kept dying.

It was a trap or a trick; it had to be. But what kind of idiot wasted so many lives on a ruse? Her people must have loosed a thousand arrows, ten thousand. There could hardly be a man left unharmed in the Brotherband camp.

She let the lethal wooden rain continue all the same, until it began to thin and she knew her people were running out of arrows. She gestured to her signalman and the green and yellow flag was raised: stop.

It wasn't silent afterwards. There was a murmur among her own people, getting slowly louder, and moans of pain from the camp they surrounded. She strode forward, but Hilda mumbled a protest round her mutilated tongue and Cwen gestured for her clutch to follow as a guard. She'd had to grow used to treating her own life as if it was more valuable than other people's.

When she was at the outskirts of the Brotherband camp, she saw another group approaching. The grossly fat form at its centre was easy to recognise and she paused, waiting for him to join her.

'Not quite the way I expected this day's events to unfold,' Sang Ki said when he huffed to a stop beside her.

'It isn't over yet,' she warned him. Her muscles were twitchy with unease and she could see that her hawks felt it too. Their eyes darted around and their weapons shifted, pointing first one way, then another.

'Well,' the Ashaneman said, 'onward?'

The first corpse was at the borders of the camp. There were three arrows in him, two in his legs and the one in his chest that must have killed him. The ground beyond was thick with the shafts of more arrows – and another half-dozen bodies. Not one of them had a weapon in hand.

A few more paces in they found their first survivor. He'd taken an arrow in the shoulder; it quivered with every laboured breath as he sat on the ground and wept. When she stopped in front of him, his eyes crawled up her body to her face, as if they found the journey wearying.

There didn't seem to be anything worth saying, so she took her knife and slit his throat. She wasn't sure these men deserved the mercy but she'd have done the same for any animal, no matter how savage.

The whole camp looked like that: full of corpses and living people waiting for her to turn them into corpses. She carried out the task grimly and after a while her hawks gave up their guard duty to sweep through the camp and do the same. Only Sang Ki stayed beside her, forehead wrinkled above his clever eyes. He didn't say anything. What was there to say? The only people who might have answered her questions were dead or dying.

After a while, though, she realised that some of the Brotherband weren't injured at all. She knelt beside one warrior who sat cross-legged between the corpses of two other tribesmen. He seemed indifferent to the flies gathering to lay their eggs inside his dead brothers.

There was a knife in his hand. He was using it to score long, bleeding lines in his own palm.

'You,' she said and he looked up, blinking incuriously. 'Why didn't you fight? Why didn't you fucking fight?'

He looked back down again, cutting another oozing wound in his own flesh. 'It's hopeless. It's all hopeless. I'm nothing. Just a failed experiment.' He lifted the knife and ran it across his own throat, drawing a thin red line that gaped like a second mouth to spew blood all over her.

Cwen scrambled back, horrified.

'Let's get out of here,' Sang Ki said. 'The battle's won.'

'Won?' she asked incredulously.

He sighed, eyes scanning the carnage. 'Well, over at least.'

*

'Poison?' Sang Ki said that afternoon, to the burnt woman.

She watched him pace her tent, ten strides one way and ten another. He wasn't sure why he'd given her a home so big, second in size only to his mother's. He was even less sure why he'd come to speak to her. He would far rather have lain down, perhaps with a mug of sorghum tea to soothe his agonised back. But if he took the drug for the pain once, he would take it for ever. Far better not to begin.

'It doesn't sound like poison,' she said. He thought her face was now as healed as it would ever be, and still hideous. The skin had frozen as it had melted, in red rivulets and deep fissures. Her eyebrows were gone and half her hair, never to grow back. The burns extended over most of her body, and the pain was clearly still with her. He'd thought once she was healed it would be easier to see who she truly was, but the fire had transformed her into a new person, nothing like either of the two women she might have been before.

'And how would you know what poison does?' he asked. Nethmi's father had died of snake venom, an 'accident' arranged by his own brother Puneet, if the rumours were to believed. There was a good reason *Nethmi* might have made a study of the subject.

'The Queen's Men sold poisons,' she said. 'If you knew the right people to ask. I heard of some that drove men crazy – made them kill, or think they could fly. Thora of the Drovers threw herself out of a window after she drank a tea Su Bin gave her. She'd slept with Su Bin's husband, right? She was smiling as she jumped. Everyone in the Drovers was talking about it for weeks.'

This was the way it was. Every question he asked, she had an answer. And her replies were growing more elaborate the longer they travelled together. It might have been that her memory was clearing as her wounds healed. Or it might have been all the time she'd spent with the other survivors of Smiler's Fair on their journey. Their travels into the Moon Forest had brought them close enough to Eom lands for Min Soo to leave his patient behind with a last few stern words to Sang Ki about her care. Since then, and despite his mother's frown, he'd left her free to wander and speak with whom she chose. Soon enough that freedom would end – her pregnancy was very obvious now: a ripe bulge of her belly.

'But you didn't use poisons yourself,' he said. 'It could be one you haven't heard of.'

'If it is,' she said, 'who poisoned them?'

'An army must drink. A few droplets in the waterskins or wells . . .'

She shook her head. 'An army knows its food and water is its life. Any good general sets guards on his supplies.'

And there she went again. Nethmi had travelled with her father's forces in her youth. She would know such things. But there was no point pressing the issue. On some earlier occasion, she'd claimed her mother was a camp-follower of that same army, making her a whore's daughter rather than the commander's, but in a position to imbibe the same knowledge.

'If it wasn't poison, what was it?'

'Maybe they realised the evil of their ways. Does it matter why they're dead?'

'I would prefer to understand what overthrew them so that my own forces don't, at some future point, suffer the same fate. There are too many mysteries here: the fate of the Brotherband, the monsters of the Moon Forest. Did you hear what the smith Alfreda said? Someone has begun to armour them, but who would do such a thing? Who could?'

'The Brotherband.'

'Had never been in the forest before their attack.'

'Other enemies of the Moon Forest folk, then – their problem, not yours. Your battle is over. You don't need to stay. You've won – you can go back to Ashanesland and bring the news to the King.' She looked down at her hands and added quietly, 'We can go back.'

Go back for the birth, and then her death. He found it hard to imagine now, the moment when he would hang her. He made himself think of his father's body, so still on the floor, his neck bruised and his eyes a network of broken veins.

'I suppose you're right,' he said. 'Krishanjit's force is defeated, and of the boy himself there is no sign. Those are both things our king should be informed of and I can hardly quarter the entire plains in search of the errant heir.'

'But it's still a victory you're carrying back. That's good, isn't it?'

She was right. She *was* right. The sight of the despairing Brotherband dead had not been one that was easy to celebrate, but a true pitched battle would have left much the same carnage in its wake, and far more of it on their side. There was every reason to be joyful, and yet his heart wasn't as glad as he told it to be. His life in Winter's Hammer had been so confined. He'd seldom been anywhere but his room or the library. It was hard to imagine returning to it.

'It *is* good,' he said firmly.

But it wasn't, it seemed, entirely over. The hawk who came into the tent was panting and exasperated. 'Oh there you are,' he said, with the utter lack of courtesy they all seemed to have learned from Cwen.

'Indeed,' Sang Ki said.

'You're wanted,' the hawk said, adding a snapped, 'Now!' when Sang Ki didn't move.

'Perhaps you'd care to explain what I'm wanted for, and by whom?'

'By Cwen. There's a visitor you both need to talk to. Come on!'

Sang Ki sighed, bowed ironically to the burnt woman and left the tent.

The man led him through the Ashane enclosure to the centre of the hawks' own section – where Sang Ki paused to study the three huge, splay-legged lizards cropping the grass outside Cwen's dun-coloured tent. Their visitors were Rah.

There were four of them inside the tent, all men of middle years with proud but strained faces. One of them rose as Sang Ki entered. 'You are the Ashaneman?' he asked a little doubtfully.

'I am Sang Ki, the son and heir of Thilak of Winter's Hammer, may he find good rest.'

'Just tell him,' Cwen said, with her usual abruptness. 'You need to hear this, Sang Ki.'

'And you are, sir?'

'Rah Uin. I have information for you – about Krishanjit.' His voice, which had been smooth and strong, now hissed venomously on the name.

'You know him?' Sang Ki asked.

'He was a guest in my home, before he betrayed me and all my people.'

'He's in Rah lands now?'

'He *was* in Rah lands. Fled like the coward he is, after setting a blaze among the coinless scum who were ready to listen.'

Sang Ki sank into the one free chair, disappointed. It creaked beneath his weight and he felt all the Rah men's eyes on him, marvelling at his bulk. There might come a day when such a gaze left him wholly untroubled.

'You look like a moose that shat a thistle,' Cwen said to him. 'Don't despair just yet: there's more. Finish your tale, Uin – the end's better than the beginning.'

'Krishanjit left by sea, that much I know. And I passed on the news of his presence before he fled.'

'Passed it on?'

'King Nayan has an agreement with the Four Together.'

'I'd heard that was the case.'

'He won't push the boundaries of his land beyond Winter's Hammer and they allow him to keep a few carrion riders on the plains to carry any news back he needs to hear.'

'You've told him that his errant son is – or rather was – here?'

Uin nodded sharply. 'I told him, and your King Nayan sent news back. He was mustering anyway, once he knew Krishanjit lived. Now he's bringing his army through the Blade Pass. It must be halfway across the plains by now.'

Alfreda's wagon was on the edge of the encampment. Cwen seemed to understand why she preferred it there, though she'd ordered some of her hawks to stand guard. Alfreda hadn't learned their names and seldom looked at their faces. They changed most days and none of them tried to speak to her. She thought Cwen might have had orders for them about that too.

The hawk leader came to spend time with her when she could, though not since the battle with the Brotherband that hadn't been a battle and then the visit from the strangers that had set the whole camp frothing like a river in spate. But despite the upheaval, Alfreda's meal had arrived at noon as usual, the same good supplies the armies' leaders ate.

Cwen took care of her. Cwen needed her weapon, so of course she wanted Alfreda well, but it still felt so strange. No one had cared for her since her parents died of the carrion fever. Taking care was *her* job. It was up to her to protect Algar, and feed him and keep him happy. But Algar was dead. The thought struck her, each of the hundred times a day she thought it, with the same piercing pain.

But there was Cwen to worry about now. Alfreda had come to feel she owed the other woman some words. She owed her thanks if nothing more. Yet each time she tried to speak them, they stuck in her throat like a fishbone. What if it offended Cwen to be thanked for what she saw as a duty? What if Alfreda's silence was what the hawk valued in her?

And then there was Jinn. The boy was walking towards her now, through the crowded camp. Usually he had a smile for those he passed and the hawks often stopped to ruffle his hair, but today he dodged their reaching hands with a stony expression on his face.

It was soon clear he was making for her and she stepped away from her forge to meet him. The notched swords could wait.

She tilted her head when he reached her, which he'd learned to take as a question.

'It's my mamma,' he said. 'I can't find her.'

She pointed at the sun and he added, 'All afternoon. I know it ain't long, but we were meant to go draw water together. There's soldiers here don't respect a woman.'

Alfreda knew that was true: the rapists weren't confined to the Brotherband. Two Ashanemen had even tried to force themselves on her. One she'd driven from the army with a broken arm and shattered nose. The other Cwen had hanged. But Vordanna was far less able to defend herself.

'I can't go to the Ashane camp,' Jinn said. 'They remember the words I spoke against their king. I've tried before and they won't let me pass.'

She nodded and pointed to her own chest. No one tried to stop her going where she chose.

He smiled for the first time. 'Thanks, Freda. I'll see you back here, shall I?'

The Ashanemen and the remnants of Smiler's Fair were by far the smallest element of their force, but she took her time about the search. People shouted when she thrust her head inside their wagons and tents but most stopped when they saw who she was. Cwen had told everyone whose weapon had brought them victory at Aethelgas and Ivarholme.

She saw people fucking, haggling, sleeping and eating, but she didn't see Vordanna anywhere. By the end her guts felt knotted. Her footsteps dragged as she walked back to Jinn. She was afraid to let him know what she hadn't found. She kept imagining his face, his tears.

But when she approached her wagon, the boy wasn't looking at her. His gaze was fixed on the small party leaving the camp nearby. It was the Rah, mounted on their ugly lizards. The leader was the one Jinn was watching. Alfreda looked at him too, back at Jinn, and then back at the Rah man again. He was only a few feet away and his face turned to them as he passed. She could see it all, every feature.

Jinn couldn't seem to tear his eyes away from the Rah man, but she didn't think he understood. She did, though. Jinn had told her his history and his mother's over all the weeks when he'd chattered on and she'd listened.

The Rah man frowned as he caught Jinn's stare, before turning his attention back to his mount. He clicked his tongue and the little party moved forward, swiftly drawing away on the bow-legged but fast-moving lizards.

'I know him,' Jinn said. 'But I ain't ever met him before.' His face was so innocent, very unlike Algar's when he'd been a boy. Her brother had always had a mischief in him, but Jinn was often so solemn.

'What is it?' he asked, staring at her. His voice was trembling.

She had to clear her throat twice before she could speak and her voice, when it did come out, was little more than a whisper. 'That man was your father,' she said.

28

Krish looked like a child when he slept, the lizard monkey curled in his arms like a child's toy. Dae Hyo sat on the bench opposite his bed and thought. When the thinking got too hard, he took a swig from his flask of fine Ashane brandy, which he'd always found greased the process. It didn't help much this time, though.

His brother was unhappy, that much he knew. He hadn't emerged from his room for three days, only sent the slave Dinesh to fetch his meals for him. The first morning, Dae Hyo hadn't noticed. Mirror Town was no Smiler's Fair, but the mages seemed to know how to enjoy themselves. There was a place near the centre of the town that served wine and didn't even charge for it. One of the customers, a man who spoke the tribes' language, had told Dae Hyo that the woman who ran it was experimenting with different mixes of grape – she and some mage of another house were competing to see whose vintage was best. It all tasted the same to Dae Hyo and all the better for being free. He'd spent a day there happily clouding his mind and a night without dreams after it.

The second day he'd continued his exploration of the city. The place made him itchy: strange buildings and stranger people and the sun shining like it meant to beat them all down into the sand. And the walks among the complex, sprawling buildings, the dusty fields and the crumbling monuments had left his throat so dry that afterwards there'd been little choice but to return to the inn that wasn't and drink more free wine.

Today, though, he'd gone straight to Krish's room. And here was his brother, sleeping, near midday. A square of light passed over him, the work of a mirror master outside his glassless window, and when it crossed his delicate eyelids he twitched but didn't wake.

Dae Hyo went to Krish and shook his shoulder, once softly and twice hard. That didn't work and so he took the glass of water from the table beside his bed and upended it over his head. When Krish had finished spluttering, he glared from beneath soaking hair. He'd cut it short again while he was in Rah lands and it barely curled on to his brow above his strange silver eyes.

'What's wrong?' Dae Hyo asked.

'You just woke me up by pouring water over me!'

'It's midday, brother, and we need to talk.'

'About what?'

'About what's wrong with you.'

Dae Hyo's calm seemed to defeat Krish's anger. He slumped back on to the bed, suddenly looking on the verge of tears.

'Has something happened?' Dae Hyo asked.

'I spoke to Olufemi. She told me . . . I spoke to Marvan too. He says my father will come for me, even here.'

'So? That rat-fucker knows nothing.'

'He knows my father – he's met him. And Olufemi says the runes don't work and the mages won't fight. If my father comes, she thinks I should surrender to him.'

'He'd kill you, brother!'

Krish shrugged, rolling on the bed until his back was to Dae Hyo. The lizard monkey chittered, clinging to his chest. 'Maybe that would be best for everyone.'

'It wouldn't be best for me,' Dae Hyo said fiercely.

Krish rolled back to look at him and then sat up, arms hugging his knees. 'But it's hopeless. The runes don't work, Olufemi says, and magic was the only defence this place had.'

'Then we'll fight.'

'Just you and me?' Krish asked, smiling a little.

'A cornered animal will fight for its territory. I tell you what, the mages will put down their games and take up arms if there's battle on their doorstep.' He frowned, less certain than he pretended. They hadn't struck him as a martial bunch.

'They won't,' Krish said with certainty. 'It's like Olufemi said, I'm nothing to them. They'd kill me themselves and hand me over.'

Dae Hyo didn't have a quick reply to that. It seemed all too likely Krish was right.

His brother lay back down on the bed. 'It's hopeless,' he said again, and refused to say anything else.

Outside, Mirror Town continued with its business, indifferent to his brother's worries. Dae Hyo wandered the streets, looking at the mages the way a general might look at his troops. His conclusions weren't encouraging.

These people had a city ancient and strong. It should have been beautiful but instead it was ugly and ill-arranged, because they couldn't leave it alone. On every street, mansions were being torn down and built back up again, and only so they could be made to outdo their neighbours. Dae Hyo moved between two houses and into the shadow of the spires on each, both teetering a hundred paces high and growing as slaves crawled up their precarious sides. The mages of each family looked on frowning as this pointless competition between them progressed.

Most streets were lined with tables where pairs of mages sat hunched over circular boards for hours on end, moving the many different pieces of the game they called Night and Day. Even children no taller than his chest chalked the outline of a board on to the pavement and mimicked their elders with rough stones in place of the intricately carved playing pieces.

There were larger boards at nearly every crossroads, paces wide and paces high, shaped like a stepped mountain with a fort on top. Some were so large the mages used slaves in place of counters, snapping their fingers to move them from square to square. Olufemi had told him these were a part of the great tournament between houses, which never ended and never had a victor, only a temporary leader, a position the mages fought over as fiercely as starving wolves over a rabbit.

Life was a game to these people, more serious than any work. And everywhere on every building were the mirrors, shedding light on it all. The mages seemed able to ignore their own multiplied reflections, but Dae Hyo felt stalked by his, staring around him in disapproval.

Krish hadn't been quite as far wrong as Dae Hyo had hoped. The mages liked to win, that was certain, but only at games where all they risked was their pride. He didn't like to think how those soft, unworking men would deal with the higher stakes of battle.

After a while, though, it occurred to him that the crowd weren't all mages. In fact, barely a tenth of them were. They were hugely outnumbered by their slaves.

The slaves worked as they were told, and the bliss made them love it, but they weren't *loyal*, not in the way a brother or even an Ashane servant must be. Or they were loyal, but only to whoever gave them the drug. And there were a whole lot of them: an army in waiting.

Dae Hyo stood in the centre of the street, people streaming by on either side, and smiled.

The next day he got up, poured himself a brandy to get him going and went to the big dining hall where Olufemi's family started their day.

Breakfast was some strange concoction he couldn't imagine he'd ever grow to love: a fruit with the texture of bread mixed with a meat so sweet it must have been cooked in honey. Four generations of the family sat round the table digging into it and barely spared Dae Hyo a glance. He took his own portion of food and watched as the household slaves trooped in.

They marched in a line past the windows, dark then light then dark again as the broad streaks of sun crossed over them. There were near a hundred, crowding out one end of the room. Usually their faces were so blankly happy it was hard to notice them, but at this time of day, and again in the evening, there was an intentness about them. The mages sensed it too, he could tell. Mostly they ignored the slaves unless it was to give an order, but quite a few turned to watch as the oldest woman at the table hobbled towards the silent crowd.

They knew, though Dae Hyo doubted they ever admitted it to themselves – they knew these people weren't truly theirs. And so they half-watched, little flicks of their eyes, as the old woman handed out the red pills one by one. The slaves knelt down, mouths open to receive the substance that enslaved them.

'Where do you keep it?' he asked, when the old woman was halfway down the line.

A number of glances snapped his way and he cursed his own mouth. Perhaps that half bottle of brandy should have waited until after he'd had this conversation.

'Where do we keep what?' Olufemi asked.

'The bliss,' Dae Hyo said, unable to think of a convenient lie.

She eyed him assessingly, then said, 'Stick with the drink, tribesman. It will kill you sooner but harm you less.'

He let himself look guilty. 'I'm not that much of a fool,' he protested half-heartedly.

Her look suggested she thought he was precisely that much of a fool. 'It isn't kept in the mansion. So there's no need to tear the place apart looking for it.'

'We leave bliss to the Chukwus,' said a young man at the far end of the table. Olufemi glared at him and his throat bobbed as he swallowed.

'The Chukwus?' Dae Hyo asked.

'They discovered it,' the young man said.

'So they claim,' another relative drawled. 'You know the Chukwus. They'd claim they invented breathing if they thought they'd be believed.'

'But they've often excelled at botany,' a chubby cousin said. 'And they're too idle to lift their own hands if they can find someone else to do it for them. I believe they might have invented bliss.'

And so the conversation went on. He'd noticed how much the mages enjoyed arguing, though they liked to pretend they didn't truly care. Dae Hyo really *didn't* care. He'd heard what he needed. He waited long enough for Olufemi's suspicious gaze to slip away from him and then rose from the table and left.

The Chukwu mansion was near the centre of Mirror Town. He'd passed it a hundred times and never spared much time to look at it, but now he settled down on a low stone bench opposite and observed.

It was bigger than the Etzes' place, and growing. The breakfast conversation had also revealed that a member of the Chukwu family had invented glass-stone. A whole wing of the house was made out of the translucent green material, like frozen seawater.

Around that wing of the mansion lay heaps of crumbled orange debris. Dae Hyo realised they must have been slave huts, demolished to make room for the expanding house. More were being knocked down as he watched, with the slaves themselves carrying out the work. Of course they were; slaves did all the work in Mirror Town. He wondered if it was the huts' inhabitants who were being used to demolish them. It seemed like the kind of cruelty that wouldn't bother the mages.

The sun sank and reddened and his head had almost nodded into sleep when the group of slaves emerged, a good fifty of them with only a couple of mages to look after them. There was something about the way they moved, the easy routine of it, the bored expressions on the mages' faces. And there was something about the way so many of the slaves on the street turned and watched.

He soon realised that five of the slaves had been set as guards. Their eyes scanned the crowds, as alert as they could be when they were hazed with bliss. Their gaze stopped on any slave who seemed to be taking too much interest – and on Dae Hyo when they caught him watching.

But he wasn't a slave of Mirror Town. He'd tracked deer on the plains and wolves in the mountains. He could follow fifty men through a crowded city.

He took back ways, parallel to their course but mostly hidden from it. They weren't bothering to disguise their direction. If it had been him, he would have weaved through the streets, left, right, up, down, anything to throw off observers. He would have taken a different route every time.

But then, he wouldn't have used slaves to fetch and carry the stuff that enslaved them. He wasn't sure what annoyed him more: that the mages were so confident of their power, or that the slaves had proven them right.

He followed them all the way to the edge of Mirror Town. There he thought he might have a problem, but they led him through a tall field of corn, its swollen heads ripe with a crop not yet picked, and it couldn't have been easier to hide between the stalks. They carried on through that field and into an orchard, where green oranges waited for the sun to turn them the right colour. After that it was apples and then a fruit Dae Hyo had never seen, plump and pink.

When they reached their destination, he waited a while, just to be sure. Then he headed back to Mirror Town and the inn with the free wine. He felt like celebrating.

The next day, Krish finally left his room. Dae Hyo took that as a good sign. He found his brother in the central square, beneath the pillar where that murderer Marvan was trapped. That was less good, but he didn't let it discourage him. He'd give Krish something better to think about.

'I've found it,' he said, walking towards him with the dust swirling at his feet.

Krish looked at him, incurious.

'The bliss,' Dae Hyo explained. 'I've found where they hide it. Well, to be fair, it's barely hidden: a house made of glass-stone out by the pinkfruit orchard. There's a key the Chukwus keep to themselves, but that's a small matter. The important thing is that we know where it is.'

Krish shifted his eyes back to the tall pillar. Far above, the brown oval of Marvan's face looked down. 'Important?' he asked.

'Of course, brother. There are ten, twenty times as many slaves here as mages. What does it matter if the masters won't fight if the slaves will? If you've got your bliss, you've got your army.'

He had Krish's full attention now, but Krish wasn't smiling.

'I tell you what,' Dae Hyo said, 'this is happy news. You could try looking happy about it.'

'Dinesh,' Krish said, still looking at Dae Hyo.

The slave was close by, as he often was. He drifted forward with that vacant smile that frequently made Dae Hyo think about hitting him, until he remembered how defenceless the slave was and felt ashamed.

Still, he wasn't expecting Krish to say, 'Punch him,' to Dinesh.

Dinesh stared at Krish, puzzled.

'Punch Dae Hyo,' Krish said again. 'I command it.'

But Dinesh still didn't move.

'Do it!' Krish snapped and finally the slave's arm moved, a feeble slap like a man swatting a fly he secretly hoped would escape him. Dae Hyo barely felt it. It was Dinesh who looked as if he was in pain.

'You did well,' Krish said to the boy. 'That's enough. You've done well.'

Dinesh dropped his arm with clear relief and Dae Hyo frowned at him.

'They can't fight,' Krish said. 'There's no anger in them. It's one of the things bliss takes from them, along with their freedom.'

'But if we gave them weapons—'

'They'll never be an army. I could only send them to die.'

'Well, we'll keep working on it,' Dae Hyo insisted.

'Thank you,' Krish said, and Dae Hyo was shocked to hear that his brother's voice sounded a little choked.

'No need for thanks, I've done nothing to help you yet.'

'You tried.' Krish clasped his arm, his fingers bruising. There was far more strength in that thin body now. 'Listen, I want you to know. Before you, I never had a brother. I never even had a friend. It's been . . . since I left the mountains . . . there hasn't been much good. I haven't made many good choices. But becoming Dae was the best thing that I did. And I'm glad, now. I'm glad . . .' He swallowed, clearly fighting back tears.

Dae Hyo punched him lightly on the shoulder, as a brother should when another man was loosing tears when he should be loosing his sword. 'I'm glad too, but no need to write a grave-speech on it yet. We've desert all around us, strong walls, and most of all my blades and your brains. We aren't finished yet.'

'No. You've done enough, brother. I won't take you down with me.'

He beckoned to Dinesh and moved away and Dae Hyo didn't try to stop him. He'd never been good with words. But he wouldn't let Krish die, whatever Krish seemed to think was right. His brother had honour, and that was good. Now Dae Hyo just needed to force some sense into him.

29

Wingard and Wine moved to flank Cwen when she strode out of the moot tent. They knew her well enough to recognise her mood. But then, they also knew her well enough not to care.

'Well?' Wingard asked when they were far enough away not to be overheard.

'The same,' she told him.

'Maybe—' Wine said and snapped his mouth shut when she turned her head to glare at him.

'Don't say it.'

'May I think it?' he asked with a grin.

She couldn't smile back. 'More war? And for what? So that Uin can spill still more of his own people's blood?'

'So that we can find this Krishanjit,' Wingard said. 'Uin has said he'll help us capture him, hasn't he? And Uin's enemies are Krishanjit's people, the moon's people – you can't argue with that.'

'Krishanjit's gone from Rah lands. Uin told me so himself. Enough, now. Enough. I've heard the arguments from him. I amn't ready to hear them again from you.'

They knew what that tone meant too, and this time they honoured her desires, dropping back to let her stride on alone. She wouldn't get peace to think, though. Alfreda was ahead, waiting in the growing gloom of twilight with the tents of the resting army shadows all around.

'Anything?' the smith asked. She was speaking now, but to Cwen only the barest she needed. It was Jinn who got the greater gift of her words. At least she wasn't asking about the council meeting. She didn't seem to care much for their war. She meant Vordanna.

'No word,' Cwen said. 'I've sent scouts to every compass direction there is. I'd send them up into the sky if I could, but his mother isn't to be found. No doubt she took one look at Uin's face and ran as fast as she could in the opposite direction.' Uin, the father of her child, her owner and her rapist. And this was the man whose alliance Cwen must make. Whose war she must fight, if she couldn't think of a better plan.

She pictured him, the smug look on his face when she told him that yes, she would fight for him. This man who sat at dinner every night beside his wife and two daughters, one distant and the other shy. Jin had tried to talk to the girls when he'd realised they were his sisters and Uin had driven him away. He'd told Cwen she must keep the boy away from them. His own son!

She came to the edge of the joint encampment, where the prison cages had been built. There were hundreds of the Brotherband in them, those the arrows hadn't finished or her own people killed. She wouldn't have minded if they'd taken knives to all those butchers, but they'd sickened of the slaughter before they'd run out of men to kill. The tribesmen didn't look glad of the reprieve. They'd mostly stopped their weeping but few of them bothered to eat. She could see two lying still, flies buzzing around their eyes. She'd order the bodies taken out tomorrow. Let the rest live with the corpses a while.

The second cage was different, its occupants angry or fearful but still holding tight to life. These were Uin's captured enemies, leaders of the rebellion against him. He meant to trade them for his own captives back in Rah lands, else they'd all have been as dead as the rest. But she could see another use for them. She'd seen it the first day she'd learned of them and she'd thought of it and rejected it every day since.

One man stood at the cage's edge, thin hands gripping the wooden bars as he glared out at Cwen. One half of his face was a bruise, the ear half torn off and festering beneath ragged grey hair. That wound would kill him if it stayed untreated, and Uin wouldn't treat it. What harm could it do, set against the possible good?

There were Rah guards on the cages. They sat in a circle to one side, playing a game with dice that she didn't know and swigging wine from a nearly empty skin.

'You,' she said, to the one who seemed most sober. 'Get this man out for me.'

'Why?' he asked, not moving.

'Because I say so.'

'And who the fuck are you?' His hand rested on his sword hilt.

She shrugged and whistled, an imitation of the blue lark's call. The man sneered at her and she sneered back until, only a moment later, two dozen of her hawks came running.

'I'm the woman who outnumbers you five to one,' she said. 'And *we're* all sober enough to hold our blades. Uin's given me leave for this' – he hadn't, but he needed her too much to complain – 'now bring him out for me.'

The old man said nothing as he was released, nor all the way through the camp as she led him to her tent. She couldn't think where else to bring him. She should have taken time to prepare, but she knew if she did she might lose her nerve.

When she got to the tent, she waved all but two of her hawks away. It wasn't an accident that one of them was Hilda, tongueless and unable to tell of what went on here. The other was a boy whose name she didn't know. She didn't choose to ask.

'Strip him,' she said.

The boy looked doubtful, frowning beneath curly, honey-coloured hair. He had a young face as pretty as a girl's and she wondered if she should send him away. The old Rah man hadn't the strength to resist. But Hilda was already ripping his clothes from him and the boy went to assist.

The body they revealed had once been strong, but hunger had wasted it to little more than bone and skin. The bruises spread downward, over his chest and stomach and thighs. Uin had told her he'd already questioned the captives. If this man's tongue could be loosened, it would take more than a beating to do it. Her stomach clenched and she urgently wanted to take a shit.

'Tie him to the chair,' she said.

The boy had begun to realise what this was about. His freckles looked like a rash across his too-pale face. But he obeyed, and when the man was bound Cwen had to either begin or not.

'I need to know where Krishanjit has gone,' she told the old man, using the trade Ashane she'd learned as a child.

She guessed that he understood it, although his mouth didn't move and his face showed nothing but contempt.

Hilda drew her knife. She knew what they were doing here, and she pressed the knife against the old man's face, blade flat, but Cwen said, 'No.' Bachur had given her the leadership. This was hers to do and to bear.

She drew her own blade and went to kneel between the old man's splayed-open legs. 'Just Krishanjit,' she said. 'That's all I care about. Give me his hiding place and me and my army go after him. I amn't interested in your war and from what I hear, your side has won it. Tell me where Krishanjit is and I'll leave you to Uin. He means to exchange you for his own people. You can enjoy your victory and your freedom.'

'And if I don't tell you?'

'Then I'll join my army to Uin's and we'll take back the Rah lands for him. You can't resist us – you're too few and we're too fresh. Everything you fought for will be lost.'

He swallowed hard. 'I'd tell you if I knew. The moon's heir left us without a word.'

It might be true. It sounded convincing, but the fact that she wanted to believe him made her doubt her own judgement. She raised her knife and rested it flat against his cheek where Hilda's had been. The point was very close to his eye. 'Are you sure about that?'

His eye flickered, as if he wanted to close it but couldn't bear to look away.

'Last chance,' she said.

He said nothing and she knew she'd have to do it. It was the only way to be sure. She was shaking so hard, she could see the tremors in the knife. Its edge shivered and nicked the skin of his cheek so that a thin thread of blood fell from it. She firmed her grip, turned the blade until its sharpest edge was against the skin and sliced.

For a moment, the cut was nothing but a line. Then it split, gaping open to show the flesh beneath and he screamed. The sound was high and thin and horrible.

Cwen jerked back, shocked. 'Tell me,' she said, when his screaming had reduced to a whimper, but he only glared.

There was a commotion outside and the tent flap was thrown back. Faces peered in, drawn by the scream, but Hilda waved them away. Cwen didn't look at them. She couldn't stand to see their expressions as they realised what she was doing.

She couldn't bring herself to touch the old man's cheek again. She looked at his bruised chest and her eyes fell on his nipple. The thought that came to her then horrified her, and she knew for that exact reason it was the thing she needed to do. She pressed her blade into the flesh above his nipple. 'Tell me,' she said again, and when he didn't answer she cut swiftly downward.

Bile rose in her throat as the little peaked scrap of skin fell away. It landed on the groundsheet of her tent, a firm red blob. The old man was crying now and she pressed her blade against the other nipple. He said nothing and she gritted her teeth and took that one off too. The wounds beneath the symmetrical cuts looked like meat. People *were* only meat on the inside, after all. It made it easier to do, if she thought of it that way. If she didn't look at his face, she could almost pretend he was a moon beast.

He'd lost the energy to scream. His whimpers sounded like a small child. 'Tell me where Krishanjit is,' she said. Her voice wasn't as firm as she would have liked. She sounded as if she was begging.

'I don't know,' he sobbed. 'I don't know!'

She wanted to believe him. How could she ever be sure? She lowered her knife until it was pressed against the root of his cock. 'Tell me,' she said, her own voice choked.

'Please no, please, please,' he babbled through snot and tears, but it wasn't an answer and she tightened her hand and cut.

She wasn't prepared for the gout of blood. It hit her in the face and made her gag. She heard the sound of vomiting as the young hawk emptied his stomach. Even Hilda looked pale.

But the old man still wasn't speaking. His mouth was open, gasping, his eyes wide and appalled. She was appalled too. They both watched as his heart pumped the blood out of the stump of his manhood, long spurts and then shorter as it drained out of him. She saw the moment when he died. There was something behind his eyes looking out, and then there was nothing.

The boy had finished emptying his stomach. He came up and pressed himself against Cwen, his head against her neck. He kissed it as his hand fumbled for her breast and she knew what he wanted. She should give it to him, the comfort of rutting. A part of her wanted it as well. Clutch-mates fucked after a hunt, that was the hawk way. This boy wasn't from her clutch but no one would care. She held him for a moment, but then she felt the hardness of his cock against her and she couldn't. She just couldn't, so she pushed him away.

His face was wounded. He looked desperate and she made herself be gentle as she took his hand and pressed it against Hilda's body. 'Get rid of the body when you're done,' she said. 'The blood too.'

But there was blood on her as well. She walked to the river, stripped and dived into the muddy water. It left her coated in a brown film, not clean but feeling less filthy. She let the warm air dry her and then pulled on her clothes. They were caked in drying gore too and she needed to change them, but that would mean returning to her tent. She shuddered and sat on a rock by the river, trying to think of nothing for a while.

It was impossible. The images of the morning refused to be banished. The worst was that there were more prisoners, a dozen at least, and there was no use stopping at one. His death would be pointless unless she questioned them all. She stood, stiffened her resolve and walked back towards the cages.

People turned to stare at her when she passed, hawks and Jorlith and Rah alike. She felt as if they all knew what she'd done and were judging her for it. When she passed Alfreda's wagon, the smith paused at her forge to watch Cwen too. Cwen flinched away from her eyes but found herself dawdling to a halt, head lowered. She could stop here for a while. Alfreda had tea brewing.

Alfreda took the kettle from her hearth to pour them both their tea. They sat on the lip of the wagon to drink it. Alfreda's silence had often made Cwen uncomfortable but she welcomed it now. She was surprised when the other woman spoke.

'You didn't learn where Krishanjit is?'

Cwen shook her head.

'Do you think you will if you question the rest?'

She shrugged.

'But you're going to try.'

Cwen looked at her, to see if there was criticism hidden in the words, but they seemed to mean just what they said. 'I have to try. It's that or fight Uin's war for him.'

The smith's mouth twisted and her massive shoulders hunched. She hated the Rah leader more passionately even than Cwen. '*You* don't have to do it, though.'

'I can't ask others to do what I won't do myself.'

'That's nonsense,' Alfreda said and Cwen stared at her, taken aback by her sharpness. These were already more words than the smith had ever spoken to her.

'It's duty,' she said.

'It's foolish,' Alfreda insisted. 'There's tools for each job. If you were carving a joint, I wouldn't hand you a peeling knife.'

'What I did today didn't take much skill,' Cwen said bitterly. 'Any knife would have done.'

She was surprised when Alfreda put her arm round her and pulled her closer. It was only as she leaned her head against that broad shoulder that she realised she was weeping.

'You're the wrong tool for this job,' Alfreda said. 'There must be some among all these men who were made for it. There's people who enjoy giving pain. There was a Wanderer once, travelled everywhere in his wagon on his own. Algar . . . Algar was only a lad then, he wandered off while I was working. I went looking and

I found this man . . . He had Algar's arm twisted up behind his back. Algar was crying and this man was laughing.' Her face twisted and Cwen wondered what the smith had done to the man who hurt her brother. 'There's people like that everywhere.'

But it seemed wrong to give this job to anyone who could enjoy it. It felt right that she suffered in carrying it out.

'People are good at the things they enjoy,' Alfreda said, as if she knew what Cwen was thinking. 'You hate this task and it will make you bad at it. If the job needs doing, pick someone who'll do it well.'

Cwen had always loathed Gest. He wasn't in her clutch and if he had been, she might have seen to it that he met with a fatal accident. She hated the way he enjoyed killing the moon beasts and the marks she saw on his own mount that didn't look like they came from battle. She hated the way he looked when she told him what she needed him to do to the prisoners, and she hated even more his sly smile as she told him to set up his tent out of earshot of the rest of the camp.

She made herself watch as he got it all ready. He shook his head when she offered a chair and ropes and instead he ordered a frame made with costly chains on it and a winch to raise them higher. Alfreda put it together for him without complaint and sharpened all the blades he wanted. She made a furnace for him so he could heat the instruments. Cwen made sure it was all ready, but she walked away as the first prisoner was brought in. She didn't need to watch; she'd imagine it all well enough.

Cwen found the boy hawk instead, still pale and silent, and took him back to her tent to rut. She slept with him all night, curled round him and pressed between others of her clutch when they joined her. It helped her forget what she'd done there. She wasn't sure it helped *them* forget it, though. She didn't think even Wingard and Wine saw her in quite the same way now. It was a cost she hadn't counted when she'd decided to do it, and it pained her.

For three days, Gest worked his way through the prisoners, Uin ranted at her actions and wheedled when that didn't work, and Cwen spent the nights with her clutch and the days with

Alfreda and Jinn. She was sitting by the smith's wagon when Gest finally came to her.

He'd washed before he did, but she saw red beneath his nails. She imagined him using them on the captives, tearing into flesh his instruments had already worked on, and shuddered. 'I've information,' he said.

She felt light-headed with relief. If it could not be for nothing, she thought she could bear what had been done. 'They told you where Krishanjit is?'

'No.' Gest grinned. She'd never seen him as happy as he'd been since she'd given him this task. 'Something else. Did you know that Uin's own daughter was one of them?'

'His daughter?'

'The youngest. I've seen her about the camp, pretty as a bluebell. She was one of their leaders, would you believe, and still loyal. He says she's been sending information back to their people about Uin's forces. Might explain why he couldn't seem to win a single fight, eh?'

The girl was so meek, Cwen found it hard to imagine. She found it hard even to picture her. Short, she thought, with brown hair often kept in a plait and eyes that seemed to be looking beyond you. 'It's interesting,' she said. 'It's not helpful.'

'But this girl – Ensee – she was close to Krishanjit. Loved him, maybe. If anyone knows where he is, it's Uin's daughter.'

Cwen went to wait for Gest in the tent he'd set up beyond the edge of the encampment. It crouched in a hollow between two stands of stunted trees. Inside, the wooden frame was stained with blood. The whole place stank of it but the knives and other instruments were sparkling clean. A man was slumped beside the frame, still breathing but not conscious. He must be the one who'd told Gest about Ensee.

'Take him to a healer,' she told Hilda.

The Rah man groaned as Hilda lifted him and left a stain of shit and piss on the ground behind him.

'Shall we clear that up?' Wingard asked.

'No, leave it.' The whole place was monstrous. That served her purpose: she'd rather use fear than pain. But she'd use pain if she had to – especially now, when she was finally so close.

Uin looked angry when Gest led him to the tent. It had become a habitual expression over the days in which Cwen had refused to fight his war. The anger shifted into puzzlement when Wine led his two daughters into the tent beside him.

'This is no place for you!' he snapped at them, and then – seeming to realise it hadn't been their choice to come – turned to Cwen and asked, 'What are they doing here?'

'Perhaps you should ask Ensee,' she said, watching the girl very closely.

There was something, a flicker of an expression, but she kept her head lowered demurely as she said, 'I don't understand.'

'Neither do I,' Uin said to Cwen. 'Explain yourself.'

'Oh,' Gest said, 'It's her has some explaining to do.' There was a dreadful eagerness in his face as he looked at the girl.

'She's been working against you,' Cwen told Uin. 'She's with those who fought you – she's sending them messages even now.'

'Don't be absurd! My daughter? Whoever told you that was a liar.'

'I don't care if you believe me.' Cwen clicked her fingers to bring her hawks forward, the round dozen she'd made sure were here for this.

Uin's expression changed from anger and disdain to fear. 'No, you're making a mistake.' He looked at Ensee, but she didn't speak and Cwen saw the moment when he realised it might be true. 'No, please, don't hurt her. She's only a child.'

Cwen thought of his other child, born of rape and unacknowledged by him. She felt a pleasure that disgusted her as she said, 'It's not her I mean to hurt.'

She gave him this: he didn't struggle as they tied him to the frame. If it was to be him or his daughter, he was clearly prepared to take his child's pain for her. But Cwen reminded herself of everything else he'd done and nodded to Gest. 'Slowly,' she told him. 'We can't have him dying too soon.'

Uin was silent, but his eldest daughter screamed as the thin-faced hawk brought the pliers to his smallest nail. He screamed too when Gest pulled it out.

'You know what we need,' Cwen said to Ensee. 'Where is Krishanjit?'

The eldest girl was crying with ugly gulping sobs. Ensee's face was calm, though, and she shook her head.

'Another,' Cwen said to Gest, looking away from his glad smile.

Uin screamed again, and wept when the scream was over.

Cwen made herself look at him, to face what she was doing. She let Gest take two more of his fingernails and a toenail. He was hard to hate when he was like this, so pitiful. She felt herself despising him and tried not to feel that either. He wasn't to blame for what she'd reduced him to.

When he looked close to unconsciousness, she turned back to Ensee. At first she mistook her expression, then she realised. Ensee's thin lips were pressed together and her face was being held so carefully motionless to hide not distress, but pleasure. This girl *hated* her father. She was glad to see him suffer.

She turned to Gest to tell him to cut Uin down, and the other daughter finally spoke. 'Stop it!' she shouted. 'Stop hurting him and I'll tell you. Ensee told me and I'll tell you.'

'Don't!' Ensee tried to grab her sister but the older girl pushed her back, hard enough to send her to the ground.

'She told me – she said he'd deserted them,' the older girl said to Cwen. 'Promise you'll let my father go if I tell you.'

'I promise,' Cwen said.

'No!' Ensee yelled. She scrambled to her feet, lunging for her sister before two hawks grabbed her arms and pulled her back. 'I'll hate you if you do!'

'I don't care,' her sister said, still sobbing. 'Krishanjit sailed away from us,' she told Cwen. 'He's gone south, to Mirror Town.'

30

The first day Drut didn't appear, Eric thought she was still in a snit with him. He decided to let it lie and wait for her to come back to him, a policy he'd always found worked in the past. But she didn't come as another day passed and then another, and when he finally asked one of the other Servants where she'd gone, she only looked at him gravely, shook her head and moved away.

That set a nasty feeling gnawing at his stomach, but he ignored it. He told himself she was away on some mission of the Servants like the one that had parted them before, and he got on with his explorations below ground and acted like everything was fine. But when the day of his oroboros came that he had to lie with his wives, and afterwards there was still no sign of her, then he had to stop pretending to himself.

In the end, it was Bolli who told him. Eric was late for dinner, having been wandering Salvation in search of Drut, and when he came the only place was opposite the other lad. They'd barely spoken since Eric had been brought back from his ill-fated attempt to escape, and there was a sulky dislike in Bolli's face when he looked at Eric now. His guilt at what he'd done to Eric had hardened into resentment at not being forgiven for it.

Eric kept his head down and concentrated on eating. The meat didn't taste like the normal reindeer and he wondered if the Hunter had been out killing more bears.

'Enjoying it?' Bolli asked.

Eric grunted non-commitally.

'It's a wonder you've any appetite given the news,' Bolli added snidely.

Eric realised that most of the other husbands were watching

him from the corners of their eyes. He didn't want to give Bolli the satisfaction but he had to ask, 'What news?'

'About your wife. You hadn't heard?' Bolli had a nasty, self-satisfied grin. 'She took the long walk into the ice.'

'It's a very sad thing,' Abejide said, glaring quellingly at Bolli and changing to a sympathetic look when he turned to Eric, which was somehow much worse than Bolli's smugness. 'Your wife was troubled and she took the Servants' way of ending it.'

'Which wife?' Eric asked, though he already knew.

Bolli made a weak effort to look less hateful. 'The one you got up the duff. And you two seemed so particularly close.'

'I'm sorry, Eric,' Abejide said, and then something more that he didn't hear because he was already up from the table and rushing out of the hall.

He found himself outside without quite remembering how he'd got there. He felt an urgent need to do something, the sense that Drut was in danger *right now* and if he didn't act it would all be over. He told himself not to be an idiot, that she could have been missing for hours already or even days, but that just made it worse. Why hadn't he realised sooner? If he'd asked for her when he'd first noticed her absence, he could have run out and saved her straight away. Instead, he'd let her—

No, she wasn't dead. The Servants were strong. He knew it first-hand – she sometimes left bruises when she clasped him in the heat of her passion. And the cold didn't hurt her the way it did him. She was still alive. Lost maybe, but out there somewhere. He could find her.

Only, how did you find someone in a thousand miles of snow? He trudged around in it for a while, desperate and unorganised at first and then more orderly, moving out from the pear orchards in a series of zizags so there was no bit of ground he couldn't see. But he realised very soon that it was pointless. It would take him weeks and weeks to find her this way, and even a Servant wasn't strong enough to survive that long without food or drink, especially if she was trying to die.

With that thought, all the will went out of him and he sat down on his arse in the snow. His tears froze on his cheeks before they could fall. He wasn't quite sure what he was crying for. The death of his baby maybe, and definitely the fact that he'd never now find a way to leave Salvation. But most of all he was crying for Drut.

Why hadn't he run after her when they had their row? A lover's tiff, that's all he'd thought it was – only he hadn't really, had he? He'd sensed something deeper in it, some current beneath her words pulling her away from him. And why had she suddenly begun to question him about his home? She'd never seemed to care before.

My sisters think they treasure their husbands but they do not understand you. He heard the Hunter's words in his head, loud as if she'd just spoken them. It was *her*. She'd turned Drut against him, he knew it with sudden certainty, and he turned round and marched back to Salvation.

The Hunter wasn't hard to find. She was on the new parade ground the Servants had flattened from the snow to one side of Salvation, drilling them in their swordwork. There was an eerie beauty to it, all those golden forms moving in perfect time with her. But when the Hunter caught sight of Eric, she dropped her sword and waved her sisters away so that she was alone when he came up to her.

'What did you say to Drut?' he asked, not bothering with any lead-up to it. He knew she'd understand.

'I only told her the truth,' she replied, proving that she did.

'And what truth would that be?'

'I told her that you were dangerous.'

'Dangerous?' He laughed harshly. 'You're the one what's a danger to her. She's taken the long walk into the ice, did she tell you that?'

He was pleased to see the shock on the Hunter's face. 'But she was with child!'

'Yeah – my child! And now they're both gonna die because of you.'

She remained still for a long moment, her booted toe resting against her fallen sword and her gaze on the horizon. Standing that way, she looked just like the statue of her they'd had in the village of his birth and he had to fight an urge to bow. But the statue had been of a god. She was just a Servant like any other, and she'd done wrong.

'I do not wish her dead, nor the child inside her,' she said at last. She reached round to the back of her neck and took off a chain from which hung a small golden whistle. 'Blow on this and it will summon my wolves. If you have an article of her clothing, something with her scent, present it to them and they will find her for you. But she cannot return to Salvation. My sisters will not accept her now that she has admitted her fall into error by taking the long walk into the ice. Do you have somewhere that you can take her?'

'Yes.' He didn't offer any more and she didn't ask it. Their eyes met as he took the whistle and some kind of understanding passed between them, maybe a sort of truce.

Everything in him wanted to rush straight out, but he wasn't such a fool as he had been. He meant to stay out until he found her, and so he dressed in his warmest furs and made himself a pack of food and warmleaf-wrapped water to keep it from freezing. The Servants in the kitchen looked at him oddly, but they didn't ask what he was about. Questioning wasn't the Servant way. That was what made Drut different; if only he'd had the guts to answer her questions honestly.

Outside he made himself walk until Salvation was distant enough that no nosey Servants – or more likely nosey husbands – would guess what he was doing. Then he put the whistle to his lips and blew. It made a noise too high to hear but somehow piercing all the same. The fine hairs on the back of his neck stood up in a way that wasn't entirely pleasant

The moment after the whistle wasn't filled with the howl of wolves as he'd half expected. It was only the not-quite-silence of the snow, with the subtle creak of ice and the murmur of the wind. The wolves, when they came, seemed to form out of the snow, their fur almost the same white and their tongues lolling.

They sat in front of him in a long neat row, yellow and green and blue eyes unblinking.

He'd always known wolves were the Hunter's creatures – that's why they howled at the moon, who was her enemy. It didn't stop him shivering as he reached out towards those tooth-filled jaws, holding one of Drut's dresses between finger and thumb. When one of the wolves lunged forward he dropped it in a hurry, but they all just sniffed it, polite as you please, then turned their backs on him and sped away, fanning out in all directions as if they knew precisely what they were doing.

And it seemed they did. He'd only just had time to wonder if he ought to go back to Salvation to wait for them when one of the wolves came trotting back to him. It was a bit of a mangy specimen. When it opened its mouth to pant he saw that half of its teeth were rotten.

'Found something then?' he asked it.

Of course it didn't reply, but it nuzzled its nose into his palm and then took the sleeve of his fur coat between its teeth and gently pulled. The message was pretty clear, and when it loped ten paces away and then turned its head round to look at him, he followed after.

The mangy wolf ranged ahead, sniffing, while one by one the others slunk back out of the snow to join him, so that soon Eric was at the centre of the pack. He was glad of their warmth. They walked for hours while the sun sank towards the horizon it would never cross, and his fears started to eat at him. Drut had gone a long way and been missing a long while. Could she possibly still be alive?

He slogged on, trudging through the snow as it numbed his fingers and nose even through his furs, and he began to wonder if he was going to die the cold death he'd only narrowly avoided before. He wondered if that was what the Hunter intended. He was so numb, it was hard to care. And then, when only a sliver of sky remained between sun and horizon, he finally saw something other than snow in the distance.

He began running, a painful exhausted jog. A little further and he realised what the building was: that place of the moon's he'd found on his wanderings in the city below. It seemed strange that Drut should have come to this one tiny place in all the broad land, but he soon saw her figure sprawled on the lead floor beneath the high, peaked roof.

He remembered in a moment of terror the burns on the Hunter's foot from treading on that metal and he found that he could run full tilt after all. But when he fell to his knees beside Drut he saw no charring or blisters or any other wound. And when he took off his mitten and held his mutilated hand in front of her mouth, the soft warmth of her breath brushed it. He pulled her into his arms and sobbed, more relieved than he knew how to feel.

She didn't wake, and after a while he calmed himself and looked at the wolves, who were sitting in a patient ring around him. 'Thank you,' he said. 'You saved her life, but you can go now – I don't need you no more.'

He thought they might disobey him, that the Hunter might have told them to keep their keen eyes on him. But one by one they turned and loped away, the one that had found Drut for him pausing only to lick her face before running off.

She wasn't light with the baby inside her. He felt his back strain as he lifted her and his boots sank deeply into the snow with each step. He'd never have been able to carry her back to Salvation, but that wasn't where he was going. The entrance to the city below was only fifty paces away and he made himself stagger forward, one step at a time, until he reached it.

Descending the stairs was easier and when he reached the bottom, he found the worm men waiting for him. A part of him had known he would. Drut had lain on the moon's metal and not been harmed by it. She'd been drawn to that place. Maybe it was the child inside her or maybe it was some change in her own nature, but she wasn't purely a creature of the sun any longer. 'Can you carry her for me?' he asked, and the worm men reached out their grey, spindly arms and took her.

It was another very long walk but Eric hardly minded. He felt as light as air. The worm men carried Drut to the end of the tunnel and beyond, through the dark streets of the buried city. They didn't stop until they came to the room they'd shown him before, the one painted with pictures of a woman who looked like the Hunter. He reckoned that was a good choice: somewhere Drut could feel at home.

'You can leave us here,' he said to the worm men. 'And listen, mates, can you keep out of sight? I ain't saying you ain't pretty, but you take a bit of getting used to. Better if Drut just sees me when she wakes.'

They didn't seem offended by this. Their moon-silver eyes blinked at him and one of them pointed at a doorway near the back of the room he hadn't noticed before, then all of them slid out, back into the silent streets of their dead city.

Drut wasn't showing any signs of waking. Eric took off his furs to make a bed for her, leaving his skin goosepimpled, and then tried the door the worm men had shown him. Behind it he found a room with a bath and a few other odd contraptions. He thought the tall pot with the tube snaking out of it might be meant for pissing in, but the things attached to the wall that looked like a twist of intestines served no purpose he could work out.

The bath seemed useless too without water to fill it, but when he leaned against one of the metal knobs on its top that he'd taken for ornaments, a jet of water spurted out. There was one on the other side too and, when he cautiously turned it, the water that came out was hot. As steam clouded the room, he found a plug and let the bath fill.

It was difficult to get Drut out of her clothes, but he knew warmth was what she needed. Her flesh was like marble to his touch. There was none of the black sickness that had taken his fingers after his foray into the snow, but who knew what invisible damage she'd done to herself or to his child.

Her eyes flickered behind their lids as he lifted her up, and when he eased her into the water she sighed, though her eyes still didn't open. There was no washcloth or soap in the room, but he tore off a corner of his jacket and used it to wipe down her face and arms. Colour flowed back into her with each brush of the cloth, turning her skin from a sickly yellow white to its natural glowing gold.

She really was beautiful. She might not have the right equipment to set him aflame, but he could appreciate the smooth perfection of her skin and the elegant line of her bones. If he hadn't been a molly, he could have lusted after her. If he wasn't a molly, he'd be lucky to have her – and maybe he still was.

It was only as he looked up from washing down her feet that he realised her eyes were open. 'Eric?' she said. Her voice was whisper-light and when she lifted a hand towards him, its fingers shook.

He took it in his own and clasped it tightly. 'You're all right, Drut. I got you.'

'Am I dead?'

'Course you ain't. I wasn't going to let anything happen to you, was I?'

'Why not?' She stared at him, puzzled and a little blurry, like a woman who'd just woken from a long sleep.

He looked into her sun-gold eyes and knew that this answer mattered; that if he said the wrong thing, one day soon she'd be walking right back into the snow. And he saw that she'd know if he lied. All those weeks he'd spent courting her, he'd thought he was the one in control, doing what he wanted and getting what he wanted, but that sort of thing never went one way. As he was learning her likes and dislikes, all the things he might do to please and win her, she'd been learning the same things about him.

'Because I love you, you silly girl,' he said, and knew that it was true. It might not be the love he'd felt for Lahiru; there wasn't any passion in it, but there was tenderness and a fondness that had made his heart ache when he'd thought he might lose her.

She was crying, though he thought they were happy tears. He wiped them away with his fingers and kissed her on her lips.

'Where are we?' she asked as he leaned back.

'We're in the city beneath. I brought you in from the ice. You can't go back to Salvation, but I can take care of you here. There's water and it's warm enough. I can pinch food for you until the baby comes and then we'll go away together, just you and me.'

It wasn't the future he'd wanted for himself, but it was better than the present and he thought he could make something of it. If he had a few men on the side what would it matter, as long as he cared for her and his child?

'Leave Salvation?' There was more wonder than dread in her voice. When he nodded, she smiled and said, 'I'll go anywhere as long as it's with you.'

He reached his arm round her to hug her to his chest. He thought of telling her what her baby would be, but it didn't seem like the time. They had weeks yet for him to break it to her gently. 'I'm gonna take good care of you,' he told her. 'We're going to be all right together, you and me. I promise.'

31

The New Misa had run broad and sluggish and brown when they first set sail. Sang Ki looked at the water beneath the ship's bow, so lively it was more white than blue, and wished it had stayed that way.

'Don't worry, fat man, my ships can take it,' Little Cousin said. The man's eyes – always bright, always in motion – darted between him and the water.

'Perhaps the ships can. My stomach is faring somewhat less well.' He'd vomited with wearying regularity since their army's embarkation onto the Ahn trader's fleet. The nausea distracted him from the ceaseless pain in his back, though it was hardly much consolation. He understood the logic of using this method to bridge the distance between his and Cwen's forces and King Nayan's own, but he didn't much enjoy the reality of it.

'I can slow down,' Little Cousin said, 'but it's you who told me the journey was urgent.'

'And so it is.' Sang Ki turned from the rail to study the other man. It struck him anew, as it did every time, how very short Little Cousin was. He couldn't have topped five feet. 'We carry a message for the King of Ashanesland. Kings, on the whole, don't like to be kept waiting.'

'And you're quite sure you'll find him here, this Ashane monarch, travelling our plains?'

'Following the New Misa from its roots in the mountains to its spreading branches in Rah lands. So I've been told by the man who summoned him there.'

'Well, good then,' Little Cousin said. 'And even if your voyage never finds him, it's brought us into each other's company, not so? So the time hasn't been wasted.'

Sang Ki was surprised to find himself in agreement. The captain of the *Misa's Master* had often kept him company below decks in the first and more nauseating days of the journey, when the ship was lurching on the tides of the river's estuary and he thought that he might never eat again. On the other hand, after the one time he'd thrown up on her boots, Cwen had stayed on her own ship.

Little Cousin hadn't seemed to mind. He'd brought Sang Ki history books, from a collection that wouldn't have disgraced an Ashane shiplord. It was strange to find a fellow enthusiast so far from home and in so odd a shape. The fables said Jaspal the Raven had sometimes taken human form. Sang Ki thought he must have looked much like Little Cousin: small, neat and dark-haired, mind and body constantly in motion, face round and eyes alert.

The ship, he had to admit, wasn't a bad boat. Uin had recommended this as the fastest way to reach King Nayan, once Sang Ki had dragged the man away from Cwen's torturer. The dragging had been a little drama he'd arranged with Cwen herself, but the Rah man didn't know it and he'd been most forthcoming with information on how to locate the Ashane king to the man he believed had rescued him. Besides, now Uin could tell Nayan the location of his son he clearly thought he had something to bargain with. He was probably right. Uin thought the Ashane king would lend him troops to win back his land and that might even be true as well. Nayan would be very grateful indeed to the person who helped him locate his son. Sang Ki was relying on it.

And so here he was, enduring the discomforts of a journey that sometimes felt endless. At least he was making it in the greatest comfort circumstances allowed and in the best company. The Water Ahn ran all the trade along the great river, and Little Cousin was the foremost among the tribe's merchant captains, while the *Misa's Master* was the foremost among his ships.

The wind was in the wrong quarter and its sails were furled, but the great banks of oars still pulled it through the water at an impressive pace. The men stood two to an oar, sweating and singing as they pulled. Sang Ki found the songs tuneless yet oddly soothing. Elsewhere, women worked the decks and climbed in the nest of wood and lines above. The nearest sat cross-legged at his feet, coiling ropes into neat piles. His eye was drawn to her skirts, where embroidered snowflakes sparkled.

'Ho there, Songbird – you have an admirer,' Little Cousin said, good-humoured despite the fact the woman was his wife. Most of them seemed to be. The man claimed to have thirty-four.

'Your lady is admirable, to be sure, but it was her clothing that caught my eye. That's a Chung design, is it not?'

The woman shifted so her broad back was to Sang Ki and her face hidden.

'I apologise,' he said, 'if the question was improper.'

Little Cousin watched her, his expression grave, but he was smiling again when he turned back to Sang Ki. 'There are no bad questions, only bad answers, not so? The clothes are Chung, you're right, and so is she. All of my wives are and a good dozen in my crew.'

Sang Ki studied the men labouring at the oars, but the people of the tribes looked much of a muchness without their clothes or accents or customs to distinguish them. 'The Brotherband . . .' he said cautiously, and saw the woman's back stiffen.

'The Brotherband aren't the Chung, any more than the decay in a rotten apple is the apple itself. Not all the tribe followed Chung Yong, how could you think it? No rule is absolute, as history teaches. Did the reign of the despotic Carrion Kings not end? And that bloody-handed bastard Yong didn't leave my wives much choice. Knife women have no place in the Brotherband.'

'*Knife* women?' Sang Ki looked down at Songbird, then across the deck. He supposed it was possible. They seemed pretty and ugly in the same proportion as any group might, but perhaps they were a little taller than the average; every single one of them towered over her husband. 'So you took them in when their own people cast them out.'

'Or they took me on, I'm sure that's what they'd tell you, those that made it out alive. It was a brutal time. The New Misa ran red with blood that year, and all my ships carried as many swords as oars. But I like women. Who doesn't? If a man can afford a hundred wives he'll have them, every man on the plains, don't tell me it isn't true.'

Sang Ki strongly suspected it wasn't, but thought it best not to say so. 'Are all your wives knife women then?'

Little Cousin frowned at him, looking for the first time a little offended. Then he clapped Sang Ki on his belly, laughing as it wobbled. 'Ah, you Seonu have your own ways, but a woman's a woman no matter what she's born with down below and I've married myself some of the finest. My first wife was different, of course. She bore us twelve children, nine still living. She's gone too, died in the fighting when the Brotherband first formed, but I've found thirty-three good mothers to raise her daughters and sons. The oldest captain their own ships now, carrying the rest of your army. Only three underfoot on the *Misa's Master* these days.' His eyes suddenly snapped away, sharpening. 'Ho there, Horsehide – there's mudflats up ahead, are you blind? Steer left. Left!'

He dashed to the wheel, leaving Sang Ki to sweep his eyes over the ship. The burnt woman had emerged from below decks. She leaned against the rail, watching him, her face unreadable beneath its mask of scars. All around her, the Chung men and women worked.

As he'd hunted the Brotherband it had been easy to think of them as beasts. Here, among their sisters and brothers, he was reminded that they had been men, and his actions had killed them. The river sang as it danced beneath the ship, rushing them onward, faster than he liked.

His presence had brought fire to Smiler's Fair and slaughter to the Moon Forest. He'd never been much of a traveller, but he'd always wanted to visit Mirror Town, where so much knowledge and history lived. Now he would, but it wouldn't be to read. When he told his tale to King Nayan, the Ashane army would be turned south, into the Silent Sands. They'd march through the desert and bring war to another people, and Sang Ki wasn't certain how much he should feel responsible for it.

The next morning, he woke to a quieter ship. It was the first time his stomach had begun the day without emptying its contents. He waited for his breakfast to arrive in the cramped cabin he shared with his mother, savouring the return of his appetite; he'd almost forgotten that food was something he enjoyed.

He'd barely taken a bite of the fried fish when Little Cousin's round face peered through his doorway.

His mother frowned – she seemed to find the Ahn man's garrulousness offensive – so Sang Ki smiled for both of them.

'You're feeling better,' Little Cousin said.

'Your boat is better behaved today.'

'*Misa's Master* is always obedient – it's the water that's not under my command. But it's smooth here and the wind's brisk; we'll be at the lake within the hour.' He said it as if he thought Sang Ki should know what he meant. No doubt his expression conveyed that he didn't, because the other man added, 'Mideulle Lake.'

'Miduelle Lake.' The name *was* familiar. Sang Ki snapped his fingers as recollection came. 'Miduelle Lake, of course: the watery grave of the Lost City. The home of the losers in the great war that emptied these lands before our peoples came to them. Victims of a goddess's wrath, or so the legends tell us.'

'Exactly so! But not so lost a place as it once was. No, not quite so lost.' Little Cousin grinned, a man with a secret.

'You've entered the city? Have you emptied the lake?'

The trader's smile widened and he left without replying.

Sang Ki followed, unable to resist. The Lost City was that most precious thing, a remnant of the mysterious civilisation that had inhabited this continent before the Ashane came to it, and been destroyed in the war between the sun and the moon. The *last* war between them.

Little Cousin was waiting for him at the prow of the ship as it clove the river into white peaks. The lake was already in sight, huge and dark-watered. Water lilies fringed its shores but their leaves were withered and their flowers drooping. Birds hovered over the beach that slipped past on the ship's left side as it entered the lake proper, but none ventured over the water itself. They travelled in an eerie silence and through an improbable scent of burning that brought back unpleasant memories of the demise of Smiler's Fair.

'Look down,' Little Cousin said.

From afar, the water had seemed murky; from above it was almost transparent and the city startlingly clear below its surface. It had been drowned centuries past but neither water nor time seemed to have eroded it. The ship dropped its anchor above some drowned hill. Twisted spires thrust up from domes only a score of feet below and beyond them other shapes marched down into darkness. It was impossible to tell how far the rest of the city stretched. Something about the place unsettled Sang Ki and he soon realised why: there were no right angles here, not a single square or rectangle. His mother, who had spent her girlhood in round hide tents, might have found the place familiar. To the child of a shipfort it seemed all wrong.

'This is quite astonishing,' Sang Ki said. 'Thank you.'

'Oh, this any traveller can see. For this I wouldn't have woken you.'

'There's more?'

'Of course, and we'll be the first to see it – the very first. What do you say to that now?'

'I say I've a body more suited to floating than diving, if that's what you had in mind.'

'Ha! Well, you won't need to worry about that. It won't be you who's doing the diving, fat man. Come. See!'

The Ahn's excitement was so palpable his body seemed to quiver with it. Sang Ki followed him back from the bow of the ship, experiencing a jittery sensation that might have been excitement too, but was more probably trepidation. He trusted Little Cousin as much as one could trust a near stranger, but he didn't quite trust his smile.

As he stumbled and jarred his back, he realised that his walk towards the ship's stern was a walk *downward*. The ship was listing and soon he saw why. The contraption contained more metal than he'd ever seen in one place, a huge round sphere of it, no doubt worth more than the ship its weight pressed down. There were glass portholes lining its sides and chains attached to winches above. Sang Ki very much feared he knew what this was.

'A subaqueous sphere,' he guessed. 'The Wanderer Afra Silversdochter wrote of this in her journal.'

Little Cousin beamed. 'Yes, yes, yes – I knew you'd know. I have the volume myself, copied from Afra's original.'

'Hmm . . .' Sang Ki circled the sphere, running his fingers along the sun-warmed metal. 'Afra designed devices she never intended to make or test. And, of course, she was entirely insane.'

'Pah, only the Moon Forest folk would say so, afraid of a woman's wisdom. You don't need to fret. I've tested it already, though not here. No, in this you and I will be jointly the first. But I took it a hundred paces down the Misa's Mouth, and lived to tell you about it. I'm telling you about it now!'

Sang Ki made another slow circuit of the device before asking, 'And it truly holds in the air as she claimed it would?'

'Well . . .' Little Cousin took his arm and pulled him to one side, where he saw a collection of leather bladders lined up on the deck. 'The air's held in but it's . . . squashed. It would be, wouldn't it, all that weight of water above? It feels the way I would if you sat on me! But we'll bring more air down to fill it out. All will be well, I promise. And we'll see what no person's seen in a thousand years. What do you say to *that*?'

Sang Ki's eyes scanned the deck until they found the burnt woman. She was watching him. He thought she might be smiling, but her mutilated face made it hard to tell.

'Your woman can come too,' Little Cousin said, following the direction of his gaze. 'There's room enough for three.'

Sang Ki thought of protesting that she wasn't his woman, but he saw no reason she shouldn't share his danger. He beckoned her forward and she joined him by the subaqueous sphere without hesitation. Perhaps such bravery was admirable. Or perhaps there was little to fear in death for a woman who had suffered – no doubt was still suffering – as she did.

Little Cousin gestured to a gaggle of his men standing by the winch that held the sphere's chains. They clattered and tightened as the winch was turned and then, with a pained groan, began to raise its great weight from the deck. When the sphere was high enough, Sang Ki stooped beneath it with Little Cousin and the burnt woman. He closed his eyes as it was lowered over them. It seemed far smaller from the inside and he could feel the heat of the others' bodies, pressed close against him. He could smell unwashed flesh and feared it was his own.

'Sit, sit!' Little Cousin said. There was a platform ringing the sphere's interior, which Sang Ki realised must be intended as a bench. It was too narrow for his bulk but he squeezed himself on as best he could. He shut his eyes when the sphere began to rise and squeezed them tighter as it descended. They flew open when his feet were suddenly plunged into water, an icy shock that shivered up his spine.

The burnt woman was watching him. She reached out a hand, tentatively. Perhaps she meant it for comfort but he ignored her. 'And now the test begins,' he said to Little Cousin, clamping his mouth shut when he heard how his voice shook.

'The test is already done,' the Ahn man said, politely oblivious to Sang Ki's fear. 'Now the exploration begins. History, fat man, in a land so much without.'

But for a while there was nothing except water. It was very clear and fish hung suspended in it, jewel-bright. Sang Ki watched as a larger approached a smaller, gaped its jaws and swallowed it whole. Free-floating plants drifted past, their leaves like green ribbons.

'It's beautiful,' the burnt woman said.

Little Cousin paused from hauling in fresh air bladders to look at her. 'We're not there yet.'

'She means the fish,' Sang Ki said, eyeing a little purple school of them. 'She's right – I've never seen their like before.' It came to him suddenly that he was here, scores of feet below the water's surface breathing air, and he laughed in delight.

'Oh, fish,' Little Cousin said dismissively. He released the air and the water beneath them, which had been threatening to soak their feet, dropped a little further. 'I'll eat them, I don't want to stare at them. But ah – ah! Look!'

He paused in his hauling in of air bladders and the water rose as the sphere continued to sink, but Sang Ki barely noticed his wet feet. They were descending through the Lost City.

Neither time nor tide had worn away a single fragment of the original structures. Many buildings were cracked and some toppled, but whatever cataclysm had laid low the Lost City seemed also to have preserved it in the moment of its destruction. The sphere descended past tiled spires, their colours muted beneath the waves but the pattern of leaves painted on them still clear, though they belonged to no tree Sang Ki had ever seen.

He stared at an open tower, the bell within it swaying in the invisible current. A crab scuttled up its dark grey side and Sang Ki's ears rang with a deep, throbbing note. For a wild moment he thought the bell had somehow pealed. But it was the sphere, rocking and shaking, and Sang Ki lurched forward, only stopped from falling by the desperate grasp of Little Cousin's hand. The water below them sloshed from side to side and reached up white-tipped fingers to grab them, but after a few moments the motion stilled and Sang Ki saw what had caused it.

Peering in through one porthole of the sphere was a vast stone eyeball. The statue it belonged to stretched down into indigo shade, scores, maybe hundreds of feet below. The sphere scraped along the statue's cheek as it descended but left no mark behind.

The face, seen only one small fragment at a time, was hard to discern. Sang Ki thought that it was narrow, high-cheekboned and not entirely human. He thought it might be the same face as that carved into hundreds of rocks scattered over the plain that held Winter's Hammer. The moon's face, or so he'd always been told. It wasn't a kind one.

And then the ship above moved them away from the statue and they sank further still.

'Are we too deep?' Sang Ki asked Little Cousin. There had been no air bladders for some time and the air they breathed now felt stale and unnourishing.

'Just a little further,' Little Cousin said. His face was rapt as he gazed over the city whose lowest buildings were now sliding by to either side. These must be the homes of the city's long-dead residents. They looked gloomy and forbidding. There were narrow, sickle-shaped windows in the walls, angled so that only the rising sun could penetrate them. Or, Sang Ki realised, the rising moon.

The walls were scribed with patterns whose form he didn't understand. Was that one there, picked out in shimmering mother-of-pearl, meant to be a horse? But no man would ride a beast that snarled so viciously. It seemed to be a scene of battle. The sprays of gems were rubies, more valuable than he could ever fathom using for such profligate decoration. But he thought their profusion was meant to signify gouts of blood.

The bottom approached, illuminated by a green light whose source he couldn't see – perhaps it was the water itself. There were figures below, arms outstretched as if to reach for him. Something many-tentacled rose from between them, thrashing up towards them and stirring the silt in which it had slept into a brown fog that defeated all attempts to see through it.

The creature's many eyes peered in through the glass and its suckers clung as if it meant to squeeze the metal sphere until it popped. It seemed large and strong enough to do it, but in a flick of jointless limbs it was gone and the sphere jolted and stopped, finally at the end of its long rope.

For a long while there was nothing to see outside except the stirred-up sand and the occasional flash of fin as something half-hidden swam past. But imperceptibly the silt began to settle and the water shaded back from yellow to a deep, clear blue. Forms hovered all around the sphere, half-seen and terrifying, and then sharper, more obviously human – and then, with startling abruptness, they were entirely clear.

The destruction of the city must have been instant, and for the first time Sang Ki truly entertained the idea that it had been the act of a god. Some force he could barely imagine had struck down not just the buildings but every person in them. Killed them and frozen them in the moment of death, jet-black statues that had once been people.

Not just people – children. There were a dozen of them, ranged around a grid that someone had scratched into the pavement, a collection of circles and squares in swirling line. One child was crouched in the middle square while around him his fellows leaned forward in encouragement or leaned back, mouths open in what must have been laughter but now looked like silent screams. Sang Ki knew the game they were playing: grasshopper. He'd played it himself with other children of the tribe when he was a boy.

It was such an ordinary scene. He'd expected . . . something else. These had been the moon's people and the sun's folk had done this to them. This was how the last war between sun and moon had ended, with children scorched into cinders as they played.

He stared at them as the water and weeds swirled about them. Water and something darker: a stain diffusing through it like smoke through air. The burnt woman groaned and he thought it was her reaction to the dead children until more of the dark substance spread and he realised that it was coming from them, from their sphere, and that it was blood.

The burnt woman groaned again, louder and more desperate. He wrenched his eyes from the blood in the water to see it pouring from between her legs. Her arms clasped her rounded stomach and she was sobbing without tears. Perhaps the fire had robbed those from her too.

'She's bleeding!' he shouted, panicked. 'There's so much blood!'

'It's the baby,' Little Cousin said, and as he spoke there was another jerk and then the sphere began to lift, but slowly, much too slowly.

'Help me,' the burnt woman begged. Her eyes were pleading but what could he do? He was no physician, certainly no midwife.

'We need to get to the surface,' he told Little Cousin.

'We will.'

'But faster!'

'We have no way to tell them,' the trader said.

'Then *find* a way! If we send a bladder up – see, there's one here. A message scratched in it—'

But Little Cousin was already shaking his head. 'It's no use, fat man. Even if I could tell them, I wouldn't. It would kill us all, to rise too fast.'

'You can't know that! No one's ever gone so deep before!'

'I'm sorry,' the Ahn man said with sad finality. Through the whole exchange the burnt woman groaned and whimpered.

Sang Ki awkwardly shuffled himself round the bench that ringed the interior of the sphere until he was near enough to reach her. Her rasping breath counterpointed his own gasps and the blood continued to fall, dripping into the water and leaving a trail that drew creatures he'd never dreamed lived beneath the waves, bug-eyed fish and razor-clawed, twig-limbed things that snapped and gobbled at the bloody water and circled round and round, waiting for the body itself to fall.

She might have fallen, if Sang Ki hadn't kept hold of her. She was weakening fast, far faster than the sphere moved on its ponderous rise to the surface. Her skin was waxy and her eyes half-closed. Only her hands seemed to retain their strength, one gripped round his and the other round her stomach.

'Hurry,' Sang Ki said uselessly. He could only hold her hand and murmur soothing nonsense words as inch by inch they neared the surface.

Then, suddenly, bright sunlight struck them through the water and a moment later they broke the surface – and then it was almost too fast. As soon as his crew could hear him, Little Cousin yelled and they pulled the sphere aboard the ship. They held it hovering while sailors crawled beneath to lift the burnt woman down.

Sang Ki wanted to follow but knew he couldn't ask the crew to bear his weight. He had to wait until a stall was brought and he slid down onto it and then on his knees beside the burnt woman and the small, red, horrible form that now lay between her legs.

'The baby?' Sang Ki asked, but he already knew the answer. He knew what that little, broken thing was.

'Dead,' his mother said. She must have been drawn on deck by the commotion and now she cradled the burnt woman's head in her lap, almost as if she cared.

'And her?' Sang Ki asked, shocked to discover that the answer mattered to him.

His mother's face was cold as she looked down at the woman in her arms, whose whole purpose and protection had perished with her unborn child. 'Not dead yet.'

32

Krish felt the sea pulling at his feet. It wanted him to go deeper and he intended to oblige, but not quite yet. The water was calm today, the waves a light ripple on its surface, reflecting the sun in fragments. His people had crossed this ocean once, back when the tribes had been united and women had still ruled them all.

He'd filled his saddlebags with rocks. They hung from his neck, bowing him over, but he'd wanted to be sure they were heavy enough. He'd failed at so much; he couldn't risk failing at this.

It was over and everything was lost. He'd believed so fiercely in his god and his god had betrayed him. His god was nothing and so was he. And the things he'd done in his god's name . . .

His memory was full of blood and screams. It sickened him to recall how much pleasure he'd taken in his victims' fear. He'd known no fear himself until he saw his brothers die by their own hands. It was his fault. His presence brought death, and more death would follow as long as he remained. There was only one right thing left to do.

The cold of the water began to seep into his bones. Sometimes discomfort faded with time and sometimes it grew worse. Perhaps when the whole of him was in the water he'd be warm again, but whatever he felt, he wouldn't feel for long.

The water lapped against his calves, his thighs; a wave came and drenched his chest, throwing salt into his eyes and mouth. He shut them and moved deeper as his clothes billowed around him, filled with air and moved by currents. The trapped air tried to lift him but the rocks in his satchel were heavier. They kept his feet pressed to the seabed as he walked on. There was sand beneath him at first and then stone and the soft give of unseen creatures crushed beneath his heels.

If he dropped the satchel, he could still rise to the surface. He could live. There was some part of him that wanted to: the boy who'd gown to adulthood among the tribe, who'd taken pleasure in the hunt and pride in his skill. But a stronger part felt otherwise. A part of him had grown up cold and hungry in the mountains, unwanted by his da, dismissed by his neighbours. That part knew that nothing he ever did could go right.

He opened his mouth and the waiting water rushed into his empty lungs. His body was heavy with the water he'd breathed and was still breathing. He thrashed in panic until movement became impossible and the peace and warmth he'd hoped for came. Then he lay back and let his body float to the rocky ocean floor as the life floated out of him.

It was said that in the last days of the old Empire, when the war was won and the cost of it was finally being counted, the mages of old had devoted themselves to pleasures of the flesh. They'd sensed what was coming and turned their backs on it to enjoy the time they had left.

Olufemi wasn't precisely enjoying herself. The physical pleasure was there – it was mounting in intensity as Eniola's mouth worked competently between her legs – but her mind was elsewhere. It drifted on the hot air wafted into motion but not coolness by slaves stationed beside the bed.

Eniola had been nothing but seeds in her parents and the lust that would one day unite them when Olufemi had last been in Mirror Town. Now she was a heavy-featured youth who had been happy to share Rah rice wine and then her body with the returned traveller. The Chukwu family always had been notorious gossips. No doubt Eniola hoped to wheedle a few titbits of Olufemi's history out of her and share it with her kin over dinner. Olufemi would probably oblige. What did she have left either to hide or to lose?

Eniola swiped her tongue one more time and Olufemi's body

finally surrendered to her persistence, clenching with pleasure as she trapped the younger woman's head between her thighs. When the climax was passed, Eniola leaned up on her elbows and grinned smugly, a very irritating expression.

Still, she'd done what was required and Olufemi pulled the other woman to her and kissed her. She could taste herself on Eniola's mouth – it wasn't unpleasant and she could enjoy this. She had to enjoy something, in whatever time she had left. She didn't believe Krish would give himself up as she'd asked. She didn't know what he'd do, but she doubted it would be anything she approved.

She didn't want to think of him now. She looked into the brown eyes above her and lowered her hand to return the pleasure she'd been given. She looked into brown eyes and tried not to think of ones that were muddy green. Vordanna was dead or rotting in an Ashane prison, Olufemi's ambitions were thwarted and her future dark. All she could have was this moment.

Eniola buried her face in Olufemi's neck as her own pleasure crested. She bit, hard. Olufemi yelped and tried to pull away, and they were still tangled inelegantly together when the door opened and Vordanna walked in, almost as if Olufemi's thoughts had summoned her.

She looked so out of place, framed in white marble in the one place she and Olufemi had never visited together, that Olufemi doubted her own eyes. Vordanna seemed frozen in place, staring at her lover and her lover's lover.

It was the sudden anger in Vordanna's expression that convinced Olufemi this was no hallucination. Vordanna was never angry; years on bliss pills had left her incapable of the emotion. And yet those narrowed eyes, pursed lips and flushed cheeks could mean little else.

'Will you leave us?' Olufemi said to Eniola.

The younger woman's spine stiffened with indignation.

'Please,' Olufemi said. 'This woman is a friend I haven't seen for a very long time.'

Eniola, from a family unused to being disregarded, held

Olufemi a moment longer, her lips pressed to Olufemi's, before rolling from the bed. She stooped to gather her robe but didn't bother to wear it as she walked from the room. Vordanna's brittle gaze followed every step until she was through the passage and out of sight.

'I thought you were dead,' Olufemi said.

Vordanna eyed her naked and sweaty body. 'Really? And this was you mourning me?'

'Vordanna, what *happened*? How are you here? And where's Jinn?'

The other woman turned her gaze from Olufemi to the two men standing to either side of the bed. 'Your slaves?' she asked.

Olufemi felt herself flush hotly. 'Get out,' she said to the slaves, her flush deepening as she heard the careless command in her own voice. 'My family's slaves,' she explained weakly as the men bowed and left the room.

She felt herself growing angry too, at the judgement in Vordanna's eyes. She'd always known how Olufemi's people lived. Olufemi had never lied to Vordanna about the source of the bliss powder that had enslaved her. And gentle, placid Vordanna had never cared. And yet here she was, in a place she'd never visited, wearing an expression she'd never worn.

'What *are* you doing here?' Olufemi asked.

'I came to warn you,' Vordanna said. The silver moon's rune Olufemi had given her glittered on a chain round her neck. 'I came because *he* called.'

Dae Hyo was trying to teach Dinesh to pull a bow when the messenger found him. Dae Hyo had his hands resting against the slave's shoulders, though in truth he didn't enjoy touching him; he could hardly even stand to look at him. His empty smile and vacant eyes made Dae Hyo's skin crawl. But if he could be trained to fight, there was hope for the other slaves too.

'I'll be there soon,' he told the messenger and then said to Dinesh, 'Yes, you see, pull your shoulders back, not just your arms. The blades should meet in the middle – can you feel it?'

'It's difficult,' Dinesh said, his arms shaking as he held the bowstring taut.

'If it was easy, the world would be full of bowmen.'

'Your pardon master, it cannot wait,' the messenger said. He was, or had been, a man of the tribes – Gyo to judge by the scarring on his cheek – but there was no warrior's pride in him now, only bliss. Dae Hyo could hardly bear to look at him either.

'There's not much that can't wait,' Dae Hyo told him, 'except a drawn arrow and a loose shit.'

As if to prove at least half his point, Dinesh released the bowstring to slap bruisingly against his own wrist and send the arrow in the approximate direction of the target.

'Your pardon master, they said to bring you now,' the messenger persisted.

Dae Hyo sighed and turned to face him. 'And what will happen if I don't come?'

That seemed to baffle the man. His smooth face shifted into a frown with the slowness of his thoughts. 'My mistress will be angry,' he said eventually.

'I tell you what, there's a few things in this life I fear, but Olufemi isn't one of them.'

'Angry with *me*,' the messenger said.

The man didn't sound worried – bliss left no room for worry – but Dae Hyo felt ashamed. Of course a slave would be the one to suffer for it, not Dae Hyo himself. It was a terrible thing, for one person to own another. But here was a happy thought: if the slaves could learn to fight for Krish they could use those skills to overthrow their masters. Dae Hyo was doing doubly right by helping his brother.

He grinned and said magnanimously, 'We'll come now.'

The messenger looked at Dinesh, clearly uncertain about whether the invitation had been extended to him, but Dae Hyo waved him on and of course he wouldn't argue. Dinesh trailed amiably at his heels, as pleased to be doing that as he had been to miss the archery target.

Dae Hyo had taken them to the city's edge for their practice, to keep them away from the curious eyes of the mages. Dinesh wasn't *their* slave, but it was clear enough he was someone's, for all Krish liked to deny it. And slaves weren't meant to be weapon wielders.

Dae Hyo was glad to be leaving the desert. He couldn't love it. However much he told himself that this wasn't the Rune Waste, his heart wouldn't believe it. He'd skirted the boundaries of the Waste once as a young warrior, a foolhardy proof of bravery attempted by the youths of many tribes. And he'd seen there the same endless waves of sand with littler waves curled into them. The sky was the same yellow as the sand, drained of the colour that made the sky pretty, and there was nothing living, as far as he could see, for miles in any direction, except for the small pale lizards whose splayed toes seemed to float them above the dunes as they skittered about to no purpose.

Soon they were walking through fields, growing improbably with their roots in the same barren sand. Olufemi had told him the mages of old planted them, back when the runes still did what they ought, and the magic lingered here. It was fading, though; even Dae Hyo could see that. They walked through the famished and broken stalks of abandoned cornfields before they reached those that were still green and growing.

Mirror Town distressed him, as it always did, with its solidity. The wind that shaped the sand dunes dashed itself against the buildings of the city. Their whiteness was too much to look at and worse still when the turning of the many mirrors sent sunlight straight into your eyes. He kept his down as they walked the dusty streets between houses slender and ornate and squat and functional and oval and square and round. Each design marked the dwelling of a different family, but the only one he'd learned to notice was Olufemi's own.

Her kin seemed fond of maps. The surface of their sprawling mansion was covered in them, each made of tiny brightly coloured pieces of glass that must have taken a thousand slaves a thousand days to press into the plaster. He recognised a map of the Moon Forest high on the domed roof and his own plains to one side of the door they were approaching, but many others were strange to him. Were there so many places in the world? But perhaps the mages had imagined these other lands. It wouldn't surprise him. Sometimes they seemed as addled as their slaves.

Another slave, a small Ashane girl, waited for them inside to lead them past the grey-haired mirror masters to the room where Olufemi and Krish waited. There was another woman there too, whose face sparked a memory he couldn't quite grab hold of, something to do with the moon and a fight in the mud.

'I have news,' Olufemi said before he could sit down.

'Well I'm glad you didn't drag me all the way here because you like the look of my face.'

'*What* news, Olufemi?' Krish said with an exasperation that suggested it wasn't for the first time. Then his brother's gaze shifted from the mage to the other woman. Hers had never left him: she was studying Krish with an intensity that clearly made him uneasy but which seemed to Dae Hyo filled more with admiration than threat. She was attractive enough: round-hipped and fair-faced and young enough to bear children, if Krish chose to court her.

'Sit then, now you're finally here,' Olufemi said to Dae Hyo. 'There's drink, and food if you want it.'

There was, plates of sliced fruit sprinkled with a fiery spice Dae Hyo wished the mages weren't so fond of. Someone had left a game of Night and Day half-finished on the table and he knocked over one of the tall black pieces as he grabbed a flagon of wine. 'This is news we need to be drunk for?' he asked, pouring himself a generous measure.

'If you're expecting good news, you haven't been paying attention,' Olufemi snapped.

'It's *my* news,' the other woman said. 'I brought it.'

'Where did you bring it from?' Krish asked. 'And who are you?'

'I'm Vordanna, my lord.'

'Vordanna is my . . . friend,' Olufemi said, as if she'd meant to use a different word. 'And she brings us tidings from the enemy's camp.'

'You're him,' Vordanna said, her eyes only for Krish. 'You're really him.'

'I'm Krish.'

'You're *him*. It was all true. Jinn said it wasn't, but I knew it was. I felt it.' She touched her own chest, or something that rested against it, a hard lump beneath her cotton dress.

'The news,' Dae Hyo said. 'I'm sure you're very pleased to meet Krish – he's a likeable fellow. But what's this urgent news you bring him?'

'It's danger, my lord,' the woman said.

'The danger I warned you of,' Olufemi interrupted brusquely. She picked a yellow fruit from the bowl but didn't eat it, instead turning it round and round in her fingers as the skin bruised and the juice ran down her wrist. 'Perhaps if you hear it from another, you'll act as I've advised. There's an army coming for you, and any army you might have had to defend you is dead. There's no hope left, but time to flee if you choose. You might head south to Vordanna's homeland. There are no cities there whose ruin your presence will bring, only a land broad enough perhaps for you to lose yourself in.'

'Flee?' Vordanna said. Olufemi had called her a friend, but she stared at the mage now as if she were a stranger. 'That wasn't what I came to say.'

'Belbog's balls!' Dae Hyo shouted, pounding his fist against the table and sending splashes of wine to stain the white wood. 'The news, woman – the news!'

'Yes.' Krish's quiet voice sounded louder in the silence that followed Dae Hyo's outburst. 'I'd like to hear it for myself and make my own mind up.'

'There *is* an army,' Vordanna said. 'Two armies. The Hunt has come from the Moon Forest—'

'A force dedicated to eliminating your creatures and all who might serve you,' Olufemi interrupted.

'—and the Ashane are coming from their land to the plains.'

'You see,' Olufemi said, 'it's as I told you. And as for the Brotherband, whom you *might* have gathered to your side, if not for Dae Hyo here. Tell him about the Brotherband, Vordanna.'

Vordanna shot her a very unloving look, but then turned back to Krish and said, 'They're dead, my lord.'

'They were defeated?' Krish asked.

'No. They . . . there was to be a battle. Sang Ki and Cwen – that's the leaders of your enemies – they planned a raid on the enemy camp, but when they got there they were all dead. They'd killed themselves, or just sat there waiting to die.'

'*Killed* themselves?' Dae Hyo didn't know what he felt. Joy, or maybe regret. He'd wanted to be the one to put a blade through their hearts. 'Don't tell me they finally realised what evil rat-fuckers they are and decided the world was better off without them.'

Vordanna eyed him uncertainly and then turned back to Krish. 'No, it was – it was despair. I heard Sang Ki talking about one who was still alive. When they questioned him he said there was no point carrying on, that the battle was already lost and the moon would never rise. But the moon *has* risen,' she added fiercely. '*You* are the risen moon.'

For once Dae Hyo could almost believe that Krish was. His brother's eyes flashed silver and strange as he leaned forward, every line of his body tense. 'When did this happen? When?'

'It was . . . nearly a moon past, my lord.'

'A moon.' Krish leaned back, his bottom lip caught in his teeth. It was a gesture Dae Hyo had come to recognise. It meant his brother was thinking about something important.

'This army,' Olufemi said. 'Do they know where we are?'

'I don't think so.' Vordanna's eyes returned to Krish like a magnet drawn to true north. 'But my lord, the leader of the Rah is with them. There might be someone among his people who knows.'

'How did *you* know where to find us?' Krish asked.

'I . . . my lord, I felt it – I felt you calling to me.' She touched her chest, over her heart.

'What is that you wear?' Krish asked.

She pulled out a pendant from beneath her dress: a silver swirl that Dae Hyo had seen before, sewn into the robe Olufemi hadn't worn since she'd come to Mirror Town. It was the moon's rune – Krish's mark.

Krish stilled, staring at it, then abruptly leaned back. 'I think . . . I think . . . I need to think.'

'There's nothing to think about,' Olufemi said.

Krish pushed his chair back and stood. 'Please be quiet.'

Olufemi looked as if she meant to argue, but Dae Hyo glared at her and she crossed her arms and said nothing. Neither did Krish, only paced up and down the room wearing a stern frown. Dae Hyo tapped his foot in time with his brother's steps and Vordanna followed his movement with her eyes, back and forth and back and forth. Only Dinesh seemed entirely patient, leaning against the wall with a dreamy smile.

Finally Krish sat down again. His silver gaze swept them all before settling on Olufemi. 'You're wrong,' he said. 'You're wrong about two things.'

'Am I now?'

'Yes. You must be.'

'And about what am I so mistaken?'

'The runes *do* work, I know they do – I've felt it. I dreamed about what happened to the Brotherband: I dreamed that I was drowning but it wasn't like a normal dream. It seemed . . . real. I felt the death of one of the Brotherband warriors, killing himself just like you said, Vordanna. I think because they wore that rune – my rune – I think they felt what I feel. When they all died, it was the time you told me there was no point fighting, Olufemi. You told me I was bound to lose.'

'You said that?' Vordanna stared in horror at the mage.

'Yes, and I believed her. I felt hopeless and somehow I must have made them feel it too.'

'Impossible,' Olufemi said. 'Why would that rune have power, just that one and no other?'

'After what you told me, that the runes weren't working, I wanted to know more. Your family found me books from the great library, everything about the runes. A slave read them to me. I think I understand it now: the sun and the moon, they're like the ends of a piece of string, or the fingers holding the string tight. Everything else is between them, some closer to the sun and some closer to the moon. But that rune –' he pointed at the pendant around Vordanna's neck '– it's just the moon, right?'

Olufemi nodded grudgingly. 'That's all a gross simplification, but in its essentials you're correct.'

'So my rune worked because I'm here – I'm Yron. But every other rune needs a bit of the sun too.'

'I know this, boy. Why do you think I summoned you back? But you're wrong: even your rune requires the power of the sun to be sparked into life. Else the Sun rune alone would have held power until you returned, and it had none. Don't you think that was the first thing I tried?'

'But that proves it. That proves what I've been trying to say! You told me the sun, my sister, that she's still alive. That she just stepped away from the world. But it can't be true. The sun must be as dead as the moon was before I was born.'

'No,' the mage said. 'It can't be. Everyone knows the tale.'

'And tales never lie?' Krish's expression was intense, the same way he'd looked when he told the Rah they must end their slavery. 'Just pretend I am right. If I am, what would it mean?'

'Smiler's Fair,' Olufemi said slowly. 'I thought that your rune quenched the fire but . . . there could be another explanation. The sun's magic is a straightforward thing: power for power, a cost you pay and a price that's known. The moon's magic is trickier: it's the reason the mages of old preferred to deal with Mizhara and the reason Mizhara's forces won in the end. The moon exacts a price, but you won't know what it is until you pay it, and it's different for every person.

'I thought the rune quenched the fire, but did it start it? Did the fire spread so very fiercely because the rune ate the living of Smiler's Fair as the cost of its work? And then . . . yes. If quenching the fire wasn't its purpose then it must have been a call for help. *Your* call for help, of course, as it's your mark. It summoned your Servants the worm men to aid you, but perhaps it was even more than that.'

She looked at Vordanna, sudden warmth in her expression. 'You told me the monsters fled the Moon Forest on a day that may well have been the same day Smiler's Fair burned. What if they weren't driven away but pulled towards – summoned quite uselessly by Yron's need, by Krishanjit's formless, thoughtless cry for help?' And then all the excitement drained from her face to leave it weary and old. 'All that could be true, if Mizhara were truly dead. But the sun won the war – she didn't perish in it. What happened at Smiler's Fair must have been merely the last gasp of Yron's power in the world, the remnants of it that remained in his Servants igniting at your need.'

'You're wrong.' Krish rested his clenched fist against the table. 'Mizhara could have died too, she and Yron could have killed each other. It would explain why no one's seen her for a thousand years. Maybe your ancestors lied about her dying because they didn't want their enemies to know – or their followers. I'm right, I know I am.'

'This is hope, not knowledge,' the mage said. 'A theory built on the flimsiest of evidence. An excuse not to do what you know is right, to leave before you bring these armies down on us.'

'No,' Krish said. 'There's more. I think . . . I think there was one other time I did whatever it was I did in Smiler's Fair.' His voice faltered for the first time as he turned towards Dae Hyo. 'Tell me, when did the Brotherband attack the Dae?'

A sour feeling began in the pit of Dae Hyo's stomach. His brother had the expression of a man who knew he needed to draw a deep-buried splinter and couldn't face the pain. 'It was seven winters past,' Dae Hyo said cautiously. 'Just before the pivot of the year.'

'The year of the great murrain? We didn't know about that in the mountains. Our goats had no sickness, but we knew something was up with the, the savages – that's what we called you then. Because the tribes came raiding on our lands when they'd never raided before. Some of our goats were stolen away in the night and the headman's tent was slashed open. They took his stock of vegetables and meat and he made the rest of us give him ours to make up the loss. My da was furious. He—'

Krish's expression hardened. 'He beat me worse than he'd ever beaten me before. Ma tried to stop him and he threw her off. I thought he was going to kill me but I wasn't afraid. I don't know why. Maybe I thought it was the end and there was nothing worse to be afraid of. So I wasn't afraid – I was angry. I *hated* him. And . . .' His throat bobbed as he swallowed. 'I hated my ma too, because she couldn't stop him.

'My da raised his fist and he looked at me and he just stopped. He looked – I didn't believe it then, but I know now. He looked afraid. He never touched me after that. He only beat my ma.'

Dae Hyo felt sick that his brother had suffered like that and worse that his father had lifted his hand to a woman. What kind of childhood had Krish had? And, a small part of him wondered, what kind of man had it made Krish into?

Krish didn't seem to feel sorry for himself. His expression was only hopeful as he asked Olufemi, 'The Brotherband were wearing my rune even then, weren't they?'

'They were,' the mage said.

'Yes,' Krish said. 'I'm right, aren't I? That was the first time. They felt what I felt through the power of my rune. They felt my anger, and they attacked the Dae.'

'No,' Dae Hyo said. 'It wasn't your doing. It was them – it was all them.'

'It *was* me. I'm sure of it. I'm sorry, Dae Hyo, but I think it was. Maybe the anger worked on something that was inside them already, but it came from me. That's why they did what no tribesman had ever done before. They were so full of my rage they didn't care who they hurt. Maybe . . . maybe it was anger at my ma, I don't know. She told me I was too angry and I didn't understand. If I'd known, if I could have made myself feel different . . .' For a moment he sounded as anguished as he should, and then he only looked determined. 'But it proves I'm right, doesn't it, Olufemi? It proves the runes aren't dead.'

'No,' Dae Hyo said. 'No.'

But Olufemi's face glowed with new excitement. 'It might. It's possible.'

'It *has* to be,' Krish said. 'What other hope have we got? We can use my rune – we can use it to help me.'

'We can't,' she said and Krish hung his head until she added, 'Or we don't need to. If your theory is correct, the way your power channels through that mark is too unpredictable, too hard to control. But it doesn't matter. The runes are scribed from the glyphs of being and the glyphs of becoming. The sun and moon lie behind them, their source and their outcome. It's always been that way, yet I've always believed it needn't be. The runes are the language of life and power. Written appropriately, they can express the idea of Yron without the idea of Mizhara – they can draw on your power alone without hers. It will be . . . dangerous. Very dangerous and very unpredictable, as all moon-magic workings are, but it can be done. *If* what you say is true.'

'It *is*. You can do it?' Krish asked.

'I can try,' Olufemi said. 'I will try.'

And Krish smiled. His brother, the man whose rage had killed Dae Hyo's people, seemed only happy. The sour knot in Dae Hyo's stomach unwound itself and he rose from the table and fled the room, getting as far as the corridor outside before he fell to his knees and the wine in his stomach came spewing out.

33

It was a steep climb and Cwen paused often, turning her face towards the roaring falls so the fine mist that surrounded them could cool her. Alfreda trudged stolidly beside her, seemingly unaffected by the heat or the exertion. Her followers were strung out on the narrow path behind them, hawks and churls and Jorlith and reluctant thegns and those few of the survivors of Smiler's Fair who hadn't melted away into the plains.

The river churned through the gorge its relentless rush had carved into the hard grey stone to spill in hissing white sheets to the plains below. Cwen licked the fine droplets of water from her lips and climbed on until the final rock was crested. The path led onward to a charmless, undulating terrain – scrubby hills and the great mass of people encamped on them.

She'd known what to expect. When they'd abandoned the river at the start of the rapids, Little Cousin had headed into the Silent Sands with Sang Ki and his retinue and Cwen had sent scouts ahead. They'd told her about the Ashane army, but she still gasped to see it. It was like a vast brown stain on the grass. Cwen had always known the Ashane were more numerous than the Moon Forest folk, but she hadn't realised there was quite such a horde of them. King Nayan must have emptied Ashanesland of its able-bodied men.

'Fuck,' Wine said at her shoulder. 'It was hardly worth us turning up, was it?'

'But can they fight as well as a hawk?' Wingard asked.

Cwen wasn't sure it mattered when there were so many of them. And they weren't a rabble – or, at least, the rabble had trained soldiers to guide them. The vast force was clustered around banners, probably marking the shipforts where the Ashane thegns lived. Each group seemed to consist of a kernel of metal-armed soldiers inside a husk of lightly armed churls, thousands upon thousands of them.

She could see the perimeter defences they must be digging fresh every day, and the pickets ringing the camp, and the moment when the pickets spotted her. A horseman, made toylike by distance, rode from the outer ditch towards the grander, brightly coloured tents at the heart of the camp.

She felt a murmur of unease in the pit of her stomach. She'd pictured herself being greeted warmly by Nayan, a welcome ally, but the proximity of the meeting fed her doubts.

She brought news of Krishanjit, news that would allow King Nayan finally to find and kill his son. Nayan wanted his son dead, but would doing it gladden him? Sang Ki had told her that the King had adored his wife and been devastated by her loss. Would Krishanjit remind him of his dead love? Or would he find a way to blame his son for her death? She thought of her mother, who must have blamed Cwen for the parting of her own legs, as if as a baby she'd somehow willed herself into existence.

'Well,' she said, 'too late to polish our boots. It's time to shake hands with the Ashane King.'

The pickets wouldn't let her hawks pass, looking askance at their spears, so she entered the camp with only Alfreda and Hana beside her. The Seonu woman had chosen to stay with them when her son headed off into the desert with Little Cousin. She seemed to consider herself Cwen's co-commander, though she led a force of fewer than a hundred Ashane.

The sun was touching the horizon by the time they came to the camp's centre and the huge structure at its heart, more a fortress made of canvas than anything resembling a tent. Surrounding it were men in leather sewn with metal rings, who carried the stink of rotted meat about them. Carrion riders, Cwen realised when she heard the distant squawk of one of their birds. She felt a stab of pain, not muted by time, when she remembered poor Osgar's corpse decaying into bones a thousand miles away.

The carrion riders eyed her with the expressions of men who thought she'd trodden in shit and didn't want her bringing it into their house. The soldier who'd led them through the camp said, 'She's here to see King Nayan.'

'And who's she?' one of the riders asked.

'I'm the woman who's brought seven thousand to ally with your army,' Cwen said.

That bought her his attention, though he still looked like a man who'd found a turd floating in his privy. 'What business is this of the Moon Forest folk?' he asked.

'The same business as yours. The moon's our trade and always has been. But I'm not here to speak to some nasty-smelling lackey. Take me to your King.'

His hand fell to his sword hilt as Alfreda stepped forward to put herself between the danger and Cwen. Cwen moved her gently aside. 'If Nayan doesn't want my fighters, he'll want my news,' she said to the carrion rider, her own hands staying clear of her weapons. 'I know where Krishanjit is.'

The sneer didn't leave the man's face, but he led them in. The tent was like an onion, layer after layer of material. There was rough canvas on the outside, dyed in the blue and green checks the Ashane favoured, an antechamber beyond with more soldiers lounging in it, then a blue cotton wall hiding what seemed to be a dining area, and finally green silk that parted to reveal a rug-strewn chamber and important-looking men seated in its centre.

Alfreda hung back, like a hulking shadow at Cwen's shoulder, and Hana drifted sideways as if she meant to stand by the door and observe, leaving Cwen to stride forward alone with a confidence she didn't entirely feel.

A dozen faces turned to her. They were probably great ship-lords, captains of the carrion flock and advisors to the King, but the only one she recognised was Nayan himself. She'd seen that beaky profile staring at her from gold wheels in her childhood, but that wasn't what made it so instantly familiar. Sang Ki had shown her his drawing of Krishanjit, and if you'd plucked out most of the lank hair and added a few wrinkles round the eyes and deep grooves cupping the mouth, it would have been this man.

Her eyes moved from him to the map spread on a table between the gathered lords. It showed the far west of the plains, the land around Rah territory.

'Who are these women?' one of the lords asked.

Cwen forced herself to incline her head respectfully. These weren't Moon Forest thegns for her to bully. 'I'm Cwen, lead hawk of the Hunter and here to bring you my alliance and news of Krishanjit's whereabouts.'

The King stood, using his hands to lever himself out of his chair as if his back pained him. It remained stooped as he walked to her and she saw a fine tremor in the hand he held out. The result of an apoplectic seizure, she guessed, and clasped it in her own before realising he meant for her to kiss it.

There was a shocked hiss from the gathered lords, but to her surprise Nayan laughed. It was a young sound, far younger than his face. 'Welcome, Cwen of the Moon Forest hawks, and the five thousand three hundred men you bring with you.'

She must have shown her surprise because his smile widened. 'We've watched your approach for quite some time, hawk. We supposed you came as friends, or you might have done more to hide yourself from us. And we know that the moon is an enemy of your Hunter, and the moon is what my son claims to be. But that you know his location, this we didn't guess. We'd thought him in Rah lands. Are you here to tell me it isn't so?'

He gestured at the map. The eight men and two women gathered round it eyed her with hostility as she approached. There was a tall, grey-haired man in leather armour, surely a carrion rider, perhaps their leader. The women were clearly twins and the gangly young man beside them certainly a relative. There was a man Nayan's own age, his face closed and sour, the lines from his mouth all radiating downward. And there was the one she liked the look of least of all: a handsome man in his middle years with bright white teeth and an expression only an idiot would trust.

She looked down at the map and put her finger in the heart

of Rah territory, where the New Misa spilled into the sea. 'Krishanjit *was* here. I . . . met the man who welcomed him and then drove him out. The same man who contacted you.'

'Rah Uin,' Nayan said.

She nodded. 'The Rah tribe went to war with itself over your son. He was forced to flee.' She moved her finger, tracing it south along the coast until it landed in Mirror Town.

Nayan frowned at the map and she could guess what he was thinking. A hundred miles of the plains and another two hundred of the Silent Sands lay between him and his quarry. 'You're sure?' he asked.

'She isn't,' Hana said and Cwen snapped her head round to glare at her. She'd forgotten the Seonu woman was there.

Nayan eyed Hana thoughtfully. 'And who are you, my lady?'

'Seonu Hana, my liege, leader of that tribe among your forces.' Her bow was deeper than Cwen's.

Cwen arched an eyebrow at her. It was the first she'd known there were Seonu among the Ashane, but she seemed to remember that the Ashane had conquered the tribe, so perhaps it made sense. Still, Hana as their leader? Sang Ki would shit a hedgehog if he heard.

'Cwen heard of your son's location because of a man she tortured,' Hana said. 'From his daughter, who said it to stop the torture. Information obtained that way is worth little.'

Nayan scowled at Cwen, all his earlier friendliness gone. 'Torture? This is not the way given to us by the Five or the prow gods of our hearths.'

Cwen felt the same sick shame clench her gut that the thought of this always caused, but she made herself face Nayan without shrinking. 'I did what was needed as my mistress commanded me. And the information *was* good.'

'It's worthless,' said the sour-faced old man.

'It's a bent twig on a trail we're following,' Cwen insisted. 'Hana's son is travelling the Silent Sands right now to scout out Mirror Town and see if Krishanjit is there. He has messenger owls with him – we'll know soon after he does.'

'Mirror Town,' the carrion rider said. He had the rough voice of a man who shouted more than he spoke. 'The mages won't take kindly to our army coming there.'

'Krishanjit had a mage with him,' Hana confirmed. 'She's taken him back to her people.'

'And we all know what weapon the mages can wield,' the sour-looking lord agreed.

It occurred to Cwen that not all the Ashane were happy to be part of this army; that perhaps most of them thought the battle futile. She looked around the table at the grave faces and wondered if they'd be glad of an opportunity to back down from the fight. But without them and their thousands of soldiers, what chance did *she* have against the mages?

Alfreda sidled up to her in that awkward way of hers, as if she thought a six-foot-tall woman built like an ice oak might not be noticed. She leaned down and whispered, 'The fire javelin' in Cwen's ear.

'We have a weapon powerful enough to defeat the mages,' Cwen told the Ashane King.

'A weapon with no ammunition,' Hana pointed out. 'A black powder weapon and only the Maeng know how to make the black powder. It's a secret any Maeng woman would take to her grave.'

But Nayan wasn't looking at her; his attention was once again focused on Cwen. 'What is this weapon and what can it do?'

The Moon Forest folk and the Ashane weren't enemies, but they'd never been allies either. Was it wise to tell another nation about the fire javelin? But there were no nations, no boundaries that mattered except the one between sun and moon.

'It's a metal tube, and balls of metal come out of it,' Cwen explained. 'Very fast and very hard. The black powder pushes them out. Listen, this is all you need to know: it's a weapon that helped us to defeat Krishanjit's Brotherband when the warriors outnumbered us ten to one.'

'But it's useless without the black powder,' Hana said again.

Nayan smiled. 'It's just as well then that my spies have already learned the secret of making it.'

The terrain in the eastern tribelands was hilly, very different from the endless flatness of the plains through which the New Misa had brought them. Their horses paused to crop the browning grass at the top of one rise and Alfreda stroked Edred's head as he chewed.

Cwen had brought her clutch with her and Alfreda wished she hadn't, though she knew they were needed for the work ahead. But they spoke so loudly and so freely as they waited for their mounts to eat, spending words like clay anchors. She felt her own silence within that noise, a visible absence.

Cwen clucked at her horse to urge it over beside Alfreda's. 'Think Nayan can be right?' she whispered so the rest wouldn't hear or try to join the conversation. It was strange to get such kindness from her. Alfreda had seen Cwen fight. She wasn't a kind woman, but she was always gentle with Alfreda.

'I think he could be,' Alfreda said. 'I heard the rumour myself.'

'Bat shit?'

'Aye. Horseshit makes plants grow, doesn't it? It isn't so very strange that it has other uses.'

'And there was me thinking Nayan just wanted us out of the way. He's a strange one, isn't he? Hard to think he's a man who plans to kill his own son.'

There was something in Cwen's expression that said these words weren't as light as they seemed, a hidden weight to them like the metal core in an ice-oak joist. Alfreda would have asked more, but the other hawks came to surround them, the big shouting mass of them, and she hung her head and let their noise pass over her.

'We've found it!' a fresh-faced boy announced. 'Aebbe has sharp eyes – it's to the south by that little lake, where the trees part. You can see the black mouth of it.'

It took them only an hour's further ride to reach the cave. It had seemed small from a distance, the lake too, but up close

Alfreda saw the cave's entrance gape many times her own head-height and the dark blue of the lake's water spoke of a great depth.

'It's very dark in there,' Wingard said. The twins made Alfreda most nervous of all, with their easy closeness to Cwen and loud, confident voices.

'It's facing east,' Cwen said. 'No need to piss yourself – the sun must shine straight in every morning. It will cleanse it against the worm men.'

'I can hear the bats.' Wine looked no more happy than his brother.

'Don't be an idiot,' Cwen scoffed. 'Bats squeak as high as a thegn when he farts. You can't hear them.'

But Alfreda knew what Wine meant. There was a prickling of her skin and a discomfort in her ears; a noise more sensed than heard. At noon the bats should all be asleep, but as they drew nearer she thought she could hear the rustling of their wings in the darkness, thousands of leathery susurrations.

'We'll be quick,' Cwen said, with her usual brash certainty, but Alfreda knew her well enough now to see that she felt the unease too. These were the moon's creatures and this was the moon's place.

As they grew nearer the stench hit them – pungent and acrid, so thick it felt like it might silt up their lungs.

'We'll be *very* quick,' Cwen said, but despite her words she hesitated on the rock-strewn borders of the cave. The hawks hung back with her and so Alfreda drew a deep breath through her mouth, lit her lantern and strode forward into the darkness.

Inside, the smell was a hundred times worse. The floor was mounded with dried white droppings that cracked beneath her boots and let the fresher shit leak out. And now she *could* hear the bats, hidden somewhere high above in the vaulted roof of the cave. First one squeak and then a thousand as the creatures sensed the intrusion into their world. She heard the flutter of their wings and felt the wind of them. She was grateful for it, for anything that brushed away the choking smell, even for a moment. She turned to flee only to see Cwen behind her, a lantern held high and the shadowy forms of the bats darting away from the light.

The other hawks were behind, hefting the crates they'd brought to collect the excrement. They'd brought shovels too and Wingard dug his into the filth beneath him and then staggered back as the stench grew ten times worse. He fell backward into the shit, shaking his head and moaning.

Alfreda realised for the first time that the smell was more than just a discomfort. The same substance that made the shit so valuable might make it lethal too. She waded through the filth and stench to Cwen and whispered, 'We have to hurry.'

Cwen's expression was dazed, as if she too was in danger of being overpowered by the toxic vapours, but she repeated 'Hurry!' to all the hawks and one by one they dug their spades into the muck and began filling the first crate.

When it was piled high with the vile white stuff, Alfreda grabbed its handles and began to drag it out, taking in short gasping breaths through her mouth. It skidded over the slick ground and the bats fluttered and squawked all around, their tiny claws sometimes catching at her cheek.

Outside felt like a haven: the high blue sky and the clean wind. She would have liked to rest and ready herself for returning but she was afraid she might never find the nerve, so she took another deep breath and went back.

The work wore on with the day. One moment blended into the next while Alfreda focused on the movements: stand, shovel, stoop, lift, drag, return. The lanterns seemed to lose their power as the time passed. Or perhaps it was her eyes. After a while the white seemed grey, the black absolute and the noise of the bats no different from the nervous chattering of the hawks. And then she felt a hand on her arm, drawing her out. She looked at it, not understanding, until she stumbled out into the light of the afternoon and blinked in shock to realise that it was over.

'Thought you'd fallen asleep standing,' Cwen said, releasing her arm. She gestured over at the crates, all now full and being loaded on to the wagons behind their draft horses. The animals shied away and flicked their heads, but their harnesses held them and the smell was tolerable out here, where the wind was waiting to whisk it away.

Alfreda turned to look at Cwen and the sight surprised a laugh from her. The other woman was coated in shit, white from head to toe with smears of brown and green.

'What?' Cwen said, but Alfreda couldn't seem to stop laughing long enough to reply.

Cwen looked down at herself and then laughed too. 'You're not exactly smelling of roses yourself, you know.'

But looking at her own hand, as white and shit-smeared as Cwen's, just made Alfreda laugh harder.

'I'm going to the lake to get clean.' Cwen studied Alfreda intently for a moment and then turned to her hawks and said, 'Stay here and get the horses ready. You'll have your turn when we're done. Come on then, Freda – what would King Nayan say if we came back to him smelling like a mammoth's privy?'

They walked towards the lake through the summer-wilted grass in a silence that Alfreda was surprised to find companionable. With Algar . . . with Algar there'd always been chatter, but Cwen was a little more sparing with her words. Alfreda glanced at the hawk and found Cwen's eyes staring back beneath a shit-smeared mop of ginger hair.

'What did you think of Nayan then?' Cwen asked.

Alfreda shrugged.

'Nothing? But you must have had a picture in your mind before you saw him. I did: I saw a brutal man, a hard one. A little like Gest, I think. I hadn't imagined I'd like him.'

They'd reached the lake, the lapping of its waves against the pebbly shore a soothing sound. Cwen didn't hesitate before stripping off her outer clothes, throwing them into the water ahead of her and leaving her underthings on the shore. She sat to remove her boots and then waded in, feet a little tentative on the pebbles.

'Fuck me, that's cold!' she said when she was only up to her knees.

Alfreda could see the goosebumps already forming on her bark-brown skin. She could see the scars too. There were a score of them or more, from a narrow white line across one thigh to a deep gouge of flesh missing from Cwen's left biceps.

'You've had a hard life,' Alfreda said.

Cwen shrugged. 'Less hard than it could have been. My parents didn't want me – that's why I was born with the hawk mark. Imagine if I'd had to stay with them instead, with people who hated me so much they prayed for me to be taken away from them. Better to be where I was wanted. And besides, I like the work – I'm good at it. Well don't just stand there. You won't get clean by looking at the water.'

The shit had worked its way beneath her clothes and then dried. They pulled at her skin when she pulled them off but it was good to be rid of them. She followed Cwen's example and threw them into the water, then waded after Cwen as she moved deeper still, until she was covered to her neck and the water tickled against Alfreda's breasts.

She realised that Cwen was studying her in turn, her eyes running over the powerful muscles of her right arm, disproportionate to her left, and the white freckled scars given her by her forge.

'I amn't a pretty sight.' Alfreda crossed her arms over her chest self-consciously.

'Who cares about pretty? You're strong. I was just thinking what a hawk you'd have made. Maybe if you'd been born with the mark you'd have been leader now and not me.'

Alfreda ducked her head, blushing, and only looked up when a splash of water soaked her hair. Cwen laughed and went back to rubbing the filth from her own body. Alfreda did the same. It felt good to see it all float away from them in a white and brown cloud, though the water was every bit as freezing as Cwen had said.

'I can't imagine being a hawk,' she said after a while. 'Taken away from your family to live among strangers. Me and Algar – and Mum and Dad when they were still alive – we were all our world. We travelled to far places, but we always had each other.' It surprised her to find that talk of her brother brought a little less pain now. It felt a betrayal, but she couldn't be sorry. Maybe it was better to be able to remember him and smile. Algar had been full of joy.

'The hawks *are* my family,' Cwen said.

'But you and them, you—' Alfreda blushed and couldn't go on. She concentrated on scrubbing a dark stain from behind her knee.

'We what?' Cwen smiled. 'Oh, you mean we fuck. Of course – a clutch must be as close as can be, to hunt well together, and how else to be closer? To touch skin, to hold each other. From when I was born I was told I was filthy, never to be touched. Bachur showed me different and my clutch-mates and me, why shouldn't we enjoy what was denied us for so long?'

'But aren't you afraid of making bairns? You couldn't hunt with one growing in you. And who'd care for it once it was born?'

'Oh, we can't have babies. Bachur said it's something to do with her rune that she puts on us.' Cwen touched her fingers to her left cheek where the brown stain of the hawk mark lay. 'It's why she must mark more bairns every year, else hawks would just make more hawks.'

'I'm sorry.'

'For what? I'm mother enough to the young hawks when they join us – twelve years old and green as the forest. What need have I for an infant sucking at my tits? There's more pleasure to be had from Wine and Wingard there. You know how it is – once you've eaten that fruit and got the taste of it, all you want to do is gorge.' She narrowed her eyes, studying Alfreda. 'Or have you not eaten the fruit? I know how it is among the rest of the folk – men waving their pricks around like weapons and women guarding their cunts like forts. But I thought you Wanderers were a little more free.'

Alfreda picked water up and let it trickle through her hand. 'My brother was free, and look where that got him.'

'Aye, my mother too. Have I never told you? I was a bastard, and she didn't even have the sense Bachur gave her to lie with a man who looked like my father. The moment I popped out, the whole world knew I wasn't his. But if you lie with a hawk, there'll be nothing like that for you. The seeds that come out of them won't sprout. Wingard and Wine would be willing, I'm sure. I've seen the way they look at you.'

Alfreda couldn't keep the blush from her cheeks. 'I don't . . . I don't want . . .'

'So maybe not them. Wine's an ugly fucker, I'll grant you. But there's others in my clutch handsome enough to moisten a grandmother. When the war's over, we'll find what's to your taste.'

Alfreda had no reply to that and they washed without talking for a while, the only noise the splash of the water and the cries of the delicate red-and-white birds that danced along the water's edge.

When she was finished cleaning herself Cwen looked at Alfreda and moved to rub her knuckles along her cheek. It seemed a casual gesture but there was a betraying tightness in Cwen's eyes and Alfreda understood that this was a test, although maybe Cwen didn't realise it. But it was easy to pass – she reached out and pressed Cwen's fingers against her own cheek.

'Mud,' Cwen said, smiling. 'It's no use if you replace one kind of shit with another.'

'I don't like this war,' Alfreda blurted as Cwen began to wade back towards the shore.

'Don't you?' Cwen looked back over her shoulder, eyebrow raised. 'You're a weapon maker. Isn't war your business?'

'I make whatever people want, aye. That's how a smith lives – but I wish people wanted something else. If Algar was alive, I wouldn't let him anywhere near this war.' She followed Cwen, walking on her toes to avoid the prick of the pebbles.

Cwen picked up her undershirt and rubbed it over her body to dry it. 'Do you think that's why Hana spoke against me? To keep her son from the war?'

'She wasn't keen for him to head into the Silent Sands, that's certain. And when he said she couldn't join him . . . That was an angry woman.'

Cwen nodded, though she didn't seem entirely convinced. 'It's not as clean as the fighting I'm used to. The moon beasts will eat a person if they can – what woman would judge you for killing them? The Brotherband were piss-poor men, it's true, but then so was Uin. And for all his good cheer and smiles, Nayan's a man who was willing to kill his own newborn son just to save his own life. Why must one die and another live?'

'I don't know,' Alfreda said. 'I've never been one for causes. I left Algar to do the big thinking. I just took an idea and made it work.'

Cwen looked down at her boots as she laced them, her bottom lip trapped beneath her teeth. When the bow was tied she nodded sharply and looked up. 'I'm the same – I listen to what Bachur asks of me and make it happen. And Bachur says the moon must die. But listen, Alfreda, there's no need for you to fight. If you make us more of your weapons you can take Jinn and head far away, back to the Moon Forest where you'll both be safe. You've done enough.'

'And leave you to face this alone after what you did for me?'

'I have my hawks and all the thousands of Ashane. I won't be alone.'

'No, you won't. You'll have me.' She folded her arms and set her chin. Algar would have known what that meant: the decision was forged and the point of argument passed.

Cwen seemed to realise it too because she smiled, a more gentle expression than her usual fierce grin, and clasped Alfreda's shoulder. 'Well then, you'll be like a hawk to me – like a clutch-mate. I'll see you safe, I promise you that, and my word's worth more than gold in a hovel. We have your weapon and we'll have the black powder for it soon. We know where Krishanjit is and we've the army to master him. We'll win this war together, you and I.'

34

Olufemi was surprised to see her hand shake as she drew the figure of the rune on the parchment. She squinted, noticing for the first time how hard it was to make out. It had grown dark while she worked. Perhaps it had grown dark more than once; she couldn't remember when she'd last slept.

'You need to eat,' Vordanna said, and Olufemi had forgotten about her too. Her lover sat opposite her at the scarred wooden workbench, holding herself with that peculiar stillness that had always drawn Olufemi, though it must have been the years on bliss that had taught it to her.

Olufemi shook her head. 'I'll eat later.'

'You said that two hours ago. You can't work if you're hungry. You can't concentrate.'

She was unaccustomed to that forcefulness from Vordanna, the certainty of her own opinions. 'I'm concentrating perfectly well,' Olufemi snapped.

'You've written the same rune three times. You just can't see it.' Vordanna set flame to the lantern, and Olufemi saw that it was true. She'd scrawled the same symbol thrice and not even the correct one.

'Food then,' Olufemi agreed, and Vordanna placed a plate of steaming breadfruit and arrowfish beside her parchment. She ate while she studied her own work, using one hand to spoon the food into her mouth and the other to turn the pages, splashing grease and smearing the ink.

It was hard, so very hard, to make the glyphs into the runes with only the moon's power behind them. She imagined it might be how a warrior felt, having lost his sword hand, to be forced to learn to fight with the other. Every instinct she had was wrong, every impulse misguided. But it *was* possible. The moon had an existence independent of the sun's, as well as in opposition to it. It could be defined as a singularity, a whole.

She finished reading through her notes and then flipped back to the beginning and began again as the food she'd gobbled congealed into an unpleasant lump in her stomach. It didn't matter. Nothing so trivial did, because the more she read, the more certain she became that she'd found the answer.

Vordanna, who knew her better than anyone ever had, smiled when Olufemi looked at her. It was the first truly happy expression she'd turned Olufemi's way since her return and Olufemi felt a lightness beyond the light-headedness of exhaustion. Perhaps she was forgiven, though truly she'd committed no crime. Sexual abstinence was as needlessly self-depriving as deliberate starvation.

'You've done it,' Vordanna said.

'Yes. Yes, I think I have.' She hesitated. She would never have bothered to explain her reasoning to Vordanna before. The former slave's intellect was unequal to the challenge of understanding it. But this was a new Vordanna, changed by the drug Jinn had bought for her from the Eom to replace Olufemi's own, and which Olufemi had asked her cousin Mayowa to reproduce.

Or perhaps it was the presence of Krish himself that had so altered her, through the rune she wore every moment round her neck. 'It's the glyphs of becoming,' Olufemi told her. 'These align with the moon as the glyphs of being are in the sun's orbit. It's been customary to use both in the construction of each rune, to mark what is, and what must alter to turn it into what is desired. But if the glyphs of becoming alone are used . . .'

'Then won't what you're making constantly change?'

'Yes, but that's no problem. Living things change constantly – and so the moon wills it. It was only Mizhara who sought to freeze us into a cold perfection. And I've been –' she flicked back to her second page, when her mind had still been sharp and her writing comprehensible '– I've been looking at those works I never studied before. It was my mistake: in my study of the runes I focused on the earliest writings from before the war, when Mizhara and Yron loved each other as brother and sister should. All was in balance then and so were the runes, which were built on the joint foundations of their power. I should have studied writings from the time of the war itself. Then each side disdained to use the other's power, or was denied it.'

'So you can use those runes, from the time of war? Those runes will work and save Yron?' Vordanna leaned forward, every line in her body eager.

Olufemi felt that eagerness like a blow. The smiles and the pleasure weren't for her. They were only for the hope she could offer Krishanjit. 'No,' she said. 'The runes are meaningless scribbles unless they tell the truth, and the truth now is different from what it was then. If Krishanjit is correct, *if*, then Mizhara is gone from the world and the runes must reflect it. They must be rewritten – but I believe I can see how. It's not really so big a change. These later runes, the ones made during the war, they acknowledged as little of Mizhara's influence as they could. If I just remove it entirely—'

'They'll work? Have you tested it? Lord Krishanjit must know!'

Olufemi looked at Vordanna through bloodshot eyes, but there was no caring for her there, only for the god that Olufemi had taught her to love. She *could* test the magic now. She knew how the rune she wanted must be formed: of Ya, the glyph of increase married to Yag, the glyph of growth, with the glyph of water Yah to bind and slow them, so that the increase and the growth were constrained by Yaw, the glyph of joining, to unite them all in life.

It could work – it *would*. She'd devoted her life to this study, to learning how to build these smaller things into a larger and true meaning. But what if it didn't? What if Krishanjit was wrong? She'd tried everything. She'd even made herself a god to spark the runes to life. And suddenly she found that she didn't want to know if she'd failed one final time. 'I can't test it,' she told Vordanna. 'Not now, I'm too tired.'

'Rest then.' Vordanna turned to go, but Olufemi reached out to grab her hand and held her fast, until the other woman grudgingly turned to face her.

'I'm . . .' The word 'sorry' stuck in her throat like a fishbone. She had nothing to be sorry for, and a mage would never apologise to a slave. 'I'm sorry, Vordanna,' she finally said. 'It was only that I thought you were gone – you and Jinn both lost. I thought *everything* was lost and there was nothing to be done about it.'

It was unsettling to be studied by those too-knowing, too-awake eyes. But whatever Vordanna found in her face seemed to soften her. She swiped the pad of her thumb across the wrinkled back of Olufemi's hand before releasing it. 'Go to sleep, Femi. We'll show Lord Krishanjit what you've found in the morning.'

Krish was sandy-eyed with sleep when Olufemi woke him. The sun hadn't yet risen and the sky outside his window was a deep pink, but he took one look at her face, tight with excitement, and didn't protest.

She and Vordanna led him outside the bounds of Mirror Town as the day dawned, to the dusty, lifeless fields that bordered the city on its landward side. He didn't think he'd ever grow used to the heat here. In this place, it was easy to believe the sun was his enemy. It seemed determined to suck every drop of moisture out of him, parching his skin as dry as the land it had robbed of its virtue.

The grand buildings of Mirror Town shimmered on the horizon behind them, a trick of the heat that seemed to reduce them to a delusion. He was afraid that Olufemi's discovery might be no more than a mirage too. The old woman looked older than ever, stooped with tiredness, eyes sunk deep in her face. He worried that he'd set her a challenge she was incapable of meeting, and without her magic, he had nothing. He *was* nothing.

He took a gulp from his water bottle and was dismayed to realise it was already empty. He never brought enough when he wandered the scorched desert. A part of him could never quite believe how unforgiving this land was. He'd thought the land of his birth was harsh, but here the line between life and death seemed thinner than he'd ever known. One mistake, and you'd cross it.

There *was* more water, hefted in large flagons between ten sweating slaves, but Olufemi had told him it must be saved for the magic. 'Couldn't we have done this back in the mansion?' he asked her.

She shook her head, eyes scanning the barren ground. 'For a true test, we need to see the extent of the power. Small magics will avail us nothing against your father's army. But this is far enough, I think.' She drew a parchment from the sleeve of her tunic and uncurled it. 'Yes, these were once sun-pear orchards – there was fruit here even a hundred years ago. The roots should still be there. Buried and long dead, but there.'

Krish kicked at the sand, which flew away in a yellow cloud. It was hard to imagine it had ever supported life. 'How can an army cross this?'

'When the autumn rains come, the desert will bloom for a few brief weeks.'

'But you'll stop them,' Vordanna said brightly. 'You'll save Lord Krishanjit.'

'I will,' Olufemi said, looking at Krish. 'I will save you, Yron.'

It was the first time she'd seemed certain about the runes, and the first time she'd ever called him by that title. It startled him even more when she dropped to her knees in front of him, her joints creaking audibly.

She clasped his hand and bent her head until her forehead touched his knuckles. 'Yron, will you give me your blessing to act in your service?'

He laughed in discomfort and tried to pull his hand away, but she held it fast. Her expression seemed at war with itself, respect fighting to subdue her usual irritation. 'I *must* serve you in this,' she said, and he remembered what she'd told him: the use of the runes was only given to those who worshipped the sun and the moon.

'I give you my blessing,' he said, feeling like an idiot. Dae Hyo would have scoffed if he'd heard him, but he hadn't seen hair nor foot of the warrior for three days.

Olufemi rested her forehead against his hand a moment longer and then creaked back to her feet. He wanted to help her, but wasn't sure if he should. Did a god serve his servants? He watched instead as she gestured to one of the slaves and held out the parchment to show the man. 'Ten paces wide at least,' she told him. The slave studied it, smiling, and then began to hack at the ground with his hoe, carving out a deep furrow.

'*He's* drawing the rune?' Krish asked Olufemi.

She nodded, not taking her attention from the slowly emerging design: a swirling spiral that seemed to join back with itself so it never began or ended. The slave consulted the parchment again and added complex curlicues spinning away from the top and bottom of the design like twirls of smoke.

'Wouldn't it be better if you did it?' Krish asked.

'I'm not—' she began heatedly, and then seemed to recall that she was supposed to be treating him with respect – worshipping him, even – and snapped her mouth shut. 'A mage's skill is needed to devise the rune,' she said with gritty politeness. 'Drawing it is an artisan's job, and Iestyn was a scribe of Smiler's Fair before he was snatched in a raid by the Janggok.'

'And that's it?' Krish said dubiously, as the rune seemed to take its final shape. 'You just draw it and then . . .' he raised his hands in a formless gesture of summoning.

'And then I must meditate on its shape – hold it whole and perfect in my mind and call your power into it. You'll pour the water in as I do and the magic will flow through the water, as life itself is carried by it.'

'That sounds easy enough.'

She laughed, a sharp sound. 'Easy? It took me a year of training until I could hold even the simplest rune in my head. Until I could see it, and nothing but it in my mind's eye. Tell me, have you ever thought of nothing?'

'Yes, when I'm asleep.'

'And do you not dream?'

'I suppose.'

'Our minds are never silent and never empty. Learning to silence them, to empty them of all thought, all worry, all images but the rune itself – this is the true meaning of a mage's gift. Now, please, I must have quiet for this.' She waited until Krish had nodded and then sank to the dusty ground, sitting cross-legged to one side of the carved rune. The position looked uncomfortable, feet folded over her thighs, but she seemed to assume it with ease. She took a deep breath, nodded at the waiting slaves and closed her eyes.

The slaves lifted the tubs of water and carried them closer. Krish thought Olufemi must have meant them to pour slowly, setting the water running round the shape of the rune, but the slaves tipped over the barrels and let the water go in one big wave. He saw Olufemi wince at the noise of it, her eyes flickering open before she forced them shut again. The water cut through the dry earth like a knife, breaking open the carefully carved shape of the rune and then soaking through it to turn it all to mud.

He watched it sink into the parched earth, disappearing with startling speed and leaving only a messy swirl behind. The rune was gone and his brief surge of hope with it. He'd been stupid to think it could work. Better to find his prow god, hidden in some corner of his room, and pray to her.

He leaned down to Olufemi, meaning to shake her out of her trance. But as he leaned towards her, he saw something in the earth around her, green where everything else was a golden brown. And then he saw another, and two more beside it: tiny shoots, poking their heads through the mud.

It wasn't much; it might have been caused by the sudden deluge of water. He leaned back, his heart pounding with the fear that this was nothing, that he was allowing hope to return only to suffer the pain of losing it again.

He felt a shifting beneath his own feet and looked down to see a green spear pressing upward hard enough to rock him back on his heels. He stepped aside – and on to another shoot, already two inches tall. It snapped beneath the heel of his sandal, but as he watched in fascination, the little broken stump began to sprout again, a furled green leaf rising from its centre and expanding until it was larger than the one he'd killed.

There were scores of them. Hundreds. Everywhere he looked was green instead of dusty yellow, seething with life. Some of the shoots were growing into grasses or flowers and others into saplings, reaching out their limbs towards the perfect blue sky.

He was forced to hop from foot to foot, dancing to avoid the reckless growth of the tallest plants. He found himself pushed into the one stable area, a grassy, flower-sprinkled meadow centred on Olufemi. All around it was an orchard. With the trees reaching far above his head, it was impossible to tell how far it extended.

He laughed in shock and joy. The sound was deadened by the seconds-old vegetation all around, but in front of him Olufemi's eyes snapped open. For just a second, she looked like she meant to chastise him. And then she saw what she'd made.

He thought she was going to speak, but though she opened her mouth, no sound came out of it. Her seamed face tightened and then she sobbed, loud and convulsively, hiding her face in her hands.

'Lord Yron's power has returned,' Vordanna said as she put her arm round the older woman and hugged her tightly.

'Yes.' Olufemi's tears glistened along her dark cheeks. 'Yes. The runes have truly woken.'

To either side of them the slaves were wide-eyed, as if the strangeness of what they'd witnessed was enough to cut through even the numbing effect of bliss. Krish felt as if he'd taken the drug, light-headed with happiness and with relief from a fear he hadn't wanted to acknowledge even to himself.

The walk back to the city took far longer than the walk out. They had to pick their way through the tangled undergrowth, stamping the woody stems of brambles beneath their feet. Everywhere there was the rich smell of new leaves.

Vordanna stopped to pluck one of the golden fruits from a

tree and when Krish did the same he found that it burst with juice and sweetness in his mouth. Olufemi had made this. She'd made something from nothing, like the mages of old when they'd first built Mirror Town.

It was a shock when they came to the outer limits of the rune's effect and stepped from lush greenery back into the normal dusty fields. When they'd walked a little further Krish couldn't resist turning round to check that it had really happened. The orchard was still there, stretching out of sight to left and right. It was eerily silent, no wind to rustle the leaves and no birds or insects to populate its branches. It occurred to him that the flowers might die without bees to pollinate them. But Olufemi could summon bees into being too, if they needed them.

Even on the borders of Mirror Town the orchard was visible, a green shimmer on the horizon. He turned to look at it one last time, and when he turned back he saw that a haze hung over the city too, a large dust cloud near its centre.

'What's that?' he asked Olufemi but the mage, turned back towards the orchard, only shrugged, her eyes still on the distant evidence of her success.

They walked on, through the low stone buildings of the poorest of Mirror Town, mages without ties of kinship, and then through the broader streets and larger mansions of the lesser families. They passed a red-painted cube with carved lizards climbing its sides, a long hall twisted into a double spiral a little like Olufemi's rune and a strange triangular-sided building that rose to a pointed peak. Everywhere they saw the flashes of the mirrors and heard the ceaseless shouts of the mirror masters as they turned them.

Not far from the centre of town, beside a marble-fronted mansion ringed with trees, a party of mages waited for them. He recognised two members of Olufemi's family – a niece and a cousin, or maybe two cousins – along with several others who'd visited the mansion occasionally. They watched Krish approach in silence, their expressions severe.

'Wasola, you must come and see!' Olufemi said.

A thin-faced young woman replied, 'See what?' in a tone so icy that even Olufemi seemed deflated by it.

'The magic has returned, Wasola,' she said. 'Our power has returned to us.'

'So it's true then?' That was one of the old men, frowning so heavily the wrinkles had wriggled halfway up his balding head. 'We didn't think . . . It didn't seem possible.'

'It is – I've made the earth bloom again. I've brought life where there was only death. I've done it, I've proven it can be done. Come, you can see for yourselves.' Olufemi turned back in the direction of the newly grown orchard, but the other mages remained unmoving.

'No,' Wasola said. 'Olufemi, *you* should see. You should see what you've done.'

'I know what I did. I don't . . . Wasola, what is it?'

'It's our home. Or it was.'

Wasola looked towards the centre of town, towards the cloud of dust still hanging above it. Krish realised he could hear faint shouts coming from that direction, and what might have been screams of pain.

Olufemi ran and he sprinted after her, down the broad avenue and across a square filled with fountains, the tinkle of their water no longer loud enough to drown out the sounds from ahead. He ran on towards the dust cloud in the sky and the wreckage of the Etze mansion beneath it.

It was impossible to understand what had happened, only that it had been utterly destroyed. As Olufemi staggered to a halt beside him they both stared at the tumbled marble blocks, some scorched as if by fire even though no fire blazed. The roof was gone entirely, fallen into and obliterating the mansion's interior. The intricate maps that had surfaced its walls were shattered into a thousand meaningless fragments of colour. Pitiful cries came from the wreckage and slaves were crawling over it in search of their owners. They pulled out one body, red streaked over its broken limbs.

Olufemi gave a choked cry of horror. 'What happened?'

'It was you, Olufemi,' the old man said. 'Have you forgotten why we were driven from our homeland? Magic has a price, and your family has paid for yours.'

'I . . . I didn't know,' she said. 'I would never – I would never have chosen this.'

'But you did,' Wasola said. 'You did this – for *him*.' She stared at Krish with more hatred than he'd ever seen on another person's face, even Uin's.

'He must go,' the old man said. 'We've heard the Ashane King is hunting for him – would you see our whole city burn? He must go.'

'Not now!' Olufemi said. 'Not when I've—'

'He must leave,' Wasola cut her off, 'and so must you. We want you gone. If the sun rises to find you in Mirror Town tomorrow, you won't live to see it set.'

'You can't . . .' Olufemi began, but another desperate scream came from the ruins and she trailed into silence.

The scream came again and Krish felt his heart lurch. 'Dae Hyo! Where's Dae Hyo?'

Dae Hyo woke to pain and darkness. It didn't surprise him – he'd fallen asleep with more than a bottle of whisky inside him. But when he groaned and tried to turn, he found that he couldn't move. He tried again, struggling against some unseen weight, and cried out as his arm twisted and the bones grated agonisingly against each other.

He blinked his eyes, which were full of dust. It wasn't entirely dark: above him there was a sliver of daylight. He strained towards it and felt something shift, the grinding sound of stone moving on stone and then an almost unendurable weight pressing down on his chest.

He groaned again and in counterpoint heard other groans all around him. His head was full of muddy water that his thoughts struggled to swim through. He'd fallen asleep in the Etze mansion, he was sure of it. Was he still in the mansion? He tried to move again and felt a sharp pain as something splintered beneath him. Something wooden – his bed. And all at once he understood: he was where he'd always been, but the mansion no longer was. The vast stone structure had fallen in and he was trapped beneath it.

He lost some time to fear and panic. He thought he might have screamed. He certainly gasped and struggled against his confinement until the pain of his movements grew too much. After that there was despair at the thought of such a death, not even in battle, not even under the light of the sun. And then there was only boredom and the growing discomfort of thirst, somehow worse than the fiercer pain of his injuries as the long hours stretched by.

His eyes had dried along with his mouth and he shut them and tried to let his mind move elsewhere, to remember better times and people. When he died here, would he join his ancestors on the plains? Could his spirit travel so far? He tried to sing a song to cheer himself, a ballad to his mother's ponies that he'd composed when he was a child, but his throat was rough with thirst and the song faded into silence.

When he heard the voices, he thought perhaps his ancestors *had* come for him. But his ancestors had never spoken the language of the mages, as these voices were speaking, and so he forced his gummed eyes open. There was daylight above him, a circle of it as broad as the sun, and a face framed in it. It smiled when it saw him. Hands reached down and lifted, until a block of stone was gone and more light could slip through.

Time seemed to crawl past, as slow as the beetle lumbering from broken slab to broken slab above him. After a while he shut his eyes again and only listened, sometimes crying out in pain as the lifting of one block above caused others to shift and the pressure against his legs or chest or arm grew worse. At last he felt the weight lift and it seemed that he'd survived.

He blinked and found that Krish's face was above his own, his brother's sweat-streaked and desperate. And despite everything, he felt joy that Krish had saved him as a brother should.

'Dae Hyo!' Krish said. 'I hoped it was you!'

'I'm not so easy to kill,' he croaked and his brother smiled and clasped his shoulder.

'Listen,' Krish said. 'You've got to tell me – where is the bliss kept?'

Dae Hyo stared at him as slaves began to bandage his wounds. Krish barely attended to them. He hardly seemed to notice Dae Hyo was hurt. 'Please,' Krish said. 'The bliss. I need it.'

Dae Hyo didn't know how long he'd slept. He hadn't wanted to, but someone had poured liquid down his throat and too late he'd recognised the taste of purple sorghum juice. He woke still in the pleasant daze of the drug, the pains in his legs and chest like descriptions of themselves, the sensations far removed from him.

They'd placed him in a plain white room beside a window. Other beds were occupied, but when he levered himself up on to his elbows, he saw that their residents were all either asleep or unconscious. Svarog's cock, he thought two of them might actually be dead. He recognised nearly all of them as people he'd seen around the Etze house.

There was noise outside, the rumbling of many voices. It was probably what had woken him. Movement wasn't much of a pleasure, but he turned himself in the bed until he could see through the window. Outside, a crowd pressed close enough that they were blocking much of the light. He couldn't understand what they were saying, but anger sounded the same in any language. Then he heard another voice rising above theirs: Krish.

Getting up was even less of a pleasure, but once he got to his feet he found he could stay there. He took a crutch from beside the bed of a thin-faced boy who was still sleeping or unconscious, and used it to hobble down the corridor and out of the building.

He elbowed his way through the gathered mages and hobbled on. The sorghum was fading and his head felt clearer and the pain sharper. Krish was speaking again, but the murmurs of protest from all around drowned him out. And then Dae Hyo was at the front of the crowd and could see his brother clearly.

They were in the grand square that held the tall pillars where the craziest of the mages liked to perch. High above, some of them bent to watch the commotion on the ground. Around the square windows were open and mages leaned out of them. There were slaves too, many hundreds of them facing down the mages.

'We're not leaving,' Krish shouted, struggling to raise his voice above the noise of the crowd. Beside him, Olufemi repeated the words in the mage's own language and an angry wave of protest washed back over them in response.

A man near the front – another relative of Olufemi's, to judge by the shape of his chin – said something sharp to her and then something sharper to the slaves all around her and Krish. It seemed to be a command, but the slaves stared at him and did nothing.

'They won't obey you any longer,' Krish said. 'I have the keys to the bliss. They answer to me now.'

That caused some consternation but no fear. 'Do you think they can stop us from taking you?' the man said. 'They won't fight for you, foreigner.' Which was exactly what Krish had told Dae Hyo.

His brother only smiled. Dae Hyo had never seen that expression on Krish's face before: so cold and confident. He remembered all at once the way Krish had looked as he confessed to his part in the death of the Dae and suddenly it was the mages Dae Hyo feared for. In that moment, his brother seemed capable of anything.

'I don't need them to fight for me,' Krish said. 'I need *you* to fight for me. My father is coming and I can't beat him without you.'

'Your father is not our enemy,' the mage said. He took a step forward and the crowd followed. Dae Hyo knew that at any moment their anger would crest and break and Krish and Olufemi would be crushed beneath it. Krish must know it too, but his brother only smiled, nodded to the slave and shouted, 'Now!'

The mages shrank back from an attack they knew couldn't come as the slaves ran towards them. But the slaves kept on running, past the mages and towards the houses – into the houses and on top of them. And from further away, where more slaves must have been sent, came the first crash of breaking glass.

Dae Hyo didn't understand the horror it brought to the mages' faces. The sound came again and again, echoing a hundred times from every corner of the city – and from right behind him. He turned and saw a white-skinned slave swing a stick at the mirror hung beside the door. It shattered into irreparable pieces as more crashes echoed. All over the city, in every direction Dae Hyo looked, he could see the glint of sun from the shattered mirrors of Mirror Town.

'What have you done?' the old man said to Krish. 'The worm men will murder us! You've killed us all!'

There was a tumult of noise, anger and screams and the continual shattering of glass as the slaves continued their work in every street of the city.

'No,' Krish said. 'The worm men are mine. Anyone who serves me is safe from them. I'm giving you a choice: serve me and be safe, or oppose me and die.'

35

Sang Ki had understood an oasis as a figure of speech – and deployed it with some frequency – but until coming to the Silent Sands he'd had no appreciation of its reality. When he saw the shimmer of green on the horizon, he felt the draw of it in his guts: shade and water and living things after three days of shelterless dunes and the pitiless sun.

The reconnaissance mission had seemed a good idea when he'd proposed it. But that had been in the comfort of Little Cousin's ship in the immediate aftermath of the burnt woman's miscarriage. He looked at her now, swaying on a litter held between two malbeam, the scaled and horned mounts the desert Ahn used in place of horses and questioned his decision.

Little Cousin's doctor said that she'd recovered from the miscarriage, yet she'd barely spoken since. Whenever anyone approached her, she turned her mutilated face from them and closed her eyes. Though she hadn't seemed to much care for the babe when it was inside her, now she mourned its loss. Sang Ki thought perhaps that he did too. The child had been a boy. The pitiful thing that had come out of her had been far enough along for that to be clear. It might have been his brother. It was strange that while it had lived it had been no more than an idea to him. Dead, it seemed more real: his flesh and blood decaying in a shallow grave on the Misa's bank.

Or perhaps they were both simply laid low by the unbearable heat of this place. The landscape offered little distraction from it. At first there had been rocks and low drab bushes and sometimes, in the distance, other bands of Ahn, the red-and-gold scales of their malbeam and desert mammoths glinting in the sunlight.

But yesterday they'd entered the true desert and since then there had been nothing but sand: hillocks and mounds and waves of it. Sang Ki had found it beautiful at first. Now it was merely monotonous.

He'd approached the journey here with some enthusiasm. The desire to see a landscape he'd only read of had been his reason for volunteering. Or . . . his eyes were drawn to the burnt woman, her body swathed in the blue Ahn robes they all wore. She lay so still she might have been dead.

He must be honest with himself. A desire to visit the Silent Sands had been *half* his reason for coming. As for the other half – well, the Ashane army that Cwen had no doubt already met seemed likely to include Nethmi's fratricidal uncle Puneet. He'd never had any love for Nethmi, and now that she was a declared murderess and childless, he would surely leap at the chance to be rid of her.

And, curse it, Sang Ki should want rid of her too. Yet what if she truly wasn't Nethmi? What if she was no more than an innocent resident of Smiler's Fair? Sang Ki no longer believed he knew the answer; he only knew he wasn't quite ready to see her hang. And so here he was in a hot wilderness that was like a mirror to the icy waste in which he'd spent his youth.

'You don't love our land, I think,' Little Cousin said, his malbeam kicking up a cloud of sand as it trotted over to flank Sang Ki's.

'I'm surprised *you* love it,' Sang Ki said. 'I thought you River Ahn scorned the desert for the plains.'

'Well, I do like a bit of greenery, but variety is what adds the salt to life, not so? And I've travelled the desert crossing with my kin before, to see the route my goods take to the lands beyond.'

'You've been to the savannah itself?'

'The verges only – those aren't a people who welcome strangers, nor the Eternal Empire, which allows none within its borders. But if I can discover something they desire enough, well then. Most rules are far from being iron, if the right incentive can be found to bend them. One day, fat man, I shall see those distant lands and all the secrets they keep.'

'This is variety enough for me,' Sang Ki admitted.

'No – never say so! You'll grow to love this place, as a man may grow to love a woman who's fair of heart but foul of face. Auntie will tell you, there's beauty here if you know where to look.' He glanced ahead, to the woman leading their band. She was nearly as large as Sang Ki himself, though he suspected that most of her bulk was muscle.

'I'll certainly love it more when it yields some water and, if the Five are generous, fruit.'

'Those I can promise you. Huimsaeg is the foremost oasis in the northern sands. My kin have controlled it for two hundred years and travellers pay gold to stop there. But you shall sup at the spring for free, my friend.'

The sun was touching the tops of the trees by the time their party reached them. They were languid things: long, corrugated leaves drooping from the top of their hairy trunks and bunches of small brown fruit drooping from the leaves. Little Cousin leaned to pick one and passed it to Sang Ki. It was sticky and sweet, but his mouth was so dry he could barely swallow it.

The Ahn made camp with their usual efficiency. They strung sheets from branches to form sun shelters and bundled blankets beneath them for the freezing night. The burnt woman was laid gently in one such shelter while a young man, barely more than a boy, knelt to offer her a waterskin. Sang Ki saw him trickle the liquid past her mouth, but she didn't make the effort to swallow it.

Others were leading the mounts on, towards the spring that gave the oasis its life. Sang Ki hurried after and fell to his knees in the mud beside the small pool, gulping great mouthfuls of it from his hands and then pouring it in fountains over his head. He'd never fully appreciated water before. It was sweeter than any drink he'd ever tasted.

By the time he returned to the camp the Ahn had spread cushions around a cheerfully leaping fire. He settled on to a pile of them and held out his hands to the flames. Daylight was fading and with it the warmth of the sun. Sang Ki stared through the trees towards the desert, but he could see nothing beyond the circle of the fire. He felt an odd sensation of watchfulness about this place, of being observed. Perhaps it was all the life here, after days without: insects and lizards and shockingly bright red-and-blue birds observing them tilt-headed from the trees and calling out in raucous voices.

Little Cousin was deep in conversation with his kin, his normally irrepressible humour at least a little held down by the bulk and authority of his aunt, who frowned quellingly at whatever he was saying. Sang Ki knew that the Desert Ahn considered themselves senior to the Water Ahn. Or perhaps Little Cousin simply understood that in this trackless landscape he was entirely dependent on his aunt. For reasons that hadn't been explained, she was known as Mother of Wasps. She reminded Sang Ki of his mother.

They brought Sang Ki a bowl of bean and blood broth, so spicy it heated him more than did the fire. A young woman took another bowl to the burnt woman, who set it on the ground beside her but made no attempt to eat it. He tried to remember the last time he'd seen her accept food and realised that he couldn't. Sighing, he picked up his own bowl and crossed the encampment to sit beside her.

'It's really very tasty,' he said. 'Or at least, it has a great deal of flavour, though whether that flavour is an enjoyable one, I'll leave you to decide.'

He thought she might not respond at all, but finally she shrugged and said, 'I'm not hungry.'

They could have carried on in that vein, he supposed, talking and saying nothing. 'I'm sorry about your baby,' he said instead.

'Are you?' Her eyes were narrow brown slits in her scarred face. 'And why would you think I was? If I was Nethmi, wouldn't I want that baby dead? The son of the man she killed.'

'A child doesn't inherit its parents' crimes, or so I was always taught,' he said.

She spooned a little of the broth into her mouth, wincing at the taste of it. He'd noticed how she shied away from fire and torch, as if the mere thought of heat pained her now. She swallowed and asked, 'Was Lord Thilak guilty of some crime?'

'Hardly. My father was a shipborn lord.'

'But Nethmi killed him. Did she have no cause?'

'So now the victim is to blame for his own murder?' His voice remained level only through supreme effort.

She clenched her fist, the bubbled scars of her burning tightening to their limit. 'I don't know. But people mostly don't kill for no reason, unless they're mad. Was Nethmi mad? Or did she have some reason to hate your father?'

'My father was her husband!' The anger burned inside him, but beneath it he felt something hollow, a black pit of doubt. 'He treated her as a husband should,' he insisted.

'Maybe she didn't want to be wed.'

Of course she hadn't. His father had known that, as had Sang Ki. They'd discussed the marriage as a stratagem, Puneet's hatred of Nethmi as a tool and her weak position as an advantage.

He remembered the Brotherband and the human wreckage they'd left in their wake. He'd thought himself so much above them, but if a woman went unwilling and powerless to her marriage bed, how much better was it truly? Marriage was a far pleasanter word than rape, but how could he deny that his father had taken Nethmi against her will? And when he was dead, he'd meant for Sang Ki to do the very same thing. Sang Ki had taunted her with it! He remembered their conversation in the library of Winter's Hammer with vivid and shaming clarity.

In front of him, the camp carried on its business. The Ahn warriors talked among themselves, Little Cousin chattered to his aunt and the fire crackled and sent bright sparks into the growing darkness. But between him and the burnt woman was a silence louder than any of that noise. 'Who are you really?' he asked her at last. '*Are* you Nethmi?'

She only shook her head and asked, 'How much further to Mirror Town?'

'A week, I think. Maybe a little less. These lizards of theirs are fast movers and the Ahn know the swiftest ways. Wait, I can show you. I've brought my . . . my father's maps.'

He was glad of the chance to compose himself as he fumbled

in his pack. But when he unrolled the parchment on to the ground before her, he paused, startled.

'I see Mirror Town,' she said, resting her figure against the jagged coast. 'But where are we?'

He put his own finger a few inches from hers, inland and north, where the map showed the very oasis in which they sat. 'We're here, perhaps a hundred miles from our destination.' And then he moved his finger onward, only a little sideways from their course. Beneath it was scribbled a skull and a symbol that hadn't been worn by a living person for many hundreds of years. 'And here is a place I would very much like to see.'

'No, no, no,' Little Cousin said the next morning. 'Not to be done, fat man. Not even to be considered!'

'It's only a small detour.' Sang Ki ran his finger over the map he'd laid before the Ahn trader. 'I'm surprised you didn't suggest it yourself.'

Beside Little Cousin, his aunt shifted her bulk until she could turn the full strength of her frown on Sang Ki. 'And where did you get this map, Ashaneman? All our trails? All our water? This knowledge is ours, not yours.'

Sang Ki thought of saying that knowledge was no particular person's possession, which was its best quality. But the huge woman didn't strike him as someone who'd appreciate the sentiment. 'It's an old map,' he told her. 'I believe my grandfather bought it from one of your fellow tribesmen more than fifty years ago. I assure you, I have no designs on your trade routes. I do, however, have a very great desire to visit the grave of the Geun. Come now, Little Cousin, surely you must understand the appeal, to see the last resting place of the Fourteenth Tribe? I'm astonished you haven't visited it yourself.'

'Fat man, it's a *burial ground.* Spirits without children to mourn or serve them. Angry spirits.'

'Angrier than those beneath the water where you were so keen to take me? It seems to me the parents of those murdered children might be somewhat more enraged than the spirits of the Geun, who only wandered and perished from hunger and thirst.'

'Oh, but the spirits in the water are foreigners – their gods take care of them.'

'Their god is dead,' Sang Ki pointed out.

'And ill came of that visit, not so?' Little Cousin's eyes flicked to the burnt woman, huddled in the roots of a tree. 'Worse harm will come from this one. Besides, what is there to see but bones?'

'Bones and treasure,' Mother of Wasps said to Sang Ki disapprovingly. 'Don't think you're the first to ponder it. We all know the ancestors brought wealth with them on their ships, and where is the wealth of the Geun?'

'It hadn't entered my mind.' It truly hadn't, but such a denial was bound to sound false.

Little Cousin smiled at him, though. 'He's telling the truth, Auntie. It's only knowledge he wants, and the pleasure of going where no one of his tribe has gone before, not so?'

'Just so,' Sang Ki agreed.

'Then why does he have maps of all our lands?' Mother of Wasps asked.

'I'll give them to you,' Sang Ki said with sudden inspiration. 'Every chart I have of the Silent Sands. You may use them yourself – or burn them if you choose.' The foolishness of the offer occurred to him the instant after he made it. How would the Ashane army find its way to Mirror Town without his maps? He must hope it had some of its own.

Mother of Wasps frowned at him, tapping one finger against her chin. 'All your charts?'

'Every single one.' He mentally catalogued those he'd left behind in Winter's Hammer.

She looked at Little Cousin, who looked back at Sang Ki, perhaps not quite with his earlier trust. Sang Ki found it highly unlikely that Little Cousin himself would ever willingly surrender any charts he'd accumulated. 'And what of the spirits, fat man?' he asked.

'The Five will protect us,' the burnt woman said. She'd crept up to the ashes of the fire pit while they talked and sat with her head hunched, hiding her hideously scarred face.

'There you go,' Sang Ki said. 'The Five will protect us, and we'll make an offering to the spirits to keep them peaceful. We are cousins of theirs, after all – family enough for those starved of any.'

Little Cousin might still have disagreed but Mother of Wasps reached across to clasp his hand, swallowing his in her far larger one and squeezing hard enough to grind the bones against each other. 'A bargain then, before the gods.'

The site had looked close, but it took them two days to reach it. Sang Ki knew he could never have found it without help, despite his maps. The dunes rolled into the distance in every direction, low golden hills shaped by the wind that blew across them every moment of the day, shifting them from place to place one grain of sand at a time. The oasis was soon lost to sight behind them, hidden from any but those who knew how to find it.

Despite having left the life of the oasis behind, the sensation of being watched had returned, a permanent itch between his shoulder blades. He nudged his malbeam closer to Little Cousin's and asked, 'Do others of your tribe travel nearby?'

'Not travel, no. It is a shared duty among all of us, a place where there are no feuds. There is death enough here already.'

'What duty?'

Little Cousin nodded to the horizon, where the wavering heat haze gradually resolved into the outlines of a dozen riders. 'To guard that which must not be disturbed. We keep the graves of our cousin tribe free of scavengers. As Mother of Wasps said, there are many who come to steal its riches – Ashane and tribesmen and the Mangmeon, the people of the savannah. We protect the bones the spirits once animated and they spare us their wrath.'

The riders on the horizon had all turned to watch them, their blue robes flapping around them in the constant wind.

'But you've never been to visit the place yourself.'

'It's forbidden, not so? For all but the guards, and guarding duty never passes to the River Ahn. But I've always wondered, and I can't say I'm sorry for this chance, if your Five will protect us.'

It wasn't quite a question, but Sang Ki said, 'They will,' with more certainty than he felt. Mother of Wasps kneed her mount to ride ahead of them, and by the time they reached the guards she'd already said whatever needed to be said to win their way through.

The guards parted without speaking. Their faces were hidden behind the blue scarves all desert-dwellers used to keep out the windborne sand, but their eyes were watchful as Sang Ki rode between them. And then they were over the next ridge and the grave site lay before them, an expanse of bone-strewn yellow that stretched out of sight in every direction.

Any comment Sang Ki might have made sank back into his throat at the sight. The Ahn dismounted their malbeam and Sang Ki awkwardly did the same. It seemed disrespectful to remain mounted here. He raised a hand to help the burnt woman down, though the movement pained his back. She gazed over the field of death and then asked Little Cousin, 'Why hasn't the wind covered them?'

Her voice sounded shockingly loud in the silence, but it was a good question. Even now, grains of sand were shifting and settling over the pure white of the bones.

'Our people keep them clean,' Little Cousin told her.

Sang Ki knelt beside one pitifully small skeleton, a child of surely no more than five. The skull had separated from its neck and lay a little distance away, empty sockets turned up to a sun that would have blinded the eyes that once lay within. 'It would seem kinder to let the sand bury them.'

Little Cousin shook his head. 'No, no. Buried they would be forgotten by the living, and then the spirits would truly rage. This way they are remembered, at least by us.'

Sang Ki shivered despite the baking heat. He hadn't thought much of Little Cousin's talk of spirits; he'd been taught all his life that the Ashane gods were ten times more powerful than the tribes', or how else would the lowlanders have conquered them? And he'd read the works of Cathura of Fell's End, who claimed that the gods were nothing but dreams. But that had been before the moon rose. Here among the bones of a whole tribe it was easy to feel the restless presence of their spirits.

Scraps of dried flesh and clothing still clung to their skeletons and Mother of Wasps had been right – there were jewels and gold at bony wrists and draped across sunken chests. Sang Ki wandered among them, looking but never touching, until he began to see some pattern to the grim arrangement of bones.

They hadn't fallen where they marched. In fact, now that he thought of it, it made no sense that they could all have succumbed to hunger and thirst in the same place. There should have been a long, sad trail of bones over miles of the desert, but instead here the Geun all were.

Once he'd thought that, the bones began to tell their stories. He saw that they were arranged in groups: one larger skeleton with smaller ones all around. The smaller were arranged with arms by their sides as if they'd fallen asleep on the ground. But when he looked closer, he saw nicks in their spines, near to where their living throats must have been, as if those throats had been slit.

The largest skeleton in each group was less orderly, a jumble of bones that might once have stood upright. And somewhere in each adult skeleton there was a blade. Finally he came to one that made it all clear; the hilt of the blade driven between its ribs was still clasped in its own hand.

'They killed their children and then they killed themselves,' he whispered.

Little Cousin's expression was as sombre as he'd ever seen it. 'Yes, fat man. This was known to us. Remember this was just after the ocean crossing, when there were only women to rule and no boy older than five years old. When it became hopeless, men might have gone on, but the women chose a quick death for their children. You see now why we fear the spirits here?'

Sang Ki shook his head, not to deny Little Cousin's words but perhaps to deny the reality of what had occurred. 'To slit your own child's throat . . . How could they know they wouldn't find water or rescue over the next dune?'

'Perhaps they sent scouts ahead and knew there'd be no relief. When your own child is dying the slow death of want, then you may judge, fat man.'

Sang Ki nodded, shamed. He walked on, trying to imagine how it must have been for them, to end their long journey over the ocean in this arid place. Despite all the care of their Ahn guardians, many of the skeletons had been reduced to fragments. One day all semblance of life would be gone from them and this would be nothing but a vast field of smooth white stones. There were such stones here already, but when he knelt to inspect one he realised it had never been part of a person. And was there . . .? Yes, there seemed to be writing on it. It was only a pace away from the outflung arm of a skeleton.

'Leave it, Seonu,' Mother of Wasps shouted as he reached for it. She strode over the sand towards him, her blue robes billowing.

He ignored her, picking the stone up delicately between his fingers. 'There's a message here,' he said to Little Cousin. 'This woman's last words, do you see?' He pointed at the delicate scratches on the white surface of the stone. 'She used her final moments to write this. Don't you think she meant for it to be read?'

Little Cousin hesitated a moment, then came to kneel beside him. He cocked his head to the side, very like one of the colourful birds of the oasis, as he puzzled out the writing. 'Oh, I see!' he said at last. 'It's a little like the writing of the Eom. The lines are strange but I think I can . . . yes. It seems to be: Geun Ha Eun asks – no begs – her . . . This could be gods or ancestors. Both perhaps. Geun Ha Eun begs the gods and her ancestors to forgive her. You were right, fat man, this was her last message – but not for us, I think.'

Many of the stones must have been lost beneath the sand, but Sang Ki soon found another, beside a skeleton whose ribs had been torn apart by some predator. 'Geun Su Bim begs the gods and her ancestors to forgive her,' he read. 'I suppose they must all be the same.'

'Yes.' Little Cousin stooped over another small heap of bones. 'Here it is again. Oh!'

'What is it?' Sang Ki asked when the trader remained silent, bent frowning over the small stone.

'Perhaps my understanding of the script is not so fine,' Little Cousin muttered.

There was something in his voice, a jagged tone very unlike him, that made Sang Ki hurry to his side. He studied the stone himself, but he'd read it three times before the import of the words sunk in. 'Seonu Min Ju begs the gods and her ancestors to forgive her.'

'Perhaps she had friends among the Geun and chose to travel with them.' It was obvious Little Cousin didn't believe his own words. He and Sang Ki exchanged a troubled glance. They began to hunt by unspoken consent, lifting all the stones they could find while Mother of Wasps glared and the burnt woman watched.

Soon they had more than a dozen stones between them, but Sang Ki couldn't bring himself to read them. Was this knowledge he couldn't face? He didn't want to think it of himself, but he handed the stones to Little Cousin and closed his eyes as the other man spoke.

'Geun Sang Hoon begs the gods and her ancestors to forgive her,' Little Cousin read, and Sang Ki gasped in relief until he continued, 'Seonu Mi Kyung begs the gods and the ancestors to forgive her. Seonu Sun Young begs the gods and her ancestors to forgive her. Geun Kyung Hee begs the gods and her ancestors to forgive her. Seonu Ha Eun begs the gods and her ancestors to forgive her. Seonu Sook Ja begs—'

'Enough!' Sang Ki shouted, and Little Cousin dropped the remaining stones in shock at the anger in his voice. 'I'm sorry,' he said more quietly. 'But there's no need to read any more. It's clear what we have here.'

'Is it?' Little Cousin asked.

'Of course.' Sang Ki was surprised at how steady his voice remained. 'This is the grave site not of one tribe, but two. The Seonu no more survived the desert crossing than the Geun.'

'But you *are* Seonu,' Little Cousin said. 'Perhaps some died here. Perhaps the tribe split . . .'

It was perfectly plausible, and yet Sang Ki knew in his gut it wasn't true. He thought he might have known it his whole life. Because if the Seonu lay here, then his people weren't the Seonu. And if his people weren't the Seonu, who were they? He remembered the monumental rocks, scattered across the high, cold plain that was his people's home, and thought that he could guess. The rocks with the moon's face carved into them.

Some premonition made him turn away from Little Cousin and look back over the bonefield they'd crossed. He was watching the horizon when the figures appeared on it: first one, then a dozen – then more than he could count. None of them wore the blue robes of the desert tribe and the sun flashed silver on their drawn swords.

'Mother,' he said, when the riders had come close enough that he could smell the strange gingery scent of their mounts. Hana's presence here felt so unlikely that the events took on the quality of a dream, in which one thing could follow another without explanation. Little Cousin seemed more intrigued than alarmed, but his aunt watched the interlopers with narrowed eyes and a hand near her sabre.

'Sang Ki,' his mother said. 'My son.'

'What are you doing here? How did you find me?' He took a step towards her and then stopped, still ten paces short. The warriors beside her were Seonu – or whatever his people truly were – and none of them had sheathed their weapons.

'I only waited until I could gather some of our tribe before I followed after you,' she said. 'I've seen the same maps you use. I know you. I knew where you'd come.'

'And did you know what he'd find here?' Little Cousin asked. He sounded genuinely curious.

Hana turned away from the Ahn trader, as if he was nothing

to her, and answered only Sang Ki. 'I knew. And you'd know too, if you'd waited just six more weeks.'

'This is the Seonu secret, then?' Sang Ki said, more bitterly than he'd intended. 'That there *are* no Seonu.'

'There have been no Seonu for many hundreds of years. They never stepped foot on the plains.'

'But we took their name. We pretended to be them. Why, Mother? So vast a trick – a trick you played even on your own children. Why ever would you do it?'

She raised her head, a glint in her eye that seemed like anger, but might have been pride. 'We are the Yronim, the people of the moon god. A thousand years ago Mizhara's followers tried to snuff us out. I know you know it. You saw our slaughtered children at the bottom of Miduelle Lake. But a remnant of a remnant survived and hid in our last strongholds in the high mountains. We hid because we knew that one day the Mizharim would come to finish the job they'd started. And so when the tribes came to these lands, and we saw that they looked so very like us, we knew what we could do. We dyed our hair to match theirs and we hid in plain sight. We hid and waited for the day that Yron would return, as he'd promised us he would.'

'This is *fascinating*,' Little Cousin said. 'Such a huge lie, so boldly told, as all the best lies are, not so?'

'Please,' Sang Ki said to him, 'don't . . . don't listen.'

'No, listen,' his mother said. 'Let all the tribes and the peoples of these lands listen. Yron has returned and we have returned to his service. We sent warriors to our lord's forest, to serve his creatures as we did in days past – to armour them against their enemies. And we joined with the forces that would oppose him. I allowed you to join with them, Sang Ki, so that we could know their plans and thwart them. And now we do and we will.'

'Just go,' Sang Ki said to Little Cousin. 'Please, just go.'

But he knew that it was too late, and Mother of Wasps did too. She also knew that it was hopeless, but like the women whose bones littered the sand, she chose a quick death over uncertainty.

With a fierce cry, Mother of Wasps drew her sabre and charged at the line of warriors who cut off her escape. She was big and strong and she wielded the sword like she knew how to use it. Her first stroke half-severed the leg of one warrior. He fell from his saddle screaming, and her back-stroke gutted the next warrior's malbeam. She was through the line and she ran on, towards the Ahn guards, who must surely be dead already. It almost seemed like she might make it. But she was afoot and a moment later a mounted warrior rode her down and slashed his sabre across her back, sending her sprawling on to the bones below.

'None must know this but us,' Sang Ki's mother said.

Now Little Cousin finally understood that he should be afraid. He drew his own axes and backed away. Sang Ki reached out to him, to protect him or to stop him, he wasn't sure. It was futile anyway. The arrow that lodged in his chest couldn't have been stopped. There was no moment when Little Cousin was dying. That didn't seem right. He seemed like a man who should be allowed some last words. But the instant the arrow struck him, he was gone.

'Enough!' Sang Ki screamed, flinging himself in front of the burnt woman. 'Leave her be! She can't go to the Ashane. She has to stay with us!'

His mother frowned, then waved her warriors back. 'She will come with us then. Let Yron decide her fate.'

'Where . . . where are we going?'

She looked at him with something like affectionate pity, as if he was too foolish to be allowed to manage his own affairs. It was so like the way she always looked at him that he choked out a desperate laugh.

'We go to Mirror Town,' she said, 'to join our god at last.'

36

On the seventh day after the mirrors were shattered, Krish walked down the grand central avenue of Mirror Town. Broken glass crunched beneath his sandals and he felt the fear all around him. Some of the mages had begun to fashion new mirrors, but they'd never make them in time.

He saw twenty sweating men and five women armed with a mismatched assortment of weapons scavenged from the walls of mansions and the cellars of the city's museums. There was a sword so heavily jewelled it must surely have been ceremonial, a rusty halberd and an axe that the mage who hefted it could barely lift. In their centre stood a slave, a tribesman who'd once been a warrior. He spoke to the mages around him, instructing them in the arts he'd once practised, and smiled mindlessly as they demonstrated their incompetence at them.

Krish knew that weapons alone couldn't save them. But Olufemi had sent for him this morning, after days of silent study. The mage was waiting for him in the Garden of Creation at the heart of the city. He'd wandered among the twisted sculptures before. Their eye-bending colours were hideous and the sun glanced at dazzling angles from the shiny glaze of their ceramic surfaces.

Olufemi leaned against one of the sculptures, a twisted blue-purple shape that might almost have been human. Beside her was another mage, so small and frail she seemed in danger of blowing away in the desert wind. Her hair was sparse and a pure, snowy white, a brilliant contrast to her dark skin. Looking at her, Krish wondered how he could ever have thought Olufemi old.

'Krishanjit, this is Yemisi,' Olufemi said. 'She's told me she has something to show us. Though why you brought us here to do it, Yemi, I don't know.'

'No indeed, you *don't* know,' the ancient woman said in a querulous voice. 'That's why you should listen. So, boy, has Femi told you what this place is?'

'She said it's where Mirror Town was first created – something from nothing.'

'Ah yes, yes, so we've always believed. A marvellous work, each sculpture not a whole rune but a fragment of it and each mage holding only a piece of the whole in her mind. See here – come, boy, lean inside! Now note the markings all around, and the way that mirrors are arranged so that the reflection seems to form a complete shape, the form of the rune each mage was meant to contemplate.

'We couldn't do it now – we don't remember how. And even then, it was perhaps the greatest work of magic ever attempted, certainly the most complex. Not quite so powerful perhaps as the working that destroyed the great city of the Yronim, but . . .'

She turned her rheumy gaze suddenly on Olufemi, her finger upraised and shaking between them. 'She knows. I told her – many years ago. The runes can express big ideas, or little, but the more complicated the idea, the more complex the rune and the harder it is for any person to hold inside their head. A simple thing, a charm for sharpening a knife, that might occupy only two dimensions. Do you understand what a dimension is, young man? Length and breadth, those are two. More subtle ideas require a third: depth. The difference between a circle and a sphere, do you see?'

'I think I do,' Krish said, fascinated. Olufemi's explanations had never been so clear.

'This is all very interesting.' Olufemi's tone made it obvious she thought the exact opposite. 'But you *did* teach it to me, forty years ago when I first grew interested in the runes. I've learned much more since then and I was hoping you would tell me something new.'

Yemisi tssked and turned back to Krish. 'So impatient. The

thing you must understand, both of you, is that the dimensions don't stop at three. There is a fourth: the distance from one moment to the next; the gap between what a thing was and what it has become. Runes may occupy this dimension too. So my studies over the last few years – my studies while *you* have been gallivanting about in the uncivilised lands, Femi – so my researches have told me.'

'You truly think so?' Olufemi asked.

'I'm sure of it. And so this place, this Garden of Creation, is not just that. But don't take my word for it. See what I found when I searched the oldest archives in the library, the writings of Baderinwa herself, who founded our great city a millennium ago.'

She'd left a parchment lying on top of the sculpture, a narrow roll almost as tall as she was. She fumbled to unwind it until Olufemi snatched it from her, laying it out on the marble flagstones between the sculptures. It was a map. After a moment Krish realised that it was a map of Mirror Town itself, though the city whose streets he'd walked was far larger than the one shown on the parchment.

'See here,' Yemisi said, kneeling gingerly on one end of the map. 'This is where we are. You see every sculpture is marked. But do you see what's written beside this place?'

'"When all hope is lost",' Olufemi read, frowning. 'This is an old map, perhaps as old as Mirror Town itself. Our people fled here as exiles. It's no surprise they named things less cheerfully then.'

'Ah, but have you seen the name of the map?' Yemisi asked. 'Oh no, wait. I'm kneeling on it.' She shuffled awkwardly aside, until the words at the very bottom of the page were revealed. 'There! "The defences of Mirror Town". Now do you see?'

Olufemi's frown deepened. 'I'm not sure that I do.'

'This, this Garden of Creation, of making – it was a rune in four dimensions, and the fourth could be reversed. If Mirror Town were ever to be attacked and defeated, our ancestors could use these runes to unmake what they had made, and deny the victor their spoils.'

Krish looked back over the scattered sculptures, trying to imagine that they held such enormous power within them. 'But that's no use to us. We don't want to destroy Mirror Town.'

Yemisi glanced sharply up at him. 'Don't you, young man? You didn't seem too bothered by the prospect when you shattered our defences against the worm men.'

'He's right,' Olufemi said. 'Even if you're correct, this was a weapon of last resort. We can't plan our battle on the premise that it will end in our defeat.'

'Use your eyes, girl. This garden was the *last* defence, but our ancestors left us others, to save us from that final resort.' Yemisi moved her finger to another point on the map, and then another, scores of them. 'This city is not as undefended as you think.'

She held out her arm to Krish and after a moment he realised what she wanted and helped her to her feet, her slight weight barely a pressure against his hand. When she was upright, she snapped her fingers. A group of slaves rushed forward and lifted her into a litter they carried on their shoulders. It shamed Krish to realise he hadn't noticed them; that they'd become as invisible to him as they were to their old masters.

The litter-bearers led them along the statue-lined avenue and then left into a side street past a courtyard fringed with dusty trees and into the less wealthy areas of Mirror Town.

'Do you think she knows what she's talking about?' Krish whispered to Olufemi.

'She knows a great deal about the runes,' Olufemi said. 'Though not as much as I. And her family are direct descendants of Baderinwa. If anyone would have access to this information, it would be her.'

At the next cross-street the litter stopped and a burly, red-haired slave knelt beside it so that Yemisi could tread on his back to dismount. Krish clenched his fists, but said nothing.

The old mage went to stand beside a fountain from which a thin stream of water was flung up and then fell down into a shallow basin. The whole thing was pale pink, like the flesh of a salmon, and seemed to be made of the same substance as the sculptures in the Garden of Creation. Yemisi unrolled her map and snapped her fingers peremptorily to summon Olufemi and Krish.

'There it is!' she said, pointing between the fountain and the map. 'Another of the defences, and exactly where the map says it should be.'

Krish could see an illustration of the structure before him, very neatly drawn. But the drawing showed something far larger: a spiral of bowl-shaped objects curling away from the fountain. 'Where's the rest of it?' he asked.

'Gone, alas,' Yemisi said. 'Some fools before us forgot its purpose and demolished what should have been preserved.'

Olufemi squinted at the map. 'Water, water and breath, that's what the rune scribed here means. I think this was intended to drown enemies as they walked, filling their lungs with fluid.'

'And now it's nothing but a fountain.' Yemisi shook her head and tutted. 'Our people never cared enough for their own history, I've always said so.'

'If the defences are all like this, they're no use to us,' Olufemi said. 'We've lost the skill to rebuild them.'

But Yemisi's wrinkled face didn't look discouraged. 'Well, we shall see.'

The little procession went on, through the dusty streets and into the fields and orchards beyond. The trees were heavy with fruits, pink and red and green, and one violently striped in orange and blue. Krish had lost all track of the seasons in this ceaselessly hot place but it seemed autumn had arrived.

The next sculpture was in the middle of a stand of cherry trees. Krish had learned to love the intensely sweet taste of them and he picked some now, reddening his lips with the juice as he watched Olufemi and Yemisi slowly circling the structure, comparing it to what was shown on the map. It seemed to be intact: no one great structure but a hundred little ones, like gourds stuck upright in the ground. Each was pierced with a dozen holes on its upper surface, and there was an indecipherable squiggle, different on each one. Looking again at the map, he guessed that together they might add up to the rune shown there.

'Well?' he asked. 'Will it work?'

'It seems to be whole,' Olufemi said, the caution in her voice undercut by the excitement in her expression. 'The rune itself is useless, of course – it draws on the power of the sun.'

'You changed that other rune,' Krish said. 'The one that made the plants grow. Can you do that for these?'

Yemisi sniffed and turned away, as if the whole thing had ceased to be of interest to her now that she'd proven her point. 'You had better hope so, young man. Otherwise you've condemned us all.'

For days as he lay in his sickbed, Dae Hyo had told the mages attending him to send Krish away whenever the boy came by. But it seemed he couldn't put off the meeting any longer. There was a commotion outside his door, and then it was thrust open and Krish strode in.

The boy looked concerned, but his face was a liar; it looked innocent too. 'What do you want?' Dae Hyo asked.

'I want to see if you're all right.' That was a lie too. Dae Hyo knew it before Krish added, 'And to see if you're well enough to walk around. I need your help.'

Of course he did. Why else would he come to Dae Hyo when he was lying bruised and in pain after Krish's pet mage had worked her magic for him? Dae Hyo knew what had happened now. There were many other members of the Etze family being treated in other rooms around him. And many more taken to their graves.

'We need to train the slaves,' Krish said when Dae Hyo didn't reply. 'Olufemi thinks she can put up some defences but we need soldiers too, and the mages are useless.'

'So you mean to send the slaves to die for you,' Dae Hyo said.

'Not to die – not if they're properly trained.'

'They can't be trained, boy. You showed me that.'

Krish hesitated a moment, clearly taken aback by his tone.

Then he sat on the end of Dae Hyo's bed, twisting so that he could face him. There were shadows under his eyes and his face was as drawn as it had been when they'd first met, when Dae Hyo had thought he might cough himself to death at any moment.

'I'm sorry I haven't spoken to you about my plans sooner,' Krish said. 'They told me you needed to rest. But with the slaves, there's . . . a way. Olufemi's found a way to free them from the bliss. A rune.'

'Well, that's good,' Dae Hyo allowed. 'But if they're free, why would they fight? I tell you what, if someone kept me in chains for twenty years, I wouldn't pick up an axe for them the moment they were struck off.'

Krish's eyes seemed caught by the shards of shattered mirror still littering the far corner of the room. They reflected back the sunshine and the plain white walls in a dazzling muddle. 'No, that's what I said. Listen, I know this isn't perfect. We'll work something better out when we've got time. But for now Olufemi thinks she can put a rune on their skin that will make them not need bliss. A way to stop them being so . . . the way they are. So uncaring.' Krish hesitated a long moment and then added very quietly, 'But it will let them feel happy as long as they serve me.'

'You mean to make them your slaves even without the bliss.'

'It's not like that!'

'Isn't it?'

'No! This is their home too. What do you think would happen to them if we lost?'

'They'd be set free. Belbog's balls, boy, the Ashane keep no slaves. They're your people – you ought to know that!'

'I thought the Dae were my people?'

And there it was. Dae Hyo was glad it had been said. Dancing around was all well and good at the spring festival, but it never got you far in a conversation. 'You killed the Dae,' he said. 'How can you be one of us?'

'I . . . I understand you're upset.'

'Upset?!'

'I didn't mean to do it – you know that. I didn't know I *was* doing it.'

Dae Hyo's body was so battered it hurt to move, but he pulled himself up in the bed and his knees into his chest. He didn't want any part of him to be touching Krish. 'And you think that makes it better? That the murder of my brothers and sisters wasn't even something you meant? Everything I loved gone because *you* couldn't control your temper.'

'My temper?' And there it was, flaring. 'My da was beating me! Wasn't I meant to fight back? You were the one taught me that's what a man should do.'

'That's before I knew what you were!'

'And what am I? I let you take a knife to my cock, Dae Hyo! I did everything for you. I let you kill the Brotherband when they could have served me.'

'Rapists and child killers. I should have known then.'

'I'm not like them!'

Dae Hyo laughed, though it hurt to do it. 'Tell someone who hasn't been with you all these months. I saw what you did to the Rah. I can see what you're doing here. And you're not sorry for any of it. All you care about is what helps you. Well, I'm done helping you, *brother*.'

They were both on their feet, though Dae Hyo didn't remember rising. Dae Hyo had his hand against Krish's chest and he used it to push him away. But he was too weak, and instead of sending the boy staggering back it was himself he unbalanced so that he fell back on to his arse on the bed. With that all the anger drained out of him, leaving him nothing but cold. 'Go,' he said. 'Just go, and don't come back.'

It seemed the boy might argue even with that, but Krish turned on his heel and stalked from the room without another word.

As soon as he was gone, Dae Hyo rang the bell they'd left by his bedside. The bush-haired man who'd been nursing him came striding in soon after. Tending the sick was the one thing these mages seemed to treat with any urgency.

'Are you not good?' the nurse asked haltingly in Ashane.

'No, I'm not,' Dae Hyo told him. 'I'm in pain and the herbs you're giving me aren't working. I tell you what, I think some bliss would make me feel better. Can you fetch me some?'

By the time Olufemi found the third defence, buried under a thin layer of sand in the dry stream bed, she knew this might work. But as she puzzled over the rune on Yemisi's map and its echo on the device itself, she wasn't entirely sure *how* it would work.

Unlike the previous devices, this one wasn't ceramic. It was almost organic, a stack of bulbs made out of a porous material resembling coral. Its roots seemed to travel deep underground and Olufemi suspected the device might underlie the whole field. But the rune itself . . .

Hähes, the glyph of spirit mediated by Yaj, the glyph of stone, which was also the symbol of hardening. But what did it mean? What had it been intended to do? She thought that she could see a way to capture almost the same meaning by using only Yaj, twisted back on itself through Yagh, the glyph of gain. She sensed there would be power in that working, but she had no idea what it would achieve. And these weren't lesser magics. They weren't even as limited as the rune she'd formed to make the forest grow, whose working had destroyed her family's ancient home. The cost of these magics would be greater. The moon always asked for more each time his power was used.

She remembered the story of Taiwo Aleshinloye, who first worked the moon's magic to fix the flaw in his eyesight. The rune performed its function, but afterwards he had a nightmare: a thin, white figure lurking in every doorway, which would consume his spirit if he ever met its eyes.

When Taiwo next worked magic, to fix a broken leg, the nightmare returned to haunt his sleep on the first day of every month. Another moon spell used and he suffered the dream weekly, and then nightly. And when he carved a rune to cure his own lung fever, he began to see that white figure even in the waking world. His physical health restored, he lived to the age of ninety-seven – in an asylum for the insane.

Olufemi knew that the price for these defensive magics would be higher than just nightmares. Such a price could only be paid once. There could be no experimentation, no testing of her theories. She must devise a rune to replace the one already scribed here, and the entire defence of Mirror Town would rest on her being right.

She was so focused on the device, she didn't see the figures until they were nearly on her, their long-legged, red-scaled mounts churning up the sand beneath their feet. Fear weakened her. Was this the vanguard of King Nayan's army, come while they were still entirely unprepared?

But when they reined to a stop, she saw they weren't Ashane at all. They were tribespeople. Ahn, she would have guessed from their mounts, but their faces were too pale and their expressions not quite right: too close-faced for the exuberant Ahn.

'Greetings, mage,' the lead rider said, a plain woman in her middle years.

Olufemi nodded, cautious. It wasn't out of the question that these were scouts in the employ of King Nayan. 'What's your business here?'

The woman straightened, proud and defiant. 'I was once called Seonu Hana, but my true name is Janiina of the Yronim. We are the Yronim, and we seek our god, the moon reborn.'

Olufemi took them to Krish. She found him in the central atrium of the great library, limned in light by the setting sun with Adofo curled asleep on his lap. 'Tell him,' she said to Janiina.

The other woman's face was ecstatic as she sank to her knees in front of Krish. 'God-lord, we were ordered by your enemies to find you here and send them news of it.'

'They have birds,' Olufemi told him. 'Messenger owls. The Ashane army is waiting to hear from them before they march.'

'We'll tell them we didn't find you, God-lord,' Janiina said. 'We'll send them away.'

'And where will they go then?' Krish asked. For the first time Olufemi noticed how grim his expression was. His eyes looked bruised and there was a hard set to his normally soft mouth.

'It doesn't matter where they go,' Olufemi said, 'as long as it isn't here.'

'They'll find me eventually. I can't run for ever.'

'We'll protect you, God-lord,' Janiinna said fervently.

'You'll fight for me?' Krish asked.

'Of course!'

'Good.' He looked at Olufemi. 'And the runes, the defences, they can be made ready?'

'But we won't need them if—'

'Can they be made ready?'

'Yes.'

'And the slaves can be freed?'

'I believe so,' Olufemi said hesitantly. She'd never feared him before, for all that she knew what he was, but she felt a little fear now. There was no warmth and no give in him, only determination.

'Then send the messenger owls,' Krish told Janiinna. 'Tell them that I'm in Mirror Town. I won't run any more: I'll make my stand here. Let them come for me. We'll be waiting.'

37

Eric had thought of most things. He'd thought of being found, and of fleeing down the long dark tunnels, and of travelling over the wild sea, but the one thing he'd never thought of was the child coming early. In all his plans, he'd never imagined Drut would have her baby before he could tell her what it truly was.

He was walking one of the narrow alleyways with her when it happened. She'd been chattering away, quite happy for once, when she leaned her arm against the smooth granite of the nearest building and gasped.

'What is it?' he asked, supporting her as she bent forward.

Her cheeks paled from golden to a sort of sickly lemon-yellow. 'I don't know. My stomach's been hurting. I thought it would get better, but it's getting worse.'

And then he saw the pool of liquid, spreading across the flag-stones between her legs. 'It's happening,' he told her. 'The babe is coming out.'

'It *can't* be – it's not time.' But she had to gasp for breath before each word and he knew that he was right. If he could have taken his hands and shoved the babe back in, he would have, but there was never yet a person who could be kept from the world once he'd decided to join it.

'It hurts,' Drut said, sounding startled. She hadn't known much pain in her life, and he ran his hand tenderly through her hair. It mustn't happen here, out in the cold dark street. Her home was only a few hundred paces away and he put his arm round her waist to guide her. He didn't think much about what would happen beyond that. He couldn't. He just set one foot before another and rubbed soothing circles against Drut's back as they approached the grey rock building.

She stumbled over the doorstep and let him guide her down to the bedding. 'I'm not ready,' she said, looking up at him with a face as innocent as any babe's.

He wasn't ready either, but he didn't think it was wise to tell her that. 'It might not be just yet. Sometimes the pain comes a day or more before the child. There ain't no need to go panicking.'

'You've helped at a birth before?' she asked with desperate hope and he nodded. The truth was he'd stood outside the door while Fat Pushpinder screamed inside and sometimes ran for water when Madam Aeronwenn shouted for it.

Water! He rushed to get it, relieved to have thought of something, and set a pot boiling over the fire. Then he brought more blankets, and some of her spare robes to wipe her. He knew there'd been a lot of blood and shit too. He might not have been in the room while Pushpinder delivered her unwanted little gift, but he'd seen the place after. They'd had to stop using it for clients. The stains in the floor and bed just wouldn't come out.

'Eric, I'm afraid.' Drut reached out her hand and he clasped it between both of his and brought it to his lips. He was afraid too, but excited as well. He was about to be a father – Drut was labouring to bring his child into the world.

He kissed her hand again, letting his lips linger over the knuckles. 'I'll take care of you. Here, let's get you out of these clothes.'

She tried to assist him as he eased the robes down her arms, but she kept having to stop and cry out as waves of pain washed over her. That wasn't right, was it? The pain shouldn't be coming on this quick.

'Am I dying?' Drut's face was even paler now, almost the same colour as his, and there was a sheen of sweat all over it. Her hand when he took it again was slick and hot.

'You're not dying,' he said. But she groaned and convulsed, and he knew he needed to see what was happening. He swallowed and said, 'Open your legs.'

She hadn't the strength to resist as he pushed her legs apart; she only cried out again. He put a folded blanket under her back, which seemed to ease her a little, and then bent down to look at her cunny.

For a terrified moment he saw the ball of matted wet hair between her parted lips and thought that something had gone horribly wrong. Her bowels had loosened too, the stink of it spreading out. And then she cried out again, her stomach clenched and the hair came out a little more, until he could see that it was the soft round crown of a head. 'It's happening!' he yelled. 'He's coming!'

'He?' she gasped, but the question turned into a scream and the head came out a little further. There was blood too. She must have torn herself with it all going so quickly. Eric shied away from touching the hair that was sticky with blood and other fluids, but then Drut pushed again and suddenly his child was coming, he was slithering all the way out.

Eric gasped and grabbed him, holding the delicate neck and cradling his slimy body. A yellow cord stretched out from his belly towards the mother he'd finally left. Eric's hand shook as he cut it, severing the last link between Drut and her child.

'Is it . . . is it over?' she asked, sounding dazed.

But Eric couldn't reply. All his attention was on the newborn, on the wonder of it, that here was a whole life he'd helped to make. He wiped a smear of fluid away from the dark grey lips and the babe cried out and blinked open eyes that were as silver as the moon. He wasn't a monster. He wasn't a monster at all. He was a baby, and Eric's son. Eric clutched him against his chest, which felt like it was growing, stretching to make room for this little thing inside it. It felt like falling in love, but so much purer and more perfect.

'Eric . . .' Drut said weakly, and he shuffled over until he could sit beside her, cradling the babe in one arm and her in the other. This wasn't just his son, he was hers too. He was *theirs.*

'Look,' Eric said. 'Look how perfect he is.' He rested his finger beneath the baby's hand and the tiny fingers clasped round it. It caused a feeling so strong it seemed to suck all the air out of him. The nails glinted like silver.

And then Drut screamed, more weakly than when she'd been birthing their son but with more horror, and Eric remembered what he should have thought all along: that he'd never found the moment to tell her what their child would be.

'It's all right,' he said. 'Look. He's fine – he's healthy. It's only that he's a boy.'

'He's . . . what is he?' She reached out for the child, her fingers shaking, and ran them carefully along the soft roundness of those grey cheeks.

'He's our son,' Eric said.

'Oh, Mizhara, what have I done?'

'You did great, Drut – I ain't ever heard of a birth going so easy.'

'The birth of a – a monster. Eric, this is an abomination!'

Her fingers, which had been so gentle, curved into claws and Eric snatched the babe away. Drut tried to come after him but she was weak, falling forward on to her hands so that she had to peer up at him through the tangled fall of her sweaty gold hair.

'You're not thinking straight,' he said. 'You don't really mean it. He's your son.' But he kept backing away, until there were several paces separating them.

'It's evil, Eric. We have to kill it.'

'*Kill* him?'

'I should never have done it. I should never have lain with you outside the oroboros. I should never have let you save me from the long walk. It's my fault, Eric. It's all my fault but we can put it right. Kill it, Eric, and no one ever has to know.'

'Don't talk crazy, Drut. He's a *baby*.'

'He's a monster! Please, if you love me. Please, Eric.'

He did love her. It hurt him to see her so distressed, her perfect face streaked with tears and snot and such a desperate look on it. 'No,' he said. 'I'm sorry. I won't kill him. But you can come with me. We can be a family together.'

'Come where, Eric? Where are you going?'

He stepped back, until the arch of the door was right behind him. 'I have to leave Salvation, Drut. I want to go home.'

'You told me *I* was your home. Don't leave me, Eric.'

Maybe she'd change her mind, given some time and a chance to hold their son, but he couldn't risk waiting. 'I'm going, Drut,' he said. 'I want you to come with me. But I'm going to leave either way. I won't let no one hurt our son.'

'That . . . that thing isn't ours. It's the moon's!' Her chest heaved as she sobbed and a thin trickle of liquid leaked from her nipples: not milk-white but red, like blood.

'Then I'll take him to the moon,' Eric said as he turned his back on her and fled the room.

Outside he hesitated only a moment. He could take the long dark route that led away from Salvation. But the Hunter knew it already; he felt in his gut that she'd be waiting for him there. It was the portion of the day when the Servants slept and they never stirred until it ended. Only the other husbands might be wandering the halls at this hour and he could deal with them. He'd fight them if he must. It was a terrible risk, but when a boy had only bad options he took the least awful of them.

The walk back to the staircase seemed to take for ever, the walk up it even longer. His son was warm where Eric clutched him against his chest, but he was wriggling and beginning to whimper. He should have suckled at his mother's tit but – no, Eric wouldn't think of that. He pressed that small, ash-coloured face against his bosom and whispered, 'Soon. I'll feed you when we're free.'

They passed the great machine, whirling vastly in the centre of the city, and Eric knew the booming noise of it would drown out any sound he or his son might make. When they were above it and into the upper levels of Salvation, his son cried louder and Eric whispered, 'Hush, please, hush now,' and broke into a run. His footsteps splashed in the meltwater that seemed to be everywhere these days.

Those thin cries echoed down the icy corridors and Eric's

heart beat a swift march, but no one came. He cradled his son and hurried on, until finally the entrance was in front of him and he gasped out a great relieved breath and sprinted towards it.

The Hunter was waiting for him outside. The sun, low on the horizon, outlined her body in a red glow as she leaned on her spear and watched him. He skidded to a halt in the snow, clutching his precious bundle tighter against him. The swaddling clothes hid the baby, but his cries grew loud and shrill, as if he sensed the danger he was in.

'Your child?' the Hunter asked.

Eric nodded jerkily. Behind the Hunter, in the blood-red sky, the dark shape of Rii winged towards him. It didn't mean hope, not really, with her bound to the Hunter's service, but it was the only stick he had to cling to as he drowned.

'Your son,' the Hunter said quietly, and Eric backed away, but she was too fast for him. She flipped back the swaddling clothes to reveal the purse-mouthed, ash-grey face below.

'He's only a baby,' Eric said.

'A Servant of the moon.'

'He ain't serving no one. All he cares about is putting milk in his belly.'

'And it is to the moon you mean to take him.'

'I have to. Where else can we go?'

'I cannot permit you to leave.'

'You ain't stopping me without killing me.' Eric's voice shook so hard the words almost shivered into pieces, but he meant them. He'd give his life for his son.

'I do not wish to kill you,' she said. 'And I will not have to.'

She probably wouldn't. She could probably just grab hold of him with one finger and take his son without Eric being able to stop her. 'But you'll kill my boy,' he said.

For the first time, she looked a little unsure of herself. 'I would never kill a child.'

'But *they'll* kill him. So you giving us over to them is as good as you killing him yourself. You know it's true.'

She hesitated, and perhaps she would have stood aside after

all, but in that moment of hesitation Rii came. The great sweep of her wings blew snow over them both. Eric clutched his baby against his chest and closed his eyes until the storm was over and only the smell of mouldy cinnamon remained, and Rii's shadow over them all.

'Creature.' The Hunter stood tall and determined once again. 'This is none of your concern.'

Rii hissed, as if steam were boiling through her black lips. *'I have made it my concern, Bachur.'* She leaned forward, until her fanged head was between Eric and the Hunter.

'Stand aside. I command you.'

'Dost thou command me?'

'By the rune I carved into your flesh, I do.'

Rii hissed again, an angrier sound, like scalding metal doused with water. *'And what if I were to use my claws on thee, Bachur? To carve more scars into thy face.'*

Eric backed away, as he'd always done when two bruisers were working themselves up into a fight. But the Hunter didn't respond with anger or violence as he'd expected. Her face twisted into an expression almost of fear and she took a pace back.

'So many years past,' Rii said, *'thou toldst this tale to the cursed Servants, knowing that I would never hear it. Thou hidst thy face from me, deep in the Moon Forest, knowing that I would never see thy scars.* I *put those marks upon thy face, that no common wound could sully?* I *who could not overcome thy power?* I *who was bound by thee? Thou and I both know this for a lie.'*

'I never claimed as much,' the Hunter said.

'Liar,' Rii said. *'My hearing is far better than thou knowest – I heard the words Mizhara's Servant spoke to thee and then I knew what a fool thou hadst been. To summon me to thy stronghold in my master's forest, to show me thy house where thy mistress's light cannot touch and yet my brethren cannot come from beneath the ground? Whose body lies there, that poisons the land against my kin? Whose nails scored those tracks upon thy face? Whence came the power thou useth to enslave me?'*

The Hunter clutched her hand so tightly on her spear that

Eric saw her fingers whiten. 'This is nonsense, beast. I command you to silence.'

Rii laughed, a wild, discordant sound. *'Such a command does not lie within thy power. And who might I speak to, that thou wouldst silence me? And what might I say? Release me from thy binding, Bachur, or I will spill thy secret to thine own.'*

'I don't understand,' Eric said. 'Rii, what don't she want you to say?'

'I did it for your sake,' the Hunter said to Rii. 'For you and all your kind. I did it to spare the world more bloodshed and the utter annihilation of your master's people.'

'Did *what*?' Eric asked. He could see that everything had changed: the power had somehow flowed from the Hunter to Rii. His son squirmed in his arms and he held him tight, hoping.

'Thou art a murderer and a traitor,' Rii said, *'thou who stood in judgement over me. Deny it if thou canst, Bachur, and free me if thou canst not. Mercy wast thy aim when thou didst kill her who should have been most dear to thee? Then free me and I will fly this babe from the reach of those who would kill him. Revoke thy binding upon me, Bachur!'*

Eric still didn't think he understood, except that whatever Rii was claiming must be true. Its truth was written in every agonised line of the Hunter's face. It twisted, as if she was in pain, and then she said, 'Go then, beast. Be free – I unbind you!' And afterwards a word in a language Eric didn't know, which seemed to hum with the same deep power as the machine beneath Salvation.

Rii shrieked in triumph and Eric ran towards her, to mount and finally escape, but she didn't wait for him. She flung herself into the air, still shrieking, and turned towards the white towers of Salvation.

'No!' the Hunter shouted, but there was no stopping Rii. She fell on the nearest tower and ripped into it with her claws, tearing it down before moving on to another. Showers of ice fell on Eric and he backed away, wanting to turn and run but unable to look away from the savage destruction.

When she'd toppled two more towers, Rii turned her claws on one of the great white domes that lay beneath. With terrifying speed she ripped it away and continued burrowing, into the heart of Salvation. There were screams coming from inside the buildings now and Eric saw the golden forms of Servants running in disarray. He saw splashes of red too and knew that Rii's claws must have found flesh.

Eric had always known what she was. He'd trusted her because he had no other hope. But she was a monster, and now she was free she was doing what monsters did. He lost sight of her as she burrowed deep into Salvation and the screams grew louder. The noise disturbed his son and the baby screamed too.

'Take him,' the Hunter said. 'Take him and flee, before the beast destroys him too.'

She didn't wait to see if he obeyed. She hefted her spear and ran towards Salvation, dodging the jagged lumps of ice tumbling from the ruined structure. Eric watched her, frozen with indecision. Where could he run to? And how could he outrun Rii? But in the end terror won and he bent his head and sprinted through the snow heading nowhere but away.

He almost thought he'd make it. The screams were lost to distance and his breath was gasping out of his mouth in white clouds when he heard the leathery flap of wings above him and sank to his knees in despair. He curled himself round the baby. It was all he could do as Rii landed in front of him and thrust her great, ugly head towards him, her fangs dripping red onto the white of the snow.

'Where goest thou, morsel?'

'Please. Don't kill him. He's one of yours, ain't he?'

'Indeed, and so art thou. My vengeance here is done. My master's stolen machine is broken and all its magic denied the cursed Servants. Mount, morsel, before our enemies rally and pursue us. The moon awaits our coming.'

38

There were nine bronze fire javelins. Every scrap of metal King Nayan had provided had gone into making them and Cwen wondered if they'd be enough. She watched her hawks as they clustered in small groups around each weapon, miming the motions required to work them: loading them with canisters of small iron balls and the bags of black powder, using a flint to strike the spark that would ignite it and running back, away from the possibility of an explosion – and then doing it all over again.

'They're quick,' she said to Alfreda.

The smith shrugged. 'It's easy to be quick when it's done this way.'

'We can't afford to waste the powder or the metal on doing it any other.'

'Aye, I know. But the black powder makes the metal hot – too hot to hold. And that's if we're lucky. Maybe it will destroy the javelins and kill your hawks as it does. And even then, what if the enemy don't come from straight ahead? How fast do you think they can turn those things round?'

'You're saying the fire javelins are useless? But then why did you make them?'

'I amn't saying that. I'm saying they have *one* use – one chance, one flight of those lead balls into the enemy and then it's over. They'll be too close by then anyhow if they keep coming, and your hawks will have to flee. But for all those balls don't fly far, they fly hard and Krishanjit's people won't have seen their like before. You saw how it was in the Moon Forest. An enemy charge meeting my fire javelins will be broken, I promise you that.'

'If they don't use magic against us,' Cwen said.

As if in answer there was a loud boom, a little like the noise of the fire javelins, and a moment later a flash of lightning. A storm had blown in while they talked, darkening the sky to the colour of her mood. 'Away!' she shouted to her hawks. 'Get those things covered and the black powder in out of the rain.' It had begun to come down already, long darts that stung as they hit.

'What's that?' Alfreda asked. Her hair was plastered to her head in long, dripping strands and her tongue darted out to lick the water flowing past her lips.

'A fucking great storm,' Cwen said. 'Let's hope the tents survive it.'

'No, *that*.' Alfreda pointed up.

It took Cwen a moment to find it, the black dot far above, growing larger as it hurtled towards them. A bird maybe – but what bird would be in the sky in such weather?

'It's an owl,' Alfreda said, long before Cwen could make out any more than the outline of its wings. Then Cwen heard its ululating screech, a thin sound almost lost in the roar of the storm. 'It's the red-and-white bird you sent with Sang Ki. He's found the lost prince.'

Cwen had thought an army this size on the march would be impressive, but when you were caught in the middle of it, it was just a crowd of smelly, shouting, jostling people, the lashing rain they all walked in and the mud beneath their boots and hooves.

'I don't see why we couldn't have waited a day to set off,' Wingard said. The Moon Forest folk travelled like a clot of weeds in the flowing stream of the Ashane force, the hawks all mounted, Jorlith marching with their spears held high and the churls and thegns trailing after.

'Krishanjit is in Mirror Town *now*,' Cwen said. 'He might suck in his balls and head off if we're not quick. We don't want to give him time.'

But it seemed time was precisely what they would be giving him. By midday, the back of the huge army had only just broken camp, or so the harried messengers riding up and down the straggling line of march informed them. The carrion riders might have done the job better, but the ugly great grey birds were kept on the ground by the storm. Cwen looked at them where they walked beside their armoured riders and thought that if she'd seen one in the Moon Forest, she would have hunted it down as a monster.

By the end of the day she was soaked through and hungry. She was so tired she could have slept on the muddy ground, but when she saw the Ashane noble approaching, his eyes seeking hers through the crowd of hawks, she sighed and reined her horse round to meet him.

'Cwen the hawk?' the man asked, though he'd been present when she'd first come to King Nayan. She remembered his smooth, not-to-be-trusted manner.

'Yes,' she said. 'And you are?'

'I am Lord Puneet of Whitewood, Quartermaster to the Oak Wheel.' His eyes scanned her forces, and then again as if he was looking for something he couldn't find. 'Where are your supply wagons?' he asked eventually.

'We carry our supplies in our packs.'

'For the whole march?' If his eyebrows could have crawled off the top of his head, they would have.

'We hawks are hunters – the Jorlith too. We'll hunt our food.'

'In the desert? I admire your confidence.'

She ground her teeth. 'And I suppose you've brought enough to feed all of your men for the next year.'

He smiled. 'Half a pound of peas, a pound of meat and a pound and a half of bread for each man every day. We don't have enough to feed us for a year, of course, but our supply line is secure through the Blade Pass and my son-by-vow persuaded the River Ahn to bring us what more we need. Lahiru may not be much of a man but he could charm a crow into song. We've enough food to feed us all for the length of the campaign.'

'Truly?' she asked, too surprised to stay angry.

'Indeed. My brother commanded the campaign that pacified those Seonu savages who now travel among us.' His eyes cut sideways, to where the thousand of Sang Ki's people were making camp away from the bulk of the Ashane force. 'My brother was a great military leader, of course, but who do you think kept his army supplied in those cold mountains? They might have lost some men without his tactical genius, but they would have lost them all without my food. Well, don't worry. We have enough to spare you some – should your hunting not prove as fruitful as you anticipate.'

'Thank you,' she said, almost sincerely. If truth were told, she *had* begun to worry about feeding the helpless thegns and churls.

He inclined his head graciously. 'And now, if you will – King Nayan desires your presence.'

The King's tent had been set up in the centre of the camp, as neat as the first day Cwen saw it, as if they'd travelled nowhere at all. With Puneet by her side, she was allowed to stride straight through the guards to the inner, silk-walled room where Nayan sat hunched over a map with sour Lord Nalin beside him.

The King's brow was furrowed as she entered but his expression lightened when he saw her.

'I've brought you your hunter, my liege,' Puneet said.

'Thank you,' Nayan replied. 'You may leave us now.'

Puneet clearly didn't like that, nor Nalin either when Nayan added 'You too', but neither man disobeyed his King. Cwen was soon left alone with him, standing awkwardly at the opposite side of the large map. She looked down at it, though she'd memorised every line by now.

'An unimpressive day for us,' Nayan said.

She shrugged. 'We'll get better.'

'Maybe. Our progress from Ashanesland was little faster. It's the landborn levies: no discipline, no training and no mounts. And none of them wish to be here – they're less interested in serving the Oak Wheel than in tilling their soil.'

'Then why did you bring them?'

He laughed, abrupt and startled. 'I'd have a tenth of the army without them.'

'The tenth that can fight. I know you Ashane do things differently, but I'd never got into a hunt with a hawk who wasn't willing. Fuck, I remember one time—' She snapped her mouth shut, suddenly realising just who she was talking to.

'No,' Nayan said, 'go on. And sit, for the love of the Five.'

She settled uneasily into the chair Nalin had vacated. It was still a little warm from his arse.

'Well? What about this hunt of yours?' Nayan asked.

'It was meant to be training for the greenest hawks. We went after a little beast, not much bigger than a boar but with fangs like a snake's. Only what we didn't realise was that was just a baby and its mother was waiting nearby. She was as big as a house, and dripping poison so strong it smoked when it hit the ground.

'A clutch of grown hawks could have taken her. Even those green hawks could have taken her. Except that one of them, this boy called Aesc no taller than my armpit, he panicked. Screamed and ran off. And as soon as *he* showed his fear, the others all realised they were terrified too. They turned tail and ran and left me with a spear and a beast that could have taken my head in one bite.'

She pulled aside the collar of her shirt, showing the beginning of the long, puckered scar that ran from her neck to the top of her right breast. 'I took her in the end but she left me with this and a fever that nearly killed me.'

Nayan tapped his fingers thoughtfully against the map. 'You think my landborn levies will panic and run?'

She shrugged. 'I say nothing about your men. But for me, I'd never again fight beside an unwilling hunter. I want to know I've got my back to something solid.'

The march went on, two more days of dragging progress through mud that only grew deeper as the rain fell without cease. And then disease began to appear, as of course it would, and men started to fall as they marched. It seemed to be only the bloody flux, which came from living in such mud and filth, but Cwen could see in all the faces around her what they feared it could turn into: carrion fever.

That evening, King Nayan came to see her himself. His whole retinue rode into the midst of the hawks and his shipborn men, armoured and severe, pushed Cwen's people back to make room for him.

'I'd be gutting our forces,' he said to her without preamble. 'As we stand, we'll strike fear into the mages with our mere numbers. I've had reports of Mirror Town – they can't muster above five thousand fighting men, and most of those slaves.'

'The longer we take, the longer Krishanjit will have to ready his forces,' Cwen said.

'But not to expand them. He can't grow new men out of the sand.'

'Maybe not, but he can train them. And the mages have their magic.'

Nayan's smile twisted. 'So a hundred thousand men or only a hundred, you don't think we can stand against them.'

Cwen shrugged. 'I say we'll be facing things no one among us has ever faced before. Better to do it with those who might be more than wheat before a scythe.'

It took a whole day to separate out the grain from the chaff. But the next morning they rode from the camp in good order, a force of barely eight thousand, but every one of those armed with metal and half on some form of mount: mammoth or carrion bird or horse.

Cwen had chosen in the end to leave her churls and most of the thegns behind. She'd given them leave to return to the Moon Forest but she didn't know if they'd ever see its trees again. The army had left all the sick behind – and hopefully the sickness with them – and they'd taken the bulk of the supplies onward to see them through the desert. It was a hard choice and Cwen was glad that Nayan had been the one to make it. She couldn't look her own folk in the eye as she left them to their uncertain fate.

That night Nayan summoned her again. He and his lords talked about strategy and looked at their maps of Mirror Town and the desert all around, but the truth was there was little they could plan until they knew what they faced. When the others left, Nayan asked her to remain.

'I summoned an idolator from the Moon Forest,' he told her, 'when I heard the prophecies about my unborn son. It was said the folk of the forest knew more about the moon god than we Ashane.' He caught her expression and sighed. 'It wasn't just my own death they prophesied, you know. They told me his coming would tear the world apart.'

She nodded cautiously. Was he trying to justify himself to her? She didn't see why a king should care what a hawk thought. 'The Hunter told me the same,' she said. 'And on the journey here, Sang Ki – the leader of the Seonu – he saw the ruins of a place destroyed in the last war.'

'I could have stopped all that. Babies are stillborn all the time. We could have buried him as parents do and had another. But . . .' He shook his head, an ageing man in distress. Then his expression tightened and he was once again a king. 'I failed then, but I won't fail again.'

They spoke every night after that, on a journey that was now far swifter. Cwen liked the King despite herself, and more than that: she was coming to trust him. He and his generals came from a nation that enjoyed battle. The Ashane had been humiliatingly defeated in the Fool's War against the Eternal Empire, but they'd won far more often than they'd lost. She could see why. Even without the landborn levies, they were a formidable force. Her own hawks drilled with them daily, the faster progress leaving time to spare in the evenings. And if her hawks were perhaps better fighters, the Ashane were certainly better soldiers.

A little more than a week after they'd set out, when she'd begun to think of them all as an army and not just an unhappy merging of mismatched forces, they reached the borders of the desert. The maps told them so; and the grasslands of the plains flowed upward to a series of hills shaped like waves that broke against the Silent Sands. But when they reached the crest of the last hill, what lay before them wasn't sand at all.

From horizon to horizon, the desert was blooming. The

rains that had brought mud and illness to their army had given life to the Silent Sands. Cwen stared in wonder at the lush abundance of what should have been a wasteland. Forage would be no problem here; perhaps her hawks would be able to hunt their food as they'd planned.

Wine and Wingard rode to either side of her, more comfortable on horses than they'd been when the slaughter of their own mounts first drove them into the saddle. Her hawks and the Jorlith were ranked behind her, a neat block within the Ashane army. She'd promised Bachur that she'd fight this battle, but she hadn't known it would be *this* battle fought in *this* way.

The green of the desert seemed welcoming, as if it was accommodating itself to their needs. But the greenery was the product of the same relentless rain that had bogged down the bulk of their army and led to them abandoning nine-tenths of their fighting strength. She distrusted its welcome. There were plants that grew in the Moon Forest, bright and beautiful, that held a sticky poison in their hearts for any insects drawn to them.

But Mirror Town lay ahead and her duty with it. She nodded to her hawks, then shook her reins and led them onward.

39

Eric spent the first day of the flight in terror, expecting pursuit at any moment. Every bird in the sky was the Servants come for him and the baby cried and cried as if he felt that fear too. It was only when they landed on a lonely stub of rock in the heart of the ocean and Rii said, *'Thy son hungers,'* that Eric realised what the real problem was. And what kind of father was he, to have forgotten that?

'I ain't got breasts and I ain't got milk,' Eric pointed out. He eyed Rii's teats, drooping from her matted fur. You could milk a cow and a sheep and a goat, and he'd even heard that you could milk a deer, if you felt the need.

'It is not milk he craves,' Rii said. *'It is blood thy son desires.'*

'Blood?' Eric looked down at his boy's face, grey like the worm man he was, but as chubby-cheeked and soft as any baby born of woman.

'Blood thou hast, hast thou not?'

True enough, but he generally liked to keep it on the inside of him.

'Give me thy hand, morsel.' She hissed impatiently at his hesitation. His fingers trembled when he finally held them out to her and he had to fight not to snatch them back as she lowered her massive fangs towards him.

'It ain't going to hurt, is it?'

'Dost thou think a mother's breast gives no pain when it gives milk?' Rii didn't give him time to reply, only slashed her fang along the tender skin of his wrist. He gaped at it as the blood welled. A droplet fell onto his son's lips and a little pink tongue darted out to lick it up. Silver eyes opened to gaze unfocused at

Eric's face and he lowered his wrist until his baby could latch his mouth on to it and suck.

It *did* hurt, worse than the cut itself. The babe sucked like he was starving for it. Eric gritted his teeth and let the tears leak from his eyes as his boy drank. When the babe was done, he fell away from Eric's wrist with a contented sigh and tiny red bubbles frothing from his mouth.

'Come,' Rii said. *'Our journey has only just begun.'*

They flew for hours, and the next time his son cried, Eric tore open the cut on his wrist with his own teeth. By the third day the pain of it was less and the pleasure more: he was giving life to the life he'd made.

On the fifth day they left behind the crawling sea with its flyspeck islands and flew to the coast. It was a green blur far beneath and then a clearer view of tall, tall trees, some with ice-white trunks and others the gnarled old limbs of giant oaks.

'It's the Moon Forest,' Eric said, shocked, but the wind snatched his words before Rii could reply to them. Her flight followed the ragged line of the coast, and mile after mile of trees passed beneath them. Then finally there was a paler green below, a great half-moon like a bite taken out of the forest. Rii's wings dipped down and she flew them towards its border with the sea. As they drew closer Eric saw the rocks that made up that margin twisted into high improbable shapes along the cliffs and scattered broken on the golden sand. Rii landed with her feet in the frothing water of the sea, where a cave-mouth gaped in front of them.

Eric's legs wobbled as he dismounted. 'Our stop for the night?' he asked. A cave would be nice, a bit of shelter and maybe even warmth if he could find wood to burn. His old ice-walled room in Salvation had started to seem cosy after nights spent wet and shivering under furs, his son clutched to his naked chest to share his body's meagre warmth.

Rii didn't answer and when he turned to look at her he saw the most peculiar expression on her leathery face. He'd learned to read her over the months, but he couldn't read this. He might almost have thought her melancholy, except that she'd never been one for such halfway emotions. It was all rage or disdain with her. Or – in the destruction of Salvation – a simple, savage joy.

'Well?' he said eventually. 'Are we going in or just staring?'

She shivered all over, seeming to come back to herself. *'Enter then, morsel – and be welcome to my home.'*

'I thought the city beneath Salvation was your home?'

'When I was driven from my first. No more questions – enter.'

He'd thought it would be dark inside, but something grew there, a bulbous moss that filled the space with an eerie silver glow like moonlight. And it was beautiful, not at all the rough cave he'd expected. The rock of the walls had been carved everywhere, twisting patterns of vines and flower after flower faced with crystal that made them glitter blue and red and purple. Who would have guessed that Rii liked flowers? But then there'd been none in the frozen north.

Rii shuffled to the far end of the chamber, and after pausing for a while to gawp he followed. This must be her bedroom, to judge by the long bar hanging high above, scored with a hundred claw marks. There was a wardrobe too – or at least he thought that's what it was, though it was the size of his old home in the Moon Forest. Rii pressed one of her long claws against some hidden latch and its door swung open.

There was armour inside, silver-chased and huge. 'This is what you came for?' he asked.

She reached in to pull out the first piece, a curved disc she pressed against her chest. *'Wilt thou aid me?'*

He found leather straps hanging from the sides of the metal, scaled like no leather he'd ever seen and undecayed after all these years. The armour she already bore, seemingly fused to her skin, had matching rings where the buckles could fasten. After the breastplate came silver netting to hang over her wings and a complex of pieces to fit round her face and neck. There were even two leather hoods to drape over her ears.

When he was done she looked dazzling and terrifyingly martial, and still one whole suit of armour like hers remained in the wardrobe.

They both stared at it in silence. The question was obvious; but then so was the answer, and he was afraid to hear it. A boy didn't need to invite grief into his life, especially someone else's.

'Bachur's husband took thy place in the time long past. It was he who armoured me.' She paused a moment before adding, *'It was he who armoured my mate.'*

And then there was a question he could ask, one he'd asked before only to get the brush-off, but he thought maybe she and he were closer now. 'Why *did* you surrender to the Servants then, when you'd lost everything? I know you was waiting for Yron to come back, but a thousand years is an awful long time to wait alone.'

'But I was not alone. I have not been alone for a single year of all those thousand.'

He darted a quick look around the chamber, wondering if a dozen more Riis were going to leap out at him, and she yipped her laugh.

'Place thy hand upon my belly, morsel, and thou wilt understand.' She lifted her wing and tipped herself sideways, until her breast was exposed. It was encased in armour now, but he slipped his mutilated fingers between the join of two plates and settled them against the matted hair.

The next instant he snatched them away again. There'd been movement against them, wriggling like worms beneath her skin. Or – no, he knew that feeling of life below the surface. He'd once felt it when he touched Drut. 'You're pregnant!' he said. 'But how, if your bloke's been gone all this time?'

'My children have slept inside me for the moon to rise upon their wakening. I first felt them quicken when I battled accursed Bachur on the day of my master's death, and I knew then that their lives were more precious by far than my freedom. Dost thou not know it too? Is thy son not worth more to thee than all the world's wealth? When Yron arose they stirred afresh, and then thou camest, and I knew that the day of their birth approached at last.'

He looked to her for permission and then reached out to touch her again. The life inside her didn't startle him now and he left his hand there as he felt it shift beneath her skin. Soon he sensed something more: the flutter of small hearts. Many more than one. 'How many kids you got in there?' he asked.

'Twenty-eight, my master's number.'

'Twenty-eight? And I thought I had it rough with one! So when's the happy occasion? It's not . . . it's not now, is it?'

'My children are not yet fully grown nor are they ready for the world. I will keep them inside me yet awhile, safe from the fight that is to come, for my master's life is threatened and his need calleth to me. Thou hast armoured me for war, morsel, and now we go to fight it.'

Eric clutched his son tighter against him, so tight the babe whimpered and nuzzled against his wrist, searching for another meal of blood. 'What about him? You can't take him into a fight – it ain't right.'

'I will guard him as I have guarded thee – as I guard all my master's servants. I shall be a mother to thy son, and thou wilt be a father to my children, and together we will serve the moon and aid his rising.'

40

They tried the rune on Dinesh first. When Olufemi told him she was ready, Krish asked the boy if he wanted to be free. Dinesh only smiled and said he'd do whatever Krish wanted, just please don't take the bliss away from him. So Krish nodded at Olufemi and walked away as she inked the mark into the slave's flesh. This would be better than bliss – it must be.

When he returned an hour late, Dinesh was still smiling and Krish felt angry disappointment. But Olufemi smiled too.

'It worked?' Krish asked her.

'See for yourself.'

Dinesh turned his wide brown eyes on Krish. The rune was on his cheek, a complex black shape beneath his left eye that warped as he spoke. 'I feel . . .' he said. 'I feel . . .'

'Happy?' Krish asked. That had been part of the magic Olufemi tried to weave: to remove the terrible addiction of bliss without taking away all the contentment that went with it.

The boy shook his head. 'No. It's . . . Not, not, not happy. But not sad. I feel . . . There's so much in my head. I don't, I don't, I don't know how to think all these thoughts.'

'I gave him bliss after I put the rune on him,' Olufemi said. 'A triple dose. Before, it would have left him lying on his back smiling at the sun. But now – well, you can see.'

'Do you understand what's happening here?' Krish asked. It had never been clear before how much the slave really knew about the world, or cared.

Dinesh nodded, his eyes still wide but no longer distracted: focused in a way they'd never been before. 'There's a war coming. You want us to fight.'

'Yes. I need you to fight, or we'll all die. Do you think you can do that?' Dae Hyo's angry words echoed in his head, but what choice did he have? He was as much a slave as Dinesh, in his own way: imprisoned by a destiny he hadn't chosen.

'I think so,' Dinesh said. 'If you want me to fight, then I want to fight. But . . . I don't know how.'

'We'll teach you,' Krish said. It would be weeks yet before the Ashane army could reach them. There'd be time to do more than put a spear in the slaves' hands and teach them which end was pointed. 'And the defences,' he said to Olufemi. 'Are they nearly ready?'

'Almost. I've found assistance, but before that there's – there's something you need to see.'

Krish followed her inside Turnabout, the great library where the remnants of Olufemi's family had made their home. The building was unique: it was entirely without mirrors. Olufemi told him it was thought the light would damage the thousands of ancient books inside. Instead, the library had been constructed on great rotating discs of rock, turned every evening by slaves.

Krish knew why Olufemi's family had chosen to stay here. However much they might nod and do as he commanded, he felt their hating eyes on him and Olufemi whenever they walked past. These people would never serve him in their hearts and only here, where the worm men wouldn't come, could they be safe.

There were a dozen of Olufemi's cousins in the first room he came to, helping to mix the ink that would be used to tattoo the slaves. But at the back of the room was a far paler face.

'Dae Hyo!' Krish said, glad despite himself. He hadn't seen the warrior since their argument. He'd been afraid Dae Hyo had fled Mirror Town entirely.

'Dae Krish.' The warrior smiled. But the smile was too wide and the eyes above it too glassy.

'Is he drunk?' Krish asked Olufemi.

'The fool's taken bliss.'

'And who gave it to him?' Krish asked, furious. 'He's not a slave!'

'Bliss is for anyone who wants it. Among our people, if someone wishes to leave the responsibilities of freedom behind, it's allowed. Their house loses a mage and Mirror Town gains a slave. We understand that freedom is harder than slavery.'

'I'm happy now.' Dae Hyo's speech was slurred and a thin trickle of drool was seeping from one corner of his mouth. 'I thought I was happy before, but I didn't know what happiness was. *This* is happiness. This is . . .' He waved his hand, his eyes tracking the movement as if they found it fascinating.

'You have to cure him,' Krish told Olufemi.

'He doesn't need curing, not yet. He's only taken the drug for a few days. If he stops now he'll have a fever and head pain like he's never known, and then he'll be well again.'

Krish looked at Dae Hyo, still smiling as he watched the movements of his own hand. 'But now he knows what it feels like, he'll use it again. He can't even stop drinking. How can he stop taking bliss?'

'Perhaps he'll find the strength,' Olufemi said, but they both knew he couldn't.

'No. We need to help him. Can you do what you did for the slaves, make it so that bliss won't work on him any more?'

'I can give him the *same* rune as the slaves,' Olufemi said, carefully expressionless. 'Is that really what you want?'

'No! Not the same – not so that he has to be loyal to me. I don't want that. I just want him to be himself again.'

The mage looked at the warrior, lost in his private happiness, then shook her head and turned to Krish. 'And are you sure that's what *he* wants?'

'I don't care. It's what he needs. Can you do it?'

'I imagine so.'

'Good.' Krish turned away from Dae Hyo, unable to bear his mindlessly joyful expression. 'Good. Now you told me you'd found some more mages. Do you mean real mages – people who can work the runes?'

Olufemi took Krish to one of the great mansions, the red-tiled, crenelated structure he'd learned long ago was the home of the

Bakari family. 'I thought the Bakaris were all musicians,' he said to her.

'And mathematicians, and scientists,' she agreed as they approached the twin sculptures that flanked the entrance, huge lizards like long-legged versions of the Rah crocodiles. 'But also many melancholics, some lunatics – all the afflictions of the mind that may be found are found in the Bakari family. The Chukwus say it runs in their blood, which is probably true. The Bakaris bed cousin with cousin and think nothing of it.'

'But we want mages – not musicians *or* lunatics.'

'There *are* no more mages. For centuries the runes have been dead and my people no longer believed they could be woken. No one studied the runes for their power except Yemesi and I – but as I told you before, some found another use for them. Many among the Bakari sought the peace that came with their contemplation. They can't devise new runes as I've been doing but, as I once did, they've learned how to hold the shape of them in their minds, to drive out all other thoughts. They can't make new runes, but they *can* use the ones I make. Come, let me show you.'

She led him through the narrow corridors of the mansion. Shards of broken mirrors crunched beneath their heels until they came to an inner courtyard, open to the sun and with a withered apple tree, brown-leafed and sad in its middle. Two dozen men and women sat round it, each of them studying a sheet of parchment scribed with a different rune. Some turned to watch as they entered, but others only rocked in place or stared fixedly at nothing. One stern-faced woman tended a younger man, gently mopping the drool from his slack mouth.

'Them?' Krish whispered to Olufemi. 'Really?'

'Perhaps the emptiness of their minds is a gift, to leave room for the runes. Let me show you. Begin!'

Magic took place out of sight, in a hidden place only its user knew. Very quickly, though, Krish saw its effects. The wilting tree in the courtyard's centre creaked as its twisted limbs straightened. Buds began to swell and open on the newly vital branches and soon there was the lively green of new leaves and sweet-smelling white flowers dropping petals to float in the air.

Olufemi smiled. 'I took the rune I devised before and divided it between them. And made its effect less, of course – we don't want an orchard growing here.'

'And they can do more?' Krish asked. 'They can work the runic defences you've rebuilt.'

'I believe so. We'll have to teach them the new runes of course, but once they know them – yes, they have the skill.'

He looked over them again. There was a low humming sound in the room and he realised it was coming from one of the mages, a list of meaningless words repeated over and over. Several of them were weeping.

'If they do do this for me,' he said, 'they'll pay the price – or their families will. Do they even know what it is they'll be doing, or what it might cost?'

'Don't ask the question when you don't want to hear the answer. You've made my people your tools – at least have the courage to use them.'

Sang Ki should have been happy. A visit to Mirror Town had been among his few ambitions before this whole enterprise began. And here he was, wandering among buildings that were the stuff of legend to any student of history. To his left was the monumental structure he knew must be Turnabout, resting on its giant, improbable discs. And near the horizon he could see the tall, glass tower in which Baderinwa, the founder of Mirror Town, had spent years of madness after magic fled the world.

But wherever he chose to go, three Seonu warriors trailed behind him, because his mother didn't trust him enough to walk free. And he knew that this distrust was entirely justified.

After so many years of believing himself to be in control, it was strange to be utterly at her mercy. His mother held all the power here – or all the power that the elusive Krishanjit would allow her. Sang Ki had yet to see the boy he'd been pursuing for so long. He felt a curious mixture of apprehension and anticipation at the meeting.

That was easier to think about than his mother lying to him his whole life. Sang Ki had often believed himself a disappointment to her, never felt that she respected him, but he saw now that he'd never for one moment truly doubted her love. And yet . . . she'd allowed him to believe that he was one thing, when he was the exact opposite. She might love him, but it seemed she loved her god more. And what was that kind of second-best love really worth?

He'd chewed it over and over, the idea that Krishanjit was his god too and this his side in the battle, but he remained unable to swallow it. The only image he could summon when he wrestled with the dilemma was of Little Cousin's face as he'd died. It had been too quick for much pain, but when Sang Ki pictured him now, he saw a flash of disappointment before the man's spirit fled. There was so much of the world still to see, so many books to read and secrets to ferret out. Little Cousin had been denied them all by Sang Ki's mother – and on behalf of these people.

'They're getting ready for war,' the burnt woman said.

She was right: many of the broad and dusty squares of the city had been turned into training grounds, the dark-skinned mages swinging weapons they clearly had little idea how to handle. Just today a flood of slaves had joined them, each bearing a black tattoo his mother claimed was a rune to free them from the slavery of bliss. Despite all he'd seen, Sang Ki found it hard to credit the power of such magic.

'They know what force is riding to face them,' he said to the burnt woman. 'They know they're outnumbered a hundred to one and out-armed too. If this is the best they can muster, I fear we've been forced to align ourselves with the losing side.'

'They have magic,' she pointed out.

'Perhaps, but can any power compensate for such a ramshackle and ill-trained force?'

Glass crunched beneath their feet as they walked and the burnt woman frowned. It wrinkled the scars on her face into something even more hideous. 'It looks like there's been a war here already. This Krishanjit's spent more time fighting his own than fighting the enemy.'

'Such is the nature of rule – even, I imagine, for a god. It is seldom uncontested, and one has to admire his cleverness at least in playing that particular card. To force the mages to his side so absolutely: it was something of a masterstroke. And in that same act, to make any resentment of it a lethally bad idea. I must say . . .'

He trailed off, realising that the burnt woman was no longer listening to him. They'd reached the widest square yet, surrounded by marble-walled mansions and ringed with red-leafed trees of a variety he'd never seen before. It was what stood in the centre of the square that had caught the burnt woman's attention: a dozen or so tall pillars. But no – it wasn't the pillars she was looking at, it was the figure standing on the pinnacle of the nearest.

'The famous stylites of Mirror Town,' Sang Ki told her. 'The mages from time to time like to perch up there in the hope that inspiration will come to them, or so I've read.'

'But that one isn't a mage,' she said.

And nor, Sang Ki realised, was the man approaching them across the square. They were both Ashane, and one of them at least he recognised.

He wondered if he should bow as Krishanjit drew nearer but it would have seemed dishonest – and besides, the man didn't have the bearing of a king. He was barely even a man, still with the gawky awkwardness of a boy about him and the hollow-chested, scrawny look of the goatherd he'd been not so very long ago.

Krishanjit was also watching the man on the pillar. When he looked away, his gaze sought the burnt woman rather than Sang Ki. 'That's Marvan of Fell's End. But you know that, don't you?'

'Marvan of the Drovers?' the burnt woman asked. 'What's he doing here?'

Krishanjit's smile was twisted. 'He was following me. But if you mean what is he doing stuck on top of a pillar, I didn't want to leave him free – not after he tried to kill me. Him and you together.'

'I don't know who you think I am,' the burnt woman said, 'but I've never met you before. I've never tried to kill anyone.'

'I'm afraid you won't get any other answer out of her,' Sang Ki said. 'She claims to be Mahvesh, formerly of the company of Fine Fellows.'

'And is she?' Krishanjit looked at him at last.

'I think,' Sang Ki said carefully, 'that the Nethmi who killed my father and tried to kill you died in the conflagration that consumed Smiler's Fair.'

After a moment Krish nodded, either accepting Sang Ki's answer or resigned to the lack of one. 'And you're Sang Ki of Winter's Hammer.'

Now Sang Ki did bow. 'I have that honour.'

'Your mother wanted to give you another name – she says it's your true name among your true people. But you wouldn't accept it.'

'I have no need of a new name. Sang Ki has done me perfectly well so far.'

'She said you wouldn't accept *me*, either.'

And here it was. Sang Ki realised that he was afraid, terrified even. He had been from the moment this thin young man approached him. 'I would hardly put it that way. I accept that you are the moon reborn.'

'But you don't accept that I'm your god.'

'I . . . accept that you are my people's god.'

'It's all right.' Sang Ki could see the lines of tension in Krishanjit's face and the tired bruises beneath his eyes. He looked entirely mortal. 'I'm not going to hurt you – you've never done anything to me and anyway, your mother wouldn't like it. I just want to understand. Would fighting by my side be so bad? Or do you just think I'm going to lose?'

That wasn't a question it would be politic to answer. 'I've met some of your followers,' Sang Ki told him instead. 'The Brotherband.'

Krishanjit's face twisted in what looked like anger, or perhaps pain. 'I didn't want the Brotherband to do the things they did. I didn't ask them to follow me.'

He sounded sincere, but Sang Ki had met many plausible liars among the nobility of Ashanesland, and the moon was said to be the god of deception. 'Well, the Brotherband are no more, as I'm sure you know, so the point is moot.'

'Yes, the Brotherband are gone, and I've got your people instead. Are they any better?'

Sang Ki thought again of Little Cousin's face, his blood. But that wasn't all his mother was. There were a thousand memories of childhood: when she'd comforted him after a fall or chosen treats for him from the kitchen; when she'd loved him, at least a little. The Brotherband had seemed to know only hate. 'My people are like any other,' he told Krishanjit. 'Composed of good and bad – I suppose that's the purpose of leaders, to encourage one impulse or the other within them. So the question isn't whether they're worthy to follow you, but whether you're worthy to be followed.'

'You're wrong,' the burnt woman said, her rough, wounded voice startling them both. 'The leader and the follower are both responsible, aren't they? Him for what he commands and them for choosing to follow it. Everyone has a choice.'

Krishanjit nodded jerkily. 'Yes. I think that's right. But you'd both better make your choice soon. My da's army will be here within weeks, and your people will be fighting for me. So you'd better hope we win. Because if we don't, the son of a traitor won't get a welcome with the Ashane.'

'Here within weeks?' Sang Ki said, looking up at the sky. Dark against the pale blue, he could see the outlines of birds: tiny at first, but falling lower, and as they fell he could see how large they truly were. 'I don't think we've got weeks.'

Krishanjit frowned, and then he followed Sang Ki's gaze to the sky. 'Carrion mounts! But they can't be here – your ma said it would take them two months to make the journey!'

The birds were lower now, low enough that Sang Ki could see the glint of metal armour across their chests and hear their harsh screams, unlike any sound his Laali had ever made – a battle cry.

'My mother was wrong,' Sang Ki said as missiles began to fall, flung by the unseen riders. The first landed at the far side of the square, just a small puff of dust that looked no more menacing than a raindrop. And then another landed on top of the tallest pillar, and the whole structure cracked.

Another rock was thrown, and another: black dots swelling into spheres in the sky. Sang Ki didn't wait to see them fall. He grabbed the burnt woman's hand and fled in terror towards the nearest building.

41

The dusty tranquillity of Mirror Town shattered like the jagged fragments of glass that littered its streets. Krish spent a moment feeling nothing but shock. This couldn't be happening now. It couldn't – he wasn't ready.

But it was, and an animal instinct for self-preservation sent him running as rocks fell from the sky all around. One struck the paving a pace in front of him, sending shards of stone to score his cheek as he dodged left and past and ran on.

He could hear screams, not all of them from the square. The carrion riders must be attacking the whole of the town. Perhaps soldiers had already entered on foot as the birds attacked from the air. Krish felt again all the terror of those cold, hopeless weeks as the carrion mounts pursued him through the mountains of his home.

When he reached the edge of the square he found himself in a crush of people. Some were pouring out of the mansions to find the cause of the noise; others who knew what it was were trying to push their way inside. He shoved his shoulder between two old women and forced himself through, as mindless as anyone else in his panic.

A hand grabbed his arm. He tried to shake it off, but it only clung on harder. And when Olufemi's voice said, 'Krishanjit! Krish!' he came back to himself.

'We have to get out of here!' he said. They'd reached the portico of the mansion and he heard the crash as a rock landed above and was stopped by the solid marble of the building. But his instinct was still to flee.

'Where should we go?' The old woman's eyes were pleading and he realised she expected him to lead.

What did he know about leadership? 'Are the Ashane here?' he asked. 'Are they in Mirror Town?'

Another mage answered him, a tall man stooped with age. 'There's been no word from the watch. Why didn't the guards warn us?'

Yes, that was the right question. Though Krish hadn't thought the attack would come for weeks, he'd set a guard already. They would have reported if the army had come into view. The birds must be ahead of the main force. There was still time.

'Get the mages you taught the runes,' he said to Olufemi. 'I'll find the slaves, the marked ones, the ones with weapons. We'll go to the defences.'

'What about the birds? They'll kill us!' Olufemi's face was stark with fear.

Krish felt it too, but he couldn't let it overcome him. He'd brought the Ashane here – he'd summoned this destruction. He grabbed a man as he fled past and shook him until his eyes focused on Krish. 'Get everyone,' Krish told him. 'Fetch shields, tables, anything we can hold above us to protect against the rocks. Go! I command you!'

When Mirror Town appeared on the horizon at last, Alfreda felt an icy shock of fear she hadn't expected. Cwen had asked her to stay at the rear with Jinn and the supply wagons, but she'd refused. She'd thought she was ready for battle, that death held no more fear for her. She was a fool. Her life held more value than she'd realised until she prepared to recklessly risk it.

The carrion mounts had flown ahead. She could see them above the brightly coloured buildings of the city, circling as they dropped their missiles. King Nayan hoped they'd drive out whatever army Mirror Town had, force them into battle on a ground and at a time of his choosing. Their own force was drawn up in good order – far better than she could have imagined when this long march began.

The Jorlith took the front rank, their long spears a defence against any mounted charge, while the Ashane horse and mammoth riders clustered on the wings. Hawks stood with longbows ready while grim ranks of sword-armed shipborn troops held the middle ground. The Seonu hefted their axes to defend the army's rear.

The fire javelins were poised for action. She'd devised a sling to hold each one between two mammoths, ready to be moved, emplaced and used with speed. But there was no one to use the weapon against. As their army marched towards Mirror Town through the withered cornfields, there was no sign of any opposition at all.

Finally, groups of people began to emerge from the city. Alfreda could see the glint of metal, but nothing else about them seemed martial. They travelled in clumps rather than ranks, separating as soon as they'd left the streets for the surrounding fields.

Carrion mounts followed them, dark silhouettes against the sky. Rocks dropped and dust clouds sprouted where they landed. Some fell short of their targets and then Alfreda heard the deep clang as they landed on top of whatever shield the Mirror Town forces must be holding above themselves. In every other way they seemed utterly vulnerable.

The Ashane King seemed to think so too. He sat on a stallion in the middle of his men, his banner snapping above him and his lords all around. He gestured, a messenger trotted away and a moment later a large group rode from the Ashane flank towards the nearest cluster of Mirror Town people. Their hooves pounded the hard earth, the tempo increasing as they sped up to a gallop.

White and brown and black faces turned towards the mounted troops and there were distant yells of alarm. But the Mirror Town forces didn't retreat. They didn't even form a line to defend themselves and the mounted troops thundered on, sabres raised to slash.

And then there was no boom, no flash, no sign that black powder had been ignited – but suddenly every Ashane rider was on fire. Their cries were shrill, the tortured screams of the horses louder as they too caught light. The charge fell apart into a panicked mass of burning men and beasts and the terrible smell of scorched flesh washed back to the army.

There was panic in the army too. Alfreda could sense it, like another sickening stench in the air. They'd all spoken of the mages' power and tried to plan for it, but none of them had quite believed it could be real. None of them but Cwen. She was gathering her hawks around her, detaching them from the army.

'What are you doing?' Alfreda shouted.

'What Bachur commanded me,' the hawk said grimly as she and her people ran towards the Mirror Town mages and whatever awful magics they had ready.

If ever there was a time to get drunk, it was now. Rocks fell from the sky, paving stones cracked and flesh tore where they struck while the mages ran around screaming, as useless as goats in armour. Dae Hyo took another swig from the bottle, and found he was sucking nothing but air. He'd drunk it dry and he felt nothing. There wasn't the slightest blurring of his vision, the faintest happiness. There was only this horrible, unrelenting clarity.

Fuck Olufemi and fuck Krish. Bad enough they'd denied him the pleasure of bliss, but it seemed they'd denied him all other escapes too. He scratched at the still-bleeding tattoo on his chest, but the black ink remained sunk into his skin and the pain was sharp enough to stop him.

He didn't want to see so clearly. He'd spent years making sure he couldn't. And suddenly his traitorous mind was showing him everything. It showed him that he'd given nearly a decade of his life to drinking and fighting and fooling himself that he was plotting a revenge he'd never take. That he never *could* take. He saw that he'd have died with a blade in his gut somewhere on the plains if he hadn't met Krish. That Krish had saved him.

And he saw that Krish would never be Dae. That the Dae were bones and could never be brought back. It showed him what kind of person his brother was: a person who could do, who *had* done terrible things and would do more.

And most of all he saw himself: the awful, dark hole in the centre of him that nothing could ever fill, not drink and not

Krish. He saw his own guilt. Because where was he, on the day his people died? And he saw too that it wasn't his fault. If he'd been there, all he could have done was die beside them. But wasn't that what he'd been meant to do? Why had he lived when all these others had died?

So many questions. The drink hadn't answered them, but it had allowed him to stop asking them.

He looked at the sky through the bottle. The glass distorted the blue, softening it. It wasn't the same as the softness alcohol brought and he threw it away. In the moment it shattered he heard something else, a whoosh like flame and distant, desperate cries. Almost at the same instant, screams began all around him.

He reached for his weapons and realised that he'd brought none. The army had come and he was without even an axe. But there were no enemies here, only mages. All of them clutched at their faces, though they weren't injured as far as he could see. Then one of them took his hands away and Dae Hyo saw what lay beneath: a milky blank nothing where his eyes had been. There were a dozen or more all the same, all suddenly blind and screaming in panic.

This was Olufemi's work. Her magic had done this, the power Krish had commanded her to use.

Olufemi had never meant to find herself in battle. All her dreams of reawakening the runes had never been meant to lead to this. The slaves pressed close, shielding her with their bodies and her head with the thick wooden board they held above. The ugly croaks of the carrion mounts sounded from on high and she heard the thud of rocks hitting sand and then dull ringing as one struck the board itself.

Two slaves fell to their knees and it seemed they'd all topple, that she'd be crushed into the sand beneath the board meant to shield them. But others braced themselves. They held their feet and shuffled forward, towards the orchard and the runic defence.

Twenty more paces and they were sheltered from the carrion birds beneath the trees. The slaves formed a ring round her, some with spears or swords and some just with sticks, pointing them outwards. She stumbled towards the device, her new rune daubed on it in fresh paint. *Soften*, that was its meaning, though she still had no idea what it was meant to accomplish – or if her new design would work at all.

But she mustn't think about that. Worry would stop her working the rune. And she knew she'd got at least something right. She'd seen the bloom of fire where a young Bakari cousin had worked another of the runic defences.

Their enemies were almost here. She saw flashes of their clothing through the trees and heard voices both male and female. Perhaps these were the Moon Forest hawks Vordanna said had come to hunt Krish down. But Olufemi shouldn't be thinking about that either. She had to concentrate on the rune.

She sat cross-legged beside the device as all the books advised. The complex curves of it filled her vision, but when she shut her eyes all she could hear was the shouts of the hawks and the chatter of the slaves. The rune slipped away from her like water through her fingers. It was no good. She couldn't do it. Now, when it mattered most, she proved that she was no mage at all.

Her breath was coming in desperate, panicked gasps. She tried to slow it. She clenched her fist, relaxed it and tried to think only of the one thing that could save them.

Cwen had Wine and Wingard beside her, her hawks all around and terror freezing her mind. She'd never thought herself a coward. She'd taken down monsters that would make Jorlith spear-leaders shit their britches and never broken a sweat. But the fear of battle seemed to grow worse with each one she fought. Now she knew what could happen, how easily an arrow could find flesh, how wounds could fester, what hate looked like in the face of the enemy. If she'd known then what she knew now, she might never have obeyed Bachur's command.

But this had to be done. The mages were fighting with the moon's magic and her hawks alone had faced the moon's forces before. It was her duty to fight them. That drove her on, that and the thought of what would happen to her people if she abandoned them.

She hived off clutches of hawks to attack each group of mages. Her own target lay ahead, fewer than a score of them, but she'd already seen the lethal work their magic could do. The mages fled into an orchard and she and her hawks ran after them, the smell of the fruit sickeningly sweet as they crushed it beneath their boots. At any moment she expected the air to turn to fire, her flesh to burn and the agony to start, but the flames never came.

Then the enemy were right in front of her: a ring of blades guarding something in their middle. She stopped her headlong rush and raised her spear. For the first time she could see who she faced and her heart lifted. These weren't hardened warriors. Some of them were older than her grandmother, others young enough to be her child, and none held their weapons like they knew how to use them.

Her hawks gave the ululating call of the Hunt and charged. The distance narrowed to fifty paces, then twenty, and now there was fear on the faces of their enemies. Ten paces more and suddenly Cwen was sinking. She tried to lift her leg, to move forward another step, but something had happened to the ground. Baked earth had turned to quicksand, thick and sucking and pulling her down.

Her people shouted in confusion. All of them were trapped. Her spear was useless, the butt deeply buried. She tried to reach down to draw her blade, but the sand grabbed her arms and wouldn't let go. She was sinking and every flailing, desperate movement she made only drew her deeper.

She could see the Mirror Town fighters watching, as shocked as her hawks. Then their shock passed. They laughed, wild and terrifying, clutched their weapons and charged.

Krish was fleeing towards the ruins of the Etze mansion when the ground fell away beneath it with a sound like the world ending. One moment he stood beside shattered masonry and the next a black hole in the ground. Its lip began to crumble and he turned and ran back, speeding when he saw long fissures zigzagging out from the pit that had consumed Olufemi's home. She must have worked her magic and her family's home had paid the price. He wondered what the cost would be of the next magic she tried – if Mirror Town itself could survive it.

He didn't know where else to go. Mages from all the great houses of Mirror Town were working the runic defences. Nowhere was safe. But the lethal stones rained down and the streets were littered with their victims, the lucky ones dead and the unlucky screaming at crushed limbs or numb with shock, nursing ragged wounds from flying fragments of the rocks.

The carrion riders were everywhere. One hovered overhead and Krish darted down a narrow alley where the bird couldn't fly. When he emerged he found himself back in the vast square of pillars. Only one remained upright. Most people had fled, but he saw a dazed Ashane slave staggering through the rubble – until a carrion bird dived and its claws snatched him into the air.

It was only when another bird swooped towards him that he understood. They were chasing everyone with Ashane features. They were looking for *him*. He threw himself desperately to his left, rolling beneath the scant protection of a pottery fountain, tall and delicate and shaped like a bouquet of flowers from the distant plains.

The carrion bird's claw lashed out, cutting the flowers and leaving Krish exposed. He drew his knife and rolled to his knees as the carrion rider grinned. The bird reared back, flapping its dingy grey wings. In the moment before it struck, it screamed.

The bird fell to the ground thrashing and the carrion rider fell with it. Krish saw that he was tied to the saddle with leather straps. He struggled to free himself but the leather held fast and he rolled helplessly against the pavement. He reached for his belt – he was reaching for the sword sheathed there. Krish gasped and darted forward, slicing his own blade across the man's throat and falling back as the blood spurted out and the bird's frantically beating wings splashed it all around.

Finally both bird and man were still and Krish staggered to his feet. Dinesh stood behind them, clutching the haft of the spear he'd used to kill the bird and laughing with horribly incongruous delight. 'I saved, I saved, I saved you!' he said.

But there were more carrion riders, and now they were two Ashane, an even more tempting target. The library of Turnabout lay beyond the square – a place not owned by any one Mirror Town family and perhaps immune from the consequences of their magic. There was no better option and Krish grabbed Dinesh's arm and ran towards it.

The square had become a maze, filled with blocks of fallen masonry and the bodies of those trapped beneath. Some of them were still alive. Their cries for help were wrenching but Krish couldn't spend his own life to offer it. He and Dinesh ran on, towards the one pillar still standing – and then another rock was flung from above and that too was falling.

It was falling towards them. Krish veered sideways, but bricks were plummeting down as it disintegrated. He ducked out of the reach of one and another hit his arm, a numbing blow that left it hanging limply at his side. Dinesh grabbed his hand, pulling him on. There were seconds of blinding panic and then a great crash only paces behind them, and he knew that the pillar had fallen and they were free of it.

Turnabout lay ahead, but so did another man. For a single, shocked moment, Krish stared into the battered face of Marvan. Krish's knife was still in his hand and the other man was dazed and bloody. But then there was a raucous cry above, another carrion mount dived towards them and Krish and Dinesh ran left as Marvan ran right with the carrion mount in pursuit. Krish didn't turn to see if it caught him. The path to Turnabout was clear and he gasped in a breath and sprinted towards it.

Alfreda didn't see what happened to Cwen and her hawks, but she heard the screams and the laughter coming from the trees – the terrible sound of people taking joy in slaughter.

The Ashane army had resumed its march towards Mirror Town. Perhaps King Nayan thought their numbers were too many to crush with magic. Perhaps he meant to offer support to Cwen's hawks in their fight against the mages. It seemed he had orders for Alfreda and her five javelins too. She saw a messenger riding towards her but she didn't wait to hear his words.

The mammoths were slow to move but relentless once they were in motion. The hawks who'd learned to work her weapons didn't argue with her decision. They wanted what she wanted with the same urgency – to save Cwen from whatever she was facing.

A horse would have struggled to pass through the orchards, but these were the largest mammoths in Ashanesland. They lowered their massive heads and butted the trees aside, crushing branches and fruit beneath their feet as they charged. The fire javelins swung between them, the weight of metal knocking aside any saplings left standing. The screams continued but there were fewer of them now, worryingly few. The mammoths lumbered on and then the last trees were knocked aside and their feet found clear ground – and began to sink in it.

The mammoths raised their trunks and trumpeted their distress. The Mirror Town forces cried out too, startled by the sudden intervention, and Alfreda saw Cwen at last, waist-deep in the same muck that had trapped her mammoth.

But the mages had recovered from the shock of their arrival. They raised their weapons and charged. She saw a slim Ashane woman laughing with joy as she cut the head from a hawk only five paces in front of Cwen with a rusty sword, chopping and chopping at the bloody neck until it rolled free.

There was no time to free the mammoth. Alfreda slid from the beast's back. Her legs buckled but she forced herself to her feet and turned to the fire javelin. She slashed the ropes tying it to the mammoths and flung herself aside as it fell to the ground.

Luck was with her. It fell with its nose pointed towards the trapped hawks and the men and women attacking them. Her hand shook as she shoved the canister of metal balls and the charge of black powder down, then poured more powder into the firing hole.

She couldn't shout to warn the hawks. She could only hope the mud that trapped them would also save them. She took her flint and struck a spark, backing away as the fire ate the black powder. A man was stalking Cwen, laughing, an axe held high – and in the moment when its blade descended, the fire javelin spat out its charge.

The noise was deafening. It left a brief shocked silence in its wake. Then the screaming started and Alfreda saw that the fire javelin had done its bloody work, scything through the enemies nearest to the hawks. Those who hadn't been hit were running, terrified. They were fleeing and leaving the hawks behind.

'Freda!' Cwen shouted. Her friend had sunk almost to her armpits.

Alfreda took her knife to the rope that still flapped from the side of the fire javelin, sawing off a long section. She wound one end round her waist and flung the other to Cwen. It fell short, slapping against the mud, and she cursed and threw again.

This time Cwen managed to catch it. Alfreda gripped the rope, stiffened her shoulders and stepped back. Beside her, the mammoth struggled to free itself, kicking mud into her face. It was succeeding but Alfreda wasn't. The weight of Cwen was too much: she couldn't shift her against the ruthless downward sucking of the earth. But the mammoth was strong enough. It was dragging itself out of the mud and Alfreda untied the rope from her waist and knotted it round the mammoth's leg. The beast snorted hot breath from its trunk but kept pulling. And then all in a rush it was free and Cwen was free with it.

The hawk lay gasping on the solid ground beside Alfreda, her entire lower body smeared brown with clinging muck. Alfreda didn't care. She reached down to help Cwen up and then threw her arms round her and held her tightly, too relieved to find any words.

Eventually, Cwen pushed herself free. 'Thank you,' she said, but her face was grim. The mud she'd escaped had swallowed many of her hawks, her friends and lovers. Wine and Wingard were no longer by her side.

'I've still six fire javelins,' Alfreda said. 'We can take them and save all the rest.'

'You do that,' Cwen said, clasping her arm before letting her go. 'I'm going on.'

'On? On where?'

'To Mirror Town. This was the ring of their defence and we've broken it. Send word to Nayan he can pass his forces through this gap without fear of the mages.'

'Then wait for them,' Alfreda said. 'They'll be here soon.'

'I can't wait.' Cwen touched the dark brown blot on her cheek, the rune that marked her as a hawk. 'I can feel it burning, drawing me on. I can feel *him* – Krishanjit. Bachur told me it was my job to face him. Look after my hawks for me, Freda. I'm going to kill the moon.'

42

Olufemi heard screams behind her. She spun to see two mammoths bursting through the trees, there was a sound louder than thunder, and then something swept through the slaves she'd left behind and tore them into pieces. As she ran desperately on, she smelled the stench of black powder carried on the wind. It must be some dreadful new weapon. And there were more mammoths behind those first two, closing in on each group of slaves around each runic defence and the mage who could power it.

Her headlong flight took her through the next circle of defences. It should have formed a second unbreakable ring round the town if the first was breached. But she'd found half the defences broken by time or carelessness and she'd been able to refashion the runes on less than a quarter of those that remained. She'd hoped – she'd foolishly assumed – that the shock of the runes' power would drive the attackers away.

There was no choice but to keep trying. If the Ashane came into Mirror Town itself, all was lost. She heard a raucous cry above and a carrion mount dived towards her. There was nowhere to run, but as she shrank away another group of slaves flung themselves around her, shields and pikes held high.

Sheltered by them, she ran to the nearest rune she'd re-inscribed. The sculpture was a horrible thing, a model of a cockroach as big as a man. She'd been able to understand nothing of its meaning. She'd hoped not to have to use it, but what choice did she have? Galloping towards her were two more huge mammoths and whatever deadly weapon they carried between them.

They'd be on her in moments and she barely even remembered the shape of this rune. But she'd scrawled it on the head of the sculpture and she'd been training all her life to do this. This was what her life had been *for*.

The mammoth was very near. The ground shook to the pounding of its massive feet over the cornfield. Olufemi closed her eyes to banish the sight and tried to close her ears to it. Her mind must be empty, a blank with nothing in it but the rune. She let her thoughts trickle away, like water through her fingers, until only that one shape was left.

Triumph tried to wriggle its way in, but she couldn't allow that either. She must see and feel and hear nothing but this. She pictured the rune and she called Yron's power into it. There was resistance, a barrier as strong as an iron door. Everything in her wanted to push against it, to break through the door, but the strength lay in letting go. She opened her mind and released the image of the door. There was nothing inside her but the rune, and the magic flooded through her and out of her, a thrill more powerful than any drug or climax.

She felt the moment when it loosed from her and was gone. When the screaming began, she opened her eyes. The nearest slave staggered towards her and she recoiled in horror. His face had been destroyed. There were mandibles where his jaws should be and split and bleeding flesh around the faceted eyes bulging from his forehead.

Two slaves stood staring in mute horror at arms that were encased in a chitinous black carapace. Others tore at their own clothes to expose the twisted bodies beneath: eight spider legs sprouting from a pink chest; the stumps of wings torn off by the desperate slave's hand; a five-foot beesting emerging from the shattered remains of a penis.

And the mammoths were still coming. There'd be no stopping them now. Olufemi turned her back on the horror and ran.

The hawks around Alfreda cheered when they saw some of the Mirror Town forces turn and flee at their approach. But their cheers died when they saw what had truly driven them away, the deformed corpses lying all around.

'What . . . what is that? What *did* that?' a fair-haired hawk asked.

'It's the moon's evil,' another replied, spitting on the corpse of a thing half-man, half-roach. 'It kills even his followers.'

The way was clear now. Alfreda could see no more mages between them and the streets of Mirror Town. She turned her head at shouts behind her, afraid the mages had sprung a trap, but it was only a force of Seonu sprinting towards them.

'Hold up!' the lead warrior shouted. 'We'll add our axes to yours.'

Alfreda felt a little of her tension unknot. The hawks she had with her were so few and there looked to be a hundred Seonu. With them and her fire javelin to send the enemy running, the battle could be won.

'Where have you been while we've been having all this fun?' the blond hawk asked, almost succeeding in sounding light-hearted.

'We've been waiting for the right moment,' the lead Seonu said. The tribesmen were among them now, mingling with the hawks and all around the mammoths. Their weapons were drawn and their eyes bright. Alfreda felt a flash of unease she couldn't understand. Her mammoth felt it too, edging sideways away from the newcomers.

'And what moment would that be?' the hawk asked. 'When all the fighting was done?'

'When you were separated,' the Seonu leader said, and then shouted a sentence in a language she didn't know. She understood only one word: 'Yron'.

The hawks didn't even have time to scream. The Seonu axes swung and the hawks fell where they stood. Only one of them managed a blow in return, a slash across the arm of the Seonu warrior who attacked him. A tribeswoman put her knife in his back, and the Seonu all turned their eyes on Alfreda.

The mammoth saved her. While she sat frozen with shock, the beast trumpeted its rage and galloped away from the sudden and unexpected violence towards the safety of the massed Ashane force.

★

Mirror Town was in chaos. Cwen had expected opposition. She thought she'd have to fight to reach Yron's heir. But once she was among the buildings and running down the broad streets, not one of the frantically milling people spared her a glance.

There were Moon Forest folk here already. She saw some sitting in doorways, glaze-eyed, and others armed and running who knew where. They must be slaves, and she was being taken for one of them.

She began to believe this could really be done. She was no longer sure of anything, except that she was Bachur's, and this was what Bachur had commanded. Krishanjit was like an itch inside her head drawing her on. She could feel exactly where he was, ahead and to her left, and the itch grew and burned as she drew closer. From the day of her twelfth birthfeast, she'd known this was what was expected of her. This was the moment she'd been meant for all her life.

The feeling pulled her onward, towards one of the largest structures in this city of monumental houses unnaturally rooted in the ground. Its bright white marble seemed little damaged and its door was open and unguarded. It sat there, a series of rooms balanced on huge stone turnstiles, and dared her to enter.

The thought of stepping out of the light of the sun into that darkness unnerved her. She touched the rune on her cheek, but it felt just like ordinary skin. It didn't matter; she knew its shape as well as she knew herself. She was the beloved of Bachur.

Inside, the building was full of books. There were none among the hawks, but her father had collected them. He'd set aside an entire room in their mansion for his library. She hadn't thought about that place in eighteen years. As a small child she'd liked to sneak in to hide beneath the desk, surrounded by words she'd never been taught to read. Her father's hounds had liked it too. They'd lie curled up together, waiting for the moment when her father would find them and shout and drive them all out.

She felt a prickling between her shoulder blades, the animal sense of being watched. But when she spun, spear ready, she saw no one. Maybe it was Bachur she could sense, watching over her in these moments. The thought comforted her as she entered the centremost chamber.

Yron's heir was there. She'd known he would be. He looked exactly like the drawings Sang Ki had showed her, an ordinary young man with shadowed eyes. Another Ashane boy stood by his side, holding a spear of his own, but he was weak and thin and he held it too limply with the wrong grip. He'd be no match for her.

Perhaps Krishanjit might have been, but he only wielded a knife and she knew that she could take him. His eyes widened when he saw her and his throat bobbed as he swallowed.

It was such a youthful face. She hadn't expected that. Although she'd known he was born on the day she was made a hawk, she'd never thought about how young that made him. Some of the Brotherband warriors she'd killed had been younger than him, but their faces had been hard. His was almost innocent. It was a boy's face, not a man's.

'I'm sorry,' she said. 'You have to die. I have to kill you.'

He looked like he might say something. And then his eyes, which had been fixed on hers, flicked behind her.

She spun, twisting her spear to parry the blow she sensed coming, and the blade of the axe that was meant for her neck struck her shoulder, severing skin and flesh and bone. She screamed as the axe was wrenched free and then the blade fell again and she had a terrible disorienting moment when her view tilted and she thought that she was falling. But her body wasn't falling: it was her eyes, her head. She thought she saw Bachur's face, smiling at her. And then she saw nothing.

Krish stared at Dae Hyo as he stood above the body of the dead woman, his axe dripping with her blood and a spray of it all around the room from her half-severed neck. Krish couldn't tear his gaze away from her face. Her expression seemed shocked, as if it had never occurred to her that this might end in her death. Her white skin belonged in the Moon Forest and Krish thought suddenly of the things he didn't know, of what had brought her such a very long way to kill him. All those questions her death would leave unanswered and her long voyage ended here, on a cold marble floor in Mirror Town.

'Oh,' Dae Hyo said. 'It's a woman.' He looked sick.

'She said she had to kill me,' Krish told him. 'You saved me. Thank you, brother.'

Dae Hyo's face twisted and Krish thought the warrior might deny him, even after that, but he just nodded.

'I'm sorry,' Krish said. 'For making you kill a woman. For . . . for everything. I'm very sorry.'

Dae Hyo gently closed the dead woman's eyes, then hung his axe back at his waist. 'Words don't mean anything. Actions have a louder voice. What are you doing hiding here?'

'They're after me – the carrion riders. They're hunting all the Ashane men.'

'I killed, I killed, I killed one myself,' Dinesh said and laughed. 'I saved my master.'

'I'm not your master,' Krish insisted.

'But saving you made me happy – it made me feel as good as bliss.'

Krish turned away from his grinning, blood-spattered face, but he couldn't pretend he hadn't known that Olufemi's rune might replace one kind of servitude with another.

'You've done ill,' Dae Hyo said. 'Do better.'

The warrior was more stern-faced and serious than Krish had ever seen him. 'I'll try,' he promised.

'I had to save you. The magic won't work without you and without magic we're lost. I've seen what men do to those they've defeated. The mages are worthless rat-fuckers and the slaves aren't much better, but they're all fighting for you. It's not right for them to die that way.'

'No.'

'It's not right for you to hide in here while they're fighting your battle. Are you a child or a man?'

'I'm a man,' Krish said. 'I'm a Dae man.'

Dae Hyo sighed. 'No you're not.'

'I want to be. I want to be your brother or – or at least your friend. I've never had a friend before. I don't think I'm very good at it.'

That startled a laugh out of Dae Hyo. 'Belbog's balls – you're fucking terrible at it. But I haven't been too fine a friend either, if we're talking honestly. And I'm not so sure we'll have time to learn to be better. It's not looking good out there: your father's forces are nearly at our door. Do you want them to find you here, hiding like a rabbit? Or will you leave this life with your weapon swinging?'

Sang Ki held the burnt woman's hand as they fled, but he wasn't sure who was leading whom. The city had confused him even when it wasn't being attacked by the King's carrion riders. Now he was utterly lost. The birds seemed to be everywhere, while their missiles had left the wreckage of houses and people flung all over the broken streets. The sun beat down without pity for their plight and he didn't know if he had the strength to continue.

'This way!' the burnt woman said. She at least appeared not to have given up hope. He let himself be led, gasping and drooping behind her.

A carrion rider flew overhead, the shadow of its wings passing over them. Sang Ki flinched, stumbling against the marble wall of a building, and when he righted himself he saw that the burnt woman had stopped.

A man stood in the mouth of the alley, blocking their exit. He was bruised and bloody like so many others they'd passed, but when he saw them, he smiled. It was that smile, crooked beneath a long nose, that sparked a flash of recognition. This was the man who'd tried to bargain for Nethmi's life in Smiler's Fair. The man the burnt woman had claimed she didn't know.

'Nethmi,' Marvan said. 'I've found you.'

Her back was to Sang Ki. He couldn't see her face, but even if he had, he knew he wouldn't have been able to read it. Nethmi had revealed more than she knew. The burnt woman kept her feelings locked tight. 'How did you escape?' she asked.

Marvan shrugged and smiled wider. 'The pillar fell and funnily enough, no one seemed that bothered about recapturing me. But one advantage of sitting up there for months: I had a wonderful view of Mirror Town and nothing else to look at. I can get you out of here.'

'And what about him?' She and Marvan both turned to Sang Ki. The burnt woman was hideous but it was the Ashaneman's face that frightened him. Marvan might have looked on a rat with more warmth.

'He's kept you prisoner all this time, hasn't he?' Marvan said.

The burnt woman's eyes, hooded in the melted folds of her brow, were fixed on Sang Ki. 'He thought I was Nethmi.'

'So he's right about one thing.'

'But what if I'm not Nethmi?'

Marvan pressed his body against hers, as close as a lover. Sang Ki thought he would kiss her, but instead he grasped her hand, curling his fingers round hers to draw the knife that was sheathed at her belt. Little Blade, the weapon from which she'd once taken her name. Sang Ki had returned that knife to her when she'd risen from her sickbed. He'd meant it as a statement: an insistence that she was the woman she claimed not to be.

'You're Nethmi,' Marvan said. 'This is the knife your father gave you all those years ago, when he knew you'd need to fight to live. I don't care what you look like. It was never your face that mattered to me. You are the woman whose knife this is.'

He held the knife between them, the blade pressed flat against their chests, and now he did kiss her. Sang Ki had to look away. His stomach rebelled at the sight, though he wasn't sure what the nauseous feeling was. It felt like disgust, but he feared it might be jealousy.

'You think I'm a killer?' the burnt woman asked when she pulled back.

'I know you are. We're the same, you and I. That's why we found each other. It's how we'll always find each other. Come away with me now – a war is a good time for people like us. Who notices a few more corpses?'

She looked back at Sang Ki. He wished her face were unburnt and whole so he could read it. But the unburnt woman had killed his father. 'I don't believe that you're a killer,' he told her.

The knife's blade looked dull in the shadows. The moment seemed to stretch or perhaps to be preserved, like an insect in amber. His heart was the only thing in motion, thudding against his chest. Then she opened her fingers and dropped the knife to the ground.

'You're mistaken. I don't want to be like you,' she told Marvan. 'You are a mistake – no one should be like you.'

Marvan stared at the knife, dusty on the ground, as she took Sang Ki's hand and led him away.

43

It didn't take long to find the battle. Dae Hyo followed the sound of screams until he saw his first Ashane soldier, running towards the low outer buildings of Mirror Town. He opened the man's chest with one swing of his axe, but there were a lot of his friends behind him, and not much that was going to stop them. The wheat fields lay trampled beneath a thousand boots and the ill-armed slaves were fighting a desperate rearguard action. The men they faced clearly knew their business. Probably only their fear of the mages' power held them back – but that fear wouldn't last long. The runic defences had already been passed.

'It's not going well,' Krish said and Dae Hyo laughed.

Krish smiled tremulously in return and Dae Hyo felt something so complicated he couldn't name it. There was some hate in it and anger, but there was more affection. He supposed it was how most people felt about their brothers. It was how he'd once felt about his own brothers and sisters – the years of drinking had allowed him to forget that. 'I've gambled on better odds,' he agreed. 'Think we can turn the tide?'

'Probably not,' Krish said.

Dae Hyo pulled out both his axes, testing the weight of them in his hands. 'I tell you what – I'll try if you will.'

His brother drew his knife, which really was a pitiful little thing, so Dae Hyo passed him one of his axes. They hefted their weapons and ran towards the fight.

The Seonu seemed to be everywhere, in front of Alfreda as well as behind. The mammoth trampled those in front and outran those behind, but it couldn't outrun their arrows. Some were tangled in its hair and others seemed no more than beestings to it, but there were so many. Arrows struck flesh and joints and the mammoth let out a terrible bellow as one drove into its eye.

It reared, legs lashing out at its tormentors. Alfreda clung to its back, but now the Seonu were all around and not all of them were being trampled. She saw an axe slash at the mammoth's legs, severing the tendons, and the huge creature fell to its knees.

She had her hammer, the largest of her forge. She lifted it and slid from the saddle, balancing for a moment on the slope of the mammoth's back and then leaping off and on to two Seonu warriors. They all fell to the ground together in a tangle of limbs and weapons, but she rose first and her hammer mashed their skulls into bone and blood-streaked grey fat.

There were a dozen Seonu around her – two dozen – but she saw them step back in the face of her anger. And then something passed overhead, some vast shadow that blotted out the sun and nearly all the sky. Her enemies looked up at it. Some of them flinched and others shouted with joy. They shouted something else, which must have been an order in their own language, because suddenly they were turning their backs on her and running towards Mirror Town and the battle that raged on its borders.

They'd driven her far to the rear of the fight, where the camp-followers' wagons sat. But the Seonu had got there before her. As she limped towards the wagons she saw the first corpse, his arms splayed and his throat slit. A horse bent its head towards him, snuffling at his blood-streaked face. Behind were more corpses, overturned wagons – and somewhere among them Jinn. Jinn, who they'd left here to keep safe.

Her ankle was trying to tell her that it was sprained and in pain but she couldn't hear the voice of her body. She could hear nothing but the pounding of her heart and the terrible fear – the terrible certainty.

She felt the shock of the sight like a wound, a knife plunged into her stomach and twisted. They'd dragged Jinn from his wagon and beaten him before they killed him. There were cuts and red marks on his cheeks that would never blossom into bruises. She could see the deep wound in his palm where he'd raised his hand to try to protect himself and the slash in his throat because he'd failed.

His shirt had been ripped off and there were cuts on his chest too deliberate to be the marks of rage or frenzy. Someone had carved words into him, but they were in the tribe's language and she couldn't read them. She thought she knew what they'd say, though: 'Traitor'.

His corpse when she lifted it in her arms was heavier than she'd expected. He wasn't truly a boy any longer; he'd gained two inches of gawky height since she'd first met him, his body straining to turn into the man he'd now never be. She rested her forehead against his and breathed, in and out. There were no tears. There was only anger.

One moment Eric had been looking at Mirror Town shimmering on the horizon, the final stop on their very long journey, and the next moment Rii shouted '*Yron*!' in a voice so loud it vibrated right through him and they were plunging towards the ground.

His son cried out in shock, huddled in blankets against Eric's chest. 'What are you doing?' he yelled over the leathery flap of her massive wings.

'Our master requires us!' she said.

The baby wriggled in his arms, screaming as the wind scoured past them. 'You're hurting him!' Eric said, but Rii didn't reply.

The ground rushed up to meet them. There were thousands of people below and the vicious sounds of battle drifted up, the clash of weapons and shouts of rage and pain. Rii hovered above it all, her wings beating. Some of the fighters looked up and Eric could see the expressions of shock on their faces. A few loosed arrows, but they cluttered uselessly against the armour on Rii's breast.

'I do not know which men fight upon our master's side,' Rii said desperately.

The battle certainly was a terrible mess, not two armies facing off but just knots and swirls of people all hacking at each other. 'There – look!' Eric shouted. 'Those are Moon Forest folk. My folk serve the Hunter, don't they? And the Hunter hates the moon.'

Rii hissed and turned her wings, plunging towards the fighters with her claws outstretched.

The slaves seemed to sense Krish's presence. When he and Dae Hyo came to the field of battle, they turned their heads and ran to rally at his side. They fought without skill but with a dreadful enthusiasm, and Krish saw Ashane soldiers recoil from the joyful sound of their laughter whenever their weapons found flesh.

He raised his axe but found no target. The slaves crowded around him, shielding him with their bodies. The Ashane pressed forward and a boy half Krish's age darted in, taking a spear that was meant for him. The boy doubled up, gasping, over the mortal wound and smiled with pleasure as the life slipped from him. When he fell, Dinesh moved forward to take his place.

Another charge came against them, mounted men slashing down with sabres, and Krish's force fell back. He felt the ground give softly beneath his feet and looked down to see that he was treading on the body of the fallen slave. His gorge rose but he swallowed it back.

They were surrounded, the fierce faces of the Ashane soldiers focused on Krish. They must have seen the way the slaves clustered around him. They knew who he was and there'd be no escape for him. He'd fight this battle out to its end and the end seemed near.

But as the time stretched he realised that his own force was swelling. More slaves were flocking to him, and a band of pale-skinned tribesmen who fought the Ashane with savage skill. Though many died as they drove through the surrounding soldiers, some made it through. Gradually the group around Krish transformed from a rabble to the remnants of an army, undisciplined but stubbornly still alive.

There were mages among them too. Krish felt a flare of hope that magic might save him, but the runic defences had long ago been passed. No magic could be used in the chaotic heat of this fight. Unable to reach for that power, an old, dark-skinned man clutched a kitchen knife in his hand and waved it at the Ashane soldier who confronted him. The soldier sneered and gutted him with his sword.

They were more but they were losing – they could only lose. The slaves were fighting with a ferocity their enemy couldn't match and a lack of skill that would ultimately see them defeated. Their uncanny laughter mingled with their screams and Krish shouted, 'Retreat! Retreat! Back to Mirror Town!'

Olufemi was lost in the city of her birth. Streets she'd spent decades walking became unfamiliar when battle raged through them and half the houses were shattered by war or magic. The runes had slipped through her grasp entirely. Broken mirrors crunched beneath her feet and shards pierced her. She felt no pain, only the squelch of her blood inside her shoes.

They had lost, although for a short while she'd ceased to believe that they would. She swerved to avoid the corpse of a cousin she'd barely spoken to since her return and choked down her guilt. She wanted to blame Krishanjit, but the blame was really hers. It was she who'd brought death to Mirror Town.

There was nothing left to do but flee. The desert might kill her but it would be a gentler death than the Ashane would grant her. She was nearly at the city's southern edge, among the low, sprawling houses of those without family. The streets ahead were empty even of corpses. She'd finally outrun the conflict and the way ahead was clear. She pulled in a deep breath and stopped, suddenly unsure. Vordanna. Vordanna was still in Mirror Town.

But why should she care? Her lover had been like a stranger since her return. All her passion had been reserved for Krishanjit. And yet Olufemi found herself turning, running back the way she'd come, towards the library of Turnabout.

When she saw Vordanna, it was already too late. The Ashane soldiers surrounded her, swords drawn and expressions that said they planned to have some fun before they used them. One stepped forward, reaching for Vordanna's breast – and a red streak shot towards him and latched on to his hand. He screamed and shook his arm. It was Adofo hanging there, teeth plunged into the soft flesh of the soldier's palm. The lizard monkey bit deeper and then let go, scurrying to fling himself into Olufemi's arms and screech his fury at the Ashane men.

They turned to her, rage replacing lechery in their faces. Olufemi tried desperately to calm her mind, but the desperation itself made the task impossible. She grasped for the runes of fire, of water, of pain, but all she could see was what stood before her: men ready to kill her.

And then there was a noise like a cracked bell ringing. The sound reverberated through her bones as if it meant to shake them apart. It vibrated in her mind too, shaking her thoughts loose. It felt like careless fingers sifting through them: her guilt was picked up and tossed aside, her childhood discarded along with her many years of wandering. And then the force had moved on, through her and out.

She blinked her eyes, stunned, and saw those the force hadn't released. The Ashane soldiers shook with unnatural speed, a blur of motion accompanied by high, quivering screams. The scream rose higher and higher as the vibration grew faster and faster until all at once it ended as the men simply . . . fell apart. Scraps of skin and hunks of flesh and shards of bone dropped on to the cobbles below like gory rain. Behind them was a young woman, her arms raised in the attitude of meditation, the pose of a woman who'd summoned the power of the runes.

Olufemi didn't know her – and then all at once she did. This was her mentor Yemisi in the flower of her youth, with a crown of oily curls and plump, unlined cheeks. Yemisi's arms fell to her sides and then reached up to her face, feeling its new-old shape. 'What happened?' she said. 'I can't remember anything. Why can't I remember?'

Something stirred on the blood-soaked ground between them, and Olufemi realised that whatever rune Yemisi had summoned hadn't finished its work. The fragments of the Ashane soldiers shook and moved and began to cohere again, reforming themselves into patchwork approximations of the men they'd once been. Five ears dangled from the chin of one rough, globular head. Another had a face made of tongues, while three had no heads at all, only ape-like bodies formed of torn flesh. Rock and fragments of mirror rose from the ground to join the living tissue, glittering shards standing out all over the makeshift bodies.

Vordanna whimpered and Olufemi took her in her arms, Adolfo's scaly body pressed between them. They watched as the rebuilt men shambled towards the sound of battle, flesh flaking from them as they walked.

Eric leaned sideways as his stomach emptied, but Rii swerved unexpectedly to snatch another man in her claws and the vomit splashed to join the blood matting her fur.

He'd seen men die before. He'd lived in Smiler's Fair, where death was often a daily occurrence. But he'd never seen men die like *this*, ripped in two from crotch to shoulder and tossed aside like meat. He'd feared Rii's fangs but he'd never before seen them do their work on living men, plunging through armour into breasts, spearing them from ear to ear and sucking out what lay inside with a horrible slurp. When she shook her head, droplets of blood sprayed across Eric and his son, and the baby's pink tongue flicked out to lick them up.

Rii turned again, cupping air beneath her wings to push herself higher. Eric wondered if she'd tired of slaughter, and then saw that there was no one left to kill. The ground was littered with the ravaged corpses of the Moon Forest folk. But the living had moved away, into Mirror Town itself, where the buildings hid them from Rii's view.

'Where is my master?' she cried desperately. *'How can I save him?'* She threw herself forward, above the city and the roiling fight that filled its streets.

'There!' Eric called. 'In that square ahead – the one with all the fallen pillars. You see that banner? It's the Oak Wheel, the Ashane King's sign.'

Rii yipped her battle cry and swooped towards the ground.

*

'Fuck me,' Dae Hyo panted, 'we're back where we started!' Blood streaked one side of the warrior's face and his turban was long gone, his hair loose and wild. But he and Krish were uninjured. There were few around them who could say the same.

They'd been pushed back to the heart of Mirror Town. The Ashane were herding him and he could do nothing about it. They were all around, and now he saw another group bearing down on him, all mounted and fresh, their weapons gleaming and the Oak Wheel streaming on a banner above them. They'd suffered two charges already and the slaves' spears had held the horses off, but Krish wasn't sure they could survive a third. These were his father's men and his death had been saved for them.

The Ashane knew that victory was theirs. They pressed forward and the slaves weren't laughing now. They were falling to the skill and the blades of the metal-armoured men. The horses reared, their hooves lashing. A slave fell, his skull caved in, and a horse followed with a spear in its flank. The madness of battle seemed to consume everyone. The choking scent of mouldy cinnamon filled the air around them, stronger even than the smell of death.

Krish swung his axe and it found flesh because there was nothing but flesh all around. The wounded Ashane soldier cried out and fell back. They were all falling back, though they outnumbered Krish's force ten to one. The horses screamed and bucked and he didn't know how he could be winning, until he saw a group of bowmen kneel to fire upward. He looked up too and understood.

The creature was vast and ugly. Its wings beat thunderously as it held itself above the Ashane soldiers and used its claws to rake them. Krish saw a man lifted from his saddle with a claw through his stomach. He hung suspended, and then the creature flexed its leg and flung him away to tumble down among his comrades and knock still more from their mounts.

The Ashane weren't fighting Krish's people now. All their attention was on the monster destroying them. 'Quickly, brother,' Dae Hyo said, his teeth bared in fury. 'We can take them now!'

'No, no, no, no, no,' Dinesh said. The slave had fixed himself to Krish's side throughout the battle, wielding his spear with clumsy enthusiasm. 'You can run – you can run now and they won't see you.'

'I'm not running,' Krish said, and Dae Hyo's grin widened, flecks of blood on his white teeth.

'But you'll die!' Dinesh said, anguished.

That might be true, and yet Krish didn't feel it. Maybe that was what it meant to be a god: that you believed yourself immortal right until the moment a sword sliced through your throat. Or maybe it was the anger, the heat burning in his gut. His father had come to end the life he'd never meant to be started. If Krish couldn't prevent his own death, he could at least take his father with him.

Dae Hyo yelled, the battle fever on him, and Krish followed on his heels as he carved a path through the Ashane. Foot soldiers fell screaming until they found themselves facing a cluster of horses with the Oak Wheel banner held above them and the winged monster hovering above that.

The monster screamed as one of the men raked its leg with his sword. Arrows had found the joins in its armour and still it seemed that it wouldn't stop, that it would press the attack and finish this. But a moment later it veered up and away, piping a pitiful cry as its black blood fell on the upturned faces of the men who'd driven it off.

'Svarog's cock!' Dae Hyo yelled. 'Come back, you coward!'

The man at the centre of the group shook his blade in triumph, and in the instant he turned towards Krish, Krish knew him.

This was his father. Here, now, the prophecy that had driven Krish to this moment could be fulfilled. His father raised his arm, and Krish knew that he meant to order his men to kill Krish, that he didn't even have the stomach to do it himself. But his men weren't looking at him. They were looking outward, to where they could see another force approaching.

At first Krish thought they were soldiers, bloody from the battle. Then they shambled nearer and he realised they were something else: something built of magic from mismatched scraps of flesh. He saw reflections of the Ashane soldiers in the fragments of mirror embedded in their chests and arms. The creatures fell on the Ashane and some of them screamed and more of them turned and fled.

Only the mounted men seemed to find their courage. Krish heard the call for a charge but the horses were wiser than their riders. When the rune-made creatures stumbled closer the horses reared. The men yelled curses and fought for control and to the right of the group, pushed out by the tide of battle, his father lost control entirely and fell from the saddle to the ground.

Krish raised his axe and ran forward. A few of the Ashane realised what had happened. They threw themselves in front of their king, but Krish wasn't alone and his people's weapons hacked them apart.

And finally Krish was there, standing above his father. A face a little like his own looked up at him, with eyes a hundred times more tired than his. They widened in fear and Krish felt his rage heat. His father *should* fear him, for all the months of fear he'd given Krish. For the *life* he'd given Krish, so different from the one he might have had. He raised his axe high, savouring the moment, and felt something surge out of him, some force or power whose leaving seemed to make him stronger still.

He cried out his anger and heard the cry echoed from a hundred throats. It was the slaves. All around they raised their weapons in tandem with his own and their faces twisted with his rage. Dinesh snarled beside him, a bestial expression Krish had never seen on his face before. Krish realised it must mirror the expression on his own.

It was the expression the Chun must have worn, when his rage had driven them to kill the Dae – to slaughter women and children. He remembered that moment now, when he'd stood up to his da for the first time and the joy he'd found in his own anger. He remembered with terrible clarity the way he'd murdered him, and how he'd felt nothing after.

'Kill him, brother!' Dae Hyo said, and Krish hesitated.

Everywhere, the slaves did the same. The shambling creatures stopped, while high above the monster hovered and the Ashane paused, seeing the mortal danger their King lay in.

Krish should kill him. He'd tried to kill his own newborn son – if any man deserved death, this man did. His father had done a terrible thing. But Krish had done terrible things too.

'Finish it,' his father croaked.

All around the battle was poised, waiting to resume. At Krish's stroke it would, and maybe his people would win and maybe the Ashane would, but it wouldn't end here. A bitter seed was being planted whose harvest could only be more of the same.

'I don't want to kill you,' Krish told his father. It wasn't true. He hated this man. But if he killed his father again, what would he do next? Dae Hyo was right: he had to do better. He had to be better.

Slowly, his father scrambled to his feet. He wasn't a young man; it was clear the movement pained him. 'It's one or the other of us. I've always known that.'

Krish looked around him, at the frozen battlefield. Some men stood with swords upraised for blows they hadn't delivered; others flinched away from wounds they hadn't yet received. 'But why can't it be both? I don't have to kill you – I've already killed my da. The prophecy's had its blood.'

His father took a step closer, until they were face to face. They were the same height, though there was more flesh on his father's bones. 'What do you want?' he asked.

'I want this to be over. I don't want to take Ashanesland this way. How can I reign in peace if I start with murder?' Krish looked at the abominations that had turned the tide of battle, their bodies made from the flesh of the dead, the twisted work of the runes he'd woken. 'I don't want to be the moon's heir. Can't I just be yours?

His father's face wasn't a trusting or a happy one. Maybe his own wasn't either. But with those words he wasn't lying. If this war continued, it would make a thousand Dae Hyos, men and women warped by anger and empty of everything but the thirst for revenge. Krish had that same emptiness inside him. He'd filled it with the same anger – and it had brought him here. It would always bring him here.

He couldn't be like Dae Hyo, or like his da, or even like his father. He had to be like Uin. Uin had been a better ruler than any of them, giving his people what they wanted and showing them a brighter future. Krish could never admire him, not with what he'd done to Dinesh. But he could imitate him. He could hide his anger behind his smile and do what he needed, not what he felt.

'My heir?' his father asked.

'Yes. You can teach me to be King after you. We can do things the ordinary way. That's all I want.'

'My heir,' his father said again. He looked at his men and then reached out his hand. Its skin was wrinkled and there were liver spots of age on its back, but it looked strong. Krish's hand was slender in comparison, yet the fingers were the same length. He curled them round his father's and felt the warmth of the grasp.

The silence of the battlefield was eerie. They seemed poised on the brink of a precipice. Krish was afraid they might tip over and plummet into depths they couldn't escape. But then Dinesh dropped his spear and moved to clasp hands with the Ashane soldier nearest him. The man looked startled, his own sword still in his grasp, sticking out at an awkward angle. Another slave followed and then somebody cheered. It was a ragged sound, taken up by only a few voices. The hate hadn't given way to love or even liking, but the joy of soldiers spared death in battle might be enough.

His father studied him, clever brown eyes travelling over his face and down his body before climbing back up to meet his again. 'Before I heard the prophecy, I meant to call you Tanvir, after my father.'

'My name's Krishanjit. That's the name my ma gave me.'

'Krishanjit. Do you truly believe we can do this?'

Krish looked round at the battlefield littered with corpses and the monster hovering above it, ready to strike if he commanded. 'I think we have to.'

And if they couldn't, there was always poison or an assassin's blade. He'd do better than he had – he'd be wiser. He'd do his darker deeds out of the light of the sun.

Epilogue

Sang Ki had found two malbeam, perhaps the same beasts they'd ridden into Mirror Town. There'd been no one to guard them in the chaos of the battle, nor to guard the water and food he'd taken from a half-wrecked mansion. They'd secured the supplies to their saddles and ridden the lizards south until Mirror Town was no more than a distant mirage. The ocean was to their right, a lifeless blue pounding against a shore littered with the bleached bones of unknown beasts.

'Where are we going?' his companion asked. 'Where *can* we go now?'

He noticed that her accent was less coarse than it had been, more like a shipborn lady's. It didn't concern him. 'We can go wherever you like, Mahvesh,' he said.

'I can't return to the Ashane.'

'Nor I to my own people. It seems the north is closed to us, and Mirror Town is a ruin.'

'And what lies south?'

'The exiles, the people of the savannah who don't welcome strangers in their lands. It's said they live out their lives on the backs of giant beasts and abhor killing so much they'll shun a man for stepping on an insect – but these are only travellers' tales and not to be relied on. I've often dreamed of visiting them.'

'I like the sound of people who hate killing.' She pulled on her reins until the malbeam was walking parallel to the shore, picking its way carefully through the shattered remains of a giant ribcage.

'South then,' he agreed, and turned his own mount to follow her.

*

Alfreda buried Cwen's body beside Jinn's. So few hawks were left alive that there was no one to protest the joint grave. Perhaps she should have put Wine and Wingard in the ground with them too, but the land outside Mirror Town was littered with corpses and she didn't have it in her to search through them all for Cwen's friends. Cwen might have wanted her to, but Cwen was dead and would never ask anything of her again.

The sand slid in on top of them so easily, their faces were hidden within moments. It didn't matter. She wouldn't forget the expression of agony on Jinn's or of shock on Cwen's. She'd heard that there was peace now between the two armies. What did it matter, when it had come far too late?

Her wagon had somehow survived the battle and she harnessed Edred to its front. The autumn rains were past and the brief flowering of the desert had ended. The grass that had sprung so startlingly green from the unpromising sand was withering. To the horizon, the ground was covered in a brittle, browning coat that it would soon shed. She must leave now to have any hope of surviving the desert crossing.

She hadn't gone far when the man stepped in front of her. He was Ashane, with a long, hooked nose beneath over-bright eyes. 'I'm in need of a ride,' he said, 'and you're in possession of a wagon.'

She thought of ignoring him, even of riding him down, but there was something in those eyes of his she both did and didn't like. It was something she recognised. She thought she wouldn't be able to find the words, but for once in her life they came easily to her. What did it matter if they came out wrong? What did anything matter? 'I prefer to travel alone,' she told him.

'I can be quiet,' he said, and climbed on to the seat beside her without asking her leave. He stared at her as they rode in silence across the dying flowers and wilting grass. 'Or I can talk,' he added.

'I don't want to talk.'

'And what do you want?'

She knew her rage was burning in her face, but he didn't turn away from it. 'I want them to die.'

'Who?'

'Everyone.'

He smiled and leaned back, turning his face to the blank blue sky. 'Then it's as well that I've found you. Together we can make the world bleed.'

Drut was dying. There was a black hole in her middle where her child had been, and the blood was draining out of it, like poison from an infected wound. There'd been pain at first and she'd wept, but now she didn't feel very much of anything.

When she heard the footsteps approaching through the dark of the buried city, she thought it must be Eric returning for her. Then she did feel something: a joy she hated. Eric had bred a monster inside her and chosen it instead of her. When he came for her, she'd reject him. She'd rather die than be with him.

But it wasn't Eric; it was the Hunter. Her sister knelt beside her and gently pushed her legs apart. It hurt and she screamed when the Hunter's fingers probed at the torn flesh through which her monstrous child had entered the world.

'You are haemorrhaging,' her sister said. 'You have lost too much blood.'

She meant that Drut was dying. But no, she wasn't Drut. The name had been Eric's and she must abandon it as he'd abandoned her.

'I am sorry,' the Hunter said. 'I thought that I could prevent this, but perhaps it can never be stopped. I thought my hawks could nip the bud before it grew this poisonous fruit, but now they all lie dead. My beloved Cwen is gone.' There were tears on her cheeks, though her voice remained calm.

'Not your fault,' she whispered. She knew whose fault it was. 'Eric.'

'Your husband loved his son as you loved him. That is no cause for shame.'

'Monster,' she gasped, as the Hunter stooped to lift her, cradling her like her own child in her arms.

The Hunter looked around, at the golden paintings on the

rock walls. Now that she stood beside them, it was clear that they were paintings of her. 'Your son was no more a monster than our husbands were. This place Eric brought you was my husband's home. The war parted us, but he remembered me and I . . .' The Hunter began to walk, her footsteps loud on the stone floor of the undercity. 'I loved my Guhtur, with his gentle hands and his clever smile. We made three sons together and she would have killed them all.'

'Who?'

'Mizhara. After she had slain her brother she meant to destroy his Servants too, every last one of them, though Yron's death had driven them to madness. I begged her not to. I told her that the war was won and the killing could end but she had grown drunk on blood and she refused to heed me. And so we fought.'

'You – you fought Mizhara?'

The Hunter ran her fingers along the four deep scars across her face. 'I killed her. I did not mean to – or perhaps I did. I can no longer remember. And I have spent all the long years since trying to atone for her crimes, and for mine.'

Perhaps this was delirium. She could feel her mind drifting, sometimes present in the now and sometimes elsewhere, lying beside Eric as the sweat cooled on his body, or in a future she had once imagined, raising her daughter with him. 'Mizhara can't be dead,' she said, in a time while she was present. 'We'd be . . . we'd be driven – insane. Like . . . We'd be insane like them. Like . . . the monsters.'

'Your madness is the sun's, not the moon's and it does not take the same form as theirs. But madness it is: the search to erase your selfhood, the endless following of endless rules that have no meaning. Only I was spared your insanity with that spark of Mizhara's power inside me that I took from her when she died. I used it to place two footprints in the ice, footprints that would never fade, and I told my sisters they were hers. I told them that she had left the world in horror at what had been done in her name. And so she should have, if there had been any goodness left inside her. But godhood had driven it from her.

They have always been born human, each time they come to us, and each time they forget what that means.'

They climbed the stairs to Salvation, first rock beneath the Hunter's feet and then ice and the welcome glow of the sun. But the light was fragmented and the walls stained with darkness.

'What happened?' she asked.

'Rii took her revenge,' the Hunter said. 'Salvation is no more, but perhaps it can save you yet.'

Others of her sisters were here. Some stopped to stare at her bloody form in the Hunter's arms, but there were wounds among them too and twice the Hunter stepped over a still and broken body. They were alone when they reached the great machine at the heart of the city.

It was as wrecked as her body, its wheels smashed and its cogs broken. An energy seemed to linger around it, sometimes visible as jagged flashes of light, the residue of the power that had once animated it.

'Mizhara left a little of herself in this device,' the Hunter said. 'If it is possible for you to be healed, it is possible this will accomplish it.'

The Hunter walked through the wreckage, heedless of the jagged spikes of metal and the lightning strikes of power that spat and hissed all around. When she reached the very centre, she laid her burden down and stepped back. 'I believe the choice may now be yours. Do you wish to be saved? If so, the power is here to do it – you have only to reach out and take it.'

She wasn't sure. Did she want to live? She'd wished to die before, and Eric had saved her. She'd betrayed her sisters and her goddess and brought a monster into the world. But that had all been Eric's doing. He'd told her that he loved her, but he'd only cared about the thing growing inside her. Why should she die when he lived? She must undo the things he'd done.

The power was all around her. She felt it sparking against her skin and it was easier than she'd imagined to reach out with some hidden part of her and touch it, to draw it *in*. It was a trickle at first, warm and pleasant, and then it was a flood. She felt it flowing in her veins and through her nerves. It healed what had been torn and bound what had been broken, until she felt her body as perfect as it had always been. As perfect as her law.

Her power flowed back into her from where she'd left it, so many years ago. She'd been absent from the world, and now she knew what that absence had done. She'd won a great battle but the war was still to be fought and she knew her enemy's face.

Mizhara rose from the centre of the machine her brother had made and that she'd turned to a better purpose. Yron had been reborn and it was only right that she'd returned to face him. She felt a moment of disorientation as she remembered two lives, a god and a god's Servant. She remembered two childhoods, one in warmth and one in cold, two homes, two husbands, two loves. But there was only one hate: Yron and all who served him, and in that hatred she found wholeness.

MERRICKVILLE PUBLIC LIBRARY

Acknowledgements

This book wouldn't exist, or would exist but would be much worse, without the help and patience of a lot of people. Matt Rowan, Matt Jones and David Derbyshire all provided brainstorming assistance while writing and brilliant feedback on an early draft. Naomi Alderman enabled me to understand Cwen, Jared Shurin was invaluable in sorting out my magic, Josh Rice gave military advice, Ian Farrington helped me with coastal features (and general loveliness), and David Bryher spent many long walks talking it all through with me and also just putting up with me.

At Hodder, I've hugely appreciated the work and support of Fleur Clarke and Ellie Cheele. And finally, as ever, my fantastic agent James Wills and editor Anne Perry have gone above and beyond to make the book as good as it can be, and encourage as many people as possible to give it a go. I owe you all big time.

WANT MORE?

If you enjoyed this and would like to find out about similar books we publish, we'd love you to join our online SF, Fantasy and Horror community, Hodderscape.

Visit our blog site

www.hodderscape.co.uk

Follow us on Twitter

Like our Facebook page

Hodderscape

You'll find exclusive content from our authors, news, competitions and general musings, so feel free to comment, contribute or just keep an eye on what we are up to. See you there!